I0772332

To Dylan,

For all your love, support, and confidence in me.

And to Dani, for loving and understanding my characters as much as I do.

Sea of L[...] Souls
Ruins of Andanova
The Eldritch Moutains
Hiraethean Woods
Eclidian Sea
The Faceless Forest
Larimar
Wreiss
Aestus
Moonwater Ridge
Rënimo
Pool of Pondering
Brimry
Calarinn
Durcova
Uvandor

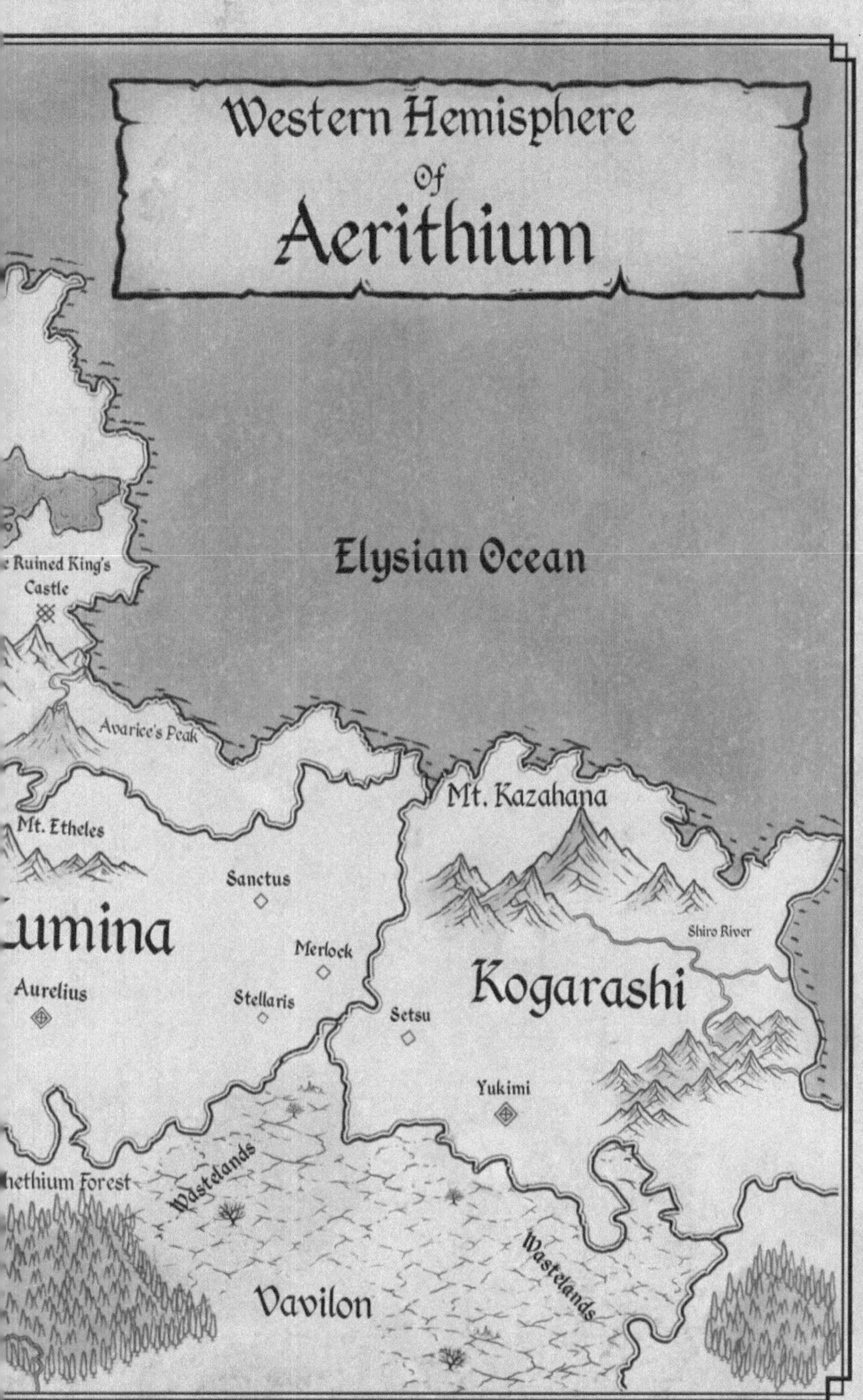

Western Hemisphere
Of
Aerithium
Elysian Ocean
e Ruined King's Castle
Avarice's Peak
Mt. Kazahana
Mt. Etheles
Sanctus
Shiro River
Lumina
Merlock
Aurelius
Stellaris
Kogarashi
Setsu
Yukimi
nethium Forest
Wastelands
Wastelands
Vavilon

THE RUINED KING

K.C WASSEM

Prologue

Rain trailed down the stained-glass windows, tracing paths like tears on the face of the fragile goddess. She was beautiful, her skin as pale as snow and her hair as silvery as pure starlight. From her back, feathered wings spread across a star-kissed sky as though she were poised to take flight into the heavens.

But it was her eyes that always made Seren look twice. There was something in the way they seemed to follow him, burned into purple glass, always watching, always waiting. At times, he could have sworn they moved—shifting, swiveling in his direction.

Yet, she was nothing more than a glass depiction of something long gone and dead. It was almost fitting that she had been immortalized in something so delicate, so easily broken.

Seren's back ached against the wooden chair. He sighed, resting his chin in his palm, trying to find a comfortable position. There weren't many ways to ease the discomfort of sitting on a stiff, uneven chair for hours on end.

If only the rain would stop, Seren thought. On days like this, when his mind hummed with a hundred stray thoughts, it was impossible to focus on the tasks at hand. The words on the pages of the book before him blurred into incoherent strings of nonsense.

It was the height of summer, and the sun should have been shining—an open invitation for Seren to slip away into the groves. He could almost feel it, if he tried hard enough: the warm sunlight on his skin, the birds exchanging songs in the branches above, the sweet taste of plums on his tongue.

His head hit the desk with a dull thump, and he groaned inwardly.

"Seren?"

Seren met Aiden's onyx eyes. Black hair framed the High Priest's thin face, and a subtle smile tugged at his lips. He took a seat in the chair beside Seren.

Aiden wore his customary deep blue priest robes adorned with embroidered golden suns, moons, and stars along the hems. Not as if he ever wore anything else. Water droplets dotted the fabric, and a glossy sheen clung to his hair.

"You look like you're lost in a daydream," Aiden mused. His gaze traveled to the open book on the table, still sitting on the page Aiden had left it on over an hour ago.

Seren sighed and fought the urge to roll his eyes as he pulled the book closer. He stared at the endless words on the aged paper, fighting a scowl.

"The Mother is beautiful, isn't she?" Aiden asked softly, tilting his chin toward the stained-glass image of the goddess.

Seren lifted his head, nodding. "Why...do you call her that?"

Aiden smiled, his long finger landing on Seren's book. "Perhaps, if you were reading as I instructed, you'd have the answer to that question."

Seren rubbed his throbbing temples with a groan. "My head hurts," he whined. "I don't feel like reading. I'm *always* reading."

With an affectionate touch, Aiden ruffled Seren's ink-black hair. "Why don't I tell you a story, then? We've been stuck inside for days. You can close your eyes and listen if you wish."

Seren grinned, resting his arms on the cool table and nestling his cheek against them. Aiden seemed to be in a good mood today. He closed his eyes with a sigh of relief.

"Long ago, before the days of the Veil, there were creatures known as the otherlings," Aiden began. "Unlike humans, they were born from magic. It flowed in their veins and lived in their flesh."

Magic.

The word surged excitement through Seren.

"I'm sure you remember the paintings in the west chapel. Your mother and I couldn't tear you away the first time you saw them," Aiden chuckled.

Of course, Seren remembered. Images flitted behind his eyelids—creatures he'd memorized. Majestic horses with twisted horns atop their heads, manes gleaming like moonbeams. Lions that shimmered as if forged from gold with jeweled serpents' for tails. Humanlike beings with pale blue skin and dragonfly wings. They were strange and amazing all at once.

"Humans lost their connection with magic, a consequence of the banishment from the Garden of Aetheria. Do you remember what Aetheria is?"

The tone in Aiden's voice was light, like a teacher trying to turn a story into a lesson. It was typical of him.

"It's the realm of the gods and houses the fount of magic," Seren said.

Aiden beamed. "Yes, and it is said that the purest of magic comes from the Mother Tree and the fruit it bears. When Eden ate the apple, after the gods had already deemed it forbidden, she had stolen from them , embedding a great sin within her. A human was never meant to consume the fruit of the gods, and for that, humanity was punished."

Seren frowned. It seemed harsh that the act of one woman fell upon all of humankind.

"Humans are creatures of sin, Seren," Aiden said as if plucking the thought from his mind. "No human is born innocent. We are impure from the moment we take our first breath."

Seren didn't believe *that,* but held his tongue. He had a hard time believing that a pink-cheeked infant, fresh in the world, was anything *but* innocent.

"Sin festered after Eden's mistake and spread like a virus," Aiden continued. "Envy is one of the deadliest sins of all. It was jealousy that shattered our harmony with the otherlings. They were capable of magnificent things, living immortal lives. A terrible man will do many things to live forever, and many terrible people exist in this world. People will go to extreme lengths to attain what they cannot have, especially that which does not belong to them."

Seren lifted his head, opening his eyes. "What happened?"

The rain intensified, drumming against the windows, while the wind made the glass shudder. Aiden stared at the reflections in the window, the image of the Mother Goddess glimmering in his eyes, and let out a long, drawn-out sigh.

"War," Aiden said, his voice distant.

"But the Mother saved everyone, didn't she?" Seren asked, perking up. "She stopped the war and created peace."

Aiden nodded faintly. "She certainly tried. The Mother, Alernaea, was driven by love for both humans and the otherlings. After all, she is just that, a true mother who would do anything to protect her children. And so, she sacrificed herself, her divine essence forming the Veil that separated us from the otherlings, granting each of us our own realm. And yes, for a short time, there was peace. But it wasn't long until the corruption spread. The otherlings twisted into grotesque forms, their magic warping alongside them." Aiden clasped his ghostly hands on the table, tilting his head to Seren. "One day, she will return—reborn into the world, heralding a cleansing that will restore harmony and absolve us of our past sins."

"How do you know?" Seren slipped, his voice barely above a whisper.

Aiden's dark brows furrowed. "Because it is what the gods promised."

"What if she never comes?" Seren asked, biting his lip, his heart racing with uncertainty. "What if the gods break their promise?"

Seren's eyes traced her mighty wings, wondering if they would be large enough to spread across the entire sky. If the Mother was reborn into the world, she could be free to do what she wished. Would the goddess truly come to save humans? If everything Aiden said was true and humans had disobeyed the gods, only spreading sin throughout the realm, why would she *want* to save them?

"What makes you say such a thing, Seren?"

Seren traced his knuckles with his thumb, biting the inside of his cheek. "The gods don't listen," he whispered. "Every night, I pray my mother will come home, and every morning I pray my father will knock on my door and tell me he's been looking for me."

Aiden set a firm hand on Seren's shoulder. "The gods hear your prayers, Seren, but they cannot always answer them."

Seren shrugged his hand off. "Then, how can you be so sure?" he demanded. "For all you know, the goddess will never come, and the demons will kill everyone. Just like Andanova." He stood up quickly, his chair toppling behind him. "I don't think they listen at all. I *hate* the gods."

It happened so fast. Aiden's hand whipped out, striking Seren's cheek with a sharp crack that echoed off the library walls. Seren cradled his face, tears stinging his eyes.

"I... Seren, I'm sorry," Aiden began, his voice thick with regret. He extended his hand but quickly pulled it back when Seren flinched.

Seren stumbled backward, clutching his throbbing cheek. His feet moved before he could form a thought. He sprinted, bursting through the carved oak doors of the library and down the corridor to the right. Without slowing, he ascended the winding staircase.

When Seren reached his room in the Eastern Tower, he slammed the door so hard the hinges rattled and fumbled with the lock. Leaning against the door, he sank to the floor, pulling his knees to his chest. It wasn't long before he heard tentative footsteps echo outside.

"Seren, please, open the door," Aiden said, his voice muffled.

"Go away."

"Seren—"

Seren slammed the back of his head against the door so hard that stars exploded behind his eyes. "Just leave me alone!"

Wind howled outside, and rain pounded against the glass. Seren's fists tightened, waiting for Aiden's response. The silence between them was deafening.

When Aiden's footsteps began to recede down the stairs, Seren's heart throbbed painfully. He stood and collapsed onto his bed, curling onto his side, trying to stop the hot tears from flowing down his cheeks. He should have kept his mouth shut.

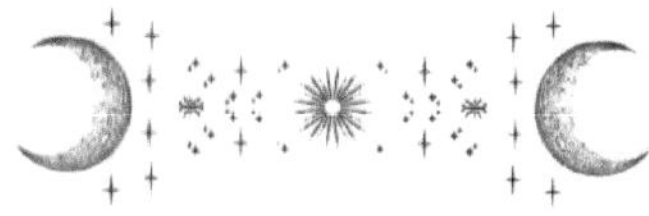

The following morning, Enid, Aiden's handmaiden, knocked gently on Seren's door, the sound echoing through the quiet hallway. The delicious aroma of freshly baked pastries wafted through the air as she entered the room, carrying a silver tray laden with breakfast.

Upon seeing Seren, her ashy eyes widened, and her lips formed a pained expression at the sight of the vivid bruise blossoming on his face. With a motherly touch, she placed a chilled cloth against his skin, the coolness offering relief, and brushed back his disheveled hair.

"He regrets what he did," Enid murmured. "The High Priest has been under an immense amount of pressure since the fall of Andanova. Do not blame yourself, little one. He plans on making it up to you."

Seren remained silent as Enid poured him a steaming cup of tea before leaving. He stared into the grayish liquid, the scent of lavender and lemon tickling his nose.

Did Aiden truly regret hitting him? Or did he believe Seren deserved it? If all humans were inherently sinful, then perhaps even priests and saints were no different despite being chosen by the gods. That would mean Seren was no different, either. Maybe he deserved it. He couldn't shake the thought that the gods might be angry with him, just as Aiden seemed to be.

Seren had said he hated the gods, but he hadn't meant it, had he?

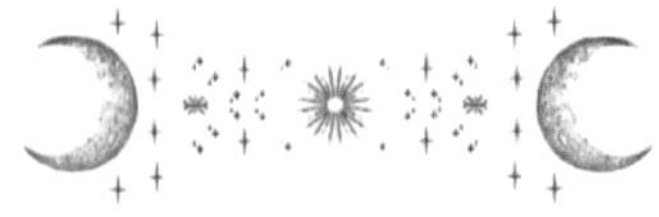

The next morning, the rain fell heavier than ever, a relentless drumming against the window panes. Seren sat by the fogged glass of his room, staring out at the dreary courtyard and wondering if he would ever see the sun again. Perhaps this was the gods' punishment—to confine him in shadow, away from the sun, the sky, and all the things that made him feel even a trace of freedom.

Just as he was about to turn away, something caught his eye. Through the rainy haze, a woman emerged, her deliberate strides cutting through the downpour. In her gloved hand, she carried a rose-gold birdcage, its top veiled by a satin cloth of deep blue. Seren pressed his face against the cold glass, captivated, as she disappeared into the entrance of the church.

It wasn't long before Aiden had the bird delivered to Seren, accompanied by a handwritten note with a hurried apology. As the dove scraped its claws against the cage bars, a pang tugged at Seren's chest. He locked eyes with the bird's ink-black gaze through the narrow slats, its elongated neck tilting as it let out a soft coo.

"We're the same, you know," Seren said, poking a finger through the cage. "I don't have friends either."

That night, Seren struggled to sleep, tossing and turning beneath sweat-soaked blankets. In his dreams, he was trapped inside a birdcage, his wings vast and white, like those of the Mother Goddess. He thrashed within the confines, stretching his wings, only for the iron bars to sear them with fiery pain. He wanted to fly. Desperately. But no matter how hard he slammed against the cage, the bars held fast. He would never fly.

Seren awoke with a start, drenched in cold sweat. The dove cooed in its cage, its gentle sound cutting through the suffocating darkness. He didn't sleep after that. Instead, he lay still, listening to the bird's soothing calls and waiting for the first rays of daylight to stream through the windows.

When morning finally came, it dawned the world in the vibrant colors of summer, washing away the gray that had stolen the sun for days. The sky was crystal-clear, as blue as polished sapphires, with not a single cloud in sight. It was a perfect day to fly. A perfect day to be a bird.

Seren rushed to the window, pressing his face against the glass with a wide grin. On this side of the church, a bird's nest clung to the eaves, and on days like this, its inhabitants would pirouette on the wind. Seren had missed them. He turned to the dove, its feathers glinting in the golden light, and approached the birdcage with careful steps. Slowly, he opened the latch.

"One of us should go out into the world," Seren told the bird. "You can make lots of friends."

Seren coaxed the creature onto his finger. The bird didn't hesitate; its small claws wrapped around him. He stroked its head with his thumb, a smile spreading across his face. Moving to the window, he pushed it open with a firm shove and lifted his hands upward, releasing the dove into the air.

For a moment, its white wings unfurled against the bright blue sky, and Seren's heart leapt in excitement. But Aiden hadn't mentioned that the bird couldn't fly—that it had been caged for so long it had forgotten how. Seren's mouth fell open in horror as the bird plummeted toward the ground. He could only watch as it flapped its wings frantically before striking the cobblestone, a bundle of broken bones and feathers.

ONE

"They say that wishes whispered to the brightest star can come true, for the God of Stars hears our wishes and sees our dreams."
—Chronicles of the Gods

The afternoon sun reflected off the golden bracelets in the man's calloused palm. He tapped a dirtied fingernail against the precious metal, his bushy eyebrows turned upward in surprise.

"Where did you get these, boy?" he demanded.

Seren failed to control the scowl that was turning the corners of his lips. "Does it matter?" he snapped. "I was told you aren't one for asking questions." He tugged the hood of his tattered cloak lower over his face.

With an ugly smile of crowded yellow teeth, the man closed his fingers over the jewelry. "People will ask *me* questions. You realize what this is, don't you? This is royal gold, and these symbols..." He traced the serpents' intertwining tails.

Seren gritted his teeth. "All that matters is that it belongs to me now."

The man's eyes roved over Seren's dirt-streaked clothes and shadowed face, his expression skeptical. Seren looked like anything but someone who owned royal gold.

"As you can see," Seren said stiffly, "I need new clothes. But I can't buy them without money." His fingers drummed anxiously on the counter. "And right now, you're not living up to the reputation I was told you had."

Seren rubbed his tired eyes, the weight of sleepless nights bearing down on him. His stomach growled, a sharp reminder of how long it had been since his last proper meal. Across the counter, the man's calculating gaze lingered on him, his fingers gliding over the bracelets as though weighing their worth. Seren's irritation flared. He could almost see the gears turning in the man's head, scheming how best to exploit him.

"Listen," Seren said, leaning on the counter. "Give me four hundred gold coins for them and we'll call it even. I was told you were not one to ask questions and that seems to be *all* that you have done since I arrived here."

The man let out a hearty laugh, closing his grubby fingers around the jewelry and pulling his arm to his side. "You are out of your mind, boy. I'll give you a hundred."

"Fine." Seren seized the man's arm, yanking and slamming it onto the table with little effort. He pried the man's hand open and snatched the bracelets away. "Then, I will be leaving. It seems you do not live up to your reputation after all."

Cursing, the man rubbed his reddened arm as Seren headed for the door. "You damn brat," he huffed. "No one will take those off your hands."

Seren ignored him, putting his hand on the handle.

"Damn it. Three hundred. Take it or leave it, kid."

Seren turned back around and smiled politely. "Okay, looks like we have a deal."

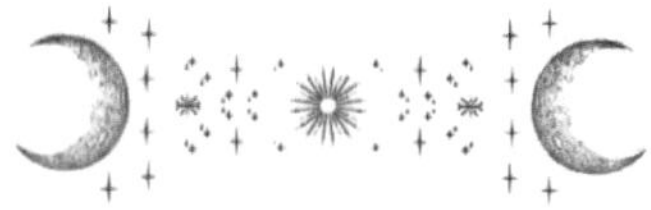

Birds sang incessantly from the treetops, their melodies weaving through the rustling leaves of sunlit maple trees. They flitted from branch to branch, their wings catching the light as if in celebration of Seren's arrival. His heart lifted with every swoop and glide, the rush of air from their wings brushing past him. Seren pulled back the hood of his new ashen cloak, tilting his face toward the endless blue sky, unmarred by clouds.

Seren let out a long sigh, his fingers tightening around the powder-blue dress in his grip. He had plenty of coin to spare, yet the only stablemaster in town had flatly refused to sell him a horse. The people of Durcova were unfriendly, offering no warmth to outsiders. He was eager to leave.

As he stepped onto the dirt path, his boot caught on something, and he tumbled forward, unable to catch himself in time. The dress slipped from his grasp, landing in the dirt beside the small container of medicinal herbs tucked into his pocket. The apothecary had promised the herbs would bring dreamless sleep. Cursing under his breath, he sprawled onto his belly, scrambling for the herbs. He breathed a sigh of relief when he found they had remained closed and untouched.

Seren sat up and rubbed his leg. He lifted his black trousers, revealing the jagged bite mark on his calf—a reminder of a demon's attack—and a half-healed gash on his lower thigh, a scar from a weapon forged in blood.

A thick layer of scabbing crusted over the wounds. Given his rapid healing, they should have faded to mere scars by now. Frustration twisted in his gut as he frowned, but he pushed the troubling thought aside.

Seren remained still for a moment, his head tilted toward the sky. A yellow-bellied bird swooped down suddenly, nearly brushing his face. He fell back, palms hitting the dirt. The bird circled around and returned, this time combing its tiny feet through his hair.

"Hey," Seren said, batting it away. "Stop that."

The bird chirped as though snickering before landing on the tip of Seren's black boot. Its beady eyes never left him as it hopped onto his knee. Seren glanced down, fixing his hair, and raised an eyebrow. "And what do you think you're doing?" he asked, a playful smirk tugging at his lips.

Leaning forward, he extended his hand, and the little creature hopped onto his finger without hesitation. Seren lifted it to his face, his grin widening as he regarded the tiny bird. "Somehow, you remind me of someone," he mused with a chuckle. "He's also quite relentless."

The bird cocked its head to the side as Seren stroked its silken belly. His gaze shifted to the dress, now covered in dirt, and a pang of guilt tightened in his chest. He reached for it, bundling the fabric into his lap.

"Think she'll like it?" Seren murmured. "I still have to wake her." He sighed, casting a worried glance. "Though...I'm afraid to face her after what I've done."

The little bird ruffled its feathers and let out another chirp. Seren frowned and looked at it. "What would you do, little friend?"

Of course, the bird didn't answer. It took flight, soaring back into the sky, leaving Seren with an empty feeling in his chest.

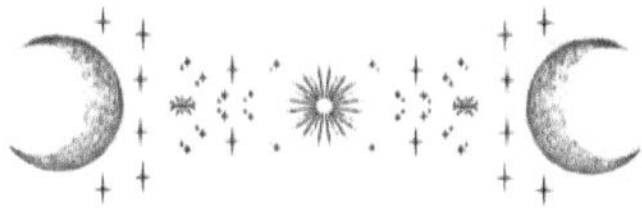

It was hard to believe that only weeks ago, Seren had been desperate to remember anything about his life. Now, the memories that had resurfaced were shoved into the dark corners of his mind, treated like unwelcome visitors. What he had once yearned for now felt like a curse. He couldn't hide from them, nor could he run. They found ways to slip into his consciousness, reminding him that they were waiting—lurking outside other locked doors, other memories sitting like demons ready to devour him whole. They had a hold on him, especially when he dreamed.

Yellow, cat-like eyes waited for Seren on the other side. Syringes lined metal tables filled with bubbling blue liquid, their cloying scent thick in the air. Feathers drifted down like snow, but not white or black—red, soaked in blood, staining everything they touched. And then that horrible ache filled his chest, overwhelming. Seren wanted to rip his ribcage open and tear out his own heart, just to stop it from hurting. And in these dreams, sometimes he did. He tore through his flesh, but he only found a mass of darkness where his heart was supposed to be.

Sleep was Seren's dreaded enemy, something to be avoided at all costs. And because of this, he almost envied Kamilah. She'd been sleeping for three days. Seren hoped that her dreams were empty, with no space to be filled with the horrors she'd endured.

Seren had woken her, only to bring her water and coax her to drink. Her movements were drunken, limbs heavy, and her mind slow. Seren would tell her to go back to sleep and to forget that she'd ever been awake.

It felt wrong.

Using her true name had given him full control, leaving a sick feeling in the pit of his stomach. Whenever the tethers between them tightened, guilt plagued him. He constantly reminded himself that he was only doing it for her well-being, and once she was better, he would never speak her true name again.

Even as Mila slept in bed with a frown on her face, Seren couldn't help but admire her beauty. Her hair was a mangled mess, sticking up in all directions, no strand matching another in size. A white scar marked the side of her cheek, a cruel souvenir from the wicked Sanguine Queen, who had inflicted it just to see Seren squirm. Though Mila's arm had suffered a brutal break, it had healed entirely. Seren didn't know what had triggered such rapid recovery, but he was thankful and too tired to seek answers.

Seren sighed, leaning in the doorway of the farmhouse, watching the rise and fall of Mila's chest. He dragged his gaze over her sleeping form, his heart pounding. He had run out of excuses to keep her asleep. She was healthy, and her body was no longer broken. He needed to wake her today.

Seren took a step toward her, fingers hovering over her cheek. "Kamilah."

She didn't stir. Seren could force her to wake now—perhaps he should. The bond between them tugged faintly at his awareness, a thread he could feel and, if he focused, even see. It pulsed with a sinister energy as though it had a life force of its own. Like a rope binding his soul to hers, it tethered them together in a way that twisted his insides. She belonged to him, in a sense—a thought that filled him with guilt. He'd been wrong to use her name, but desperation had driven him. Maybe if she'd slept, she'd heal faster. And somehow, by some miracle, Mila had healed. She was alive. Days ago, he'd believed she would die in his arms.

Despite everything, the intangible bond between them was a constant reminder: he wasn't human. Mila shouldn't belong to him, and no one should have the power to claim another. Protecting her from the Sanguine demon who had tried to steal her true name had seemed like the right thing to do, but wielding that same power left him feeling monstrous. He had saved her, and he would have done it again, but the price weighed heavily on his spirit.

"Seren."

Anna stood in the hallway, her brown curls framing her round face. She wiped a smear of fresh cream from her curved upper lip, frowning. Seren's stomach tightened as he wondered how long she had been standing there, watching him.

"Hey," he replied solemnly.

Anna's frown shifted into a subtle smile, her hands locking behind her back. "How is she? Has she woken up yet?" She cast a curious glance at Mila's sleeping form over Seren's shoulder.

Seren shook his head. "She'll be awake later, I'm sure of it."

Anna stood on the tips of her toes, her beige dress brushing against her skinny calves. "I'm expecting my dad to return tomorrow morning. Do you think you two will...stay?"

Seren could hear the strain in her voice. He couldn't blame Anna for wanting him and Mila gone.

"I heard families are evacuating the town," she continued. "The Veil is much too close for comfort." Anna moved her hands in front of her, nervously playing with her dirty fingers, stained from working in the garden. "Just this morning, two children wandered into the Veil by accident. I think...once my dad returns, we'll be leaving Durcova too."

The Veil crept along the edges of Calarinn and had swallowed the entire Behethium Forest. Seren had seen it himself after leaving the Sanguine Kingdom; the forest now belonged to the cursed realm and the demons that dwelled within it. After narrowly escaping Queen Omaira and the demon that shared her body, a portal had taken Seren and Mila to the forest's edge.

For a second time, Seren had somehow seen the barriers of the Veil and known where to run to escape. He had run faster than ever, clutching Mila against his chest until he burst through to the other side. Even then, he didn't stop running, not until he knew the Veil was far behind. After what felt like both an eternity and a fleeting moment, he collapsed in a heap by a riverbank, breathless. The eclipse had passed, and the moon shone bright, its silvery light casting reflections on the water that danced like stars.

Seren and Mila had been coated in blood from their escape, the abrasive smell of iron clinging to his skin, his hair, and even his tongue. Stripping off his clothes, he stepped into the river, the icy water sending chills deep into his weary bones. Scooping up Mila, still unconscious, he fumbled to peel away her blood-soaked garments. He held her against his chest, her skin cool and clammy against his own.

Mila was dying; her breathing was far too faint, and her once warm, brown skin had faded to an alarming, washed-out gray. The bond between them stretched too thin, fraying as if it might snap at any moment.

"Heal her," Seren had begged the sky. "Please." The strange voice that had guided him for as long as he could remember was silent. "If you ever cared, heal her, please." Whether he was pleading with the voice or the gods, he didn't know—and he didn't care. He would have given his soul to a demon if it meant saving her life. He couldn't lose her. If she died, Seren would only have himself to blame.

Seren wasn't sure how long he'd been under the light of the moon, his torso submerged in the water, with Mila cradled in his arms. He thought he may have cried and screamed at the heavens, but he wasn't sure. Time had strung together, one moment fading into the next.

Seren hardly remembered walking to Calarinn. He had come to Anna's doorstep once before, seeking refuge with Jude, and he found himself there again. Collapsing at the threshold, he slipped into unconsciousness. When he awoke, Anna had been hovering above him, her hand pressed to his forehead as she called his name.

That night, Anna bound Mila's sides, uncovering several fractured ribs and a broken arm. When her gaze fell on the red-inked serpent tattoo on Mila's chest, her lips pressed into a thin line, and her eyes flicked toward Seren.

The first night, Seren refused to leave Mila's side. He fell into small bouts of sleep, but nightmares repeatedly jolted him awake. He could feel the icy pricks of syringes sinking into his skin, the tearing of flesh from his back, and the heavy, wrought iron smell of blood.

When the sun rose the next day, he almost broke down in relief when he saw color returning to Mila's face and her wounds healing at a miraculous pace. Losing her would have ruined him, he was sure of it.

"Did you hear me, Seren?"

Worry flitted across Anna's features.

"We will leave tonight," Seren said, breaking away from his thoughts. He stepped forward and placed a velvet sack of coins in Anna's palm. "We'll need two horses. Could you get them for me?"

Anna opened the bag and gasped, quickly shutting it. "This is a lot of money," she squeaked. "Half of this should be plenty."

Seren's smile was faint but sincere. "Keep the rest. I have more than enough," he said. "Take your father and go to Vavilon. You can become a Technophage like you've always dreamed, though I think you'd make an even better Mechamagus."

Anna's hands had proven that—the way she'd repaired Jude's cybernetic limb with nothing more than a few simple tools. It was no small feat, especially for a country girl.

The thoughts came effortlessly, but Seren paused. How did he know that?

An image surfaced: Anna crafting cybernetic limbs of her own, machines of metal and false magic humming with a power unlike anything outside the Godless City. It felt so clear—too clear. Like an old memory, unbidden and unfamiliar, yet vivid all the same.

"Leave this country, Anna," Seren continued. "Go somewhere you can be who you want to be without judgment. You could have turned Mila and me in for who she is, but you didn't. You chose kindness, and I will be forever grateful."

Anna's tawny eyes met his as she clutched the bag. "Th-thank you," she stammered. "You can have a couple of our horses. And I can pack a few meals for the road for the two of you if you'd like."

"That'd be wonderful."

Anna squealed and turned on her heels. Seren was glad he had made the right judgment in coming to her. One wrong move and it could've cost him.

Seren sighed, turning back to Mila. He knelt by the bed and reached out, his finger softly brushing across her cheek. But then he pulled back, feeling his face burn. He had no right to touch her, not anymore. They were no longer in the Sanguine Kingdom, parading a false relationship.

She wasn't his to touch.

Swallowing his reluctance down, Seren stood. "Princess Ata," he whispered. "Wake up."

In a heartbeat, Seren felt a pull through the connection between them. Though he didn't fully understand it, the sensation was distinct. He held his breath as Mila's eyelids fluttered, and then her eyes sprang open, blinking as she sat up. She clutched the side of her head, and scanned the room before her gaze finally settled on Seren.

"Seren...?" she croaked.

Seren let out a heavy breath of relief. "Hey."

Mila swung her legs over the bed, placing her feet on the floor.

"Be careful," Seren demanded, his words coming out harsher than he intended. "You... you got hurt badly. Just...take it slow."

Mila nodded, her hand traveling to her side. "Yeah... I remember. Where...are we?"

"A farmhouse in Durcova. A friend's," he added. "We're safe here."

"How long have I been sleeping?" Mila's eyes wandered over Seren's messy hair. She raised her eyebrows, a silent acknowledgment of the change that had taken place in him.

A flush flooded Seren's cheeks as he ran his fingers through his hair. The new white streaks contrasted sharply with the inky blackness, a recent development that Anna had wasted no time commenting on. She had jokingly compared his appearance to that of a skunk after they arrived.

"It's been a few days."

Mila ran her hands across her arm and traced a finger across the scar on her face. "Oh, that's strange."

Seren was sure she was wondering the same thing. Why had she healed in such a short time when she should have been dead?

"How are you feeling?" he asked, breaking the silence between them.

Mila didn't respond, wrapping her arms around herself.

Seren cleared his throat and rose to his feet. "Well, I should let you have some privacy. Before I forget, I have something for you." He reached for his hip and pulled out her opalescent dagger from his waistband, placing it in her palm. Mila had kept the dagger close since he'd met her, saying it was the only memento she had of her late brother. "I know how important it is to you. And I...I have this for you as well."

He awkwardly reached for the blue dress he had bought that sat on the dresser. "There weren't many options for clothing, but I hope this is okay. I thought you'd want something new to wear." He had done his best to shake out the dirt, though it was still a bit stained and rumpled.

Mila's eyes widened as she gripped the dagger, her expression softening. "Thank you." Her fingers reached for the dress. "You didn't have to do this."

"Well, I doubted you wanted to wear that around."

Mila wore a dress Anna had given her, though it was too small, revealing her upper thighs. Her brown eyes widened, and she snatched the dress from his hands. "Thank you," she said. "Now, get out."

Seren turned around, his face bright red. "The bathroom is down the hall."

"Got it. Now *get out*, idiot."

Seren nodded and stumbled out, closing the door behind him with another weary sigh.

Anna had gone into town to run some errands, leaving Seren to wait for her return. In the quiet, he'd chosen to sit outside on the porch, leaving Mila undisturbed.

The sun dipped below the horizon, painting the sky in soft shades of pink and orange. Seren closed his eyes, letting the last rays of golden sunlight brush against his face. It was nice...too nice. His body slackened, sinking against the wall as if he might melt into it.

A loud thud jolted him as his head struck the wall, and he cursed under his breath. He had almost fallen asleep again. Shaking his head, he forced himself upright with a scowl.

"You look awful."

Mila stepped out onto the porch, bathed in the golden hour's light. Her damp hair clung to the back of her neck. She'd put on her new dress, the blue taking on a dusky hue beneath the sun's last breath. The cut was lower than Seren had intended, revealing a sliver of her red-inked tattoo just above the neckline—subtle, but enough to catch the eye.

Mila caught Seren's stare, her gaze drifting to the spot where his eyes had lingered. With a smirk, she tugged the dress higher. "Don't be such a pervert, Seren."

Heat rushed to Seren's cheeks. "I'm not!" he sputtered. "It's—your tattoo—"

Mila laughed. "I know. No need to get all tongue-tied."

Seren crossed his arms, his cheeks still burning as he muttered under his breath. "Whatever."

Mila strode over to Seren and settled next to him, pulling her knees into her chest. "You really do look awful."

Seren arched an eyebrow. "Why don't you say it a third time?" He met her glare with a sigh. "I'm fine, okay? Don't worry about me."

"Always the stoic type," she grumbled.

Mila lifted the hem of her dress, revealing a makeshift sheath made of cloth and rope strapped to her thigh. She drew out her dagger, twirling it between her fingers. The gems on the hilt dazzled in the fading sunlight.

"Will you help me with something?" She ran her fingers through her hair. "I tried to fix it myself, but I don't think I did a very good job."

When Seren first met Mila, her hair cascaded down her back like a river of silk. After the fall of the Sanguine Kingdom, her hair was choppy and chin-length, cut away by her mother as a parting gift.

"You should let Anna do it. I might mess it up," Seren said flatly, turning away.

"I doubt you can make it any worse," Mila said. "Besides, I would rather you do it."

Seren was quiet for a moment. He had never cut anyone's hair before and couldn't understand why Mila would want him to attempt it. As his eyes traced the uneven edges of her hair, he was reminded of her mother's cruelty.

It was another memory he wished to forget.

"Fine, I'll do it."

Mila placed the dagger in his hands triumphantly and positioned herself on the steps in front of Seren. He hesitated, brushing back a long strand of her uneven hair. His fingers grazed her neck, and he swallowed the lump in his throat before getting to work.

With each careful cut, her hair fell in soft, curling wisps around her shoulders, tumbling to the base of her neck. The process was slow and deliberate, Seren's fingers occasionally brushing her warm skin. When he finished, he paused, his hand resting a moment longer on her neck, feeling the subtle heat of her skin. For a moment, neither of them spoke or moved.

"Is something wrong?" Mila asked quietly.

Seren cleared his throat, handing her the dagger. "No, I'm done."

"Thanks." Mila smiled, tucking a strand of hair behind her ear. "I've never had hair this short."

"It fits you," Seren said honestly.

Mila flushed, lowering her thick eyelashes. "Thanks." Standing, she tucked the dagger back into its sheath, her gaze never leaving him. "Can we...talk?"

Seren stood and nodded toward the dirt path ahead. Anna was sauntering down the road, a basket swinging from her arm. He let out a quiet sigh of relief.

"There's Anna. Come on, you should meet her."

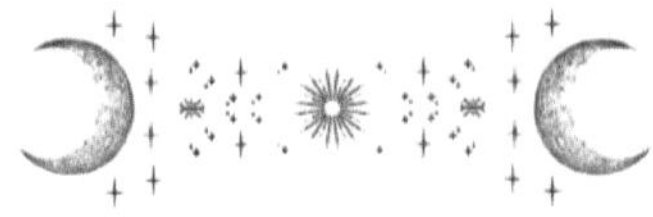

Anna and Mila got along effortlessly, their conversation flowing as if they'd known each other for years. Anna didn't mention her awareness of Mila's identity as a Sanguine Sister. Instead, she complimented Mila's hair, babbling about how she could never tame hers, while Mila returned the compliment, remarking on Anna's unruly curls.

Although Anna was clearly surprised to see Mila walking around with healed wounds, she refrained from asking questions. Sanguine Sisters were renowned for their magical prowess, so it could be Anna attributed it to that. Either way, Seren was thankful she didn't pry.

Anna had kindly prepared a delicious meal for them, mindful of their plans to leave. As they gathered around the rickety table, each with a generous bowl of stew, the savory aroma filled the air. Fragments of rosemary floated atop the frothy layer of fat that rested on the surface of the broth. Seren focused intently on his meal, doing his best to ignore Mila's penetrating gaze, which occasionally bored into the side of his head.

"Thank you, Anna. It's delicious," Mila said. "I hope it wasn't too much trouble to have us here."

"No need to thank me," Anna said. "If anything, it was nice to have company while my dad was away. Besides, Seren and I know each other, don't we?" She smirked at Seren from across the table, but her expression shifted as she sighed longingly. "I just wish you'd brought Jude with you." She planted her chin in her palm, a dreamy look in her eyes as she added, "He always knows how to lighten the mood."

Seren stirred his soup with a frown. "I do, too," he admitted quietly. He knew Jude was safe, but he longed to see his face and confirm it for himself.

"Jude is much more fun. No offense," Anna said, sticking her tongue out. "All Seren does is mope around like a sad puppy. At least he had an excuse this time." She removed her hand from her chin, leaning across the table. "He was *so* worried about you the last few days," she grinned, emphasizing it while batting her eyelashes. "I'd say the stress is catching up to you, skunk boy."

Seren tore off a piece of warm bread, slathered one half with butter, and jammed it into his mouth, though his hunger was nonexistent.

Mila laughed softly. "So, what does your dad do on his trips?"

Anna's voice lowered. "Vavilon has... advanced beyond what is possible here," she began. "We grow a lot of herbs on the farm, many of which we sell to the apothecary, but there are certain ailments that only the Godless City can help with. They have some sort of...agreement to help one another."

"That's dangerous," Seren murmured. "He could get caught."

He thought of the room downstairs where Anna had fixed Jude's leg, filled with wires and Godless City fragments brought back from her father's travels.

"So?" Anna said with a twisted frown. "How many lords go off to the Godless City to gamble and do whatever else they want?"

"Leave her be," Mila said. "They could be doing worse things."

"Yeah, like helping a Sanguine Sister." Anna grinned. "So, is that why you're healed?"

Mila's face paled, and she shot a glance at Seren. So much for keeping things quiet.

Anna flung up her arms. "Don't worry!" She stuffed a bite of food into her mouth and continued to talk. "Honestly, half the men in this country deserve it."

Seren coughed as a morsel lodged in his throat. As he reached for his drink to wash it down, he flashed Anna a disapproving look.

"I'm only kidding," Anna said. "Seren told me you ran away, and I trust him. No matter how mysterious and brooding he pretends to be."

Mila chuckled. "I like you, Anna."

Seren rolled his eyes, although a smile was tugging at the corners of his lips.

"Where do you two plan on heading?" Anna asked. "You can always stay one more night if you'd like."

"No," Seren replied firmly. "We're already intruding as it is. Besides, the sooner we get to Lumina, the better."

"What's in Lumina?" Anna asked, her curiosity piqued.

"Stellaris. Home," Seren sighed, watching the rosemary float in the bowl. The word tasted strange on his tongue. He leaned back in his chair, his limbs heavy. Gods, he was tired. Had he ever been this tired?

"Are you sure you don't want to rest a bit before you leave, Seren?" Anna asked. "You truly look terrible."

"Why does everyone keep saying that?"

"Because it's true. We should stay a bit longer," Mila said. "I'm still feeling...weak."

Guilt stirred in Seren. Looking at Mila now, she was thinner, and although she'd rested, dark purple smudged underneath her eyes. He'd been selfish, wanting to rush her out the door. She'd gone from fighting a demon to lying in bed for days, with no time in between.

Anna raised an eyebrow at Seren. "See, Seren? If not for yourself, do it for her."

Before he could respond, a loud knock sounded on the door, interrupting their conversation.

Anna's face lit up. "Dad must have returned early!" She stood up, bounding toward the door.

Seren adjusted his posture. If he wasn't careful, he'd end up falling asleep again. He sipped on his drink, bitter mulberry coating his tongue. It would be nice to see Anna's father, Andrew. He could properly thank him for his last visit.

"Isn't this his house?" Mila drawled with suspicion. Her eyes followed Anna's form as she approached the door.

Seren raised his eyebrows. "Yes, and?"

"Why is her dad *knocking* if it's his house? You don't find that strange?"

Seren jumped to his feet. "Anna—wait—"

Anna turned the handle, and the door swung open. It happened so fast; there was no time to think. Seren's veins ran cold as the blade left Anna's body, and she collapsed to the ground, blood flowing from the deep wound in her chest.

Mila let out a horrified gasp as Seren stumbled backward.

A steel-tipped boot kicked Anna's crumpled body to the side. The man wearing it hovered over her, his stormy-gray eyes clouded with amusement.

"Poor little farmhand," he said with mock sympathy. He tossed a golden bracelet shaped like coiled snakes and caught it midair. "Perhaps she shouldn't have been harboring a Sanguine sadist. Wouldn't you agree?"

Two

"The power of priests and saints stems from their faith, as the gods show favor towards those who believe and reward them accordingly."

—the Compendium of Holy Magic

Light flooded through the windows of the Church of Caelestis, illuminating the dust dancing in the air. Beneath the canopy of sunlight, the young man's unkempt hair shimmered like spun gold. His head rested against the pillow, blue eyes dull and unfocused.

He was dying.

A sudden fit of coughs wracked the boy's body, sending a chill through Lumen, who lingered just outside the doorway.

Watching the boy suffer, Lumen felt a pang of familiarity. He remembered the sensation all too well—the icy grip of sickness that had once ensnared him, coating his lungs with frost. He'd wished nothing but a swift death.

The High Priest of the church stood tall by the bedside, a cotton cloth wrapped around his mouth and nose. The room was sparsely furnished, containing only a bed draped in thin white sheets and a weathered side table where a cracked vase held freshly plucked yellow roses.

With his slender hands clasped in prayer, the priest kneeled beside the young man's bed, his dark blue robes pooling around him on the floor.

The boy's vacant eyes seemed to pass right through the priest, his expression distant. A slight moan escaped his lips, bringing with it a frosty exhale that hung in the air like smoke.

The High Priest lifted his head towards the young man. "I call upon the light to ease your suffering. I ask Helios to lessen your pain, Kallista to calm your soul, and Caelum to strengthen your mind." His hands hovered over the young man's forehead for a moment as he spoke the healing prayer. Glimmers of magic entered the boy through his tinted blue lips. The young man's eyelids fluttered shut as he slumped back onto the pillow, his breathing gradually easing as he drifted into slumber.

Lumen stroked Grimm, the raven companion perched upon his shoulder, watching the ritual unfold. *A pathetic attempt,* he thought.

The High Priest stood, letting out a long sigh. He smoothed the folds of his robes before soundlessly slipping out of the room, closing the door as he left.

Lumen emerged from the shadows of the hall. "Your prayers cannot save him, Aiden." He offered a thin smile, pushing his glasses up the sharp bridge of his nose with a delicate finger. "You're only prolonging his suffering. If anything, you're torturing the poor child."

Aiden scowled, barreling past Lumen with his robes billowing behind him. "As if you truly care. If you've come here just to mock me, then I'd rather you leave."

Frowning, Lumen ran his hand over Grimm's silky feathers, then traced the gleaming metals woven into the other wing. "Deny your little brother a place to stay after he traveled so far to see you? Now, that's just cruel."

Aiden spun around, his face flushed red. "You're lucky I even allowed you to set foot inside this church. If I hadn't contacted the Helios Legion, I never would've known Seren was in danger," he spat. "You are a disgrace. Just looking at you makes me sick to my stomach. And now the mercenary is dying in my church, and Seren isn't here as promised. Tell me, are you responsible for that as well?"

The corner of Lumen's mouth twitched. "You give me too much credit." He narrowed his eyes. "Always the hypocrite. Are you truly such a coward that you couldn't come get the boy yourself?"

Aiden ignored the question. "Why do I even waste my breath on you?" he hissed. "You're the same pathetic little brat you've always been."

"And you're the same spineless zealot you've always been."

Aiden slammed his fist into the wall, wincing at the impact. "I've about had enough of you." He squeezed his eyes shut, bracing himself as his knees trembled beneath him.

Lumen's pale eyebrows raised. "You're getting worse. Aren't you?" he murmured.

Aiden had changed little since the last time Lumen had seen him. Purple stained the thin skin underneath his eyes, a testament to the many sleepless nights he'd endured. His dark hair hung on the tops of his shoulders, longer than he'd ever kept it. The only feature that the two brothers shared was the shape of their eyes, the only sign that they came from the same mother. But Lumen could see how thin Aiden had become. His cheekbones jutted out, and even his wrists looked like they would snap underneath his weight.

"What do you want, Lumen?" Aiden finally asked. "I don't have the energy for this."

"I told you," Lumen said slyly. "I'm here to visit my older brother. Is that a crime?"

"Liar," Aiden whispered. "You want something. You always want something."

Lumen grinned. "Isn't that just human nature? Of course, I want something. Doesn't everyone?" He glided his index finger across the dusty edges of the pulpit. "When a baby is born, all it wants is its mother. When that baby grows into a child, it cries and screams if it breaks its favorite toy. When that child grows into a man, perhaps he wants money, women, or glory." He reached out and wiped dust onto the hem of Aiden's robe sleeve. "Humans are born selfish, and they die selfish. Unlike others, I have no qualms admitting the truth and no hesitation in doing what it takes to get what I want."

Aiden pushed himself off the wall. "Are you finished with your little speech?"

"Depends. Do you have what I want?"

Aiden's eyes darkened. "You're going to stay far away from Seren. You've poisoned his mind enough." His knuckles whitened at his sides. "You will *never* see him again."

Lumen leaned against the pulpit with a dramatic sigh. "I have no interest in the boy. He is your problem."

For now.

"However," he continued, "I seem to remember it was *you* who asked *me* to come here years ago. I find it ironic that you're suddenly acting so protective of a boy you once discarded like garbage."

Lumen remembered that day with a clarity he hated. Four years ago, he received a strange letter from Aiden, pleading that he come to the church. The writing had been frantic, uncharacteristically so. It had been years since his brother had so much as glanced in his direction—their last words exchanged after Ethles.

At first, Lumen ignored the letter, shoving it into a drawer. But then he read it again, a nagging feeling gnawing at him. Aiden had never asked for his help before. And though he wouldn't admit it, Lumen knew he owed his brother—if only a little. Eventually, curiosity won out.

What Lumen had found was a church and a strange boy painted in blood, with his brother left as a hollow shell of his former self. There had been no invitation this time, no hasty words penned to paper, but Lumen knew his brother was just as desperate now as he was four years ago. The circumstances had changed, but some men remained constant.

Aiden's mouth remained in a tight line. "It was a mistake to send for you that day."

"Yes, mistakes. It seems as though you've made a lot of those lately."

After the Unveiling of the church and the loss of the harp, Aiden had lost much of his respect in the eyes of the other priests and saints. Lumen knew his brother had limited options for redeeming himself. Seeing Aiden like this was unusual. He'd always been the praised one, the brother who never made mistakes and stayed in line. Now, shame flitted across Aiden's features.

The two brothers stood facing each other, a heavy silence settling between them for several seconds. They stood worlds apart, a familiar chasm dividing them. There had once been a time when Lumen had longed to stand by his brother's side, but now, he realized the folly of such desires. It was only a reminder of how pathetic he had once been.

A rush of wind heralded the arrival of an ivory falcon, swooping through the open window and breaking the brothers' tense silence. The speckled bird landed at Aiden's feet, clutching a rolled-up parchment in its talons.

Aiden's brow furrowed, his gaze lingering on the bird as though welcoming a distraction. "Eldyir's falcon," he muttered, kneeling as the bird released the letter onto the marbled floor. Without hesitation, the falcon spread its wings and soared back out into the open air.

Straightening, Aiden retrieved the letter and unrolled it. As his eyes scanned the contents, his face blanched. He cleared his throat, finally meeting Lumen's gaze.

"It seems I've been called to an emergency council in Aurelius." He tucked the letter into his wide sleeve. "I want you gone when I return. I've had enough of you for a lifetime."

Aiden said nothing more, striding toward the center of the chamber where the symbol of the Trinity was etched into the floor. At its core, a crescent moon nestled within the heart of a blazing sun, while seven radiant stars scattered across its rays like jewels in a crown. Lumen's gaze followed his brother as Aiden clasped his hands, silently preparing to leave.

"You could have stopped me. You wanted me to take him," Lumen called across the chamber. Grimm ruffled his feathers as Lumen moved toward his brother. "You practically begged me, and you know it."

Aiden didn't so much as bat an eye in his direction.

Lumen continued, "You won't receive forgiveness easily. You've always had far too many secrets." He smiled. "You're getting worse. Have you told Eldyir why, brother?"

Aiden's hands fell to his sides, his dark eyes clouding. "*Don't*."

"You've always been a hypocrite," Lumen said. "Just like your father." He ran a thin finger through his curtain of platinum hair. "I could help you redeem yourself, earn the respect of the ecclesiarch again. I know where Caelum's Sword is."

Aiden's body stiffened.

"You asked me what I wanted, and I'll tell you," Lumen sneered. "I can imagine how desperate you are to get your hands on the trinity of holy items."

Aiden's fists clenched. "You're lying."

"Am I?" Lumen said with a frown. "And why would I do that? I have no reason to lie to my dear brother. You think so little of me." He took a step closer, his toes touching the tip of the golden Trinity outline. "The sword is in Vavilon. Allow me to access the crypts of the church, and I will tell you how to access the Reliquerium. You get what you want, as do I. Do we have a deal?"

Aiden's dark eyebrows furrowed. "The Archives?" he sputtered. "Since when do you have any interest in such things?"

Lumen tilted his head to the side, the shadow of a smile playing on his lips. "As your brother, I deserve access, regardless."

"Wrong," Aiden boomed. "Do not forget that when we went to Etheles together, the gods rejected you. That *my* father rejected you. The gods chose *me*. You're an unholy, sinful man, and one day, you'll pay for your wrongs. Go back to the Godless City where you belong."

Lumen's lower lip curled. "But it was not the gods who saved you in the Veil all those years ago, was it? And I can't seem to understand that, no matter how hard I try. Why did the gods choose you, Aiden? Surely you cannot play the role of both sides, can you?"

Aiden's face paled. "I was a child."

"And so was the boy."

"You say that," Aiden said, voice icy. "And yet, you were so quick to use him for whatever motives you had planned."

The brothers stared each other down, the silence between them once again thick and suffocating. Finally, Aiden let out a long sigh, releasing them from the moment. His onyx eyes didn't waver as they remained locked on Lumen. "I've had enough of this quarreling. I have things to attend to."

He paused, his gaze narrowing. "If you watch over the mercenary until his..." Aiden trailed off as if the word *death* was a horrible taboo. "As well as tell me how to access the Reliquerium. I am not sure how long I will be gone. Do these things for me and only then do we have an agreement."

Lumen scowled. "I refuse."

"You will do it, or you'll leave now, and I will get the sword without you."

"Just let him die," Lumen said bitterly. "The boy needs no coddling before his death."

A wind rippled through the window, inky strands of hair blowing across Aiden's face. For a moment, they were children again—Aiden as distant as he had always been. It didn't take much imagination for Lumen to be transported back to that time, twenty years ago.

Lumen had been full of sorrow then, the pieces of his old self just beginning to corrode away. It had always been Aiden who possessed a wicked tongue, who spoke cruel words he believed were the gods' painted truth. Lumen had to learn to make cruelty his own, to nurture it and let it grow from the inside out until it covered him like a second skin.

I should have let you die, Aiden had said. *If it wasn't for you, our mother would be alive.*

"Have you no love in your heart, little brother?" Aiden asked.

"I have just about as much love as I was given."

Aiden's expression remained unmoved. "This is the last time I will do anything for you." He pulled a silver key from his robes, clasping it rigidly between his fingers. The end of the key was shaped into a starburst, with delicate ridges decorating it like the rolling tides of the ocean. "If you steal anything or destroy anything in the Archives—"

Lumen snatched the key from his grasp. "I am not a fool. I know the consequences of such actions," he interrupted. "Having every priest and saint after my head is something I'd rather avoid." Lumen tucked the key into his pocket and crossed his arms. "Only a Novem can enter the Reliquerium through a biometric security system."

Aiden's eyebrows shot up. "And you can access it?"

Lumen laughed. "No," he said. "I'm not a Novem any longer. I'm sure you could find a way, considering your *connections*."

For once, it seemed Aiden believed Lumen was telling the truth. What Aiden didn't know, however, was that Lumen had killed Faith—the Novem woman who had aided the mercenary in freeing Seren and had been passing information to Aiden through her contacts in the Helios Legion. As far as Lumen knew, Faith hadn't been foolish enough to expose the Legion's true purpose. To Aiden, they were just a radical faction that had splintered from the Trinity, devoted to the sun god and hoping to thwart Vavilon's expansion. What a fool Aiden was.

"Very well," Aiden finally said. "But first, I want your word."

Lumen grimaced. "I'd rather not."

Aiden motioned toward Lumen's pocket. "The key is bound by a geas; it won't unlock the door unless you speak the truth and follow your word. Is that truly where the sword lies? And do you swear to watch over the mercenary upon my departure?"

"Yes and yes," Lumen said through clenched teeth. "You have my word."

"And do you swear to treat the Archives with the utmost respect?"

A muscle twitched in Lumen's jaw. "Yes."

"Say it."

Lumen's fists curled at his side. "I will watch over the brat and will be kind to your precious books."

Aiden took a step backward. "Good. Then we have a deal." He closed his hands, and intricate runes began to glow faintly on his palms. A soft, golden light swirled around him, coalescing into a shimmering aura that traced the patterns of his robe. As the magical energy intensified, the air seemed to hum with power. Aiden's form started to blur.

"You abandoned him, Aiden," Lumen said. "You could have come to Vavilon. Four years—you had all that time to drag him back to Lumina yourself. But you didn't. Because you didn't want him back. Not truly. Do you even know what it feels like to be left behind by those you thought you loved?"

The wind whipped through the open window, tousling Lumen's hair. Aiden remained silent, his expression tight.

"What makes you think Seren will want to return?" Lumen continued. "To become what you've tried so hard to mold him into? As far as he knows, you see him as nothing more than a disappointment and a monster." His voice rose with each accusation. "Do you remember what you said to me? 'The gods chose wrong. I have chosen wrong. He will never be a son of mine.' I took him to Vavilon under your word. No matter what you tell him now, everything he has endured—everything—is because of you."

The last thing Lumen saw of his brother was the guilt filling his eyes before the spell whisked him away and the wind slammed the window shut.

THREE

"Obedience makes us the most faithful, for we are but children of the gods, and children who disobey must be punished."
—the Laws of Servius

Seren had to be dreaming. It had to be just another horrific nightmare creeping into his consciousness, tricking him. None of it was real. It couldn't be. His eyes followed the dark pool of blood spreading around Anna's limp form, and denial clawed its way under his skin. He knelt, hands trembling, and turned her body over. Lifeless eyes stared back at him. A choked sound escaped his throat as the room spun. He jerked his head away, retching onto the cold floor.

"You killed her." Seren's voice was barely a whisper. He wiped the bile from his lips, his ears ringing as his heart pounded.

With a sly smile, the man towered over Seren. His fingers slid through auburn hair streaked with gray, eyes narrowing as he studied Seren with interest.

There was no mistaking the man's stature, told by the way he carried himself. The common folk of Calarinn dressed in faded browns and creams, but this man wore an impeccably tailored suit in a deep, rich gray.

Not a single drop of blood marred his pristine attire, though the sword in his grip glistened with fresh crimson.

Standing beside the man was Thomas Glynn, a young man Seren recognized. Sweat beaded on his forehead, his reddish hair clinging to his temples. His mouth hung open, eyes wide, and a burning torch trembled in his grasp as he stared at Anna's lifeless body. Just weeks ago, Jude and Seren had shared drinks with Thomas, laughing as if they were old friends. Now, the boy stood frozen, blood creeping steadily toward the tips of his boots.

"What a mess," the man beside Thomas scoffed, cocking his head and jutting his chin forward. "Grab them."

"Yes, Lord Glynn, sir."

Two men—one short and stocky, the other tall and muscular—emerged from behind Thomas and Lord Glynn. The tall one seized Seren by the arm, yanking him to his feet. Seren remained motionless.

"Don't touch me!" Mila thrashed, struggling against the other man's hold.

Hearing Mila's cry seemed to snap Seren from his haze. He jerked his arms, but the man's grip tightened, his thumbs pressing bruises into Seren's skin.

"Leave her alone," Seren demanded. But his body was weak, the man's hold too strong. The more he struggled, the more it felt as if he were underwater, wading through an impossibly thick current of exhaustion.

"Treason," the lord said, stepping forward, "should never be taken lightly. Thomas, I must express my deep disappointment in you."

Thomas's head drooped as he avoided making eye contact with Seren. Even if he did recognize him, he made sure not to reveal it.

"Perhaps, I was mistaken in passing lordship to you. This issue should have been addressed as soon as the rumors started," the man continued, holding out the bloodied sword. Thomas hardly lifted his head as he took it, gripping the hilt before securing it in the scabbard on his back. "After all the missing young men, no stranger should be unaccounted for in Calarinn. Though, I can't say I'm surprised that Andrew and his bastard girl are responsible."

"Rot in hell," Seren spat.

Unfazed, the lord stepped forward, lifting Seren's chin with a casual flick of his fingers. A crease formed between his brows as he studied him. "You look... familiar somehow." He grimaced, wrinkling his nose. "Perhaps, you just remind me of a particularly foul creature." With a dismissive click of his tongue, he turned away. "Take them outside."

Seren and Mila's captors pulled them out the door, their feet sliding through Anna's blood. Seren squeezed his eyes shut, unable to look at her. He didn't want to remember her like that.

"Monster!" Mila snarled. She cried out as the man restraining her jerked her back with ruthless force.

Lord Glynn burst into laughter, his lean frame trembling. Moonlight enveloped them, casting a glow on the lord. His resemblance to Thomas was uncanny; one could almost believe he was Thomas's father. Seren blinked, his attention shifting to the sky. The moon hung swollen in the sky.

Another full moon?

That was impossible.

"Should we kill them now, Lord Glynn?" asked the man holding Seren. "This one doesn't look like he has much fight in him."

Thomas's eyes widened slightly, and he opened his mouth as if to speak, but when the lord stepped forward, he snapped it shut. The lord walked past Seren, placing a hand under Mila's chin. Her eyes darkened as he traced her features, a perverse smile spreading across his face.

"I don't want to kill them yet. That would be far too easy," Lord Glynn murmured. "It's such a shame that you're a devil woman. You're beautiful." He circled her like a cat, his hand sliding down to rest on her hip. "Such a lovely face..." His lips pressed against her neck, rendering her frozen in place. "Gone to waste."

"Keep your hands off her," Seren seethed.

"Oh? Have I hit a soft spot?" Lord Glynn grinned. He leaned in, bringing Mila's hair to his nose and taking a deep breath. Rage boiled inside of Seren. "How fortunate that she's being executed on my terms. I'd say it can wait until sunrise. Wouldn't you agree, boy?"

Mila's eyes blazed as the lord brought his fingers against her cheek. "I'm sorry, pretty little thing. I simply cannot allow a Sister to parade around Durcova, murdering men of Servius. You understand, don't you? It's nothing personal." With a stride, he moved ahead, his polished boots glimmering in the moonlight. "Burn everything and make it look like a tragic accident."

With a rigid nod, Thomas glanced in Seren's direction. He gulped and threw his torch atop the dry grass that surrounded Anna's home. It instantly caught fire.

"Damn you!" Seren shouted, wriggling. "You're *filth*! Damn you, and your slime of a god!"

Lord Glynn smacked Seren across the face with his gloved hand. Blood filled Seren's mouth, but he swallowed it down. He wouldn't bleed for him.

"You little shit," the lord sneered. "Watch your tongue, or I'll cut it out." He licked his dry lips, another smile creeping onto his face. "Listen closely. Here's what's going to happen." He leaned in, inches from Seren's face, his breath reeking of ferment. "If you continue to fight, I'll throw you and your pretty friend into the fire. I'll make sure she burns first, that way you can hear the witch scream." Wood crackled as flames spread across the porch, their glow casting long shadows on the grass. "Or you can keep your filthy mouth shut and watch while I peel that dress off her and check every inch of her skin." Seren's heart hammered. "And if I do, and she has no Sanguine markings, we can call this a misunderstanding." His grin deepened as his eyes roamed to Mila's chest, where the neckline had shifted in her struggles, revealing the edge of her tattoo. "What do you say?"

"Go to hell." Seren lunged forward, slamming his forehead into the lord's. The man cried out, grabbing his forehead, rage burning in his eyes.

A blow landed on Seren's stomach, and he doubled over in pain. Struggling to focus through the spots clouding his vision, he fought to catch his breath. Nausea crept up his throat as another fist struck his chest. Seren choked on the air, his eyes watering.

"Stop!" Mila shouted.

As if for good measure, Lord Glynn yanked Seren's face down and drove his knee into it. A horrible crunch echoed through the air. Pain exploded in Seren's face, white lights dazzling his vision like stars. When he finally managed to draw a breath, blood poured down his chin. He lifted his eyes, squinting through the pain, just in time to see Mila spit at the man's feet.

"We're taking them to the Glynn Estate," the lord announced. "I am going to show Thomas the proper way to instill fear when it is necessary. He's too soft for his own good."

Seren fought to stay conscious as they dragged him and Mila through the dark. His legs felt weak beneath him, and his eyes watered relentlessly alongside the burn in his nose. It was probably broken. He wondered if Mila still had her dagger or if she could even use her magic. Maybe she didn't want to give them the satisfaction of knowing she was a Sister. Or maybe she was just too weak. That was it, wasn't it? They were both too weak.

Seren hadn't slept or hardly eaten in days and Mila had been bedridden. And that was Seren's fault, too. Maybe. His head was heavy, his thoughts swirling in a muddled mess. All he could focus on was the hollow ache in his chest. Anna was dead because of him. Selling those bracelets had been a foolish decision. He should have known better.

As they were pulled through wrought iron gates, Seren's recognition dawned. He'd been here once before with Thomas and Jude, part of an ill-conceived plan that would allow Seren and Jude to sneak into the Sanguine Kingdom to rescue Mila.

Past the garden, the men dragged Mila and Seren forcefully through the cherry-wood door of a chalet nestled among the trees at the edge of the property. Inside, the decor was more modest than the chamber Seren remembered. A simple chandelier cast a warm, almost mocking glow over velvet-upholstered furniture and a table in the corner. Seren's weary eyes barely registered the gleaming metal on the table before a jolt of recognition shot through him. A golden pistol from the Godless City rested beside a lantern.

The word *hypocrite* built up, ready to spill over Seren's lips, but he was shoved forward before a sound could escape. Lord Glynn pulled two chairs out. A large elbow slammed into Seren's chest, crushing the air from his lungs.

"That's so you don't get any ideas," the man grunted.

Struggling to catch his breath, Seren was roughly shoved into a chair, his legs buckling beneath him. His wrists were yanked behind the chair and bound with coarse rope, the fibers digging painfully into his skin. His ankles were similarly secured, pinning him in place. As he gasped for air, his vision swam.

Mila was dragged across the room with a harshness that made Seren's heart clench. They forced her into a chair opposite him, tight cords binding her arms to the chair, rendering them immobile.

"Comfortable?" Lord Glynn asked, leaning toward Seren.

Seren struggled to lift his head, too exhausted to come up with a clever retort. Instead, he spat directly into the lord's face. The burly man behind him reacted, wrenching Seren's head back, gripping his hair tightly and pulling his chin upward.

"Want me to cut out his tongue, my lord?" the man asked. "It would be my pleasure."

Lord Glynn flicked his wrist. "No, I want him to keep his tongue." He smiled at Seren. "How else would I hear him beg for mercy?"

Thomas pressed himself against the red-painted wall near the door, his gaze fixed on the floor. "What are you going to do to them, Uncle?" he whispered.

Lord Glynn chuckled. "You'll see," he said. "Go grab two bottles of wine, so we can truly enjoy ourselves."

Thomas hesitated, his hand hovering over the door for a moment before he pushed it open and disappeared.

The lord walked behind Mila, his finger grazing her lower neck. She bared her teeth at him like a dog ready to rip his throat out.

Seren's pulse spiked. "Don't you dare lay another filthy finger on her," he said, his voice coming out quieter than he intended.

"Or what?" the lord asked. "You're in no place to be giving me demands."

"It's okay, Seren," Mila said. But Seren noticed the slight quiver in her voice as she spoke.

And then he felt it—a twinge between them. Seren's eyes dropped to her hands, catching the faint flex of her fingers. She was trying to use her magic, but the pull was weak, too faint. She didn't have enough energy.

"You two," the lord directed the other men, "out."

With audible grumbles of disappointment, the men nodded and left through the door. Lord Glynn locked eyes with Seren, his smirk sinister. The man reached for the golden pistol on the table. He strode toward Seren, pressing the cold barrel of the gun against his temple.

"Have you ever seen a gun, boy? They're clever little machines," he mused. "All I have to do is pull this trigger, and your brains will come out of your ears."

"Servius must be proud of you," Seren whispered.

Lord Glynn's finger hovered over the trigger. "You brat—"

Seren opened his mouth to bite off another reply, heedless of the death that might follow afterward. That's when he saw it, the room coming just enough into focus that the items above the mantle could be understood. Seren leaned forward, the barrel digging further into his skin. Could his eyes be deceiving him? He blinked through the dizzying sensation in his head.

A silver sword hung on the mantle, and just below it was a portrait. In the painting, the lord appeared much younger, undeniably handsome. The room seemed to close in around Seren, the cold press of the barrel forgotten. The young woman standing beside the lord in the picture was beautiful. She had eyes painted emerald-green, fiery red hair cascading around her, and sadness filling her features.

Lord Glynn followed Seren's gaze. "Admiring my painting?" The barrel left Seren's forehead as he strode over, his finger running over the woman's cheek. "She was my first wife. It's a shame she turned out to be a barren, useless whore. Still, I couldn't bear to take down the painting. I quite enjoy waking up to such a lovely face every morning."

Seren lunged forward, letting out a snarl, the chair teetering on the edge of toppling forward. "You bastard!"

Lord Glynn raised his eyebrows, a flicker of confusion crossing his face.

"My *mother* had a name," Seren said.

The room fell silent, save for Seren's labored breathing.

"Mother?" Lord Glynn finally said. "That's impossible. The woman was incapable of having children."

Seren fumed, straining against the restraints. All the exhaustion he had felt vanished, replaced by an all-consuming rage. "Her name was Emeryn," he growled. "And if that's true, then why am I sitting right in front of you?"

The lord's eyes widened in recognition when Seren spoke her name. His features twisted. "You're a lying little shit."

"No wonder she ran from the likes of you," Seren continued. "You're *scum*."

Lord Glynn's nostrils flared. "I knew she was an unfaithful, worthless woman," he said. "I should have let her rot in that orphanage."

"Servius must have punished you," Seren challenged, gaze traveling to the pistol. "It doesn't seem very obedient to be parading around in the Godless City. Now, does it?"

The rope started to fray underneath Seren's writhing grip. The lord's face paled, and an emotion flickered across his features, perhaps humiliation or hate, maybe even something between the two. But before the lord could say a word, the door burst open, the sound of clinking glass echoing as wine bottles rolled from Thomas's hands onto the oak floor.

"Uncle." Thomas's face was ghostly. "The town, it's being attacked."

Lord Glynn advanced towards him. "What? By whom?" he demanded.

"Demons," Thomas choked. "The Veil has merged with half the town."

"That's impossible."

Seren sucked in a breath. No, he hadn't been hallucinating. The moon was bright and full.

"I swear to you," Thomas said, his voice trembling. "We need to get out of here right now. The gates are open, and people are pouring in. It's total chaos."

Sweat formed on the lord's upper lip. "Get the horses ready and meet me at the stables."

"What about them?" Thomas asked.

"Let the demons have them. A death fitting for a son of a whore and a sadist." He kicked Seren's chair with enough force to send it toppling to its side. Seren's head hit the ground, grit and dust under his face. The lord's boot met his stomach again in an act of farewell, but Seren had no way to curl in. Then, without another word, Lord Glynn barreled past Thomas out the door, shouting demands. Thomas followed him, flashing a last look behind his shoulder before shutting the door.

"Seren, are you okay?" Mila said, fighting against her restraints.

"I'll kill him," Seren whispered, his cheek pressed against the floor.

"Forget him. We need to get out of these binds," Mila growled. She shuffled her chair around, cursing. "If I could just use my damn hands, this would be so much easier."

From where he laid, Seren could meet his mother's gaze once more. No. He couldn't bear it. She was staring at him disappointed and sad. The memory flashed again: her lifeless body sprawled in the hellebore-littered grass, blood seeping into the earth around her. He could hear the shrill screams of the demons, as if they had crawled out of that memory and sunk their claws into his mind.

"I'll kill him," Seren said again.

"Damn it, Seren. Look at me!" Mila shouted. "Stop staring at that painting. I will not have you get us killed because of some creepy lord and your dead mother. Do you understand? I tried to summon my magic earlier, and it didn't work; I'm too weak. I need you, Seren."

Seren's gaze lifted, meeting Mila's beautiful brown eyes which were somehow warm despite the cold horrors unfolding around them. Yes, she was right. He was losing it. The lack of sleep and the haunting memories were eating at his brain—rotting his good senses away. Seren twisted and pulled against the binds.

A hair-raising screech erupted from outside the door, followed by the frantic screams of men. Squelching and slopping sounds filled the air, and dark liquid began to spill in from beneath the door, staining the floor and creeping up to the tips of Seren's shoes. His breath hitched in his throat, and Mila froze across from him.

The air thickened, a sibilant hiss cutting through the silence. Something scraped at the door—sharp, like claws on wood. The door rattled on its hinges. Seren didn't dare move. A wail echoed distantly, and the rattling stopped. Seren and Mila both let out a simultaneous breath of relief.

Then, the door burst open.

Thomas stumbled through, his boots splashing in the freshly spilled blood. His steel-gray eyes glistened with terror. Thomas rushed over to

Seren, a penknife in his grasp. He cut the ropes and cut Mila's binds as Seren rose to his feet.

"You have to get out of here now," Thomas said rapidly. "There's a demon on the estate. If we can get to the stables in the back, we have a better chance of outrunning it."

"Why are you helping us?" Mila asked. Her dagger was already in her grip, pointed towards Thomas.

"Because it's the right thing to do." He stiffened. "If you want to kill me, go ahead. I'm sorry about Anna. I didn't... I didn't know he was going to kill her, or I would have tried to stop him."

Thomas and Mila stared at each other for several seconds before she lowered the weapon.

"Lead the way," she said.

Mila followed Thomas as he headed towards the door, swiping the lantern from the nearby table. But Thomas paused, hands shaking above the door handle as the demon shrieked in the distance.

"It sounds farther away," he breathed. "Maybe we're safe."

"Wait." Seren rushed to the mantle, taking one last glance at the painting. He wondered if this was the last time he'd see her like this—immortalized in doleful beauty and grace. This was how he wanted to remember her. He fixated on the painting, striving to sear the image into his mind to replace her bloodied death with the gentle strokes of paint. He reached out, a finger tracing the curve of her cheek, standing for a moment as if waiting for her face to move, to break into a smile, or for a hand to reach out and grasp his. But it didn't come.

Seren grasped the sword above the fireplace and pulled it down next. It was heavy in his grip though it wasn't any larger than the one he'd used in the Behethium Forest.

The three of them rushed out the door. Seren deliberately kept his gaze straight ahead, feeling the weight of his boots on what he feared might be human flesh. A wave of relief washed over him as he saw the estate was deserted, the sounds of the demon fading into the distance.

"Hurry it up. Follow me," hissed Thomas.

Seren's back pressed against the building as they followed the feeble glow of Thomas's lantern, the only light piercing the surrounding darkness. The night cloaked their surroundings, forcing Mila and Seren to huddle close behind Thomas, their breaths forming visible clouds in the chilly air.

Seren stumbled, his shoe colliding with something on the ground. Regret surged over him as he looked down at a severed hand, mangled and torn. The world spun around him as he struggled to keep up with Thomas through the enveloping blackness.

The horses' fearful neighs echoed through the night, guiding them to the stables. Seren and Mila stayed pressed against a tree, barely daring to breathe as Thomas motioned for them to wait. Hooves thundered against the stable walls as the creatures frantically searched for an exit.

Thomas cautiously approached the gates of the first stable, his hand extending toward the white fur of the closest mare. Her ears flattened, and hot breath swirled in front of her face.

"Calm, Estelle," he whispered, though his voice wavered. "Calm." Her breathing eased as Thomas brushed the pale bridge of her nose. He then moved to the horses with russet hides and cream-colored splotches along their torsos, calming them one by one with his touch.

"And just *what* do you think you're doing, Thomas?"

Lord Glynn emerged from the shadows, limping on a mangled leg, a bloodied brick clutched tightly in his curled fist. His auburn hair was wild and unkempt, and his stormy eyes gleamed with a feral intensity. "Trying to leave me, just like those spineless cowards, are you?" he spat, his voice edged with menace. "Perhaps you should join them," he added, glancing at the brick with a cruel smirk. "They made good distractions for the demons, after all."

Seren clutched the naked sword in his hand. "Go," he said to Mila, not tearing away from the lord. "You and Thomas, get out of here."

Thomas glanced between Glynn and Seren. He took a step forward, his hand still resting on the mare. "Uncle, just let them go," he said. "Please, we can share a horse and get out of here together."

"Shut up, unless you want to die too," Lord Glynn growled. "You're actually worth a bullet or two."

Not far away, a terrible scream echoed. Thomas's face drained of color as the lantern slipped from his grasp and fell into the dirt, the flame miraculously still flickering despite the impact.

"Go," Seren demanded. "*Now.*"

Thomas flung open the stable door, mounted the white horse, and kicked it with his heel. The horse reared up and bolted into the darkness.

Mila was next, flinging open the next gate and jumping onto the other russet horse. It stood its ground, although its hooves beat on the ground fearfully as it awaited the command to run.

"Seren," Mila said. "Get on the horse." She held her hand out. "We'll ride together."

"Yeah, run away, boy," Glynn sneered, dragging his injured leg. "I'm sure you're good at it, just like your mother."

Seren squeezed his eyes shut, his pulse racing. He turned away from the lord and grabbed Mila's outstretched hand, pulling himself onto the horse. With a firm grip on the reins, he urged the horse forward.

A sudden searing pain struck the side of Seren's head. His vision erupted into a blinding burst of white light and darkness as he was violently thrown sideways. The rhythmic pounding of the horse's hooves faded. Seren hit the ground with an unforgiving thud that left him sprawled and dazed, struggling to regain his bearings.

Somewhere in the distance, Mila shouted Seren's name. Warm blood trickled down his forehead. He turned his head to see the brick beside him in the dirt, along with his sword. The sound of hooves trampling sticks and undergrowth echoed through the night.

Seren forced himself to sit up, his head heavy. His thoughts were thick as honey, the world around him fading in and out of darkness.

"Did you really think I'd let you leave alive?" Lord Glynn hissed, towering over Seren. "Your mere existence is a sin." He delved into his pocket, producing the gleaming golden pistol that he aimed directly at Seren's chest. "I wish your useless mother was here to watch you die."

Seren's heart pounded against his ribs, his breaths coming in shallow gasps as he stared down the barrel of the pistol. "The demon will hear the gun if you shoot me," he said. "And then we'll both be dead."

"I'm willing to take that risk to see you die."

Glynn's finger pressed the trigger.

Boom.

Seren clutched at his chest, waiting for the gush of hot blood to seep between his fingers—but it didn't come. Lord Glynn's gun was raised to the sky, his forearm trembling. A wispy shadow wound around his elbow, snaking upward and coiling itself around the weapon. More darkness slithered from the depths of the trees, creeping like mist and reaching out toward them.

A frosty chill coursed through Seren, as though the entire world had iced over. Goosebumps prickled his flesh, and a shiver crawled up his neck. The air filled with whispers—a cacophony of a hundred voices—and the sensation of a thousand unseen eyes watching them.

Seren scrambled in the dirt, desperately reaching for his sword. He pushed himself onto his unsteady legs, bracing himself as the encroaching darkness swarmed closer.

"Don't even think of running, bastard," the lord demanded, his voice quaking.

As he attempted to lower the gun, the grip of the shadows seemed to tighten. With a sharp yank, his hand recoiled, and the gun clattered to the ground. An onslaught of darkness surrounded them, cloaking them in a thick, oppressive miasma. Seren felt a familiar, soul-crushing weight against his chest as a putrid stench invaded his senses. A bone-deep cold snaked into Seren's veins.

Trembling, the lord's lips quivered like the flutter of moth wings. "No, please!" he cried out. "Don't take me. Take him instead. I've been faithful and obedient. Take the *bastard!*"

A wisp of shadow curled around Seren's wrist, trailing across his forearm. He shuddered, a delicate chill traveling up his spine like the cruel lips of a lover. And then it spoke, ripping through his mind—a sound like bones snapping and flesh tearing, a symphony of sickness and death wrapped in a shroud of malignancy.

"Kill him, little prince."

Seren clasped the sword in his hand, his eyes locking onto the lord's fearful stare.

"Dig your sword into his heart. Give him his judgement."

The lord cowered and fell into the dirt, his focus slipping away from Seren as the pitiless dark swarmed.

"Kill. Kill. Kill."

The shadows chanted, each word a fresh wound in Seren's mind. His feet refused to obey him, even as the urge to run surged through his body. Instead, the word grew heavier, burrowing under his skin as if searching for a home.

"Give him your judgment, godling."

The word reverberated deep inside Seren. Lifeless tawny eyes flashed in his mind. Lord Glynn had slaughtered Anna in cold blood, without mercy. He had nearly put a bullet into Seren's chest. And Seren could only imagine what his mother had endured at the hands of this man.

Judgement.

Seren pointed the tip of the sword at the man's chest. The shadows swirled around them like a storm, kicking up dirt and small rocks. They constricted around Seren's forearm, urging him forward.

How many times had judgment gone unnoticed? Seren's fear transformed. He no longer wanted to run. No. He had always been running. But he wasn't going to run right now.

Shadows clung to Seren's shoulders, their weight lifting. He raised the sword, every cell in his body whispering the same word.

Judgement.

The dark wisps curled around the blade, swirling and whispering into the space between. And yet... who was Seren to deliver judgement? He froze, lowering the sword. Judgement was for the gods, wasn't it?

A shadow floated across Seren's mouth, whispering in a hundred voices:

"Judgment is yours, godling."

Seren's hand tightened on the blade. That's right. Judgement was for the gods. And didn't the blood of a god flow in his veins? Didn't the soul of a goddess live inside him?

"Take his soul. It is yours to judge. Yours to condemn."

He slid the sword's tip into the lord's chest, feeling it sink into flesh. Shadows crawled across Seren's torso, grazing his throat. The lord cried out in pain as Seren pressed on with renewed strength. He wanted this. He wanted to pierce the lord's heart, to seize judgment into his own hands.

But there was something more. Seren could see it—a writhing grey mass of energy pulsing at the center of the lord's chest. His soul. A deep, primal hunger stirred in the pit of Seren's belly. His left hand twitched as shadows surged forward, thin tendrils wrapping around the grey aura.

"You speak of the gods as if you know them," Seren heard himself say, his voice foreign, splintered with shards of darkness. *"As if they care for you. As if they will save you."*

His body trembled with anticipation, every fiber of his being urging him to shatter everything around him. *"But your gods are not here. Only I am. I am your god now. You kneel to me."*

Seren's knuckles whitened, the tendrils of shadow tightening around him. A choking cry escaped the lord as the color drained from his eyes.

The hunger within Seren grew unbearable. It consumed him, the world around him fading as the darkness clawed deeper into his mind.

"This is your judgement."

And then, Seren plunged the sword into the lord's heart.

"Seren!"

Mila's cry cut through the haze. For a moment, the world tilted, disorienting him. His breath hitched, the sound of her voice echoing in his mind, shattering the spell that had ensnared him. His body lurched, blinking rapidly, as if waking from a nightmare.

The lord choked on a strangled breath, a wet, gurgling sound escaping his thin lips as blood bubbled up and spilled down his chin. His body lurched forward, driving the blade deeper, and a rush of crimson spread down his front.

Seren had killed him. He'd *killed* him.

Mila called for Seren again. Her voice felt distant, echoing through the vast emptiness where darkness had dwelled. He wrenched the sword away with all his might, his breath coming in ragged gasps. Shadows curled around his throat, creeping through his hair.

"No..." Seren stepped back, his grip faltering, his heart racing. "No." He squeezed his eyes shut, panting. The sword clattered to the ground.

Another voice broke through—different from the others. It wasn't Mila's cry. It wasn't the shadows' incessant whispers. It was her. It nearly fractured his mind.

"Seren."

Pain sliced through his thoughts like a molten blade. Energy jolted across his spine. Seren recognized the feeling—the tingling sensation prickling across his skin, swelling in his chest. He didn't resist it. It filled him from the inside out. The power surged through him with a force both exhilarating and excruciating. It grew brighter, warmer, until it started to burn.

It was pain and bliss, agony and euphoria. Blinding light erupted around him, blazing like the final flare of a dying star. It was as though the very gates of heaven had swung open, casting an otherworldly brilliance. The darkness shattered and receded, the agonized screams of the wisps fading into the night, swallowed by the sheer intensity of divine light.

Seren stood, trembling and drenched in sweat. Then, he ran. He sprinted toward Mila's call until he saw the shape of a horse in the night. Seren leapt onto the horse's back, wrapping his arms around Mila's waist. His hands found the reins alongside hers, gripping tight as his feet dug into the horse's sides.

The horse thundered toward the trees. They galloped past the town's edge, fire blazing across the buildings—dying screams fading behind them. Finally, reaching the outskirts, far from it all, Seren's head grew heavy. He slumped against Mila's back, and then, he was falling. Just before hitting the ground, he heard his mother's voice calling his name.

FOUR

"The magic of harmony is a beautiful thing—it is powerful to find peace in the chaos."

—the Compendium of Holy Magic

Aiden's back was slick with sweat. It had been several years since a Sanctified Assembly had occurred. Every priest and saint from all corners of Aerithium had been called to the emergency council. Aiden could not deny the anxiety building inside of him as he approached the Caelestis Cathedral. The Grand Priest of Aurelius, Eldyir, ruler of Lumina and widely regarded as the most powerful priest in Aerithium, had sent the letter to Aiden himself. Aiden's family had held a powerful position in Lumina for generations. In fact, Aiden's father had been next in line to become the Grand Priest of Aurelius, but he passed away shortly after Aiden was anointed a priest.

Aiden knew where he stood amongst the priests and the saints after the Unveiling. The gods had not stripped him of his magic, but he was still a disappointment. A failure. He had allowed the Veil to taint his holy place of worship, a place where evil was not supposed to enter, and all the blame fell on him. On his blasphemy, his weakness. His lies. To *her*.

The Grand Cathedral stood tall and imposing, its sheer size evoking comparisons to the once-majestic castle of Andanova. Its slender alabaster spires reached towards the heavens, their tips resembling shimmering stars. Sunlight bathed the magnificent structure, casting colorful hues through exquisite stained-glass windows.

As Aiden approached the south entrance of the cathedral, whispers of hymns and prayers echoed within its sacred walls. Drawing nearer to the looming doors, he beheld High Priestess Lydia standing on the polished steps. She courteously bowed her head to Aiden, adorned in the pink and gold robes of Ravnassa, the Goddess of Harmony, revered as the primary deity of the far eastern kingdom of Oneriosa.

"It is a pleasure to see you," Lydia said, her lilting Oneriosan accent just as lovely as Aiden remembered.

"You as well," Aiden said. "It's been a long time."

Lydia frowned, tucking a ringlet of copper behind her ear. "Too long, I'd say. Though, I'm not surprised Eldyir called for an Assembly. I heard rumors that the Blue Inferno has made its way into Lumina and Koga-rashi."

Aiden sighed. "A fate that none of us could have avoided," he said. "'*The women will weep for the children of pestilence, and damned are these children of sin.*'"

"You're just as cryptic as you've always been." Lydia smiled, putting a tanned hand on his shoulder. "I wish you luck in there, Cycris. I am sure you will need it."

The tension in his shoulders eased, replaced by a wave of tranquility that washed over him. The warmth of the sun on his skin and the soft rustle of the wind through the trees soothed his mind. He turned his head, taking in the vibrant spring flowers in full bloom.

Aiden was familiar with this enchantment. Lydia, being a Priestess of Harmony, possessed the ability to calm and pacify one's emotions. The effects varied for each person, evoking nostalgic and comforting sensations in those it was cast upon.

"That wasn't necessary," Aiden said, turning his attention back to her.

Lydia began climbing the stairs, her light pink robes trailing behind her. "You're welcome."

Lumina was known for its commitment to neutrality. Surprisingly, the country had no adversaries, not even Vavilon. Even though the Grand Priest of Aurelius considered the Godless City to be an abomination, and many others shared this sentiment, war was never seen as a viable option. Lumina's core principles revolved around peace and unity. The founders firmly believed that judgment was the sole responsibility of the gods, and they encouraged humanity to unite through faith and belief. The Trinity aspired for a future where the entire world would willingly embrace these ideals.

The musty scent of incense hung heavy in the air, mingling with the murmurs of devout worshippers. Aiden's shoulders tightened again as he sat on the white pews embossed with suns, moons, and stars, symbols of his position as a High Priest of the Trinity. Multiple rows of pews filled the room, each tailored for the priests or saints who were assigned to it. Aiden was seated near the Saints of Wreiss, ocean waves carved into the wood.

Murals decorated the ceiling and walls, each telling a story with a stroke of a brush. All the gods, even those outside the Trinity, were depicted in vibrant colors across the chamber's ceiling, painted in an image of a time when they stood side by side, united in purpose and glory.

Aiden could feel the burn in his back from the piercing gaze of the Priest of Sanctus, the neighboring authority of Stellaris. Aiden straightened his posture, refusing to betray any vulnerability to the scrutinizing eyes around him.

Despite the Unveiling that had taken place, a gnawing doubt lingered. The gods spared his magic, and the Grand Priest had not stripped him of his title, but believing he was still worthy had grown more difficult over the years.

Aiden understood his worth paled in comparison to that of Eldyir. Eldyir's name held immense renown across kingdoms and continents. He was favored by the gods, surpassing all others in his mastery of holy magic. When Eldyir summoned them, both priests and saints alike answered without hesitation. Despite coming from different lands, they were all bonded by their shared ability to wield magic. In the presence of the Grand Priest, the laws of their countries and kings ceased to hold power. Those who lacked the same connection with the gods as the priests and saints simply could not grasp the significance of their kinship.

A hushed reverence filled the sanctuary as the Grand Priest made his way towards the podium. His falcon was perched upon his shoulder, its sharp eyes surveying those in the room. His robes, pale in color, gleamed with a mesmerizing display of shifting shades, reflecting the contrasting colors of night and day depending on the angle of the light. A medallion crafted from gleaming white silver adorned his neck, symbolizing his esteemed position as the Grand Priest, featuring the intricate etching of the Morningstar, the most radiant star in the night sky. Despite being older than Aiden, his appearance defied time. His flawless brown skin was devoid of any wrinkles. The gods had bestowed upon him the gift of an extended lifespan, but he remained mortal.

"Welcome, brothers and sisters," Eldyir greeted with a smile. "I cannot remember the last time that every priest and saint was in the same room together. I appreciate all of you making the journey here on such short notice." He took a step back from the podium, adjusting his pristine robes. "As some of you already know, the Blue Inferno has reached Kogarashi, Wreiss, and there have been a handful of cases in Lumina as well," he continued. "All efforts to cure this virus have proved futile. This sickness is not ordinary. No magic can cure it, and I believe those infected face more danger than death."

Eldyir's gaze shifted toward Aiden as he spoke. It was Eldyir who had arranged for the sick mercenary to be sent to Stellaris, fully aware that Aiden's church was vacant and the safest place for the virus-laden boy. A mysterious woman had left the young man on the doorstep of the Grand Cathedral a few days earlier, then disappeared into the night. When an acolyte from the city arrived with the boy and entrusted him to Aiden's care, he could hardly believe his eyes. It was the same mercenary Faith and Aiden had hired to bring Seren safely back to Lumina. Apparently, the young man had failed. He had said little, only that Seren had made it out of Vavilon but shared no other details.

"I've heard whispers that the Novem is on the brink of discovering a cure. As death looms, countless will seek solace in the Godless City. Faith is continuously waning," Eldyir said. "Even my own magic feels weakened, a dwindling light with each passing day." He lifted his chin towards the heavens, his hazel eyes glistening beneath the skylight.

Panic murmurs erupted in the chamber.

Eldyir raised his hand, motioning for silence. "I have also received information that Calarinn of Durcova and the Behethium Forest have been lost to the Veil. The cycles are unraveling at a dangerous pace, and I fear this is only the beginning. If something is not done, we all face the same fate as Andanova."

Aiden's blood ran cold. Murmurs erupted once again.

"What about the Seers?" thundered Saint Geralt of Wreiss, one of the Six Saints who protected the seas—the highest among the Saints of Illiana. "Do they not possess any answers?"

Aiden could have sworn he saw a flicker of unease pass through Eldyir's features, but it disappeared in an instant.

"The Seers see only darkness."

Aiden clutched his robes, and the entire room seemed to hold its breath.

Eldyir brought his hands together, clasping them tightly. "The Sundering draws near, and each passing day brings us closer to this ominous fate. The King of Oneriosa speaks of war—war against the Godless City, war upon Lumina for permitting Vavilon's existence. Corruption spreads like a voracious evil, consuming our faith, and soon it will sever our bond with the gods completely."

Aiden glanced over at the Priests and Priestesses of Harmony, witnessing their unease. One of them perked their heads up, his expression weary. "My king is not well, but there is nothing that can be done. I only hold so much power within the court and I do not wish to speak ill of my king."

"Neither do I," Eldyir noted. "However, it is impossible to ignore the prophecies that are unfolding around us." His knuckles blanched on the podium. "Which is exactly why I haven't given up hope." A smile graced Eldyir's face. "The real reason I've brought you all here today is not to trouble you with the world's spiraling—it is quite the opposite."

Eldyir took a deep breath. "I traveled to Etheles with Seer Mathieu, hoping to find a cure for the virus, begging the gods for an answer. Until my fingertips turned blue and my feet froze beneath me, I prayed and prayed. And right when I thought my efforts had been futile, I received a vision."

As Eldyir waved his hand in the air, a burst of vibrant colors filled the room. In the center of the chamber, the translucent vision of a decaying tree took shape. Its branches stretched toward the heavens, and from the trunk emerged a breathtaking figure—a woman with eyes that glittered like amethyst and hair that radiated like starlight. With a soft touch, she pressed her palms against the tree, causing the dead branches to unfurl with lush green leaves and blooming flowers of every color imaginable. Golden light, pulsing with magic, emanated from the core of the trunk. The mesmerizing image gradually faded, returning the chamber to its original state. Gasps and murmurs filled the room as everyone marveled at the vision Eldyir had shared with them.

"The Mother Goddess walks among us," Eldyir announced. "She has returned to cleanse the Veil."

Aiden braced himself against the pews. Prophecies had long spoken of the Mother's return, yet confirmation had never come to light—until now. Eldyir's words were certain, his eyes filled with conviction as he spoke. And Aiden knew it to be true because he had been there to see the prophecy turn into reality. When Seren emerged from the crypts, playing the divine harp, there was no doubt. Although Aiden had never dared to speak a word to anyone about it, he knew the gods had willed this. He could hide no more.

Saint Julia rose from her seat, her face twisted with skepticism. "The Mother?" she scoffed. "And how do we find out the truth of such claims? Felix Amos descended into madness searching the future for her return. If she is here, then why is she hiding in the shadows?"

Aiden sucked in his breath. As Saint Julia voiced her doubts, the truth hung heavy in the air. The fading magic of the Seers, once clear, now struggled against the corruption of the Veil. They lost their visions without the Scribes to record them. Felix Amos had been the exception. Visions had bombarded him daily, and he always remembered them. It had eventually driven him towards insanity.

Julia slammed her fists into the pews in front of her. "Can we truly believe in the return of 'The Mother' when she has yet to reveal herself? What about the Veil's relentless encroachment on neighboring lands? Did the Andanovans not fall prey to their faith in a false deity? Look at what befell Calarinn, loyal followers of Servius. I respect you, Eldyir, I do, but where is she?" Her blonde eyebrows raised. "Because she is certainly not here."

"I know you're afraid," Eldyir said calmly. "But we must remain strong. Faced with faithlessness, we cannot fall victim to our fears."

"This is ridiculous!" Julia shouted, turning toward the rest of the audience. The sleeves of her blue robes slipped down to her elbows as she raised her arms. "What are we to do? Sit around and wait for the great prophecy to be fulfilled as I watch my people die? The Devil and his demons grow stronger while our gods grow weaker." Her eyes landed on Aiden. "And *he* is the prime example. A High Priest, almost as powerful as Eldyir, and he allowed his entire sanctuary to become defiled, innocent lives lost—children included. He brings nothing but shame to us and has stripped even more security from the people, yet he may keep his title? For four years, he's rotted in his empty church. Doing what? The world is in shambles, and you expect us to wait around for a miracle when we are falling apart? Even if the Mother was here, the holy items are lost. Cycris oversaw the harp, the one and only holy item that we had in our grasp, and a demon stole it in the Unveiling. It was his duty to protect it." Julia's pale skin was splotchy and red with rage.

The room erupted in uncontrollable chatter, and Eldyir struggled to restore order. Priests and saints stood, pointing accusatory fingers at one another. Those of the Trinity faction bickered with the Priests of Harmony. Saints of Wreiss were standing beside Julia, glowering at those of the Trinity. Aiden could feel the weight of accusing stares burning into his back.

"Your king must step down!"

"This is an outrage!"

"The Veil will doom us all!"

"The Mother isn't coming!"

Aiden closed his eyes for a moment and took a deep breath. "This can go on no longer." He rose to his feet. He walked past the priests and saints, ignoring the insults spat at him. Aiden held his head high even though his heart was stuttering in his chest. He approached Eldyir, who was leaning against the podium, rubbing his temples, looking utterly drained.

"Sir, if I may speak."

"Aiden." Lines formed between Eldyir's eyes. "I am glad you came."

"As am I," Aiden said. "I know I don't deserve even a moment of anyone's time here, but I humbly ask for just a moment of everyone's attention. What I have to say will change everything that has happened here today."

The Grand Priest raised an eyebrow in surprise and placed his hands flat on the podium. "As you wish." Using magic to amplify his voice, Eldyir shouted, "Silence!"

The room fell into a hush.

"High Priest Cycris has something to say," Eldyir announced. "I ask you to be respectful and listen." Darkness on his features, a silent warning.

The eyes that followed Aiden as he came to stand behind the podium were both curious and aggravated. Aiden knew what they were all thinking. After the Unveiling, Aiden had locked himself away in the crypts. He had been scanning over ancient files, texts, and all the things he had been granted for safekeeping, praying that Eldyir would not relinquish them from the church. No one had ever truly given an explanation. Many blamed Aiden's incompetence and sin on the horrible, tragic accident.

"I'm ashamed of the behavior displayed here today," Aiden said as he stepped onto the podium.

Julia bristled in her seat along with others.

"Eldyir deserves our respect and trust after the many years he has led us," Aiden continued, scanning the crowd. "He has never let us down or led us astray. Not like I have." He lowered his head, running a hand through his black tendrils. "Eldyir speaks the truth. The Mother has returned."

Sunlight hit the podium from the skylight, small beams of light bursting across the room. Aiden took a deep breath. The smell of cherry blossoms filled his nose, and the taste of melon melted on his tongue. From across the room, Lydia offered a smile to Aiden, and he knew what she had done.

"You have every right to doubt my words," Aiden boomed, his voice strong. "You've all heard the rumors. I had relations with a married woman, breaking my holy vows as a High Priest. I will not deny it."

Julia smirked, her arms crossing over her chest.

"I often wonder if my blasphemy truly contributed to the Unveiling of Stellaris," he said. "I never believed true evil could penetrate the sacred walls of the Church of Caelestis. I was mistaken." He opened his hand, staring at the lines of his palm, focusing on the steady rhythm of his heart. "I hid many secrets within that church... And for that, I tainted it."

Aiden looked at the saints and the priests, who listened with rapt attention. "Forgiveness is not something I deserve, nor is the right to stand before you as a Priest of the Trinity. But I believe the gods want me to speak in hopes I can shift your doubts." Aiden swallowed the lump in his throat.

"When I say the Mother is here, it is because I have met her." Aiden was thanking the gods Lydia had used her magic on him. "A child played the Harp of Kallista."

"Impossible," breathed a nearby saint.

Everyone knew the truth. A mortal could not dare to play the harp, for to do so meant certain death. No living being could harness its power. The harp lowered the barriers to the Garden of Aetheria for the person who possessed the ability.

"She was born into our world as a boy by the name of Seren," Aiden said. "I raised him myself in Stellaris when his mother and he came asking for help twelve years ago. After the Unveiling and his mother's death, he was terrified and untrusting of me, and he fled." A lie. "Because of my misguided actions, he turned his back on me and ran. I was ashamed of my failure and broken by the loss of those in Stellaris. I should have told Eldyir. I should have told you all. I feared that I had failed beyond reparation."

"He's lying!" said Julia. She was on her feet, face flushed with fury. "*Twelve* years you kept this? How could you do such a thing?"

There was only one reason Aiden had kept it a secret after Emeryn's death. In the beginning, his every move was driven by his devotion to her. Then, the Unveiling occurred. That changed everything. Aiden could not reveal the horrible truth.

It wasn't his love for Emeryn that opened the Veil, nor his blasphemy staining the church. No, it was Seren who was to blame. And Seren hadn't run. Lumen had been summoned by Aiden. When he arrived, Aiden pleaded with him to take Seren away, begged him. Consumed by grief and hatred, Aiden swore to his brother that he wanted nothing to do with the boy again.

"It wasn't until he played the harp at the age of twelve that I was certain," Aiden said to Julia. "His mother begged me not to tell anyone."

"You're a fool," Julia spat.

Saint Geralt rose to his feet as well, his grey hair wild. "Your sin is inexcusable."

"Silence!" Eldyir demanded. "This is not the time for this."

Julia settled back into her seat, her face falling.

"Yes, I was a fool," Aiden said, anger coating his tone. "I lost myself to her and I have no qualms in denying it. I was more faithful to her than I was to the gods, more than I was to what I believed in. If she had asked me to, I would have worshipped her and abandoned all else. So, yes, I was foolish, but we've all made mistakes driven by love."

Saint Geralt clenched his fists, eyes darting between Aiden and Eldyir.

"I beg the gods every day for forgiveness. I know I made a mistake in keeping this to myself. And after the Unveiling, I should have come forth with the truth, but I—" Aiden stopped.

He could not tell the truth. No. Because the truth was, he'd desperately been trying to figure out what was *wrong* with Seren. That day, when Seren's hands danced across the strings of the harp until they bled or when the Veil swallowed the entire church—Aiden saw something. He had *felt* it. The Aura that emanated off Seren had caused his lungs to constrict, his heart to drop. The light did not embody the divinity of a holy being of goodness. No. He sensed something dark, something else—a *corruption*.

"I was *afraid*." Aiden gripped the podium. "But I am not afraid anymore. The gods have granted Eldyir a vision, and they've brought me here today. We need faith, or our magic will die. We need hope. I will take any punishment as given, but I beg you to listen. Seren is on his way to Lumina now."

Sun blanketed the chamber as Aiden stood taller. "Tell your kings, your lords and even tell the Auguries if you must. The Mother has been reborn to cleanse the Veil just as she promised."

As Aiden stepped down from the podium, he hoped they had not heard his fear, doubt, or desperation.

FIVE

"There are men who argue hate is stronger than love, but it is hatred born from love that is the most dangerous."

—the Personal Diaries of Felix Amos

Seren woke up with his head resting against the flank of a white horse. Blinking into the flickering firelight, his vision gradually sharpened. Groaning, he pushed himself upright, his fingers brushing against the dry grass beneath him. He turned to the horse, and his breath caught.

Estelle.

Her icy blue gaze, framed by pale, thick lashes, locked onto his. Seren glanced around, spotting the brown mare he had ridden out of Calarinn standing at his side.

"You're awake," came a voice.

Seren made out Mila's figure against the glow of the fire. Her face was streaked with dirt, and a shallow scratch curved just above her lip. She stared at him, a crease of concern etched between her dark brows deepening.

"What happened?" Seren managed, his tongue thick in his mouth. "Is Thomas here?"

Mila shook her head, her expression somber as she stroked the mare's neck. "I found her on the outskirts of town, scared out of her mind without her rider. She followed us here and hasn't left your side." Mila lowered herself across from him, crossing her legs. "I rode as far as I could until I was sure the Veil was far behind."

Seren's stomach sank. He didn't need her to say it aloud to understand what it meant for Thomas.

A small campfire blazed in the dry earth beside them, casting light over the trunks of the nearest trees. Above, a canvas of stars stretched across the sky. Seren's gaze swept over the dry grass and dirt within the clearing, encircled by a dense thicket of trees. Not a building was in sight.

He reached back gingerly, his fingers brushing the large knot where the brick had struck. A dull headache pulsed behind his eyes. "How'd you get me back on the horse?"

"You don't remember?" A finger pressed against the center of his forehead. "You gained consciousness just long enough to climb back on yourself."

Her touch disappeared as she sat up and added a branch to the flames, the fire crackling as she focused on tending it. Silence settled between them, thick with unspoken words.

"I wish we could have helped them," Seren murmured, his voice barely audible. "The town."

Mila's shoulders sank, her movements slowing. "Me too," she said. "But we would've been killed. We were both in a bad spot."

Seren sighed. The horse nuzzled his neck, nickering softly. Seren rested his cheek against the mare's face, stroking her side. Guilt welled up in his chest, and he squeezed his eyes shut.

Anna was dead. She would never go to Vavilon and become a Technophage. Her father would come home to find his entire town gone and his daughter with it. How could this happen?

Seren's head dropped between his knees, the weight of the thoughts crashing down on him. The horse nudged him with its muzzle, but he shoved the creature away. "I shouldn't have sold that jewelry," he whispered, his voice quivering. "It's my fault that the bastard killed her." His fingers scraped the dirt, grounding him, but he couldn't stop. "I'm such an idiot."

"Hey..." Mila's hand landed on his shoulder. "Seren, it wasn't your fault..."

Seren flinched and recoiled from her touch. "Don't," he snapped, his voice sharp. "You and I both know it was." His eyes bored into hers. "I killed that lord, Kamilah. I..." His fists clenched, his chest tight. "I drove that sword into his chest, and I...I..." His breaths became ragged, words choking him.

Mila didn't hesitate. She wrapped her arms around him, pulling him into an embrace that left no room for escape. "He killed Anna, and he tried to kill you. Don't feel bad, not even for a second."

Mila pulled back, her hands cupping the sides of his face as she lifted his gaze to meet hers. Seren froze, caught in the softness of her brown eyes. Why was she looking at him like that? He squeezed his eyes shut, his shoulders trembling. Bitterness surged in his throat, burning like bile.

Why was she comforting him? It was ridiculous. He didn't need to be coddled. He didn't deserve it. He was a murderer. Mila knew it. He knew it. There were so many reasons he didn't deserve her help. And yet, the bitterness continued to rise, uncontrollable, shaking his shoulders.

"Seren?" Mila pulled away, her features contorting in confusion. "Are you *laughing*?"

It was pathetic. It was horrifying. The entire scene: Mila's arms around him, offering comfort. Of course, it was laughable.

"Have you lost your damn mind?" Mila demanded.

The laughter froze in his throat, trapped between rage and self-loathing.

"Probably," Seren said, his voice brittle, strained. "Why do you even care? What does it matter to you if I lose it?"

Mila stilled.

Seren scoffed, shaking his head, the world around him swaying. He pushed himself to his feet, struggling to stay upright. Every ounce of his composure fought against the urge to collapse.

"Exactly," he muttered. "It doesn't. You know what? I should just leave." He wrenched his fingers through his hair. "I've been thinking about it for a while now, and I just... I can't do this anymore."

Why waste time with words? No. There was nothing left to say. He needed to go. Now. He turned away, but Mila grabbed the back of his shirt and stepped in front of him.

"Did that brick rattle your damn brain?" she asked. "You're in no place to leave, Seren. You need to rest."

His jaw tightened. He didn't need to rest. He didn't need anything. Mila needed to stop acting like he was fragile, like he was a child.

"You don't know what I need. Move out of my way, Mila."

"Please," Mila said, her tone softening. "Just sit down, and we'll talk. You're covered in wounds and blood. You need to—"

Her hand brushed his arm again, and something in him snapped. He smacked her hand away. "Don't touch me."

Mila stepped back, her eyes wide. "What the hell is wrong with you?"

Everything in Seren ignited, hot and uncomfortable. Every muscle burned, every fiber felt white-hot. "*You're* what's wrong with me," he hissed, stepping closer. "I don't want to rest, and I don't want to be here. Don't you see that? I shouldn't be here. You're out of the Sanguine Kingdom. The only reason you've stuck around is because Jude is in Lumina. There's no reason for us to be together anymore."

Mila recoiled, her face falling. "Do you really believe that, Seren? After everything?"

"After what?" he snapped. "After we pretended to be in love? I'm not sticking around to play pretend any longer."

Mila's voice turned cold. "Nobody's pretending anything right now, Seren. I am trying to help you."

Seren lifted his head, his fists curling at his sides. The strange desperation in Mila's eyes only fueled his anger. "I don't need your help," he said, his voice rising.

"And I suppose I should have left you when you fell off the horse?" Mila shot back.

Gods, she was infuriating.

"Yeah, maybe you should've," Seren spat. "It wouldn't be the first time you wished for my death."

"That was before—"

"Before what?" Seren cut in. "Before Jude was out of danger? Before Eden? Tell me, what difference does any of it really make?"

Mila's jaw clenched. "Of course, things are different now. We're friends. I care about you, believe it or not. You came for me in the Sanguine Kingdom—moronic as that was—and then somehow, you claimed my name from an ancient demon. Do you even realize what that means for us?"

And there it was: the truth Seren didn't want to hear. That Mila and Seren were connected, but not because of choice. It was all circumstance. All of it. The bonds formed between them weren't natural, not the ancient bond from the demon, not the bond of their friendship or the pretend romance they'd shared. It was fake. A lie.

"It doesn't matter what it means. I'll never use your true name again. We'll go our separate ways, and you'll be free of me."

"It's not that simple." Mila rubbed her temples, frustration creeping into her voice. "Please, just lie back down. We're both exhausted. We can talk about this in the morning after we rest. You're not being yourself."

Seren's head spun. "How do you know I'm not? If you know me so well, what is 'me'? How do you know what I would or wouldn't do? I'm a murderer. Isn't that what you called me when you held a knife to my throat?" His voice dripped with venom. He loomed over her, fists tightening at his sides. "And guess what, Mila? You're right. I killed that lord, and I *liked* it. Don't act like you know me because I don't even know me."

"I want to."

It sounded like a confession, and it made Seren's chest tighten. His heart pounded, each beat painful against his ribs.

"Let's be perfectly clear: I am not your Beloved," he whispered. "We're barely even friends. If you think you owe me for what happened, you're mistaken." His breath came in uneven gasps. "Stop acting like you care about me. Stop acting like you can help me or save me or whatever this is because I won't be made a fool of again."

Mila took a step closer. She pressed a hand to the center of his chest. Seren froze beneath her touch. This time, he did not pull away.

"Your heart's out of control, Seren. You need to breathe." Her voice was firm. "Let me help you."

Beneath her hand, a wave of warmth spread through him. His heartbeat, though still unsteady, began to slow. His body loosened, the roar of his blood finally quieting.

Their eyes met, and the tenderness in hers nearly unraveled him.

And then Seren ran.

The night was calm, the sky clear, but even the stars felt distant, cold—nothing like they should. In the distance, framed by the sparks rising from the fire, Mila's silhouette sat. Seren stood with an armful of branches, leaning against a tree. He'd been standing there for what felt like hours, unwilling to face her. She was right. About everything.

I care about you, believe it or not.

His teeth clenched, and he angrily dropped the branches to the ground, kicking a nearby rock so hard it ricocheted off a tree. Gods, he'd made a fool out of himself. He wished he could take back every word he'd said to Mila.

Seren sank to the base of the tree, his fingers digging into his scalp. What was he supposed to have said to Mila? That maybe he really was losing his mind? That he didn't want to rest because his dreams had morphed into his worst memories? Lumen's fox-like smile, those yellow eyes. Aiden's disappointment. Harp strings snapping under his fingers. Blood seeping into the stems of burgundy hellebores. Betrayal. Lies. Then, ice flooding his veins, his heart slowing as darkness took hold. And it would begin again—a relentless cycle, a limbo he couldn't escape.

Seren's arms tightened around himself, a hollow pang filling his chest. He could tell Mila the truth, that he remembered things he'd rather forget. But what was the point?

Besides, the two of them had a new problem. They hadn't spoken about the bond between them, and Seren had avoided even thinking about it since Mila woke. He felt guilty for using her name at Anna's, even if it had been to help. But Seren didn't know what it truly meant to them, and for some reason, it scared him.

Why had he been able to take Mila's name from a demon? The bond was forged from evil. Dark magic. And Seren knew it. And just because he had taken it, it hadn't changed. It wasn't purified in his ownership; it was still corrupted. Why was he capable of holding onto something so sinister? What did it say about him?

And that feeling when those shadows had urged him on. He shuddered at the thought. Was that truly him?

I am your god now.

Seren looked down at his hands in the darkness. There was something wrong with him, wasn't there? Even if that lord had killed Anna, wasn't it wrong for Seren to have killed him? To have felt such power? But the truth of the matter was, he couldn't dwell on it forever. He was always running—mentally, physically.

It had to stop.

With a deep breath, Seren gathered the branches back into his arms and made his way toward Mila. When he returned, she had her back to him, not acknowledging his return. Seren set the branches down and stood across from her, the fire between them now feeling less like a physical barrier and more like the unspoken words that hung heavily in the air.

Estelle stood nearby and nudged him from behind, her hot breath warming his back. Seren initially ignored her, but she nudged him again, nibbling at the end of his dirty cloak. He shook his head with a smile, rubbing the silky hair between her ears before sitting down.

There was nothing but silence between them save for the wood being devoured by the fire. He watched the flames lick at the thick branches, his thoughts still racing.

He drew his focus to Mila as she sharpened a stick with her dagger, only to thrust it into the dirt. The light of the fire cradled the curves of her face, her eyes turning into the color of warm honey.

"I'm sorry," Seren finally said into the silence. "I'm an ass."

Mila ignored him, grabbing another stick and started to sharpen it. Seren wondered if this one was destined for his head.

"I don't want to leave," he continued, hoping somehow, he could mend this. "I think you're right and that brick rattled my brain." He forced a chuckle. "I just don't know what's real anymore." They were the most honest words he'd spoken in days. Mila's attention shifted, her head lifting. "After seeing my mother's face again...watching Anna die..." He sucked in a breath. "And there's other things that I just don't know how to talk about. I never meant for any of this to happen and I can't help but think that if it weren't for me...Anna and my mother would still be alive."

Mila stood and walked over, settling so close to Seren that he could feel her warmth. "You're such an idiot. You know that, right? I really thought you'd left me."

"I know," Seren sighed. "So... Friends, then?"

Mila raised her brows with a smirk. "I thought we weren't even friends?"

"Yeah, well, I'm a big jerk who was acting like a child," he said. "And you were right about everything. Happy?"

"Good enough."

Seren smiled, but it quickly faltered. "I also think...we should talk about what happened between us. The bond."

"Well, since you refuse to rest, I suppose we can talk about it now." Her brown skin shimmered under the warmth of the campfire's blaze. "I don't know how you took my name and I'm doubting you know either. But it's important that you understand the gravity of this bond." She sighed. "It's the only reason I'm alive."

Seren's heart skipped a beat. "What do you mean?"

"Those injuries should have killed me," she continued. "You saved me through the tie we now have."

Seren blinked, taken aback. How could that be possible? "I don't understand," he said, frowning as he tried to grasp the meaning behind her words. He thought of the way he had begged to the voice that he carried with him. Had she...helped him?

"I felt your magic," Mila began. "And you felt mine, didn't you? When I tried to use it when we were captive."

Yes, that's right. He had felt something between them then, and he'd *known* that she had been trying to use it.

"Earlier, when I was upset... What was that?"

Mila bit her lip. "I asked you to let me help you, and subconsciously, you did. This bond allows us to share power—that's why Lilith...*Eden* wanted me to become queen so badly. But it's dangerous if you don't know how to control it. You healed me through the bond, whether you realized it or not." Mila reached for Seren, her fingers lightly grazing the bridge of his nose. He winced. "I think it's why your wounds haven't healed yet." Her touch lingered, their eyes locked for a moment before she pulled away, clearing her throat. She crouched, using a stick to draw two figures in the dirt, a line connecting them. "If you choose to share power with me, you can. And if you choose to siphon power from me, you can."

Seren frowned. "Is the child's drawing necessary?"

Mila poked him with the stick. Hard.

"Sorry," he grumbled, rubbing his arm.

"Pay attention. A bond like this is...spiritual. I was healed because, deep down, your will made it happen without you even knowing. It's all about intention. You wanted to share your power with me, and you just didn't know you could." Her eyes met with his, becoming distant. "Despite my own abilities, I am human, and you are...clearly not. If you were to transfer too much power to me, you could kill me. If you were to siphon too much power from me, you could kill me. The closer in proximity we are, the stronger the bond." She drew the figures again, further apart. "The bond stretches, and no amount of distance can sever it. This bond is ancient and cursed, and as far as I know, only the death of the owner can break it." Mila's voice was low. "Though, I once believed it couldn't be taken by someone else, so that may very well be untrue."

Seren's stomach dropped. He stared at the flames licking the wood, struggling to find the right words. "What does that mean, then? I don't know how to do those things."

"I know," Mila said quietly. "Which worries me. If you ever had any intentions..."

"Hey." Seren leaned forward, the heat of the fire warming his face. "I would never have ill intentions toward you or take what's yours. All I want is for you to be safe and free to make your own choices. I feel terrible knowing I have this control. It feels wrong. I..." He stopped, the weight of his words catching in his throat.

Seren still didn't know how Mila truly felt. Friends. But wasn't it more for him? Wasn't that the truth he was afraid to admit, even to himself? His fingers brushed his lips, a faint reminder of what they'd shared. He couldn't ask her if she felt the same. Their romantic act had been just that—a façade to protect them in the Sanguine Kingdom. He was a fool for thinking it might be something more.

Mila thrust her pointed stick into the ground, where it landed perfectly upright. "Then, I guess we have nothing to worry about. And I suppose I should thank you." She rested her head on his shoulder, yawning as her eyes drifted shut.

Seren blushed. "For what?"

"You changed my fate."

"That was never your fate," he whispered, leaning his head against hers.

"Then what is?" Mila asked softly, her body relaxing.

To be here, he wanted to say. *With me.*

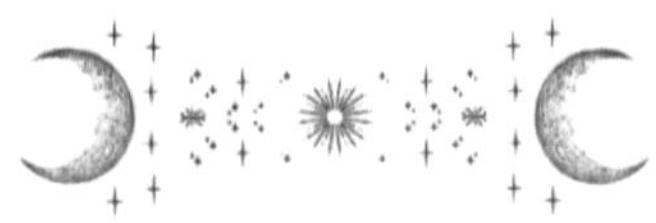

The sun rose in the distance, painting the sky in soft hues of pink and orange. Golden beams spilled over the horizon, warming Seren's skin as the morning breeze tousled his hair. For the first time in what felt like forever, he had slept peacefully and dreamlessly, waking refreshed. The heaviness that had clouded his mind was gone, replaced by a clarity he hadn't realized he craved. As his fingers brushed over his calf, he found the skin smooth and unblemished. His wounds had healed.

After Mila inspected and deemed the herbs Seren had bought in Calarinn safe, he had taken them, hoping they might help him rest. Though he couldn't recall falling asleep, they seemed to have done their job. When he woke, Mila's head was nestled against his chest, his arms draped loosely around her shoulders. She always seemed warmer in her sleep—her cold exterior softened, all her tension melting away.

As he admired the brightening sky, a flicker of movement caught his eye. Seren squinted against the morning light, a shadow briefly passing before the sun. When the light returned, an ivory-winged bird had landed at his feet. The dove carried a rolled-up piece of paper attached to its right leg, tied with an indigo ribbon.

He hesitated, glancing down at Mila, who was still resting against him. Carefully, he slid his arm out from beneath her head, settling it gently on the cloak beneath them.

Sitting up, he leaned forward, mindful not to startle the bird, and beckoned it closer. It hopped onto his calf, its small head cocked to the side. He untied the ribbon and unfolded the paper.

Seren,

I trust this letter finds you in good health and that the charmed avian has reached you safely. I'll keep this brief to prevent any misinterpretation. Please come to the Grand Caelestis Cathedral in Aurelius. You must return to Lumina, regardless of any reservations you may have.

The mercenary who accompanied you has returned and has offered no explanation. He is now safe in Stellaris.

I have disclosed your identity to the Grand Priest of Aurelius. You can no longer hide from who you are as the world continues to spiral into chaos. I know you understand the gravity of this. The bird will carry your response so I can ensure your safety and return.

Stay safe and come home. It's been much too long.

-Aiden

Seren's fingers quivered as he read the letter again. Aiden's handwriting was unmistakable, a familiar scrawl he'd seen countless times. It carried the same lack of emotion, the words precise and detached, revealing nothing of the man behind them. How long had it been since he'd last seen Aiden?

Four years?

"What's that?"

Seren flinched, startled by Mila's voice. He hadn't noticed her waking. She sat up and leaned toward him, trying to peer at the paper in his hand. Seren's fingers gripped it a little too tight.

"It's from Aiden."

"The priest who sent Jude after you?"

Seren moved the paper out of her line of sight. He nodded. "Yeah. He said Jude is in Stellaris. Aiden wants me to meet him in Aurelius."

Mila frowned. "Isn't that the capital? Why there? I thought you were supposed to go to your hometown."

"I'm not sure."

Of course, Seren knew why. Once Aiden had revealed his identity to the Grand Priest, secrecy was no longer an option. Aiden had warned him this moment would come someday, that he couldn't run forever. But why now?

He crumpled the paper in his hand. The thought of being exposed to all the saints and priests as the Mother was suffocating. How could he ever be ready for something like that? He was still trying to piece together the shattered fragments of his own life.

"Stellaris isn't too far from Aurelius by horse," Seren said. "After we get there, Jude could meet us. It'll take us roughly a week to get to Aurelius from here."

Seren beckoned the bird over again, and it jumped up, tiny feet gripping his finger. He smiled, petting the top of its head. "I have nothing to write with," he realized.

"It's completely unethical, but I have an idea." She reached for her knife, the blade catching the morning light as she turned it over in her hand. "I was weak yesterday, but I'm feeling much better."

"Hey, stop—"

"Relax," she said, already pressing the blade to her palm. "It's just a small cut."

Seren winced as a thin line of blood welled up, but Mila didn't so much as flinch. Closing her eyes, she flexed her fingers, curling them around the wound.

"Wait, Mila..." he said uneasily. "You can't. Your mother—won't she sense you?"

Her eyes flashed open. "Have you forgotten already? I'm not bound to my mother. I'm bound to you. Besides, my magic isn't hers. It's not Eden's either—it's mine. Perks of being a descendant of Adamus, I suppose."

A thin stream of blood lifted from her palm, floating through the air with surprising precision. Seren watched as she straightened Aiden's letter, blank side up, and hovered the blood over the page.

"What do you want it to say?" Mila asked, glancing up.

"Tell him I'll be there within a week," Seren said.

"Got it."

Seren couldn't look away as Mila carefully guided the blood across the paper. The words she wrote were beautiful—dainty, even—formed in crimson.

"That was harder than it looked," she said with a sigh.

Once the blood dried, he carefully rolled up the paper and tied it back onto the bird's leg. He gave the bird one last pat before watching it take flight, knowing he would soon follow its path back home.

Six

"The angels weep—one remains, his tears are gold, his heart in chains. In patient silence, not in vain. For the Golden One, his god shall reign."

—the Seer Diaries of Felix Amos

Grimm ruffled his feathers and stretched in front of the window, his movements smooth despite the metal woven into his right wing. The golden components gleamed between sleek feathers, catching the pale light that filtered through the cool-toned stained glass. An iridescent sheen danced across his plumage as his metal talons scraped idle lines into the oaken table. Boredom was setting in.

"You're welcome to go fly if you are feeling restless, friend," Lumen said, patting the creature's head.

Grimm let out a noise that Lumen considered to be a sigh as if a bird could do such a thing. "Are you going to care for that dying boy?" he squawked.

Lumen scoffed, setting a handful of toasted nuts on the table. Grimm joyfully cracked a shell with his beak.

"He will be dead in the morning. Unfortunately, I am bound by that pesky geas," Lumen responded. He pulled the key out of his pocket with a grimace, fingers running over the runes etched upon it. "I hate magic."

Grimm cocked his head, beady eyes fixed on Lumen with a silent question.

"If I go back on my word and don't care for the boy while Aiden's away," Lumen muttered, half to himself, "the Archives won't open." He ran a hand through his hair, grimacing. "Demoted to a caretaker. How charming."

Lumen drew the linen cloth sitting on the table into his hands. He carefully wrapped it around his face. "Let's get this over with."

Bypassing the geas was impossible, and Lumen knew it. He'd be a fool to think he could get into the Archives another way. A single entrance lay deep within the crypts, protected by formidable magic, and trying to break into it would only bring consequences Lumen wasn't willing to risk. Despite the humiliation, he'd deal with the mercenary until he finally died since Aiden had still not returned from Aurelius. He sat from his seat and stared out the window. It was a shame he had to spend the day this way, but it couldn't be helped. He had no other choice.

With a defeated sigh, Lumen turned away from the window and pushed open the door, squinting against the sunlight. The curtains were pulled back, and intense light illuminated the room. Lumen gave a subtle shake of his head and strode across the room, grasping the edges of the sun-patterned silk.

"No, leave them open," a voice croaked. The boy sat up in bed, his blue eyes red-rimmed and glassy. He turned towards Lumen, his breath coming out ragged and uneven. "It's...warm."

"Fine," Lumen said coldly. He stalked across the room towards the sink and filled an empty goblet with water. With a grumble, Lumen walked to the bedside and reluctantly handed it to the boy. The idea of giving the mercenary any of his time felt like a waste of dignity. Especially considering the brat had deceived him, posing as an understudy for weeks in the Obsidian Lab. Although he couldn't deny that the child had impressed him a little, Lumen was not accustomed to being outsmarted.

The young man reached for the cup, his arm trembling. Lumen watched his hands shake, and when he brought the cup to his blue-blushed lips, the water dribbled down his chin and spilled upon the blankets. Desperation flashed in the young man's eyes as he struggled to maintain control, but the goblet slipped from his fingers, clattering to the floor and rolling far from his reach.

A groan escaped his lips, a sound thick with frustration and exhaustion, as he fell back onto the bed in a shuddering heap.

"I'm not thirsty anyway," he breathed. A plume of frosty breath escaped as he let out an achy cough. Such a pitiful excuse for a mercenary. After a beat of thought, the boy seemed to refocus his attention toward Lumen, and something like recognition crossed his gaze, watery eyes widening. "I must be losing my mind..."

Had it really taken this long for the brat to recognize him? Lumen let out a heavy sigh.

Usually, he would have enjoyed taunting the boy, but he was exhausted. He wanted nothing more than to sit in the Archives and begin his research. Lumen turned towards the door, rolling his head on his shoulders. He'd done well enough, hadn't he?

"If you need anything else, I will be outside the door," Lumen said, void of emotion. "Death will be here for you soon."

"Too bad," the young man said quietly. "Quite disappointing. I had hoped to go out with a bit more excitement—a death mighty enough for the last Andanovan."

Lumen froze in the doorway, turning towards the boy, his eyes narrowed. "Andanovan?"

The mercenary coughed, his gaze distant. Lumen knew that look. The virus was prone to induce madness in its victims, causing them to come in and out of lucidity near the end. It was shocking that the boy had endured for such a long time.

"Pathetic," the boy rambled on. "I don't want to...die this way." His fingers tangled in his messy hair as he closed in on himself, gasping for breath. After a few seconds, he lifted his head, turning towards Lumen. "What are you still doing here?"

"I'm curious if you've completely gone mad. The pure Andanovan bloodline was wiped out," Lumen said, crossing his arms and leaning against the door.

Did he honestly have nothing better to do than to indulge in this young man's delusions?

"And yet I could tell you I remember the taste of the Honey Bread," the boy replied, his voice a whisper. "The smell of the chamomile, the feel of Andanovan silk on my skin. I remember the gold-threaded curtains in my room, the red-ripened cherries... I'd pick in the summer. I remember it all as if it were yesterday. Just as I remember, the autumn sky burning and the rivers...running red."

Lumen lingered in the doorway, a smirk playing on his lips. "Oh, and you managed to escape just like that?" he said with a scoff. "Now that's a tale worth hearing—if I'm supposed to believe it."

Struggling with his weak arms, the boy forced himself upwards, leaning his head against the wall and closing his eyes. "I don't...care...if you believe me or not." Lumen arched an eyebrow, noting the genuine tone in the mercenary's voice. "Sometimes I wonder if I could consider it mercy at the hands of a demon."

"A demon showing mercy," Lumen chuckled. "That's an intriguing concept."

"The world...is backwards and inside out," the boy murmured, his words stringing together in a disjointed manner.

Lumen settled onto the lone chair against the wall, his head leaning on the doorframe. He supposed he would need to linger if he truly wanted to access the Archives.

"It seems we can agree on something." Lumen clicked his tongue. "So, tell me, mercenary, how did you survive? Surely, this merciful demon you speak of gave you something quite formidable for you to make it out of that bloodbath alive."

The boy let out a rattling cough, wheezing for a moment. "Not...exactly." He looked far into the distance, a single tear streaming down his face, turning to ice on his skin. "It should've been Caius," he whispered, breathless. "He was strong. Or Caspian, he was smart. Even Armin or Raima, they were...kind. Anyone but me." Another plume of frosty breath escaped between his chattering teeth.

Lumen stiffened. He recognized all those names. King Solomon Aurevall, ruler of Andanova, had four sons and a daughter. The eldest and only daughter, Raima. The eldest son and heir to the throne was Caius, then Caspian, Armin, and the youngest, Judas.

"A sneaky mercenary like you?" Lumen asked. "You claim to be not only to be the last Andanovan but a prince at that?"

The boy lifted his head, his blue eyes holding a sadness as deep as the sea. "I am certainly handsome enough, don't you think?"

Lumen chuckled. "Judging by your age, I assume you claim to be the youngest prince, then, hmm? It would certainly be fitting for you to be named after a fool."

Judas was the ancient ancestor of the royal family of Andanova. The Andanovans had held an unwavering faith in the deity Galarithian, whom they revered as the God of Abundance and Prosperity. Legends and stories passed down through generations spoke of a prophet named Judas, who, in a moment of despair, found himself lost within the Veil. When Judas believed he was sure to die at the hands of a demon, a proclaimed deity called out to him. The divine entity, believed to be Gala, selected Judas as their chosen disciple and guided him out of the Veil, leading him to the untouched and bountiful land that would become known as Andanova.

Galarithian declared himself a lost god, forgotten in the ancient archive of time. The Andanovans created their own scripture and pledged wealth, prosperity, and bounty to Judas and to all those who would inhabit this newfound land. The deity's promise of opulence and abundance resonated within the hearts of the people, and from that moment forward, Gala became the sole deity worshiped by the Andanovans.

Judas and his people built a kingdom in Gala's name, with Judas crowned as the first king of Andanova. Yet, the ancient texts passed down through noble families made no mention of this god. Gala seemed to have miraculously appeared out of thin air. Despite this mystery, no malevolence had ever been proven; the Andanovan people had prospered for centuries. Still, it was widely believed that Judas had built his kingdom on a lie, deceived by a demon—a belief that only seemed more certain after the kingdom's fall. Or so the story went.

The young man leaned back onto the pillow, his skin losing more color. A bone-shaking cough erupted from him, blood dribbling down the boy's lips and freezing on his chin. "Shit." He wiped it away with his fingertips, his face falling in fear.

"Some say the Andanovans deserved their fate for worshipping a false god. The mourning of their death was short-lived," Lumen said. He stood up, grasping a stray cloth sitting by the sink and handing it to the boy. "What do you think?"

Judas stayed put, ice forming on the edges of his mouth as he looked up at Lumen's outstretched hand, eyebrows pinched. "The Andanovans were...good people. They didn't know any better," he choked out. "Damn...anyone who says...otherwise."

"I believe you," Lumen finally said. "A shame, truly. I can see it in your eyes—you're barely holding onto your sanity." A smile curled at his lips. "You have strong willpower, Prince Judas."

Just as he was about to withdraw his hand, Judas reached for the cloth in Lumen's hand. The boy sluggishly wiped the blood from his mouth. "No," he said, voice sharp. "Don't call me that. My name is Jude."

Lumen sat back down, and stretched his legs out in front of himself, craning his neck to the side. He twisted the key in his pocket, fingers running over the runes. They felt deeper, changed. He smirked. It was only a matter of time before the door would open for him.

"I visited Andanova once, before the Veil with...a priest," Lumen began. With the man who Lumen had once considered a father. It had been on a trip with Aiden, right before their journey to Etheles. "The king had requested a High Priest's presence, something about wanting his children to be blessed. Looking back, it was almost as if the king knew the falling of Andanova was to come—but he seemed like a common fool."

Jude shuddered. "I rarely saw my father," he murmured. "I was the youngest son...of the king. People never had high expectations of me. I wasn't the heir to the throne." His eyes watered as he coughed again.

Lumen stood up and retrieved the goblet, filling it with water from the sink, handing it to Jude. The boy raised his eyebrows, taken aback by the offering, but accepted. His hand was unsteady, but he was able to sip on the water this time. Lumen grabbed it before it clattered to the floor again.

"I was often in trouble," Jude continued after clearing his throat. "I hid in horse stables, neglected my studies, and pick-pocketed knights for fun. My father was never present. He was busy with my brothers. Raising them to be good, powerful men. We were the richest, most prosperous kingdom in the world and my father didn't want that to change." Jude closed his eyes, struggling to continue through his labored breathing. "But...I heard rumors, the servants gossiping about the castle. The crops were yielding less and less, animals were falling ill, and gold deposits in the mountains were scarce."

"How old were you?" Lumen mused. "You're still just a child. The fall of Andanova was ten years ago."

"I was ten."

"I see." Lumen adjusted the cloth on his face that had slipped. Although he was curious if he had immunity after his incident in the Wastelands, he did not intend to push his luck. After all, he only had three vials of the cure with him. "Tell me, what did the demon give you? Surely a child wouldn't have known what to ask for."

Jude sighed. "It gave me...something that has run out. As I knew it would, eventually." He furrowed his blonde brows. "Why do you care, anyway? Don't you have anything better to do?" Jude snorted, a cough creeping its way into his throat.

Lumen smiled. "I just find it rather interesting," he said. "A prince of a dead kingdom, a princess of demons, and a destined king of worlds traveling together."

"Some would say it was fate."

When the boy's eyes, as blue as the sky, met Lumen's gaze, all doubts faded away. Sunlight caught in his golden hair, shimmering like summer honey. Only now did the doctor truly see him—the gentle curves of his face and his cunning smile. Beneath the blithe confidence, Jude was nothing more than a troublesome child. It was as if Lumen was staring into a forgotten past, a relic left behind from a dead world.

"Fate," Lumen mocked, the word bitter on his tongue.

"You say it as if it is such a terrible thing," Jude replied. "But who's to say it's not fate...that has brought us here? That it wasn't fate that brought you and Seren together? Perhaps it's the one thing you cannot...manipulate."

Lumen laughed. "Then fate is crueler than I ever imagined. Do you know what Seren was like all those years in Vavilon? He was miserable. Broken. He begged and pleaded for anything but the fate the gods had chosen for him."

Jude's features shifted. "And you think you gave him a new fate?"

Lumen's mouth twisted into a grim smile, his glasses catching the faint light. "You think I gave him something? No. I took. I took everything he begged me to take."

Jude stared at him, his voice solemn. "So, you're sure you weren't just falling into the fate the gods wanted for you all along? After all, maybe this is what they intended. You...act like you're above them—could it be that you've been playing right into their hands?"

Lumen's expression faltered for just a second, anger flaring as he snapped, "You think that's what the gods wanted? That they wanted this?" He stood quickly. "They abandoned me, so *I* made the choices. *I* always have. *I* changed the will of the gods, and *I* will continue to do so!"

The last word echoed in the silence that followed. Lumen recoiled, his breath uneven as the force of the outburst rippled through him. His lips pressed into a thin line as he sat back down, slower this time, his knuckles whitening as he gripped the arms of the chair.

When he spoke again, his voice was lower, restrained, as if to tether himself. "I don't play into anyone's hands. Not anymore."

"I think I understand now. You wanted Seren to hate you," Jude murmured, his voice barely a breath. "The crueler you were...the more you...hurt him...the more he would grow to hate you. The more you would both forget that maybe...at some point, he mattered to you."

Lumen stilled. The words echoed faintly in his mind, then faded, leaving nothing behind.

"If he hates you, then it makes everything easier...doesn't it? You don't have to...face it..." Jude said. His lids grew heavier. "But beyond it all, you truly cared. And I think deep down...you didn't want this. Not really."

"You're wrong," Lumen hissed.

Jude exhaled, his body slackening, his voice fading to a distant whisper. "I...am never wrong."

Seven

"What is an overflowing cup worth if it contains only poison? What is a cup brimming with mirth if it is broken? And what is a golden cup half full if it is filled with blood?"

—Exorcist Damian Silver

As Seren and Mila rode their horses toward Lumina, half a day had already passed. Estelle was an easy steed, trotting down the overgrown grassy trail under the late afternoon sun. They had found a road leading north toward Brimry, a small town on the edges of Durcova. Both were exhausted and hungry, but thankfully, Seren had managed to hold on to the gold in his pocket despite everything. Seren knew they would need to take occasional rests, and he missed sleeping in a bed. Any leftover money he had once they reached Lumina, Seren would give to Mila.

By the time they reached Brimry, dusk had arrived, and even the horse's strides had become sluggish. Seren got off Estelle and stretched his sore body from the long ride. He pulled his cloak over his head and concealed his unusual hair.

"It isn't so bad, you know," Mila said as she slid off her horse.

Feeling self-conscious, Seren pulled the cloak tighter over himself. "Are you sure? Anna called me a skunk."

Mila wrinkled her nose, a playful smirk on her lips. "I think skunks are rather cute."

Seren's face turned hot.

In the Underbelly of Vavilon, Kitsune, the demon ruling the underground city, had pierced through his facade, discerning his identity even when he himself had not. His Aura had always been activated automatically, unbeknownst to him, protecting his true appearance. Now, he questioned whether his hair had changed due to the weakening of his Aura, the removal of the seal on his back, or because the mysterious voice that had always guided him was quieter again.

When Seren had somehow opened the Veil in the Sanguine Kingdom, that voice had strongly warned him against it. The strange seal had exerted some control over Seren and his abilities, but he had broken through it. Though unsure of her identity, he was certain of her protection. Perhaps now he had displeased her, or worse, breaking the seal had somehow severed their connection. Reaching Aurelius had become his primary aim. There, he was determined to uncover the identity of the voice that had guided him.

Brimry was a quaint town, its cobbled streets wide enough for Mila and Seren to guide their horses through. Children ran past barefoot, some stopping to pet the horses. The sun set, bleeding orange and pink across the horizon. As they approached, they passed a wooden bench worn from the weather, a bundle of dried red roses resting upon it. Buildings the color of old parchment lined the streets, decorated with window boxes full of mismatched flowers.

"Such a small town," Mila said. "If we weren't in Durcova, I'd say it was charming."

Seren nodded in agreement. "It looks like there's an inn down the road. Do you want to rest here for the night?"

"Yes, please. I could use a warm bed and a hot meal."

The two of them walked toward the building, a worn sign hanging above the doorway with the words *Serenity's Inn* etched into the wood. Seren glanced towards the side of the building, noticing the marks of hooves on the earth.

"Looks like there are stables towards the back," Seren said, handing Mila Estelle's reins. "I'll get us a couple rooms if you want to take them. Meet me inside?"

Mila nodded and encouraged the horses to move forward. Estelle threw her head back, her nervous blue eyes meeting his. He smiled, rubbing the bridge of her nose.

"Go on, you'll be alright," he told her.

The horse snorted as Mila egged her on. Seren stepped inside, greeted by the faint warmth of a newly kindled hearth, its fire ready to ward off the chill of approaching nightfall. At the counter stood a friendly, plump woman, her hands busy polishing a brass candlestick.

"Hello," the woman said with a smile. "Welcome in, young man. In need of a room?"

Seren kept his head low. "Yes, please. Two rooms and stabling for my horses. Just for tonight."

Her shoulders slumped as she frowned and said, "I'm sorry, sweetheart. We only have one room available. We've had many stragglers from Calarinn in need."

Seren raked a hand through his hair. "Okay, one room is fine," he grumbled. "How much?"

"Two golds should do it just fine, lad."

Seren nodded, pulling the gold out and setting it in her chalky palm. The copper bells above the door jingled as Mila came through the door, mumbling to herself, dusting dirt from her dress.

"Stupid horse," she muttered.

"And would that be your wife?" the innkeeper asked slowly. She bit her lip and lowered her voice, leaning towards Seren. "I just wouldn't want anyone to get the wrong idea, is all."

"Yes," Seren said quickly. He shot Mila a look, hoping she couldn't see the warmth filling his cheeks under the shadows of his cloak.

"Oh, good!" The woman smiled. "Let me show you and your lovely wife to your room."

Seren grimaced at her remark but didn't turn to face Mila as the woman led them down the hallway. The inn was in a state of disrepair, with aged pictures adorning the walls and half-melted candles placed in dusty sconces. Drying bouquets of lavender and other herbs hung on the walls. The woman stopped at the door at the very end of the hall, using a brass key to open the door.

"There's a tavern just down the road, and they serve delicious ale and food if you two are hungry. If you need anything, please ask," the woman said, placing the key into Seren's palm.

"Thank you," Mila said politely from behind.

"I hope you and your wife enjoy!"

Seren laughed uneasily as he pushed the door open. Mila followed him in, letting out a sigh of relief as the door closed. She flopped onto the bed with a contented groan, then turned to Seren with a raised eyebrow.

"Wife?"

"Sorry," he mumbled, avoiding her gaze. "I didn't want to draw any attention."

Mila slid her hands under her head and stared at the ceiling. "Yeah, I get it," she said, her tone lighter. "So, should we go get something to eat? I'm starving."

Seren sat down on the bed with a frown. "I'm not hungry. You can go ahead without me." He grabbed a few coins and set them on the bed between them.

Mila tucked a stray piece of hair behind her ear, her jaw tightening. "You haven't eaten since Anna's. You can't tell me you're not hungry."

Seren shrugged.

"Well, I'm your wife, aren't I?" She crossed her arms, cocking an eyebrow. "Certainly, you won't send me out all alone."

Seren turned away, biting the inside of his cheek. "I didn't think we were playing pretend anymore."

"You could have said I was your sister," Mila grumbled.

When Seren didn't respond, Mila snatched the coins off the bed and sprang to her feet. She opened the door, pausing in the frame as though debating whether to speak. Seren barely had time to glance up before the door slammed shut behind her, rattling the frames on the wall.

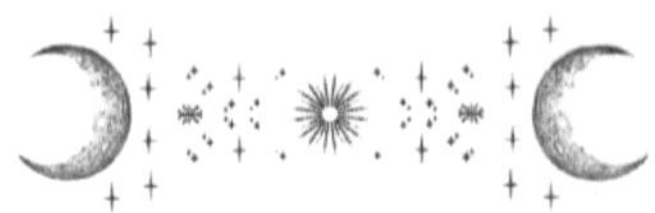

Mila returned after an hour. She said nothing to Seren, collapsed on the bed beside him, and promptly fell asleep. Seren envied her peacefulness as she lay sprawled across the beige sheets, cheek pressed against her palm. Mila's dress had shifted, fabric gathering just above her thigh, revealing a sliver of bare skin. His gaze lingered longer than it should have, tracing the delicate curve, the way the dim light kissed the warmth of her skin. A flush crept up his neck, and he pulled the blankets over her, careful not to disturb her.

Seren reached for his medicinal herbs, peeking inside the container, realizing it was empty. "Damn," he sighed, tucking it back into his pocket.

In just a matter of days, they would reach Aurelius, and after that, everything would change. Jude would resume his mercenary work, and Mila would most likely return to the Godless City. Everything would fall back into place, as it was meant to. Right?

Seren reached for the scars that marred his back, his fingertips tracing the deep marks. What if nothing could ever fall back into place? Things weren't supposed to be this way, and he knew it. Lumen had taken something beyond the physical claim he had made. Whatever it was that Seren had lost, he needed it back. He felt...incomplete.

Seren sighed and stood before a dusted mirror mounted on the wall. He watched his eyes flicker between purple and green. He frowned. It had all started with that damned harp. Everything had been much simpler before then. There had been no certainty that Seren was anything but a boy until he'd plucked those strings. It had changed everything.

Mila mumbled something incoherent in her sleep, shifting to bury her head beneath the blankets. Seren strode to the door but hesitated. He could take Estelle, leave for Lumina, and never have to say goodbye. He had always been good at running.

But then his gaze drifted back to Mila. He thought of the way her hand had pressed against his heart, steady and gentle, even when he had been cruel.

For a fleeting moment, he imagined gathering her in his arms, sinking into the warmth of her presence, and letting sleep take him for once.

Instead, he stepped into the hall and shut the door behind him.

Seren walked into the tavern, surprised by the lively buzz of activity. The scent of ale and roasted meat hung heavy in the warm, smoky air. At the center table, a group of men leaned close, speaking in hushed tones. As Seren passed, a man with a quiver of arrows slung over his back shot him a sharp glare over the rim of his mug. Another, seated beside him, offered a crooked smile full of crowded teeth.

Seren pulled his hood further over his head and strode briskly across the room, avoiding the curious gazes that followed him. He chose a table tucked away in the back, secluded and lit by the uneven glow of a dusty candelabra. As he sank into the chair and leaned against the wall, his head spun. Perhaps he did need something to eat after all.

A comely woman approached his table, wiping her hands on a stained apron. "Would you like something to eat or drink? We have delicious meat pie and blackberry ale."

As if on cue, Seren's stomach grumbled. "Both sound great," he said, his voice barely above a murmur.

The woman nodded and weaved through the crowded tavern, disappearing behind the counter. Resting his head on the table, Seren let out an involuntary groan, the noise lost in the hum of the room.

The sharp slam of a mug on a nearby table snapped his head up. A man with a bloated belly and a red-bearded face, mottled pink with drink, stood abruptly from the center table, swinging his mug in a wide arc.

"I proclaim we all take a moment of silence for the lives lost in the recent events," the man announced, his cup sloshing as he raised it high.

A hush fell over the room. Low murmurs of whispered prayers floated between the wooden beams. Seren followed suit, bowing his own head.

When the moment passed and heads lifted, the man shattered the stillness with a deep, drunken laugh, a sound so jarring it sent a shiver down Seren's spine.

"Sing us a song, Alton!" someone called from across the room.

The man—Alton—grinned, wiping his mouth with the back of his hand. "Alright, alright. If you insist."

With a mischievous twinkle in his eye, Alton slammed his mug three times against the table, each rhythmic thud reverberating through the floorboards. A low hum rumbled in his throat, building steadily. The deep tone of his voice swelled, filling the room like the roll of distant thunder. Despite himself, Seren couldn't look away, his gaze fixed on the man.

"A cupful of honey, sweet in my cheek.
A mouthful of feathers makes life seem so bleak.

A ruinous tale, and one not oft told,
So listeners beware unless ye be bold.
Oh, sing to me of treasure and sing to me of woe—
How much gold can one kingdom hold?

Oh, the pity, oh, the shame,
Not every king lives up to his name.
A thousand souls, isn't that what they say?
Sins of the fathers, the children must pay

Oh, sing to me of treasure and sing to me of woe—
How much gold can one kingdom hold?
A cup full of poison, bitter in my hand,
A mouthful of lies makes death feel so grand."

The men at Alton's table burst into laughter, ale sloshing over their tunics. Light clapping echoed through the tavern, but the noise soon faded back into faint chatter.

The woman returned, now wearing a scowl, and set a cup of ale in front of Seren.

"What are they singing?" he asked.

"A song about the Andanovans," she replied, wrinkling her nose. "Quite distasteful, if you ask me. Worshipping a false god or not, it's wrong to mock the dead—especially after what happened in Calarinn."

"And how are you so sure their god was false?" Seren asked, his voice cutting through the room, much too loud.

Silence fell over the group of men as their heads turned toward Seren. The man with the quiver of arrows on his back stood abruptly, his chair clattering behind him as he staggered forward. The woman quickly stepped aside, winding through the tables to avoid his path.

"I have a question for you, boy," he slurred. "How are we so sure that *all* the gods aren't false?" He raised his arms above his head, swaying on unsteady feet. "Where was Servius when a harpy ripped my sister's belly out? Three arrows I put in that beast, and it did nothing. Three times, I prayed, and three times, I was met with silence. And for what?"

The tavern fell silent. Heads turned, but no one dared interrupt the blasphemous words. "The Veil is going to kill us all, and the gods are going to watch."

"Enough, Varen," Alton barked, rising from his seat. "Leave the lad alone."

Varen's lip curled, but after a moment of wavering, he dropped his arms and staggered back to his table. He fell heavily into his seat, taking another long pull from his ale.

Seren sighed, swirling the ale in his cup with the tip of his finger. He had no argument for the man. How *could* they be sure of anything? After Calarinn, it made sense for faith in Servius to falter. Even Seren had cursed the god right to Lord Glynn's face—and he had meant every word.

Still, the woman was right: it was wrong to mock the Andanovans, given the circumstances. His thoughts drifted to Ambrose, the man he and Jude had met in the Behethium Forest on their way to Durcova. Ambrose had been quick to curse Andanova and its people, and it was the first time Seren had ever seen Jude truly angry. How would Jude have reacted to *this* song?

Andanovan blue.

Wasn't that what one of the Sanguine Sisters had said when she'd looked into Jude's eyes?

The chime of bells interrupted Seren's thoughts. All eyes turned toward the entrance as a figure swept into the establishment. A saint, dressed in gray-blue robes, dripping with water. Had it rained? As he entered the tavern with a purposeful stride, he kept his face concealed underneath his cloak hood. Silver thread ran across the brim of his cloak, in the designs of waves and a mighty sea serpent.

"Welcome," said the barkeep. His eyes scanned the saint's robes curiously. "How can I help you?"

The saint walked past the barkeep, completely ignoring him, and Seren could have sworn he saw the barkeep shudder. The saint approached Seren's table, his face still concealed beneath the hood. Uneasily, Seren shifted in his seat as the figure sat down directly across from him. Though he couldn't see anything beneath the hood, he was certain the man's gaze was fixed on him.

"Hello, Seren."

The blood drained from Seren's face. Just as he was about to respond, the noise of a plate being placed in front of him shattered the moment.

"Enjoy, sweetheart," the woman said sweetly. She gave a nervous, sideways glance at the strange man before walking away.

Seren stared at the food in front of him, before turning his gaze to the saint. "Who are you?" he asked uneasily. "Did Aiden send you?"

"Such an untrusting boy, aren't you?" The saint chuckled, his voice as rough as jagged stone. "Eat, and then we'll talk."

Seren found himself compelled to listen, though he was unsure why. He took hesitant bites of the pie, sipping on his cup of blackberry ale, not taking his eyes off the strange saint. The man remained motionless, sitting as Seren ate.

"You remind me of him," the saint said, leaning back against his chair. "Perhaps it is the way you carry yourself."

"Aiden?" Seren asked, his mouth full of food.

The saint chuckled. "No, your father."

Seren froze, the clatter of his fork hitting the plate echoing. "What did you just say?"

"I have a gift for you," the saint continued. He drummed his long fingers on the table. Seren noticed them truly now, the way they were wrinkled and pale as if he'd been submerged in water for too long. From his pocket, he pulled out a beautiful ring, a glistening gemstone sitting on a silver band, setting it on the table. "It once belonged to your mother."

Seren shrank towards the wall. "My *father* sent you?" he whispered. Seren stared at the ring between them, eyes tracing the pristine cut of the gem. "Why didn't he bring it himself?"

A raspy laugh escaped from the saint. "Your father said you would recognize it."

"You're not answering my question," Seren said coldly.

"Gods do not have to conform to your expectations, child," the saint warned. "I suggest you listen quietly." He picked up the ring, holding it to the flickering flames of the candle burning on the table. "*Bound by a bond both delicate and true, their dance holds the path for only you. Let strings sing their slumbering refrain, and the shadow's curtain shall wane.*"

Seren leaned forward. "It's been...*years,*" he began. "And this is what my father has to say? A stupid riddle?" He looked sidelong at the group of drinking men. "I've had just about enough rhymes and riddles."

Seren saw only a glimpse of the saint's curving smile, barely visible in the dimness beneath the cloak. Seren, unsure if his imagination was playing tricks on him, thought he saw a hint of blue on the man's lips amidst the fiery shadows.

"You can never be too sure who is listening and who is watching, little godling. Your father knows this well; he has been around a very, *very* long time. I suggest you keep this close." A wrinkled finger pushed the ring toward him. "You'll be needing it soon."

"How can I trust you?"

The saint laughed, and the ale atop the mug rippled. He turned his cloaked head toward the men drinking nearby.

"You'd be a fool to trust me," he said, his voice low. "Cynicism will keep you safe in this world. It's easy to lie to a child. To the gods, humans are nothing more than naïve children. A parent will tell lies to protect their kin. You'd do well to remember that."

Seren reached for the ring, drawing the cool metal into his palm. The stone in the band of silver was a glorious purple color that mirrored the strange shade of violet that kept flickering into his own eyes. His hand closed around the ring. Seren looked up to see that the saint was already gone.

EIGHT

"There is no judgment more divine than the sanction of lone-liness. There is nothing more cruel. Nothing more empty. Our nature is not to be truly alone. If that were so—the gods would have left us long ago."

–the Personal Diaries of Felix Amos

"It is not like you to keep secrets, Aiden." Eldyir sat at his desk, his hands folded against the polished wood. His tired hazel eyes were fixed on Aiden—questioning, waiting.

Aiden lingered stiffly in the doorway, having just arrived after being summoned. In his palm, he held the letter he had sent, now returned with confirmation that Seren would be arriving within days. Clearing his throat, he pocketed the letter without a word.

The Grand Priest gestured to the chair opposite him. "Take a seat, please. It's time the two of us finally talk."

Aiden crossed the room with deliberate steps, settling uneasily into the chair. He felt like a child again, sitting before the Grand Priest in his study. The room looked just as he remembered: an organized mess of maps, books, and magical trinkets scattered about. In the corner beside Eldyir's desk, his falcon perched silently, its snowy, speckled wings folded neatly at its sides.

"I've known you since you were a boy," Eldyir began. "Your faith has always set you apart, even as a child." A faint smile crossed his face. "When the Unveiling of Stellaris occurred, it came as a shock to many. It is known that the holy grounds of a church are impenetrable by evil, unable to be tainted. But..." Eldyir paused, his smile fading. "Would you like to know a secret?"

He fixed Aiden with a quiet intensity. "It is only the strength of our beliefs that keeps these holy grounds protected. Spells and holy crystals hold only so much power—they can be broken, circumvented. But faith—unshakable faith—is the most powerful magic of all."

A long silence stretched between them before Eldyir spoke again, his voice firmer now. "Your faith has been ruptured, Aiden. What happened was beyond devastating, and though years have passed, I imagine it will take many more before your faith can fully heal."

Aiden's gaze fell, his hands clenching the fabric of his robes.

"But it must begin somewhere," Eldyir said. "So, let us start with something that shakes faith like nothing else, shall we? The truth."

Aiden blinked, his mouth suddenly dry. "Eldyir," he began, his voice faltering. "There are things I don't understand myself. Everything I've done, I've only done to protect our faith. To protect—"

"I have known of the Mother's appearance since his birth," Eldyir interrupted.

Aiden's heart skipped a beat. "...What?"

Eldyir stood and crossed to the window. Sunlight washed over his pale robes and dark skin. "It was an autumn evening," he began, his voice distant, "just before winter's bite crept in. The vision came to Felix Amos faintly—a flicker of light in the darkness. But it was there. We didn't know where she was, only that she was a boy, born into a broken world." He pressed a hand against the glass, the motion heavy with unspoken grief.

"Felix and I were close then. More than colleagues—we were dear friends. I trusted him with my life. Faith isn't just for the gods, Aiden. It's for friends, for family, for those we love. So, when Felix begged me not to seek the boy, not to bring it to the ecclesiarch's attention... I trusted him."

"This entire time?" Aiden breathed, disbelief thick in his voice. "But what of the vision you showed everyone at the Assembly?"

"A vision gifted to me by Felix many years ago," Eldyir said. "I was waiting for the right moment to share it."

"You...lied to everyone?"

"Yes, just as you did." Eldyir didn't appear upset by Aiden's words, his gaze steady as he turned to face him. "I did what I felt was right. Felix insisted the boy needed to have a normal life. It was too early, too dangerous to expose such a small, fragile child to the fate the gods had created for him. I trusted Felix, and he trusted me. We had the deepest faith in each other."

Eldyir drew the purple drapes closed, the sunlight retreating behind the fabric and leaving shadows to claim the room. With a flick of his finger, a small blue flame sparked to life above his fingertip. He lit the candle on his desk, the soft glow casting fleeting shadows across his solemn face.

"The two of us agreed," Eldyir continued, his voice softer, "that when the time was right, I would reveal the visions, and all would be well. It was for the best."

He placed his palms flat against the desk, his voice lowering further. "But it wasn't long before the madness took hold of my dearest friend. Each vision of the Mother pushed him closer to the edge. The more he saw her, the more his mind began to fracture. His visions became unreliable, and others in the ecclesiarch demanded he be stripped of his title as Grand Seer. Still, I kept my word. I never spoke of the boy. I believed that when the time was right, the gods would bring him into the light. Even when I was forced to revoke Felix's title, I held my faith—in him, and in the gods."

Eldyir sighed, his weariness apparent. "I told the others that his visions were corrupted, that we could not trust them. Sometimes, we must tell lies to protect faith. Without it, the people fall into panic. They lose trust in the gods—and in us—and fearful people are easily manipulated." His gaze grew heavy, and his words became a quiet confession. "It is a burden I have carried for many years, one of many as Grand Priest."

Aiden's grip tightened on the arms of the chair. "Why are you telling me this?"

"Fate is a fine thread." Eldyir raised his hand, and a red thread of light appeared, twirling delicately around his fingers. "Easily frayed." The thread twisted, fragments breaking away. "And when it frays, it splits—leading in many directions." The thread divided, two strings of light spiraling through the air. "The boy's fate remains undecided, unanswered. Each possibility shifts the world in profound ways." He let the threads hang in the air, untouched. "It drove Felix mad. He sought the answer: which path is destined for us, and which is not?"

Eldyir set his hands on the table, the thread fading. "Faith is delicate. A single truth can undo it all. What would they say, Aiden, if they knew? That the boy destined to save them could just as easily destroy them? That salvation and ruin walk hand in hand?"

Aiden watched the blue flame dance, his mind growing heavier. "Felix saw the darkness in the boy," he whispered, his voice cracking. "Didn't he? I don't understand. How could the gods let this happen? This isn't what we were promised." Tears pricked the corners of his eyes, threatening to spill. "I wanted to come to you, but I was too ashamed—ashamed of my failures and what I had allowed to happen."

The Grand Priest placed a steady hand on Aiden's. "Do not let this destroy your faith, Aiden. That is exactly what the Devil desires—to sow doubt in our hearts and make us question the gods' wisdom."

Aiden lifted his gaze, his heart clenched tight. "Did you know?" His voice broke. "Did you know I was raising the boy?"

Eldyir shook his head. "By the time the boy was in your care, Felix had already descended into deep madness."

"I tried to teach him," Aiden whispered. "I tried to guide him, to do what I thought was right, but..." He squeezed his eyes shut. "The Unveiling was his doing. The bloodshed—it was all his. His hands are stained with it."

Eldyir's expression softened as he leaned closer. "I know how deeply that day scarred you, Aiden, but it is my duty as Grand Priest to understand what truly happened. You have carried this burden alone for too long. Let me share it with you."

Aiden's shoulders sank, the crushing weight of his guilt easing for the first time in years. "Of course," he said quietly.

Eldyir stepped behind him, his robes dragging along the floor. "Stare into the flame, and remember that day." Cool fingers pressed against Aiden's temple. "Relax your body and let your mind guide you."

Aiden fixed on the blue flame, its flickering light steadying his thoughts. He felt himself sinking into the chair, the tension slipping from his fingers, his jaw unclenching. The flame seemed to pulse with life, swelling brighter with each breath he took, until it reached out, glowing and pulling him in.

Voices stirred within the fire—faint, distant.

Memories.

"This harp is a piece of you, Seren. Just as you are a part of it."

Aiden's heart quickened, but he willed himself to stay calm. The room around him began to dissolve, darkness creeping in at the edges of his vision. It smothered the light, consuming everything until all fell away.

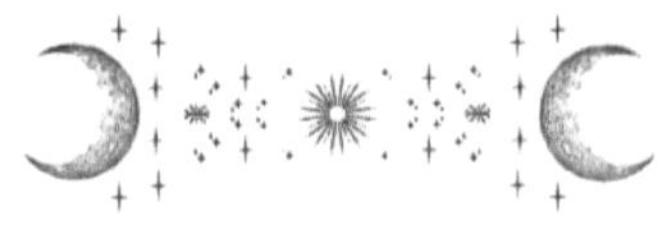

"You're not paying attention, Seren. Did you hear a word I said?"

The boy sat on the windowsill, dark hair falling into his distant gaze. His long legs dangled, feet swaying idly above the floor. He'd been quieter than usual, their exchanges mostly hollow, lacking the usual bite of bitter words or small outbursts.

"Seren," Aiden repeated, his voice sharper this time.

The boy turned with a bored sigh. "I'm sorry, what were you saying?" The apology carried no trace of resentment, only genuine distraction.

Aiden sighed. "Are you feeling alright? Enid mentioned you're skipping meals, and it seems like you're hardly present these days."

Seren turned his attention back to the window, resting the back of his head against the sill. He hovered between the stages of boy and young man, his face still soft with the edges of childhood, though his voice carried the weight of change.

"I'm fine."

Outside the window, sunlight peeked through the trees, though winter whispered in the wind. Seren watched wistfully, his finger tracing the pale-stained glass, following the gentle curve of an angel's feather.

"She's quiet," Seren said, his voice low. "Sometimes I think she'll leave me forever."

Aiden rubbed his temple. "I know she hasn't been writing as much as usual, but that doesn't mean she's left you. Perhaps when she returns in the morning, you can speak with her—tell her how you feel." He sighed. "I understand... I miss your mother when she's gone, too."

"Not my mother," Seren said.

Aiden blinked, surprised, and stepped closer to the boy. It was unlike Seren to open up, to share his feelings, unless they erupted in fits of rage. "She speaks to you often?"

Aiden would never forget the first and only time the Mother had spoken through Seren. It had happened when the boy touched the harp for the very first time. The music flowed from him effortlessly, naturally, as though it had always been a part of him despite him never having played before. The air had shifted then, growing heavy, sacred, undeniable.

Seren's eyes had changed—blazing with a radiant lavender light that pierced straight through Aiden's soul. It was no longer Seren looking back at him.

It was her. The Mother. And her voice had rung out, clear as the brightest morning in heaven.

"Faithful one, you have done well to return what was lost to me," *she had said.* "Through your hands, a piece of me has been restored. But this is a moment for us alone—my child, my harp, and me. Leave us now, and let this sacred reunion remain unbroken by mortal hands."

"She will return," Aiden said. "She is a piece of you. She will always return."

Seren was silent for a long moment before he finally turned to Aiden. "But who am I if you take her away?" he whispered.

Aiden stilled, the weight of the question settling in his chest. "You're Seren," he said softly. "A boy full of wonder, full of questions, full of life." He smiled, though it was bittersweet. "You are your mother's son, and you are mine."

Seren's emerald eyes widened before filling with tears. They streamed down his pale cheeks. "I think...I think there's a darkness inside of me," he said, his voice breaking. His hand clutched his chest. "Sometimes I just feel so angry. So..." His voice cracked into a sob.

Aiden crossed the room, and for the first time, Seren collapsed into his arms. The boy buried his face in Aiden's robes, his sobs quiet but endless. Aiden placed a hand on his disheveled hair.

"There is no darkness inside of you, Seren," he murmured. "Only fear. It's okay to be afraid."

Something twinged in Aiden's chest, his own fear. He pushed it away. He held the boy close, waiting for his sorrow to pass. When Seren pulled away and wiped his tear-streaked face, Aiden offered a smile.

"Why don't we focus on your studies next week? Enjoy the rest of your day and take some time to rest. Tomorrow, we will go to the Winter Solstice Celebration. Your mother, you, and me. No books, no memorizing spells. We'll eat Sunbread and..." Aiden rubbed his chin. "I'd say you're of age to try a cup of sacramental wine this year."

"Really?" Seren asked, his face brightening.

"Yes, really." Aiden ruffled his hair. "Now, run along."

Seren nodded and pulled himself to his feet, exiting the library. Aiden lowered himself into the chair with a sigh. His eyes flickered toward the window, to the heavens, beyond the winter blue of the sky, to the stars he could not see.

"I am exhausted," Aiden whispered. "Please, guide me in the right direction."

Perhaps it was time to take the boy to the Grand Priest. Aiden could no longer do this alone.

Aiden covered the birdcage with a satin cloth so the candlelight wouldn't disturb the resting messenger dove. He settled back at his desk and opened a drawer, pulling out a fresh ink-pot, already having used up the last one. The parchment resting on the table was nearly illegible, and Aiden's wrist ached. He grabbed his quill, dipped it in the ink, and continued writing.

A knock echoed, startling him, ink splashing on the paper. He grumbled, setting the quill down. Who could be knocking at this hour?

"Come in," he called.

The door creaked open, and red hair caught the candlelight, glowing like molten rubies. Emeryn stepped into the threshold, steam curling from the cups in her hands. She smiled, lifting them. "Cup of chamomile? I know it's your favorite."

"Em," Aiden breathed. "I thought you weren't arriving until morning?" He rose from his desk and crossed the room, taking a cup from her hands and planting a kiss on her cheek.

"Technically, it is morning," Emeryn replied with a smile. She moved to the wooden chair by his desk and settled in. "And I see you're right where I left you—pouring over your books."

Aiden chuckled, though a heaviness lingered in his chest. "I'm just compiling some spells for Seren. I believe he's ready to start casting higher magic."

Emeryn's smile faltered. "Already?" she murmured, her red brows knitting together. "I forget how quickly a lifetime can pass." She sipped her tea, a faint flush rising in her cheeks. "How...is Seren?" Her voice grew quieter. "I've missed him so much."

Aiden ran a hand through his inky-black hair, releasing a heavy exhale. "He's…a bit distant," he admitted. "More so than usual. I was hoping we could talk, but it can wait until morning. You must be exhausted." He reached out, tucking a loose strand of fiery hair behind her ear. "You should rest."

"I'm not quite tired," Emeryn said, stretching out her legs. "What's on your mind?"

Aiden frowned, the words catching in his throat. It had been weeks since he'd last seen her, and the distance had only deepened his longing. He didn't want to think about the boy right now—or anything else. All he wanted was to kiss her breathless, to lose himself in her and forget his responsibilities. But duty tugged at him, forcing him to set his emotions aside.

"I think it's time we take Seren to the Grand Priest," Aiden said slowly. "There are some things I cannot teach him. And your absences have unsettled him. He lashes out, refuses to study, and the distance between us only grows."

The memory of Seren pressing his face into his shoulder, tears dampening the deep blue fabric, flashed through his mind. Aiden's chest tightened, but he kept his tone steady. "We cannot shield him any longer from the future that awaits him. He's growing into a young man. It's time, Emeryn."

"No." The word fell with such sharpness that Aiden almost expected blood to spill from her lips. "He's not ready."

Aiden set his hands on the desk, his fingers curling against the wood. "Tell me, Emeryn—when will he ever be ready?" His voice dropped low. "I've kept him hidden because you said it was for his safety—for your safety. Yet you won't even tell me what it is I'm keeping you safe from."

He exhaled slowly, tension stiffening his shoulders. "All these years, I've been patient. I've raised him as my own. It's just as much my right as yours to decide what's best for him. He'll be safe in the Grand Cathedral. You can stay with him. Having you by his side would bring him peace. Things need to change."

Emeryn set her cup on the desk with a clink, tea sloshing over the rim. "Safe?" she echoed. "The entire world will know who he is. It paints a target on his back."

"He would be protected," Aiden argued. "What are you so afraid of, Emeryn? You and I both knew this day would come."

"There are things you do not understand," she said fiercely. "Things you are not ready to hear."

Heat surged through Aiden. "Do you think I'm incompetent? Whatever it is you think I cannot handle, I assure you—you're wrong. Help me understand why this is not the right choice." He ran his fingers through his hair. "I respect and trust you, even when you disappear for weeks without a word to the boy. But this cannot go on forever, and you know it."

Emeryn's gaze dropped to the floor, her jaw tight. "Do you think I enjoy keeping things from you? Everything I've done, I've done out of love for my son."

"And have I not done the same?" Aiden's voice rose, his anger bubbling over. "If it wasn't for my love for you, I would've taken the boy to the Grand Priest the moment he played Kallista's Harp. Have I not kept his identity a secret for you? Have I not taught him all I know and raised him as my very own? And what do I get out of this, Emeryn? Sometimes, I don't even know if you truly love me in return."

"Of course, I do—"

"But how am I to believe that?" Aiden's hands slammed onto the table. "I just want the truth."

Emeryn stood abruptly, her hands gripping the folds of her green dress. "You are a man of faith, Aiden. Are you willing to lose that piece of yourself? To question your gods, your faith, and everything you believe—all because you demand the truth?"

"Don't I deserve to know?" Aiden shouted. The candle flames trembled, casting frantic shadows against the walls. "I'm taking him to Aurelius next week—whether you agree or not."

Aiden watched as the fight drained from Emeryn's shoulders. Her trembling hands clutched the edge of the desk, and for a fleeting moment, he thought he saw fear.

"Do you know why I brought Seren to you, Aiden?" she whispered. The silence that followed was suffocating, heavy with unsaid truths. "I'd heard of the High Priest of Stellaris—of his unwavering faith, his power said to rival the Grand Priest's. I admired that about you."

She turned to him, her verdant eyes brimming with unshed tears. "I thought you'd build the same faith in Seren that you built in yourself. You trust in your gods so deeply, and it gives you strength. They favor you, Aiden. They chose you, and so I brought Seren to you because they chose him." Her voice cracked as the tears finally fell. "The gods do not care for me. They have cursed me. And how am I supposed to help my son when I cannot undo my own darkness?"

"Em—"

"More than a hundred lives I've lived," Emeryn interrupted, her voice brittle, as if the words were tearing her apart. "Each one more bloodstained than the last. To be human is a fragile existence, Aiden. But within it all, there is one thing that has always mattered. In every lifetime, love has been both my curse and blessing." Her eyes softened with a deep, sorrowful longing. "So please, believe me when I say there are things you do not understand. The things I do, I do to protect Seren."

Aiden stilled. More than a hundred lives? He didn't understand. "What are you saying?"

"If I tell you the truth," she said, "it could destroy you."

"Emeryn, please," he said, desperation creeping into his voice. "I deserve to know."

She squeezed her eyes shut. "Then, promise me you won't take him to the Grand Priest yet. The time just...isn't right." She met his gaze, her eyes pleading.

Aiden moved toward her, his heart racing, and took her hands in his. "You can trust me," he said. "Whatever it may be, we can carry this burden together."

Emeryn was quiet for a moment, and then she settled into the chair. She clutched his hand, her knuckles white. When her voice finally came, it was only a whisper. She began with her life, her time in Durcova with a husband much older than her, a man who treated her with cruelty because she was incapable of bearing children. Aiden listened intently as she recounted her escape. He'd heard bits and pieces before, but nothing like this. Next, she told Aiden of the deal she had made with the Fallen for the ability to carry a child.

And then came the truth Aiden hadn't prepared for.

As she spoke, the world narrowed. His vision blurred, and his breath hitched. Her voice faded, overtaken by the roaring in his ears.

Aiden couldn't breathe.

"Do you understand now?" Emeryn asked when she finished. "Why I was afraid to tell you?"

His heart thundered in his chest.

"Aiden, please," she said, her voice wavering. "Say something."

He staggered back, his legs unsteady, his mind reeling. "No," he gasped. "That cannot be right. That's impossible." Panic coiled around him, tight as a serpent's embrace, and he clutched his chest. "No, you're wrong."

"It is true, Aiden," Emeryn said, her eyes locked onto him. "I'm trying to protect him. But if he knows... If he knows, he will question everything."

Aiden shook his head, the words swirling in his mind, refusing to settle. "No. No, no, no."

The revelation twisted inside him, deeper with every second. He stumbled into the bookcase, grabbing a ledge to steady himself. "Oh gods," he whispered. "He already has questioned. We have to—" His voice broke. "We have to take him to the Grand Priest."

"No," Emeryn said sharply. "You promised me."

Aiden froze. Yes, they had to, it was the only option. The Grand Priest would know what to do, how to handle this. But...

This wasn't how things were supposed to be. It was wrong. What if there was no fixing it? What if it doomed them all?

"This is an abomination," Aiden breathed, his voice cracking. "If this is true..."

"*Please...*" *Emeryn's voice softened. "Calm down." She reached out, her hand landing on his shoulder.*

He jerked away as if burned. "No. Don't you see what this means?" He looked at Emeryn feeling a betrayal sear through him like no other. "And you—how could you do such a thing? Did you know?"

Emeryn recoiled.

"Did. You. Know?" Aiden's voice broke, raw and furious. She didn't respond. He gazed upon her unmatched beauty, like a perfect red rose, and now Aiden could see it, she was covered in vicious thorns.

"You disgust me," he spat, the words unstoppable. "That boy should have never been born! Gods, what have you done?"

Emeryn's jaw tightened, her expression hardening as she snapped to her feet. "Do you think the world is as simple as you believe?" she asked, her words poisonous. "That your precious books have all the answers?" She snatched a leather-bound book from Aiden's desk and hurled it toward the bookcase, over his head. It cracked, papers scattering from the shelves.

Aiden flinched.

In Emeryn's eyes, he saw it: the pain of a hundred lifetimes, the weight of choices long made, all burning in her gaze like a forest ablaze. And the question echoed in Aiden's mind.

Who was this woman that he had loved for eight years?

"You can curse me, you can curse the gods, but do not dare curse my son," Emeryn hissed.

"Mom?"

Aiden and Emeryn both stilled, their heads turning. In the crack of the door, a pair of green eyes trembled in the dim light. There, in the doorway, stood the boy, his pale face framed by his unkempt hair.

"Seren?" Emeryn's eyes snapped to Aiden, her expression smoothing into a forced smile. "I'm sorry, did we wake you? We were just…" An unbidden frown stole her calm façade. "Having an adult conversation."

The boy took a step back, his chest rising and falling rapidly. His gaze remained fixed on Aiden. "I heard you," he whispered. "I heard what you said."

"Seren, wait—" Aiden rushed forward, his hand reaching for the boy's robes that slipped through his fingers like feathers caught in the wind. But Seren turned and fled, the fabric billowing behind him like white wings, vanishing down the hallway.

Aiden dashed after him, not sparing a glance at Emeryn. His gaze darted down the corridor, but there was no sign of the boy. Rounding the bend toward the spiraling stairs that led to Seren's room, he nearly tripped over his robes in his hurry. Taking the steps two at a time, Aiden reached the door and knocked, his knuckles turning raw.

"Seren, open the door! Please." The quiver in his voice made him wince, every word betraying the fear he was struggling to contain. He gritted his teeth, grabbing the knob, but it wouldn't budge. Locked.

Behind him, footsteps echoed. Aiden stiffened but didn't turn. Instead, he knocked again.

Emeryn pressed her forehead against the door, her palms flat against the wood. "Seren, will you let me in?"

Silence.

Aiden pounded harder. "Listen to your mother, Seren. Open the door."

Emeryn rested a hand on his shoulder. "Leave him be," she said, her voice strangely calm. "We'll talk to him in the morning."

Aiden shrugged her hand off, spinning to face her. "You talk to him. I've clearly done enough."

Without waiting for her reply, he turned and strode down the stairs, his robes flaring behind him like the tail of a shooting star.

"Aiden," Emeryn called. "Wait—"

"Do not follow me," he demanded. "I need to be alone."

Aiden couldn't look at her. Not now. He stormed into his study and slammed the door shut, locking it with unsteady hands. Leaning back against the door, he slid to the floor, his fingers tangling in his hair as he buried his face in his palms. Tears stung his eyes, blurring his vision, but he refused to let them fall.

The fear and disbelief gnawed at him, writhing inside until they became something darker. It spread through him like venom, burrowing into his skin, settling deep in the marrow of his bones.

With a roar, Aiden surged to his feet and swept the books from his desk. Papers scattered to the floor like autumn leaves caught in a gust. He grabbed a book and hurled it at the wall, the thud barely registering. Another followed.

Breathing heavily, his chest heaving, Aiden yanked open the desk drawer and snatched a sheet of parchment along with a quill and ink. Quill in hand, he scribbled furiously, the words bleeding together across the page. When he finished, he rolled the parchment and crossed the room to the birdcage in the corner.

Aiden opened the cage, murmuring a spell under his breath. The dove stirred, its feathers glowing from the charm. With shaky hands, he tied the letter to its leg and coaxed the bird onto his palm. The window creaked as he pushed it open, and a chilly wind rushed in.

The stars were blinding tonight, sharp and cold, like shards of broken glass scattered across a void. Aiden lifted the dove, magic leaving his fingertips, guiding it into the night to ensure it would reach its destination in a short time.

As the bird vanished into the darkness, Aiden crumpled to his knees. He felt hollow. Lost.

"How could this happen?" he whispered as he looked to the stars. He wondered if the gods had made a mistake. The thought was terrible, poisonous, foreign, something he'd never, ever wondered.

Or maybe the world was meant to go dark. Maybe it was destined to never know the warmth of light again. What if the gods were soon to abandon them all?

For the first time, Aiden wished his brother were at his side. That maybe he could help Aiden make sense of this emptiness.

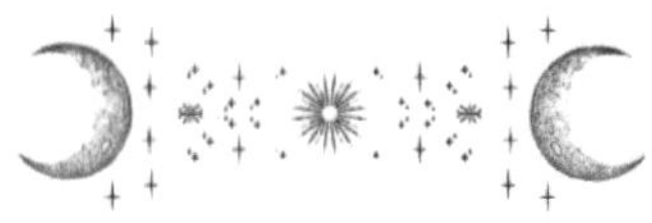

Aiden woke to three knocks at his study door. He jerked his head from his desk, blinking against the sunlight with a groan. He glanced down at his ink-stained fingertips and the disarray scattered across the study. Gods, *he'd truly lost his mind, hadn't he? With a listless sigh, he rose to his feet, straightening his robes. Cracking the door open, he was met with Enid's kind gaze.*

"Good...afternoon, Aiden. We missed you at the sermon this morning. Iroh took it upon himself to fill your place... Are you alright?" Her eyes followed the strewn papers and Aiden's disheveled appearance.

"I'm fine," Aiden grumbled, running a hand over his face. "I'm... Have you seen Emeryn?" His gut twisted as he replayed the harsh words he'd said to her.

Enid blinked and frowned, her hands smoothing the folds of her cream-colored dress. "Yes," she said, her fingers drifting to the blue rosaries around her neck. "She's been looking for Seren. The boy has been missing since this morning."

"What?" Aiden stiffened, dread clawing its way into his chest. "Missing? Why didn't you come for me sooner?" Without waiting for an answer, he rushed past her.

"She's in the gardens!" Enid called down the hall.

Sure enough, Aiden found Emeryn there, searching under the overgrown roses as if she would find Seren curled beneath them.

"Emeryn, I'm sorry for what I said—"

"Not now, Aiden," she said, lip trembling. "Just help me find him."

Aiden nodded, and the two of them searched for Seren until dusk, their efforts growing more frantic with each passing hour. Seren's room was untouched, as if he hadn't slept there at all. Enid joined them, combing through every corner of the estate, but no one had seen him. Aiden even sent an acolyte to the town center to ask around using Seren's description, but there was no sign of the boy.

By the time the sun dipped below the horizon, casting long shadows across the church grounds, Emeryn was distraught. They sat together on the front steps of the church, the winter sun painting their skin with an amber glow.

"This is my fault. What if he isn't here?" Emeryn whispered. "I shouldn't have told you the truth. I should have—"

"The fault is mine," Aiden interrupted, brushing a strand of her hair behind her ear. "He wouldn't have run if it wasn't for the things I said." He hesitated, his gaze searching hers. "I'm sure he's around here somewhere. Even if he isn't, he couldn't have gone far. We'll form a search party first thing in the morning. Okay?"

Emeryn nodded, her expression still clouded with worry as she headed up the stairs. Aiden clenched his jaw, doing his best to hide the fear creeping through him. After several minutes, he followed, pacing the church halls as his mind raced. None of Seren's belongings had been taken. It didn't make sense. Even if the boy was distressed knowing his mother was here, Aiden couldn't believe he would leave the sanctuary of his home. They had searched everywhere. Where hadn't they looked?

Leaning against the wall in the candle lit hallway, Aiden's gaze landed on the wyrm painted on the church walls. Its amber eyes seemed to mock him, unblinking in the flickering light. His fingers curled against the cool stone. He could have handled everything better—he knew that much. He'd buried himself in the search for Seren, pushing all other thoughts aside. But when they found the boy, the reckoning would come.

They'd have to speak about what he'd said. And Emeryn was right: they couldn't tell Seren. He could never know the truth.

Aiden's stomach churned, his thoughts traveling to the frantic letter he had sent to his younger brother in the dead of night. It had probably reached him by now. What would Emeryn say if she knew? That, in his lowest moment, he'd wanted to send Seren far away, to push the problem out of sight. But the truth was, Aiden was just afraid.

Because he believed her words. And it shook him to his core.

Deep down, he'd always sensed something wasn't right, though he'd never let himself admit it. When Aiden thought of the Mother, he imagined a pure being, perfect in every way. That wasn't Seren. Seren was defiant, angry, and too willing to give in to his darker impulses.

Aiden leaned his head against the wall, his shoulders heavy with weariness. Then, the lull of a distant song reached his ears. He lifted his head. The music flowed through the hallway, and even the candlelight danced in response, shifting from orange to a muted purple. Aiden's feet moved of their own accord, drawn toward it, the song like a thread pulling him forward. It was beautiful, perhaps the most beautiful thing Aiden had ever heard.

The music brought him to the top of the stairs that led to the crypts. The door was open. Blinking, his mind hazy, Aiden began descending. A thought crept into his mind. Impossible. How had Seren entered the crypts, where the Archives lay, without a key?

When he reached the bottom, Aiden stopped at the second door, which was also open. He reached out to trace its surface, feeling the faint pulse of magic hum beneath the wood. He sucked in a startled breath, then stepped through the doorway.

Aiden kept walking toward the music, past towering bookcases brimming with ancient scrolls and weathered books. Charmed sconces lined the way, their eternal flames casting flickering shadows on the stone walls. The music grew louder, seeping into every corner of Aiden's being. It was haunting, as though the sound was not meant for his ears. He felt the warmth of hot tears streaking down his face as he pressed forward.

And then, he reached the heart of the room. Haloed light flooded the space, casting its glow across the walls and the starburst rug that seemed to shimmer with a thousand shades of color.

The boy sat in a chair, bathed in a heavenly glow. Aiden braced himself against a nearby bookcase, eyes widening at the magic his Sight allowed him to see. He watched the music swirl through the room—little birds of light fluttering in the air, their feathers drifting like snow across a glimmering veil of colors, some of which Aiden could not name. It was like a dreamy night sky, pulsing with divine essence.

The beauty was so painfully perfect that it made Aiden ache, not just in his body but deep into the very center of his soul.

Seren's pale face shone with tears beneath the light of the harp; his eyes closed as if lost in a dream. Aiden could see Seren for what he truly was. His hair had bled into a radiant white, and for a moment, he could've sworn he saw the shadows of wings behind him. Aiden's heart lurched at the sight of the boy—so lost in the melody, so deeply connected to something Aiden couldn't understand.

"Seren," Aiden said, his voice trembling. He took a step forward, his knees shaking beneath him. "Your mother and I have been looking all over for you."

The boy's eyes flashed open, revealing not green, but eyes burning a violent purple. "Go away," he said.

Aiden took another step beneath the canvas of colors. "It's beautiful, Seren," he said. "I didn't know you were capable of such a thing."

Seren's fingers danced across the strings at the same pace, no emotion betraying his voice. "I told you to go away."

"Why don't we go upstairs?" Aiden urged. "And talk."

"Talk," Seren repeated, tone bitter.

The boy's fingers moved faster, the strings ringing out with much more force. A heaviness settled in Aiden's chest, a sorrow more unrelenting than anything he'd ever felt. He couldn't stop the sob that ripped through him, tears flowing relentlessly.

"And what should we talk about?" Seren said coldly. His fingers plucked the strings harder. The birds plummeted downward, only to burst like dying stars. "The fact that I should have never been born?" Blood ran down Seren's knuckles as he struck another chord.

Aiden gasped in pain.

"Or the fact that everyone always lies to me?"

Another note, sharper, louder.

The colors began to shift, their ethereal hues darkening, folding into an umbra that gradually consumed the light.

"Maybe the reason my mother is always gone is because she can't bear to see me. Because something is wrong with me."

The music warped with each passing second, growing discordant, and Aiden felt himself splintering. The sound crawled beneath his skin, unraveling him from the inside.

"Seren, stop playing," Aiden said hoarsely. But he couldn't move. His feet felt as though they were glued to the floor, his body frozen in place.

Black veins crawled up the side of the ivory harp, stretching like the roots of ancient trees.

"I told you there was a darkness inside of me," Seren said, voice cold. "And you didn't listen."

The light bent and danced before collapsing into itself—a death so swift and sudden that, for a moment, darkness consumed everything. Then it parted. Shadows stretched and grew into forms, hands reaching, tendrils of shadow licking the air.

Aiden crumpled to his knees as a piercing cold shot through him. "Seren," he choked. "Stop."

And then, one of the strings snapped beneath Seren's bloodied fingers. A strangled noise escaped the boy, but he didn't stop. His fingers kept weaving, each sound more blood-curdling than the last. Wisps of shadows curled around his hand, creeping up his arms, until they reached his mouth and nose, snaking their way in.

"Seren!"

The feeling hit Aiden with full force, stealing the breath from his lungs. His head slammed against the stone. That unbearable pressure, the raw, unbalanced fear, tore at him from the inside.

The Veil had opened.

Seren was screaming.

Fear gripped Aiden's heart, and he tried to lift his body but couldn't. The world collapsed into unforgivable darkness that had no beginning and no end.

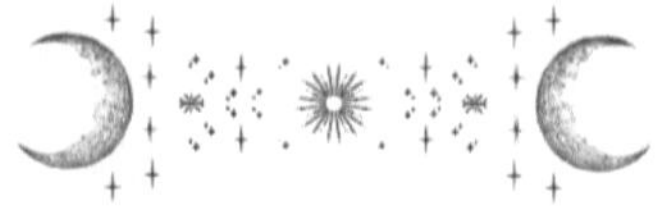

Shrill screams tore through Aiden's senses. He forced his eyes open and tried to lift his head, but it felt as though he were underwater. His vision was a blur, everything coming into focus at a glacial pace. That's right, he was in the crypts. Pushing himself to his feet, Aiden's head swiveled.

The harp was gone. And so was Seren.

Aiden stumbled toward the stairs, counting his breaths, something he had learned during his time as an acolyte. The Veil induced a primal fear that leeched off one's senses. Aiden inhaled deeply.

One. Two. Three.

Screams echoed down the stairs, human or demon, Aiden did not know. Clenching his fist, he willed his magic forward as he dragged himself up the steps. It was difficult in the Veil, here the gods' connection was faint and fragile, but the power still stirred within him. Slowly, he brought it to the surface, letting it surge through his veins.

One. Two. Three.

When Aiden stepped into the corridor, his foot splashed in liquid. He looked down, forcing himself to breathe steady, even breaths. He couldn't panic. Not now.

Enid's body lay crumpled on the floor, her hair matted, half her pale face torn away to expose bone.

No. He had to keep breathing. He had to hold onto his magic.

Aiden stepped over her body.

One. Two. Three.

A scream echoed down the corridor. It was coming from the prayer room, Aiden realized.

He broke into a run, not daring to look down as his feet splashed through more blood. The doors loomed at the end of the passage, closed and waiting. Emeryn could be in there. Seren.

How long had he been unconscious? How long had the demons been tearing through the church?

His hand stretched toward the carved doors, fingertips brushing the engravings of the Mother Tree's branches.

Something slammed into him.

Aiden was flung backward, his body going limp as he braced for impact. He hit the wall hard, the force knocking the air from his lungs. Blood dripped down his forehead as he lifted his head, vision swimming.

The demon's sickly yellow eyes gleamed in the darkness, scattered across its elongated body like a grotesque constellation, dozens of them blinking in unison. Its paper-thin skin clung to its frame, veins pulsing beneath the surface. A black-tongued serpent writhed at the end of its tail, its exposed fangs glinting with venom.

Its many-clawed arms resembled grotesquely malformed human limbs, dragging its twisted body forward like a monstrous spider. Worst of all was its face—eerily human, with cracked lips and a gaping mouth lined with jagged, uneven teeth. As it spoke, its voice slithered out, wet and rasping, the corners of its mouth stretching unnaturally wide.

"Poor little priest," it hissed. "You're too late."

The creature plunged one of its arms deep into its own throat and pulled something free.

Aiden's face drained of color. He breathed in. Out.

Dangling from the demon's claws was what remained of a child: small, bloodied, and unmistakable.

"We ate all the children," it said. "They were so very sweet."

Aiden shoved himself to his feet, his entire body trembling with wrath that surged like fire through his veins. His magic flared, rippling across his skin and distorting the air around him.

"You will pay for what you've done, demon," he growled. He swept one hand across his forehead, the other across his heart, bringing them together in a resounding clap. Power exploded outward, nearly knocking him back against the wall.

Despite everything, the gods had not forsaken him.

"I banish you to the hellish realm from which you came!" Aiden roared, his voice echoing through the halls.

Magic surged from his hands, a searing burst of light that struck the demon square in its cavernous mouth. It convulsed, its flailing arms clawing at the air, desperate to grasp something solid as the fabric of reality twisted around it. With a final, agonized shriek, the creature was consumed, hurled through the Veil-space and cast beyond the church grounds.

Aiden huffed, forcing himself to press on. He couldn't falter. Not now. He had to find Emeryn and Seren. Blood trickled down the side of his head, but he ignored it as he barreled toward the doors. With a flick of his wrist, they flung open.

The prayer hall, once a sanctuary of white, gold, and blue, was now drenched in crimson. Blood pooled across the floor and streaked the walls, the air thick with the stench of fresh death. Demons lifted their heads, their bloodied maws dripping as they turned toward him.

Aiden's vision narrowed to a tunnel of red. He screamed, a raw, primal sound tearing from his throat, and charged. His hands shot forward. Magic erupted, banishing one demon in a burst of light. Then another. His robes flared as he spun, the hem dragging through the blood, sending scarlet arcs flying with each motion.

He pushed his magic harder, forcing it to stretch beyond its limits. Another demon vanished, erased from the desecrated church. Then another. Aiden didn't stop. Not until the hall was empty and he stood alone, panting. Sweat dripped down his forehead. His legs were weak beneath him, but he couldn't tire. Not yet.

Aiden reeled around, stumbling back through the doors and down the hall.

"Seren!" he screamed. "Emeryn!"

Maybe they had made it out alive by some gods' forsaken miracle. He burst through the entrance doors. Aiden's feet sank into the blood-soaked grass, overgrown hellebores brushing against his robes. In the distance, shadows swarmed beneath the pale half-moon, writhing and snapping like living things.

Seren.

Aiden forced himself forward, his body aching with every step as he thrust his hands out, willing his magic to respond once more.

Light surged, blinding as the sun, flooding the clearing. Shadows screeched and scattered, shooting skyward before vanishing into the darkness. And there, beneath them, was Seren, his hair dark as night.

All at once, the Veil lifted.

Aiden gasped as his body felt impossibly lighter, the weight of its restraint suddenly gone. "Seren..." He trudged forward and froze.

Lying in the vermilion grass at Seren's feet was Emeryn. Her lifeless body splayed out, blood blooming behind her. Seren's hands trembled, slick with crimson as he stood over his dead mother.

No.

Aiden shoved Seren aside, and the boy crumpled to the ground. Aiden dropped to his knees, his shaking hands hovering over Emeryn's still form. He gathered her into his arms, her blood-soaked hair sticking to his fingers as he smoothed it from her face.

"Emeryn..." His voice cracked. A sob ripped through his chest. "Em, no!"

Aiden turned to Seren, dropping Emeryn's body to the grass. Seren swayed unsteadily on his feet.

"You did this," Aiden whispered. "You did this!" His voice rang out across the night sky. A wind howled through the surrounding trees, his blood-soaked robes rippling as he stood.

"I didn't mean to," Seren gasped, tears streaming down his face. "It was an accident, I didn't mean—"

Aiden's hand swung through the air, striking Seren across the face. Once. Then again. Seren cried out, tumbling into the grass. But Aiden didn't stop. Another strike, harder this time.

"This is your fault, Seren! You stupid boy!"

As Aiden raised his hand for another blow, a hand grasped him from behind. Yellow eyes met his, piercing and unfeeling.

"I'd say he's had enough, don't you think, brother?"

Aiden's heart stopped.

Lumen stood before him, his snow-white skin and long pale hair stark against the darkness. He swept over the scene, pausing first at the dead woman lying in the grass, then lingering on the boy, who had crawled atop his mother's body. Blood dripped from the sides of the boy's mouth as he clung to her, sobbing.

"What happened here, brother?" Lumen asked with an unsettling calm.

Aiden didn't speak, his heart pounding in frantic beats.

Lumen knelt and gently closed Emeryn's eyelids. Seren looked up, each sob strangled and broken. "I didn't mean to, I didn't mean to. I didn't mean..."

Lumen set a hand on Seren's back, almost mechanically. "I know," he murmured. "It's alright. It wasn't your fault."

"Take him," Aiden said hoarsely. "Take him before I do something I regret."

Lumen didn't react to the threat. His visage remained unreadable. "Come with me, Seren. I'll take you far from here." After a long pause, his gaze slid back to Aiden. "Are you going to tell me what happened here, brother?"

Aiden trembled, hatred boiling within him. "Isn't it obvious? He killed her," he hissed. He dropped to his knees, hands meeting the grass. "It's all his fault." He lifted his head to his brother. "The gods chose wrong. I have chosen wrong. He will never be a son of mine."

Aiden clasped his hands together, the words of the spell already forming in his mind. His lips moved too fast, a finger tracing over his chest, then his forehead.

"What're you doing?" Lumen demanded, rising to his feet.

"Sealing this darkness away," Aiden spat.

He thrust his palms forward. A burning seal erupted across Seren's back, the magic singeing through his clothes. The boy screamed before crumpling into the grass beside his mother.

Lumen scooped up the unconscious boy, his eyes never leaving Aiden's.

"And what do you expect me to do with this boy?" Lumen asked.

"I don't care," Aiden whispered. "Just take him away. Please."

Lumen's lips formed a tight line as he looked down at the limp boy. "What is this child to you?"

"Nothing," Aiden hissed. "He is nothing."

Lumen stared at his brother for a long minute before he turned, walking through the grass toward two hovering lights in the distance—a mechamobile waiting quietly.

Aiden didn't dare stop them, didn't let a surge of guilt or doubt creep into his mind. No. He wanted that boy gone. Forgotten. He could rot in the Godless City with his brother, for all he cared. Aiden turned to the sky, his holy robes drenched in the blood of the only woman he'd ever loved.

Clouds gathered, hiding the stars. Soon, the moon would vanish with them.

Aiden's voice trembled—not in prayer, but in a broken, bitter plea. "Was this your will?" he whispered to the heavens. "All your signs, all your promises, for this?"

The stars could give no answer. Instead, snow began to fall, the flakes drifting to the ground like feathers from a bird that had lost its wings.

Nine

*"Thou who sins without regret must ask the gods for mercy, lest
the shadows of your deeds consume your soul."*

—Book of Divine Law

The Auguries had gathered countless artifacts from across Aerithium. How they had come into possession of the Sword of Caelum,
Lumen could not say. During his time in the Godless City, the Auguries
had granted him access to anything in the Reliquerium, provided it fur-
thered their pursuit of immortality. When Lumen first laid eyes on the
sword, he'd felt a crackle deep in his bones as though the blade had momentarily sliced through his very flesh. The weapon was otherworldly, a
cruel beauty forged from materials beyond the realm of humanity.

Lumen had glimpsed sketches of the sword in his youth, alongside the
harp and the crown. They were the three holy artifacts said to have been
crafted by the Mother Goddess herself and bestowed upon her children.
These relics were believed to hold the key to the Cleansing, the promised
day when the Veil would no longer be a cursed realm. For a time, Lumen
dismissed them as mere legend. That changed the day he followed Aiden
and his stepfather into the crypts and saw the harp with his own eyes.

His stepfather's disdain had never needed words; the sin of Lumen's birth was condemnation enough. *Defilement.* The unspoken accusation lingered in the silence between their hollow exchanges. *Never meant to be born.* Lumen was no Cycris but the bastard child of a sinner, fortunate only to bear his mother's family name, Yukimura. While his brother was welcomed into the crypts and the inner sanctums, Lumen remained in the shadows.

Until that day.

Lumen had mastered the art of invisibility, slipping unnoticed beneath his father's gaze. Trailing his brother and stepfather into the crypts had been almost too easy, especially when his stepfather had carelessly left the door ajar. The harp had been beautiful and unlike anything Lumen had ever seen. Inside, the harp loomed above him, a masterpiece of pristine ivory intricately engraved with patterns he couldn't fathom. Mesmerized, he had reached out, fingers hovering over a string, ready to pluck a note until his stepfather caught him. The curiosity cost him dearly. For weeks, he nursed bruised ribs, punishment for his trespass.

So, when Lumen first saw the sword gleaming in a glass case in the Reliquerium of the Godless City, he couldn't help but feel smug. To think his brother and the other clerics were so desperate to gather the holy artifacts, and yet there it had been within his reach, hidden in the heart of the city of sin.

According to the ancient texts, only the gods to whom the artifacts were gifted could wield them, except for the reborn Mother, who would use them to cleanse the Veil. Lumen had already paid the price for using the sword and was still unsure what further repercussions he would ultimately face. He glanced down at his palms, the scrawl of black veins pulsating with discomfort. A man of radical decisions, perhaps, but Lumen was no fool. When he had wielded the weapon, he had expected the unseen cost that came with it.

"What are you writing, master?" Grimm squawked, jumping on Lumen's shoulder.

Lumen sat in his brother's study, draped in black robes he'd found in the church, the faint smell of parchment and ink filling his nose. He dipped the black quill in the ink and signed his name. "You are going to deliver a message to the Auguries for me," he said simply. "A journey would help with your restlessness."

Grimm leaned over Lumen's shoulder, his bionic eye whirring as the second, beady eye focused intently on the letter. "I am to deliver this to Vavilon?"

"Precisely."

"What does it say?"

Lumen chuckled. "Always a curious creature, aren't you?" He scratched Grimm under his chin. "I am offering the Auguries the cure to the virus. If they were to find it, they would have by now. Just as I expected, they are *useless* without me."

"And in exchange?"

"Ah, clever bird," Lumen simpered. "You know me well." He rolled up the parchment. "In exchange, I want the sword. I told my brother how to access the Reliqueriem, so now I'm free to do as I please."

The raven nodded as Lumen tied the note to his leg. Then, he didn't linger, moving to the open window at once to launch himself into the air, his wings glistening in the sun.

"Be safe, my friend."

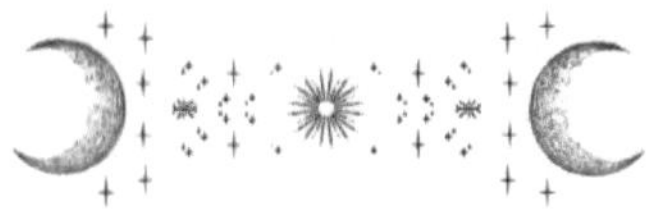

The boy had miraculously survived the night. Nevertheless, it was evident that he was running out of time. Lumen assumed he had a few hours at best before the virus took him.

Jude's teeth chattered, clanging together. Heavy clouds of frosted breath gathered in front of his face as he rocked back and forth in bed. The bags under his eyes were blue, leaving strange rungs that looked like bruises.

"I'm shocked you're still alive," Lumen remarked as he entered the room. "You could say I'm almost impressed."

"Shut up, Caius," Jude snapped.

"Ah, I see the madness has fully set in. You probably don't even remember your own name."

Jude's eyes fluttered shut. "No, no. I'm fine." He took a quivering breath. "Your name is Lumen. I'm in Stellaris. My name is Jude. I'm fine."

"Are you convincing me or yourself?" Lumen asked, settling into the chair and tightening the cloth around his face. "While you're still lucid, I've come to ask you something."

Jude wheezed, each breath ragged. "Just leave me alone."

Lumen sighed. "Is that what you truly wish? To die alone in this church?" He leaned his head against the wall behind him. "I've been told that bad company is still better than none at all."

Fear flickered across Jude's face. "And why would you stay?"

Lumen shrugged. "I've nothing better to do until you die."

"Do you hear it too?" Jude asked weakly. His frantic gaze looked past Lumen as if he could see a world beyond the church walls. "Their cries?"

Lumen frowned. "No," he said. "Your mind is simply betraying you."

Jude's lower lip quivered with fear and his body spasmed as he forced the words out. "I don't want to die. Please...don't let them take me, big brother. Please." He cowered, his twitching fingers curling into his golden locks. "I don't want to go to the Veil."

"And what happens when you go to the Veil?" Lumen asked, crossing his arms over his chest. "What happened to the others?"

If everything was true, Jude was the last living Andanovan in existence. He could be the only person in the world who knew the truth. And truth was hard to come by.

"I'll lose my soul," Jude whispered, hand clutching his chest. "It is what I owe."

Nobody knew precisely what happened to those who made deals with demons, but the belief was that their souls were damned, broken spirits forced to wander the Veil for eternity. Even without a demon's interference, dying in the Veil was another form of damnation. Within the Veil, the souls of the dead had no escape.

"My mother disappeared into the Veil," Lumen murmured. He was unsure what had caused the words to slip from his lips but tried not to let his surprise show. "It was nearly thirty years ago, when I was just a boy. I'm sure you've heard of the Unveiling of Hiraeth. We stayed on the outskirts of the village on a full moon, and it swallowed us all. My mother did not make it out, but my brother and I did."

"You were...in the Veil, Caius?" Jude asked, eyes turning to him. "How did you...get out?"

Aiden's tormented face flashed through Lumen's mind. "I suppose I was lucky, just like you."

"Lucky," Jude whispered. He looked around the room, brows drawing together. "What're you doing here? Where's father?"

"He's dead," Lumen said. "Just like Caius, and just like you will be soon."

Jude's head lifted, eyes focused on Lumen, and a recognition sparked through them. "You're not...my brother."

"No," Lumen said without emotion. "I'm not."

He stood, easing toward the door. A chill flooded the room. Death was approaching.

Jude shook his head, blinking much too fast, as if trying to dispel the fog clouding his vision. His breaths came in ragged gasps, his chest heaving, ribs stark beneath the white silk of his shirt. "Why...are you here? Where is...Seren?" His voice cracked.

Lumen remained silent, watching as Jude's gaze frantically darted around the room. The boy's stubbornness had been the only thing keeping him from completely slipping into oblivion. But that determination could only last so long.

"What did you do to him?" Jude's voice was raw now, only a strained whisper as he lunged forward. His body betrayed him as he crashed to the floor, convulsing violently. His fingers curled against the cold stone. He gasped for air, eyes gleaming with terror. "What...did you do?"

A strange lump formed itself in Lumen's throat at the boy's words.

"Seren trusted you," Jude whispered, his sorrow deeper than when he spoke of his own past.

Lumen froze in place as the young man extended a trembling hand towards him, only to retract it and curl up into a ball. Lumen remained upright, placing his hands in his pockets.

"Yes," he said stiffly. "He trusted me, but it's because he was *weak*. Every day of his life, he was told to trust the gods. I tried to warn him, but I could see it lurking underneath. He couldn't let go. He couldn't bury the gods, no matter how much he claimed he hated them. But did the gods help him when I took his fate from him? No. They watched him scream without mercy. Just like they watched every Andanovan die ten years ago. And do you want to know why?"

Jude's glassy blue eyes froze.

"Because the gods don't care," Lumen hissed. "The gods need us more than we need them. They *want* us to suffer. Where else would they get prayer? The gods laugh at us and right now..." The tip of Lumen's boot nudged Jude's form. "They are laughing at *you*."

The boy smiled, revealing blood-stained teeth beneath his blue lips. "If you...truly wanted...to strip him of his fate and defy the gods, you would have...ended his life. And yet, you chose not to..." His eyes slowly closed, his voice fading. "Why...is...that?"

Lumen tasted blood, not realizing he'd been gnawing the inside of his cheek. His slender fingers toyed with the glass vial in his pocket, twisting it back and forth. "I keep wondering when you'll finally die."

"I don't...want...to...die..."

Lumen kneeled, pulling the vial out of his pocket, and set it in Jude's resting palm. The boy's heavy eyelids lifted, his irises shaking as he focused on the vial.

"What is it?" His voice was faint, scarcely even a breath.

"It's an antidote. If you're lucky, it may work. But I doubt it. You are probably too far gone."

"Why...?"

"I am curious to see what could become of the last Andanovan," Lumen responded. "Nothing more." As he stood in front of the door, preparing to leave, he paused. "Tell me, Golden Prince, what did the demon give you that kept you alive?"

Jude's hand tightened on the vial. "Luck," he whispered. "The demon gave me luck."

Lumen closed the door, wondering how long it would be until the boy was dead.

A letter arrived in the evening from Aiden, stating that it could be several weeks before his return to Stellaris. He asked Lumen to make arrangements following the mercenary's passing and reminded him to treat the Archives with respect. Lumen crumpled the letter at his side with a long sigh and continued up the spiraling stairs toward the Eastern Tower. He pushed open the oaken door to find the room untouched and covered in dust. Piles of books lay in the corners, and a bed with cream blankets was left rumpled.

Lumen strode across the room and pushed open the stained-glass window, letting an evening breeze blow his long hair back. He gazed out, focusing on a bright star hanging in the distance. It had been nearly twenty years since he had last set foot in this room and looked out this very window. He turned and settled onto the bed. Something shifted under the blankets, and he reached to pull it out—a notebook. Lumen flipped it open to find detailed and beautiful drawings of birds scattered across the pages. He paused on a sketch of a raven perched upon a tree branch. As he continued flipping, his hand stilled at the name scrawled at the bottom of the last page: Seren. Lumen slammed the book shut and tossed it aside.

He trusted you.

An unfamiliar tightness gripped Lumen's chest. Yes, Seren had trusted him to help, and he had. Seren wanted freedom, and Lumen had given it. He had shown him that fate could be altered—that the gods themselves could not stop it. What is a god if there is no one to worship them? Nothing. A man can find purpose without gods, but a god without men is nothing.

Lumen had shown Seren the truth of the world. *His* truth. He had watched the boy's emerald eyes shift, seen that spark of something new. Lumen had seen himself in that boy before everything had been taken from him. And then, he'd ripped it away—just as it had been ripped from him.

Perhaps now, the gods were laughing at Lumen, too.

TEN

"The Mother left pieces of herself behind to remind us that she will return. When I look into the Cauldron of Tears, I see her weep for the world and what it has become."

—the Personal Diaries of Felix Amos

How was Seren to face his home again? Home was supposed to be a warm blanket wrapped around his shoulders, a kiss on the forehead, the smell of flowers clinging to his mother's hair. Home was books with gilded spines and birds peering in through stained-glass windows. It had become an echo, a sound fading into the background, an untouchable memory he longed for. Now, the thoughts made him feel...*empty*.

It had been days since Seren and Mila left Brimry, with only occasional rests. Seren had scarcely slept, plagued by his usual nightmares. Mila hadn't said anything, but he knew he'd woken her several times mid-shout. He was glad she didn't ask about them.

Returning to Lumina had filled Seren with a mixture of nostalgia and apprehension. It was just as he remembered. A land of forever green rolling hills that brushed the open sky, endless meadows of purple, white, and blue flowers. Young rabbits darted between the horses' legs, seeking safety in their burrows.

The landscape had amazed Mila since they'd arrived, and Seren didn't blame her. The horses grazed in the long grass as Seren and Mila paused to rest. Mila stood a couple of paces ahead, leaning down to pick a blue flower and holding it up, studying it between her eyes.

"A starflower," Seren said from behind her. He stepped beside her, kneeling to pick another. "They've always been my favorite. They glow at night, just like stars." He squinted against the afternoon sun. "We'll have to come back sometime when it's dark so you can see it for yourself."

"Wow," Mila breathed. "I've never seen anything like them." She picked another flower with golden petals and held it up to the sun. "I like this one."

"A sunflower," he told her.

"Pretty."

Seren studied her face, enjoying the softness that seemed to settle across Mila as she collected bundles of flowers. He picked another with drooping pale violet petals and handed it to her. "All of these flowers only grow in Lumina. This one is a moonflower. If you look closely, the petals look like crescent moons."

Mila sighed as she examined the moonflower. "Kamil would have loved it here," she murmured, voice small. "He'd have done it justice with a painting."

Seren tilted his head to the side as Mila set the flowers down, her warm expression fading. "Can I ask you something?" He ran his fingertips over the petals of the starflower sitting in his palm. "You don't have to answer."

Mila turned to Seren. "Under one condition, if I answer, then I get to ask you a question. And you *do* have to answer."

He rubbed between his shoulders. "I suppose that's fair."

Mila grinned, triumphant. "Ask away then."

Seren hesitated, wondering if he had made a mistake. With a nervous breath, he stared off into the distance, eyes tracing the rolling hills.

"What was your brother like?"

Mila's smile faltered, and she set the flowers down on her lap. "Naïve," she said. "You remind me of him."

"Thanks," Seren grumbled.

"He was blue in a sea of red," she whispered, holding a moonflower close to her chest. "He was stronger than I could have ever been. I don't think he had even a drop of hatred in his blood. I never understood it. I wanted him to be angry with me." Mila sighed, the flower crumpling in her grasp. "Maybe, then, he would have had a chance."

"What was your childhood like?" Seren blurted.

"That's two questions," Mila scolded.

"Right, sorry."

Mila gazed into the distance, her fingers tracing the jagged scars that marked the brown skin along her arms. "I was taught to never know fear," she said. "Yet, no one ever denied me the ability to love, and there is always fear in love." She stood up quickly, the flowers falling from her lap.

Seren cleared his throat, his knees shifting in the grass. "I suppose it's your turn to ask two questions, then."

"How much do you remember of your life?"

It felt as if the world was still around them, and a stiff wind blew through Seren, shaking him to his bones. His fingers curled in the grass, nails sinking into the moist earth.

"Still only bits and pieces. I can't remember much of anything directly after..." Seren paused. "I remember little of my time in the Godless City, but I know I was there for...a long time."

"How long?"

"Four years."

A sharp inhale sounded from Mila. Another gust of wind tumbled across the land, grass licking at Seren's skin. He could feel Mila's steady stare on him, causing a prickle down his spine. He knew how it sounded. Four years lost to the Godless City. Four years with *Lumen*.

"I don't know how much time I spent in that lab," Seren admitted. "But I'd rather pretend it didn't happen at all."

"Is this why you never talk about yourself?" Mila finally asked. She let out a breathy laugh and shook her head. "I feel as if you know so much about me, but I still..." She grimaced. "I still know so little about you, but I suppose it makes sense if you know little about yourself. But when we were in the Sanguine Kingdom—you remembered something important. Didn't you?"

Seren's fingers curled around the flowers. He wanted to tell her that it wasn't any of her concern, but he knew it wouldn't be fair. Mila had been open with him, vulnerable even. Her life, her secrets, and her curse had been laid bare before him. And what had he offered in return?

"No, I don't know who I am," Seren said. "I only know who I am supposed to be."

"And who is that?"

Seren sighed, laying his entire body into the grass, feeling the sun beams hit his face. Mila mimicked him, both of their faces upturned to the sky.

"Someone who wouldn't run from their fate," he scoffed. "Someone who isn't naïve. Someone strong, good, and *pure*."

"Nobody is pure, Seren."

The Mother was, he wanted to say.

"The gods say differently," Seren said. "I was taught that the world was once filled with purity and that the more we stray from the gods, the more it is lost."

He didn't have to see Mila's face to know she was rolling her eyes. "And do you believe that?"

"I have no reason not to," he admitted.

Seren turned to Mila, tracing the curve of her nose as she stared into the sky. Her soft mouth was parted, her dark brown hair falling against her cheeks. Again, Seren wanted to brush the tendrils away from her skin. He wished to stay until the sun set and show her the way starflowers twinkled across the valley.

But Seren knew nothing was that simple. How would Mila react if he told her he was the reincarnation of a goddess destined to cleanse the Veil? What would her reaction be if he revealed to her that prophecies had been written about him, promising to change the entire world?

Mila's mother shared her body with a demon that wanted to aid the Devil—which made the entire Sanguine Kingdom his natural enemy, didn't it? Every moment, the world edged closer to a future of darkness and death. He wanted to believe that it could all be stopped, but he couldn't picture himself being the one to do it. Seren was no savior. He had killed his own mother, accident or not. Seren had done nothing but make the wrong choices. He'd gotten himself locked away as a lab rat. How was he supposed to stop the Veil? He shuddered, his shoulder blades stinging. What if he had already failed? What if his fate had slipped through his hands and become unreachable?

Seren thought about the strange shadows that seemed to follow him. The deeds he had been so willing to commit.

"Mila, do you remember when we were in the sewers and we saw those shadows?"

"The corrupted wisps?"

"Yeah," Seren said. "What... are they?"

"Well, it's believed wisps are remnants of souls trapped in the Veil. But they aren't supposed to be capable of leaving the Veil or... violating your mind. I don't know what we faced in the undercity, but I think they were something else entirely. Why do you ask?"

"No reason."

Mila didn't prod any further.

Silence settled between them. Seren sat up, watching the wind ripple across the rolling hills. A pang flickered through him as the flowers swayed, their movement stirring something deep inside him. This place had once been his home. So why did he feel trapped, no matter where he went? Like a flightless bird that would never reach the sky. And once he crossed this lush land and reached the heart of Lumina, everything would change. He could feel it. Seren looked skyward, at the never-ending expanse of freedom that he felt he would never touch.

Mila broke his thoughts as she stood, the grass rustling around her ankles. "Do you remember when you told me to pray for forgiveness in the Underbelly?"

"Yeah, that was pretty stupid of me."

The wind tousled her hair while her flowing blue dress billowed behind her. "I had already tried."

Seren stilled.

"I prayed to your gods," Mila said. "They did not listen."

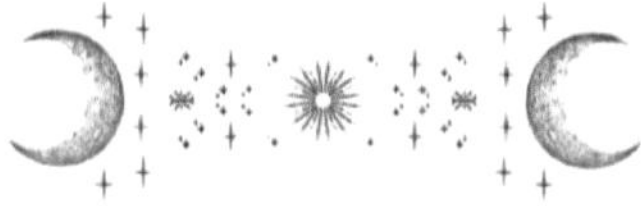

Aurelius was an impressive city, dwarfing Stellaris in size. Cream-colored buildings with merlot-red roofs marked the sides of the paved cobblestone roads. Despite the crowded streets of Aurelius, the citizens were accustomed to making way for those on horseback, allowing Seren and Mila to pass through without drawing much attention. Estelle nickered nervously as if sensing Seren's anxiety. It took everything in him to not turn around and flee.

Carts brimming with an array of fruits—crimson apples, golden pears, and lush, fragrant herbs—lined the thoroughfares. Under rich purple canopies adorned with silver moons, suns, and stars, merchants beckoned with smiles, hoping to sell various items. Seren's senses filled with the familiar smell of lavender and mint, common herbs scattered amongst Lumina's land.

"Wow," Mila said, head swiveling as she took in the sights. "It's lovely here."

"Aurelius is the heart of Lumina," Seren replied. "All the grandest celebrations are held here and it's the one place in all of Aerithium where saints and priests all gather as one despite their differences."

"Is that where we're heading?" Mila asked, pointing ahead.

At the northern crest of the city, the towering cathedral was impossible to miss. The Church of Caelestis in Stellaris had always been a mighty sight, but it looked measly compared to the Grand Caelestis Cathedral. Seren had distant memories of visiting Aurelius once or twice with Aiden to explore the markets, but he had never stepped foot inside the Grand Cathedral.

It stood tall, like a castle in a mighty kingdom, a fortress chiseled from pure white stone. Sunlight bounced off the stained-glass windows of the cathedral, creating kaleidoscope fragments and reflecting a myriad of colors.

"Yep," Seren muttered. His stomach growled at the scent of fresh bread. He slid off his horse, and Mila followed suit, grasping the reins and pulling her horse forward.

"Wait here for a second."

Mila opened her mouth to protest, but Seren was already pressing the reins into her hands, his fingers brushing hers as he stepped away. The tantalizing aroma of baked goods pulled him toward a nearby merchant's stall. A middle-aged woman with brown hair pulled into a bun stood smiling warmly at him. Something stirred in Seren, a distant memory that made his chest tighten.

"Good afternoon, young man. What can I get for you?" she asked.

"May I have a loaf of Sunbread, please?" Seren asked. The words came out of him naturally, without thought. He placed two gold coins on the table, even though the sign only asked for a silver.

The woman's smile grew wider as she handed Seren the bread, wrapped in a soft, pale yellow cloth, warming his hands. He thanked her and quickly made his way back to Mila.

"What's that?" she asked.

"Come on, I'll show you."

Seren led Mila through the streets by memory, surprised when they arrived at a small, familiar clearing with overgrown grass and cattails. This part of the city was quiet, with a pond where ducklings as yellow as dandelion fluff wandered along the water's edge. There was plenty of room for their horses to stand nearby. Grinning, he unwrapped the bread and presented it to her. The loaf was a perfect golden color, round and shaped like a radiant sun.

Mila's eyes widened as Seren broke off a piece and offered it to her. "This is one of my favorite foods," he said softly. "It's Lumina tradition to eat Sunbread in winter and spring. It's said that it encourages Helios to bless us with a bountiful summer."

Mila raised an eyebrow but accepted the bread, popping it into her mouth. Seren followed, savoring the familiar taste. Sunbread was both sweet and salty, with a nutty texture from the sunflower butter and a delicate layer of honey on top that melted with each bite.

Seren glanced at her. "Do you like it?"

"I love it," Mila said, a subtle smile tugging at the corners of her mouth. "You never...talk about the things you like. About favorites."

Seren frowned. "Yeah, I suppose I just didn't know..." he trailed off. "There's a lot I still don't."

"Well, Sunbread is a start."

They sat down together, passing the bread between them. Mila broke off small pieces, throwing them to the ducklings. Seren kept stealing glances at the towering cathedral in the distance, a heavy sigh escaping his lips.

"Are you nervous?" Mila murmured, breaking the silence. "Is that why you're stalling?"

Seren turned to her. "I am not stalling."

She raised her eyebrows.

"Okay," he sighed. "I just don't know what to expect. I haven't seen Aiden since my mother died."

Mila leaned close, her fingers brushing over his where they rested on the bread. Her brown eyes searched his face before she pressed her lips to his. Seren froze, caught off guard. The kiss was brief, too fleeting to be called intimate—more like a gentle peck on the cheek, innocent and unexpected. When she pulled back, her expression was unreadable.

"What was that for?" Seren asked, his face flushed with heat.

Mila smiled, a teasing glint in her eyes. "You didn't expect me to kiss you, did you? And you handled it just fine." She withdrew her hands. "You'll be alright, Seren. I promise. It's not like you're going to an underground kingdom surrounded by blood witches."

Seren chuckled.

Mila threw another piece of bread toward the ducklings. Seren watched her in silence, gaze lingering on her mouth.

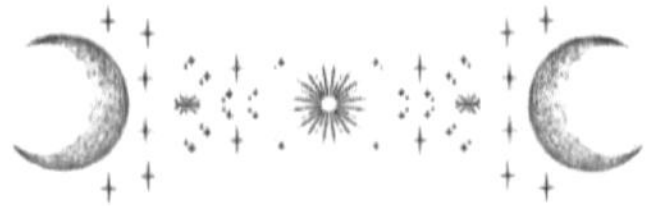

A marble walkway led to the Grand Cathedral entrance, lined with intricately detailed statues and white roses entwined among them. As Seren led the horses closer, his heart hammered in his chest. Stepping onto the walkway, he was greeted by the statue of Caelum, the God of the Stars. Windswept hair framed his handsome face, and one hand reached skyward. In his other hand, Caelum gripped a sword to his chest. Beside him stood Kallista, her untouched beauty poised over a harp, curls framing her slender face. Helios, his muscles taut with strength, wore a crown as his gaze met the heavens.

Seren's legs trembled as he passed the statues, drawing closer to the entrance. The carved doors, fashioned from dark-stained cherry wood, loomed above him. Etched onto the doors with painstaking detail was the likeness of the Mother Tree, its branches twisting and weaving across the wood.

Seren startled as Mila's voice broke the silence from behind him. "So, do we knock?" she joked.

Seren dug into his pocket, pulling out the velvet bag of coins and handing it to her. "I should go in alone. There are plenty of shops nearby if you want to look around. I'll make sure to ask about Jude."

Mila nodded. "Yeah, I didn't feel like stepping inside a church anyway," she said. "Will you be okay alone?"

"I'll be fine. We can meet back here at the end of the day."

"Alright, I'll see you later."

As she turned, Seren reached out, his hand grasping her shoulder. "Mila," he began.

She searched his face, tilting her head. "What is it?"

"It's just..." He hesitated. "I..." How was he supposed to convey what he felt? That after this, things would never be the same. That when he entered the cathedral, he might accept the fate he'd been given. And soon, they'd go their separate ways.

"This isn't goodbye yet, Seren," she said. "We can save that for later."

"Yeah," he managed, his hand faltering.

"You can tell me how it goes," she added with a smile. "If you can survive the Sanguine Kingdom, you can survive anything."

Seren chuckled weakly.

Mila urged her horse down the path, tucking the coins in her pocket. Seren lingered for a moment, watching as she disappeared into the distance. The cathedral felt much larger without her beside him.

Seren scanned the grounds, searching for a place to tie Estelle's reins, but the unusual stillness unnerved him. No acolytes hurried across the courtyard, no worshippers murmured prayers—just the heavy silence of an empty holy place.

At last, he spotted a hitching post near the door and stepped toward it. Just as he reached for the reins, a firm hand clapped his shoulder.

"Sorry, I wasn't here to greet you."

Seren turned to face the speaker. A man with broad shoulders and a worn leather apron stood behind him.

"I'm Elijah," the man continued, offering a nod. "One of the groundskeepers. We had a bit of trouble earlier—horse broke loose from the stables. I can take her for you if you'd like."

Seren blinked, then nodded, handing over the reins. "Thanks. It's...quiet here. I expected more people around."

Elijah's lips pressed into a thin line, his gaze drifting toward the cathedral. "It's been like this for days." His voice dropped, low and cautious. "After Calarinn...people are starting to question the gods' protection."

Seren opened his mouth to ask more, but before he could speak, Elijah gave a small, tight smile and led Estelle away.

Seren stared at the cathedral's doors, the weight of what awaited him pressing down in his chest. Aiden was behind those doors. The urge to run and never look back at the country he once called home clung to him like a shadow. But he steadied himself, exhaling a shaky breath. With trembling hands, he pushed the doors open.

Light poured in through the stained-glass skylight, forcing Seren to shield his eyes. As he crossed the threshold, his gaze lifted. Paintings adorned the cathedral ceiling, a masterpiece unfolding above. At its center, the Mother was rendered in pale hues—white, silver, and soft purples—threads of light woven across her milky skin. She dove headfirst between warring otherlings and humans like a shooting star streaking toward the earth, her silvery-white hair cascading behind. Seren had seen the Mother portrayed in many ways before, but this was different. She looked powerful, almost terrifying in her beauty. Her face wasn't painted with the temperance he'd seen so often, but with an unfamiliar ferocity.

Creatures lost to time and corruption swirled together in a sea of chaos beneath her. Seren's eyes were drawn to a wyrm with pearlescent scales, its two clawed legs reaching forward as if ready to strike. Its unfurling wings, feathered and vast, caught him off guard; he had never seen one depicted with wings before. Beyond it, ivory horses stretched their own wings wide while an orange fox with nine tails stood nearby, its molten gold eyes glinting and sharp teeth bared in a feral snarl.

Someone cleared their throat, snapping Seren's attention toward the sound. In the center of the room stood an elderly priest, his wispy eyebrows raised. Unlike Aiden, who always donned the robes of a High Priest, this man's status was lower. He wore plain blue robes devoid of the golden markings of the Trinity that signified a High Priest.

"Hello," the man greeted. "The Trinity welcomes you. Are you in need of help?"

Seren took a timid step forward. "I'm looking for someone," he said. "A High Priest named Aiden Cycris."

The man's brown eyes lit up. "You must be Seren." He graciously bowed. "The Grand Priest has been anxiously awaiting your arrival. If you'll please follow me to the Grand Chapter House."

Seren swallowed and nodded. He trailed behind the priest down the deserted corridor. "Where is Aiden?"

The man cleared his throat once more. "Cycris had business to attend to. He'll return later this afternoon."

The emptiness of the cathedral made Seren uneasy, twisting his stomach into knots. Its vaulted ceilings loomed overhead, their grandeur suffocating him. Each step made him feel smaller and insignificant in the vastness of the sacred space. It was beautiful, truly. If he hadn't been so on edge, he would have stopped to admire it. But as they ventured deeper into the hall, all he could think about was how the incense burned his nose and how tight the collar of his shirt felt against his throat.

Upon entering the chamber, walls of pearly marble stretched out before Seren. Sculpted horned horses adorned the stone, their majestic forms rendered in meticulous detail, as if leaping from the walls with ocean waves curling against their sides. Dozens of white candles flickered in golden sconces, bathing everything in a warm, ethereal light. Across the floor, the etching of a tree stretched wide, its branches woven with veins of gold that shimmered in the candlelight. Seren's footsteps echoed as he stepped forward. A soft hymn resonated in the air, sparking a sense of familiarity within him, something he'd heard during prayers in Stellaris. But as he continued into the center of the chamber, the hymn fell away, broken by his presence.

The weight of unseen eyes fell upon him as he crossed the threshold. At the room's center, atop the mezzanine, stood a figure draped in heavy white robes, his dark skin striking against the pale fabric.

"Welcome, Seren," the man's voice rang through the room. He inclined his head toward the priest accompanying Seren. "Thank you, Dane, for bringing him."

"Of course, Eldyir."

Seren bowed his head politely, choosing silence. He was in the presence of the most powerful priest of Aerithium. If he remembered correctly, priests and saints had their limits, but once every century, one priest was chosen to guide those gifted with divine magic.

Smiling faintly, the Grand Priest descended the stairs. His youthful appearance came as a surprise. He didn't look any older than Aiden, though that seemed impossible.

"Thank you for making the journey, Seren," Eldyir said as he approached. "Aiden tells me this is your first time inside the Grand Cathedral."

Seren didn't move, feeling eyes burn into the back of his neck.

"Yes," he answered. "Where…is Aiden?" The presence of all the figures in the room was unnerving. He searched the rows for Aiden, only to find the curious eyes of acolytes, all dressed in plain blue robes. Dane left Seren's side and made his way up the pews to sit with the others.

The Grand Priest set a hand on Seren's shoulder. "All is well, Seren." When he met the man's warm hazel stare, Seren's shoulders relaxed, and his hands unclenched. Eldyir smiled, fine lines crinkling at the corners of his eyelids. "Aiden will meet with you after."

"After?" Seren echoed.

"Come," he said.

Seren moved with a stiffness that betrayed his apprehension as he followed Eldyir across the room. They stopped beneath the rearing front legs of a horse carved into the wall, standing before an unusual cauldron elevated off the ground. It was unlike anything Seren had ever seen. The pale amethyst surface gleamed in the candlelight, and a faint mist curled from its rim.

"This is the Cauldron of Tears," Eldyir said. "I want you to look into the water and tell me what you see."

Seren couldn't help but glance over his shoulder.

"Pay them no mind, Seren."

Leaning over the crystal cauldron, his heart pounding, Seren stared into the water. It was limpid and still, glowing like liquid glass, its luminescent surface shimmering. Purple eyes stared back at him, brighter than the water's surface. "I see a woman," he began, "with white hair and eyes like gems." He reached to brush the hair out of his eyes and flinched when her movements mirrored his. "Can you see her as well?"

The Grand Priest shook his head. "We all see different truths within the Cauldron of Tears. This cauldron holds the tears of the Goddess Alernaea and is often used to bless items, typically for protection," Eldyir explained. "The cauldron can never be emptied, nor can its contents be consumed. Faint glimmers of the Mother's magic sustain it. It is a relic that the Trinity has protected for centuries. Perhaps you've heard of it in your studies with Aiden."

"I thought it was a myth," Seren admitted.

The Grand Priest chuckled. "No myth," he said. "It is but another piece of a past long forgotten and a testament of the Mother's love by what she leaves behind."

Eldyir ran his hand above the water, and Seren's eyes widened as the surface rippled and changed. A bird with wings made of multi-colored flames emerged. Horned horses with hides as blinding as newly fallen snow appeared, their beauty almost painful to behold.

Then the water moved again, twisting and churning. Dark tendrils snaked out, clutching the creatures, seeping into feathers and flesh, stripping away beauty and replacing it with cruelty. Seren stepped back, his heart in his throat. He glanced at Eldyir, who remained unmoved as though he had witnessed nothing. After a moment, Seren cautiously approached the cauldron again and saw the woman staring up at him. Everything else had vanished.

"Do you truly think it's me?" Seren whispered. Eldyir was silent. He reached out, his hand wrapped around a silver chalice sitting near the crystal cauldron. Carefully, he lowered it into the water, filling it to the brim. Lifting it, he examined the liquid.

"Many have attempted to drink from the tears, hoping it would heal their ailments, but all in vain. Though it has the power to bless, its true essence can only be accepted by whence it came."

The Grand Priest handed the chalice to Seren.

Seren peered into the cup, this time, his green eyes stared back at him from the edge of the water. He thought about asking what he was about to do with it. But he knew. He knew exactly what he was meant to do.

"Drink it," the Grand Priest urged.

Seren tore his gaze away from the water. "If I am not who you think I am, what will happen?"

Eldyir offered a kind smile. "I was told you played Kallista's harp."

"I did," Seren said, feeling small.

"Many have tried to play the harp," the Grand Priest said, "only to end up buried beneath the earth. The harp accepted you because you share the same essence, just as the tears will accept you. Have no fear in your heart, Seren."

With a nod, Seren closed his eyes and brought the frosty edge of the chalice to his lips. The liquid was easy to swallow, though its taste was strange. It was icy as it slid down his throat, only to ignite into a searing burn as it reached his chest. His muscles tensed, and the chalice slipped from his grasp, clattering to the floor.

He gasped, curling inward as the heat in his chest swelled, nearly unbearable. His fingers clawed at his skin, convinced if he dug out his heart, it would be ablaze.

Somewhere, someone was weeping, loud, and inconsolable. The ancient sorrow seeped into his bones, into every ragged breath. Gods, it hurt. He was certain he was unraveling from the inside, piece by piece.

Seren fell to his knees, arms limp at his sides. The cloak slipped from his head as he raised his tear-streaked face upward, hot tears blurring his vision.

The world around him dimmed, fading into white emptiness.

Nothing remained but her.

She stood before him like a reflection, long white hair and piercing purple eyes, swaddled in silks of pale blues and purples. Her pale lashes lowered as she smiled and stepped toward him.

"Hello, Seren."

Seren blinked against the brightness, pushing himself to his feet. "What's going on? Where am I?"

She looked amused, lips curling at the corners. *"Do not be afraid. I am always with you, Seren. You mustn't forget, even in your darkest moments. One cannot exist without the other."* Her finger brushed across his cheek, and Seren jerked back. Her touch seared him like a brand. The goddess' eyes darkened, flickering with something he could not name, unease or perhaps disappointment. *"Do not reject me, Seren."*

Her voice cut through his mind, hotter than the core of a star. The intensity was unbearable. A sob tore from him, but it felt foreign, as though it belonged to someone else.

"Stop," he begged.

"You mustn't resist."

And then, she was gone.

Seren was back in the chamber, the vision vanished. Sweat clung to the tangle of hair on his forehead as he panted, his hands pressed against the cool marble. He didn't move for a long stretch of seconds, and it was as if the entire world had frozen over, waiting for him.

Finally, Seren pushed himself to his feet, a ripple of electricity coursing through his body. When he lifted his head, his breath hitched.

The Grand Priest took a step back, an action that prompted Seren to glance at the cauldron's edge once more. But this time, the woman was absent. Instead, his own reflection greeted him, his eyes ablaze with a violent purple, his hair transformed into silvery-white, and a radiant light glowing from his pale skin.

The Grand Priest fell to his knees and clasped his hands around Seren's. Following Eldyir, the acolytes all bowed. And then, all together, in a single chant, the words echoed:

"The Mother has returned."

Eleven

"Even the coldest winter cannot freeze fate's run, and even the scorching sun cannot burn away what's undone."

–Book One of Metanoia

Seren sat on a bed draped in soft-spun muslin sheets, his fingers tracing the pristine white folds. He gazed out the lancet window, where the afternoon sun hung at its zenith.

Seren wondered what Mila was up to. She was probably waiting for him. His fingers traced his lips, thinking of the fleeting kiss they'd shared over Sunbread. A small part of him wondered whether it might be easier to disappear from her life without a real goodbye. Yet, deep down, he knew he could never forgive himself if it came to that. And he didn't want to say goodbye.

Seren had been assigned a room in a high tower on the cathedral's eastern side, reminiscent of his old room in Stellaris, but this one was much grander. Eldyir had escorted Seren to his new quarters, mentioning that Aiden would meet with him before sundown. The Grand Priest hadn't seemed surprised by the revelation of the Cauldron.

"Fate has finally come to fruition," he'd said. "Your destiny has brought you to us."

Fate.

The word stirred a bitter resentment inside of Seren.

Destiny.

A sour taste filled his cheek. And Lumen's words echoed in his mind. *"I have taken your fate from you."*

Seren raked his fingers through his silvery hair as he collapsed onto the bed. He wrapped himself in the sheets, curling into a ball, and wished his mother were here. An ache spread across his chest, threatening to climb into his throat. She was supposed to be here, beside Aiden, reminding him that everything would be okay.

After several minutes, Seren groaned, untangling himself from the sheets and looking upward. Painted on the ceiling was the Trinity, their backs pressed together, arms outstretched toward the sky.

Kallista's skin was dark as night, her curly hair ashen like the moon, with bands of white silver looping around her wrists. Helios had sun-kissed skin, with warm golden ringlets clinging to his forehead. He wore sunburst earrings and gold-plated armor that gleamed across his chest. Caelum's hair was as black as a moonless sky, his fair olive skin luminous beneath a circlet of stars that rested upon his brow like a crown.

When Seren was a child, he'd once asked Aiden if he favored any of the Gods of the Trinity over the others. Of course, Aiden had denied feeling more drawn to any of them. But Seren had once seen Aiden speaking to the stars from the church tower, a hand across his heart and somehow, Seren knew. Aiden had once told Seren that Caelum was not only the God of Stars but the Keeper of Wishes. Children made wishes on falling stars; the brightest stars in the sky, and Caelum heard them all. Every star had a name, Aiden had said, whispered to Caelum at the moment of its birth. And when one fell, it carried those wishes back to him, to be remembered forever.

The Goddess of the Moon was said to be the Spirit of Song. Many believed that the most beautiful songs were created under the moonlit sky and that when wolves howled to the full moon, they were singing to Kallista. As for Helios, he was a pillar of protection, the bright sun that always cast the darkness away, the Champion of Strength.

It had been a long time since Seren had prayed to the gods. And in Calarinn, something had stirred inside him, a resentment that had overwhelmed him. He had lost control of himself and killed that lord.

Could it be that for four years, Seren had abandoned the gods? What if, deep down, that's who he was? Someone full of hatred and anger. Someone capable of driving a sword into a man's heart.

A heavy knock broke Seren's thoughts. He rose from bed and strode to the door.

"Seren, it's me."

Seren's pulse spiked and he froze. He heard a thump on the other side, as if Aiden had slumped against the door. Seren pressed his forehead to the wood, trying to calm his heart.

"I...I understand if you don't want to see me," Aiden said, his voice muffled. "But even if you decide to never speak to me again, I just wanted you to know that—"

Seren pulled the door open. Aiden's raven eyes met his, framed by the long strands of his jet-black hair. He was thinner than Seren remembered, cheekbones sharp and angled. As always, he wore the robes of a High Priest, dark blue with golden symbols of the Trinity sewn into the fabric.

"Wanted me to know what?" Seren breathed.

Aiden fell forward, robes wrapping around Seren like a cocoon, smothering him in the unexpected embrace. His arms were thin around Seren as he held him tight.

"I wanted you to know that I'm happy you came home," Aiden whispered, his voice swelling with sorrow.

Seren was silent, arms limp at his sides. A part of him wished to push Aiden off. He felt awkward and vulnerable as Aiden held him—and he hated it.

"I'm sorry, Seren," he said. "I should have come for you. I never should have let you leave. Please, forgive me."

Seren was afraid the words would break him, that he would crumble to the floor in a hundred pieces. He should have wanted to hear those words. They should have lifted the ache in his chest, eased the burden on his shoulders. So, why did they press down upon him like a terrible weight?

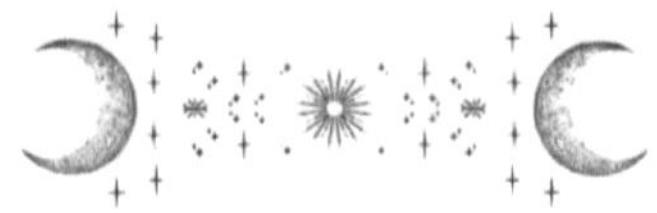

The ripened apple crunched between Seren's teeth, sweet juice dribbling down his chin. The refectory was silent, besides the clatter of Aiden setting his teacup down. Sunlight flooded in through the large open windows, bathing the arched ceilings in warmth. Unlit chandeliers dangled from the ceiling, swaying slightly as the breeze rippled through.

"Where is everyone?" Seren asked.

Aiden clasped his fingers together. "Grand Priest Eldyir has summoned a meeting with the congregation."

"Why aren't you there?"

"Because Eldyir has already discussed everything with me."

The real question. "Why am I not there?"

Aiden cleared his throat. "Eldyir and I agreed it would be best if I gave the news."

Seren said nothing, biting into the apple again.

"You've grown," Aiden murmured, tracing Seren's features carefully.

It hadn't occurred to Seren that the last time Aiden had seen him, he was a gangly boy with a quick temper.

"Yeah."

Unanswered questions lurked underneath Aiden's visage. *What did you do in the Godless City? What have you been doing since you left?* Seren prayed Aiden didn't ask.

Aiden's hands went to his lap, knuckles blanching as he clutched his robes. He noticed Seren's stare and relaxed his hands.

Had it really been four years since they'd seen each other? The unspoken question pressed on Seren's tongue.

"Seren."

He nearly flinched hearing his name from Aiden again.

"I know you've only just arrived, but may I ask you something?" Aiden asked.

"Sure."

"When you...consumed the tears? What did it feel like?" Aiden asked. He cast a glimpse over his shoulder, as if to ensure they were alone. He leaned in closer, his voice low. "You mustn't hide anything from me."

Seren wanted to breathe a sigh of relief that the question hadn't been something he'd dreaded. "It felt good," he lied.

Aiden exhaled, his shoulders relaxing. "Good."

"Why?"

Aiden smiled. "I was curious, is all. I've waited my entire life for that moment. It's a shame I missed it."

So, why did you? Where were you?

"How do you like the Grand Cathedral?" Aiden pressed.

"It's nice," Seren managed.

"The Stellaris murals pale in comparison, don't they?"

"I guess."

"I hope your travels weren't too difficult."

"It was fine."

Aiden shook his head, laying his hands on the table. "I suppose that's enough small talk. Now that you're here, we can discuss the upcoming events based on your arrival. The Summer Solstice isn't far—"

"We're going to act like no time has passed. Aren't we? Like nothing ever happened." Seren's words came out poisonous. "I'm going to parade around as the Mother, just as you've always wanted and that's it. Isn't it?"

Aiden sighed. "You *are* the Mother, Seren."

Seren slammed his hands onto the table, the bitten apple rolling onto the floor. "I haven't seen you since—"

"Do not speak of the Unveiling," Aiden hissed. "A tragic mistake. You unintentionally lowered the barriers with the harp because you were an unknowing child." Aiden's voice carried an edge, hinting at a distant fear.

"But—"

"I do not wish to speak of it. I do not wish to hear of it. We have both had our time to grieve. It is time for us to move on. We have more important matters to attend to."

It felt like a punch to Seren's chest. He hung his head low, biting his tongue. He wanted to ask Aiden the real question: why hadn't Aiden come for him in the Godless City? Four years. Seren's stomach churned. Didn't he already know the answer?

"The Veil is spreading, Seren. It's already taken over the entire Behethium Forest, and now it threatens Durcova. Faith is wavering, magic dwindles, and a deadly virus is rampaging Wreiss and Kogarashi. People are losing hope, turning away from the gods. Aerithium needs you—it needs *your* faith. We cannot afford to dwell on the past or question the path the gods have laid out for you," Aiden said, taking a deep breath. "The Mother has risen, and her power to cleanse the Veil is a beacon of hope. It will bring Aerithium together again. And within the next few days, a celebration in your honor will take place to do just that. People from every corner are coming to meet you. But understand, Seren, there will be a doubt among them. If you do not believe in yourself, nobody else will believe in you either."

Seren's throat went dry. "This is happening rather fast..."

"It should've happened years ago." Aiden's words were as cold as steel. "There is much to be done. After you undergo proper training, you'll be ready for the Summer Solstice. You'll need to be prepared before you leave for—"

"Leave? I just got here," Seren cut in.

"This is *your* fate to carry," Aiden said sharply. "It is *you* that must retrieve the holy items, *you* who must perform the Cleansing. There is no way around this, and no one else can do these tasks for you. On the Summer Solstice, you will go to Andanova and retrieve Kallista's harp."

Seren froze. Was this some kind of punishment? Wasn't it his fault that the harp was missing in the first place? But...to go to Andanova. That was a death sentence.

"You cannot be serious."

Aiden's features tightened. "Do you think heroes do not fight their own battles? Do you think the gods have others do their divine bidding? This was the reason you were born into this world."

The words stung worse than a slap to the cheek.

"You will not be alone," Aiden said into the silence. "An exorcist will accompany you and Eldyir is recruiting a group for you. I will not be joining you; I have a lead on the sword and will continue my search for the crown in your absence."

This was crazy. How many stories had been told about Andanova and the cesspool of demons that existed within it? One did not enter Andanova and leave intact and alive.

"You expect me to blindly wander into Andanova and find the harp?" Seren asked. "You can't be serious."

"We have a lead." Aiden pulled a stained map from his robes and spread it on the table. "We think the harp is somewhere in the castle," he said, pointing to the top corner. "The Andanovans were known for their opulence, so the castle is quite large. A powerful and dangerous demon who hoards heirlooms and magical items rules the ruins. Many exorcists have tried to exterminate it over the past ten years, but none have succeeded."

Seren blinked, staring at the map. "And you expect me to go there to get the harp?"

"Yes, you cannot fail."

A bitter laugh rose in Seren's throat. "Of course not," he replied. "Failure would mean death."

"I don't see what you find funny about this."

Seren threw his hands into the air. "No, 'hello, how have you been?' Just straight to it?"

"We cannot waste any more time."

"Then why didn't you bring me here sooner?"

Aiden recoiled. "I can sense your doubt. You think you're not ready."

"I have *never* been ready," Seren said fiercely. "How long has it been since we've seen each other, Aiden? Who is to say I am the same boy that grew up in that church? You think you know what I am capable of, you think you know what I feel, but you have never known. 'Read your books, Seren. Play the harp, Seren. Cleanse the Veil, Seren. Go to Andanova, Seren.' All you see when you look at me are the things you want me to do. You have never once asked me what I want."

Aiden slammed his hands on the table, eyebrows pointing downward. "You're being selfish."

"If you would just listen to me. If you knew what I—"

"It is not about *you*!"

Seren realized he was standing, his hands flat on the table.

Aiden took a deep breath, his hands falling into his lap. "Can we start over?"

Seren didn't speak, his hands trembling.

"You've always doubted yourself," Aiden said coolly. "I know we haven't always seen eye to eye, but I'm asking you to put everything behind us. Leave Vavilon and the horrors of the Unveiling behind. We've both made mistakes, but fortunately, the gods are forgiving."

"Are you?"

Dark eyebrows raised. "Am I what?"

"Are you forgiving?" Seren whispered.

Aiden stood, his lip curling. "This has never been about me or you, Seren."

"Yes, I know," Seren spat. "You've reminded me of that every moment of my life. I did what you asked. I came to Lumina. I'll retrieve the items and do whatever fate demands of me. But I didn't come here for you. And you certainly didn't send that letter for me. Just admit that you didn't want to see me in the first place."

"Seren—"

"No. I won't hear it. I won't have you lying to me and pretending you missed me. I won't pretend that things can go back to how they were. You would've left me in the Godless City to rot if you didn't need me." Seren slammed his hands down on the table, and the wood splintered. "*Say it.*"

Aiden was silent, his face pale.

"Say the truth," Seren demanded. "Admit that if you didn't need me, you would've forgotten me. If you tell me the truth, then I'll do whatever you ask."

As Seren leaned forward, Aiden's body jerked back. His dark gaze flickered, an emotion crossing his face so quickly it was almost imperceptible—but not to Seren.

A cold, unnerving realization washed over him. "You're afraid of me," Seren breathed. "Aren't you?"

There was a long beat of silence.

"I see your temper hasn't changed," Aiden finally said, his tone dismissive. "Deal with your attitude before we move forward."

"That's all you have to say?"

"You should get some rest, Seren. You have a long week ahead of you."

Without another word, Aiden exited, leaving Seren feeling just as alone as he'd always been.

Twelve

"Priests and saints proclaim magic as a divine gift, bestowed solely by the gods. Technophages harness false magic, while others must make dark bargains with demons. But what becomes of us when the holy magic wanes and we stand alone?"

—Exorcist Damian Silver

The elder priest stationed in front of the cathedral doors looked Mila over, scrutinizing her dirty blue dress and tousled hair. "I'm sorry, young lady. Unless it is an emergency, no one may enter the cathedral until the Cleansing Celebration. It is for the safety of the Mother."

"I just need to speak to my friend," she demanded. "I don't know who the hell this 'Mother' is, but I don't care about her."

The old priest flinched. "I'm sorry, young lady," he repeated. "The Grand Priest was very clear. Nobody except those of the Trinity may enter the Grand Cathedral until after the celebration." His brown eyes darkened. "I suggest you leave and wait for your friend elsewhere."

Mila realized that the priest's eyes had landed upon her chest, where the tip of her Sanguine tattoo was peeking just above the neckline of her dress. She took a step back, fists balled. "Can you at least give him a message for me?" she asked. "Please."

The priest shook his head. "I cannot do that."

"Damn it," Mila growled. "Old-timey prick." She flicked him an obscene gesture before storming down the marble walkway.

Mila headed back toward the main streets, rage boiling inside of her. Three days and not a word from Seren, and the damn priests weren't letting anyone come into their stupid cathedral. Just being near a holy sanctuary as a Sanguine Sister was a risk, but she was starting to worry. Either they were keeping him hostage, or he'd run out on her. She hadn't expected him to disappear for *days*.

Mila supposed she should purchase a different outfit, but she'd been so tired from their travels, she'd spent most of her time at the inn. Mila hadn't bothered to do much else besides catch up on sleep and meals, patiently waiting for Seren.

Mila cursed the priest again as she strode down the cobbled streets. It was far busier than the day they had arrived. As people came close to bumping into her shoulders, Mila adeptly weaved through the crowd.

Flower vendors filled the streets, their carts overflowing with the starflowers, moonflowers, and sunflowers that Mila had seen in the fields outside the city. Banners emblazoned with the sigils of the Trinity draped the buildings. Each featured a crescent moon cradled within the sun and pointed stars interspersed among the sunrays. The citizens were quite peppy, all smiles and light banter. Floral decorations adorned the rows of buildings, women donned bright sundresses, and children had flowers woven into their hair.

Celebration for the Mother?

Mila knew little to nothing about Lumina and its gods. Truthfully, she had never cared. Life had been simpler in the Godless City, where those who had abandoned the gods rarely spoke of them. Here, she felt exposed, like a wolf trying to blend in among sheep.

"A flower for the beautiful young lady?"

Jerking from her thoughts, Mila stared at the outstretched hand in front of her. A sunflower, with petals as golden as the young man's curls. Her chin lifted, blinking against the sun, only to meet with eyes as clear and blue as a summer sky. Without a second thought, Mila launched herself toward him, wrapping her arms around the nape of his neck.

"Ah, careful," Jude said. "I'm sore."

Mila pulled away, fighting the tears brimming in her eyes. "I'm so happy to see you."

"You as well," he said. "I like the new hairstyle."

The skin beneath Jude's eyes looked paper-thin, tinted an unusual shade of blue. When he smiled, his normally pink lips were blotchy and tinged with purple.

"You look...terrible," Mila said. "Are you feeling well?"

Jude rubbed the back of his neck. "Oh, I'm fine," he said. "I just came down with a nasty cold, is all." He frowned and shifted the subject. "Why don't we get out of the middle of the street before we get run over?"

Jude led Mila down a secluded alley, away from the bustling main street. They walked until they reached a quiet corner of the city, near an open meadow. "Ah, let's sit," Jude suggested, gesturing towards a wooden bench. He looked exhausted, his limbs dragging when he moved.

A well sat in front of them, a bucket dangling from a rope at its center. A couple of bluebirds sat on the top of the wellhead, scratching at the moss that was growing between the cracks.

The sun was warm against Mila's skin, perfumed with the fragrance of flowers. She closed her eyes for a moment, taking in the smells. In the Sanguine Kingdom, it had always been dreary and dark, with the constant scent of iron. Even compared to the times she had snuck out to pick flowers and bask in the sunlight of the Durcova mountains, Lumina appeared more vibrant than anything she had seen before. Although the Godless City was bright and full of neon colors, it was a city of metal, concrete, and artificial light.

Jude put his arms behind his head and closed his eyes against the sun. The sunlight caressed Jude's hair, casting a golden halo around him, as if he were an angel bathed in light.

His presence was calming. Mila had always been drawn to Jude's charm. It was easy to love his dazzling smile and honeyed words. Sometimes, when Jude looked her way, she felt a warm, pleasant flutter in her belly.

Seren was different. He possessed a cruel beauty, features that were distant and almost cold. When Seren looked her way, it was as if a hundred caged birds were flying wildly in her stomach, their wings beating against the bars of her ribs.

"How did you know where to find me?" Mila asked.

"I was fortunate to spot you on the streets not long after a very unwelcoming priest told me to leave the cathedral grounds," Jude said.

"I'm still expecting half my payment from Aiden for getting Seren out of the Godless City, but it seems I'm not exactly welcome."

"Yeah, I haven't seen Seren for three days," Mila admitted. "He went to meet Aiden, and I haven't seen him since."

Jude opened his eyes and crossed his legs. "You know," he said, leaning forward. "We could go to the celebration. He'll be there. I'm certain of that."

"What are they even celebrating?" Mila huffed. "Who even is this Mother?"

Jude chuckled. "Want to crash the celebration and find out? I heard there will be unlimited food and spirits." He raised his eyebrows with a conspiratorial grin. "You can be my date, and Seren will be compelled to join us. I've heard it's going to be quite grand, and I *do* love festivities."

"You just want an excuse to drink," Mila teased.

"What could be better than drinking and dancing on a day like this?" He raised a palm to the sun. Rubbing his chin, Jude eyed Mila's filthy dress. "Though you will certainly need to be dressed more appropriately. That attire is not fitting for a princess."

"I'm short on money," Mila said, her tone tinged with guilt as her eyes darted to the ground. She had chosen a decent inn to stay at, which had been a bit costly. On top of that, the food in Lumina was amazing, with the freshest fruits, aromatic herbs, and delicious bread. It'd been hard to resist.

"Not a problem," Jude said with a smile. He dug in his pocket, pulling out a velvet sack of coins. "Get yourself something pretty. I heard this…Cleansing Celebration is tonight after sundown in the Grand Cathedral. What do you say?"

Mila smirked. "Always ready with a plan, aren't you?"

"Why, of course. I'm a clever fox and don't forget it." He stood up, brushing his hair back. Mila took notice of his fingernails, also tinged blue. "Have fun shopping. I have a few errands to take care of, so let's meet at the cathedral."

Without a second to waste, Jude waved Mila goodbye before heading down the alley and disappearing onto the street. Mila resisted chasing after him. It'd felt like ages since she'd seen him and just like that he was gone again.

Mila weighed the gold in her hand, peeking inside with a small gasp. "I could buy a wedding dress with this much gold," she muttered. "How does he manage these things?"

Mila stood up, heading down the street, not sure where to start. She scanned the streets for Jude, but it seemed he had already scurried off somewhere. She grimaced, passing food stands as her stomach grumbled at the smell of baked pies. *No time for that,* she thought. If Jude had a hunch, they'd be able to attend the celebration and see Seren, she trusted him. He always had a way of knowing his way around things.

Mila needed to prioritize finding something suitable to wear. Truth be told, Mila had lazily washed her dress in a basin the day before and was content with that. It had been too long since she'd been able to relax and not focus on *surviving*.

Mila paused, eyes skimming a sign that hung above a winsome shop just past a fruit stand. *Lulu's Boutique.* The small shop was discreetly tucked away in the corner, adorned with pearly trim. Upon pushing open the birch-wood door, Mila was taken aback by the number of colors she saw. A wooden rack neatly displayed a sea of different shades. The deepest of blues, brightest of reds, palest of pinks. Mila's fingers skimmed the fabrics, their quality as fine as the silks and satins in the Sanguine Kingdom.

"Hi, miss. May I help you find something?" A petite woman with brown hair and dark freckled skin smiled, her face framed by her hair. "Are you perhaps searching for a dress for the celebration?"

Mila looked down at her dirty dress. "Yeah," she muttered.

The woman clapped her hands together with a squeal. "Lovely! We still have quite the selection. May I suggest a deep red for your beautiful skin tone—?"

"No," Mila cut in sharply. "Blue, please. I'd...prefer blue."

"No problem at all," she said sweetly, putting hands on her hips. "I have never let a woman leave in a dress that didn't make her look like a queen. I have just the thing for you."

The woman slipped away for a moment before returning with a dress draped over her arms. "You can try it on in the back."

Mila seized the dress, slipping behind burnt-orange drapes. She peeled off her dirty dress, struggling for several minutes to put on the new one. Grumbling to herself, Mila wrestled with the heaps of fabric, refusing the woman's offer of help with a quick 'no.'

Finally, when she put it on, she gazed at herself in the mirror, astonished. The dress was heavier than those she had worn in the Sanguine Kingdom, its shimmering midnight blue fabric dragging on the ground. Though the scars on her arms were visible, she hardly cared. She adored the dress. Silver stars adorned the hem, and sheer fabric cascaded across her shoulders. When she twirled, it resembled a spinning, dazzling night sky. There was even a slit down the side of the dress, offering the perfect spot to strap her dagger for easy access.

Mila's reflection caught her off guard as she glimpsed familiar brown eyes in the mirror—the eyes of her brother.

Mila stepped out from behind the curtain.

"Oh, my gods! You look stunning!" The young woman squealed, jumping up and down like a child. "I just knew it would look amazing on you."

"It's beautiful," Mila said. "Though I feel like it's a bit...much."

"Not at all! This celebration is a once-in-a-lifetime opportunity, it isn't just some simple party. You *must* look your best. I can do your makeup if you'd like," the woman said with a broad smile. "No extra charge."

Several minutes later, Luna, who introduced herself as the shopkeeper's daughter, had Mila seated on a white stool after flipping the shop sign to closed. Luna dipped a brush into a dusky black powder and carefully underlined Mila's eyes.

"You have such lovely features," Luna said, her voice light with admiration. "I'll bet you make men nervous." She giggled when Mila blushed. "I heard that the Prince of Kogarashi *and* the Prince of Oneriosa are coming to the Grand Celebration. Can you imagine dancing with royalty? I've heard they're both very handsome."

"Oneriosa? Isn't that at least a month's journey from here?" Mila asked, raising an eyebrow.

Luna nodded, waving her hand in the air. "Yes, well, with *magic* and all, I'm sure the saints in his court can snap their fingers and bring him here in the blink of an eye. Or perhaps they have rune stones." She sighed. "If I could afford it, I'd certainly get my hands on some."

"This celebration seems...quite important for someone to travel so far."

As confusion contorted Luna's features, Mila wondered if she'd said something wrong.

"Well, of course it is. It's been the talk of the town for the last couple of days." She dipped the brush in glimmering blue powder, dusting Mila's eyelids. Her voice became quieter, more serious. "I regret to admit that even I was losing faith. After Andanova and Calarinn...it seems days just keep growing darker. I lost a dear friend to the virus in Wreiss and...times have just been hard."

"I'm sorry," Mila murmured.

"My cousin is training to be a priest, and he told me that the Grand Priest claimed the Mother had been reborn. Before I knew it, rumors were spreading like wildfire. The Trinity confirmed the identity, and now she is in the cathedral, preparing for the celebration." Luna let out a wistful sigh. "I'll bet she's beautiful."

"Who...is the Mother?"

Luna pursed her lips, the brush stilling over Mila's eyelid. "Not from around here, are you?"

Mila frowned. "I'm afraid not."

Luna pulled back, setting the brush down. "I could tell from the moment you walked in," she said. "It's alright, your secret is safe with me. All that matters is you're away from that dreadful city now."

Mila breathed a sigh of relief, realizing Luna thought she was from Vavilon.

"The Mother is the reborn goddess from before the Great War. She's one of the three primordial gods," Luna explained as she applied a berry-colored cream to Mila's lips. "She sacrificed herself to create the Veil before it was...poisoned. But now that she's been reborn, she can undo the corruption and prevent the...you-know-what." Mila raised her eyebrows as Luna leaned in. "The Sundering," Luna whispered. "The end of us all."

"And you're saying that the evil can be undone?"

"Yes," Luna answered. "The Mother is the only one who can do it. That's what the prophecies say anyway. She created the Veil, after all." She put silver pins in Mila's hair. "They don't speak of these things in the Godless City, do they?"

Mila looked toward the window, watching a couple walk by, their hands intertwined. Cleanse the Veil? Her entire life, she had been told that the prophecies spoke of only one thing: the Veil would overtake the entire world without fail, and only the strong would remain. Those with power, those who could harness dark magic, would forge a new world. She had been told that, if she were lucky, she would have a place beside the Devil himself.

"No," Mila said. "They don't."

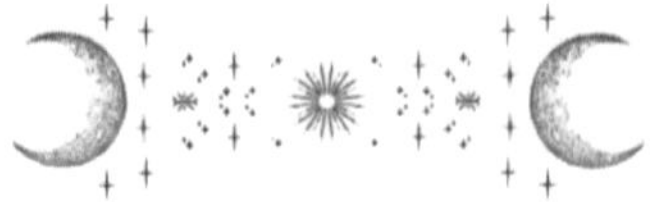

Mila stepped out of the shop, her hair brushed, and makeup flawlessly applied, the new dress hugging her curves. Beneath the fabric, a garter encircled her thigh, her dagger securely nestled in a sheath.

Mila strode onto the bustling street, a wave of anticipation sweeping over her. The fragrance of blooming flowers filled the air, mingling with the distant sounds of laughter and music drifting from the cathedral.

Women glided past in elegant dresses, their laughter trickling into the breeze. Men, dapper in crisp suits, walked with partners on their elbows, their eyes alight with excitement. In the distance, two sleek ashen horses pulled a carriage adorned with sapphire drapes toward the Grand Cathedral.

It was strange to see all the commotion, but now that Mila knew what the celebration was for, she supposed it made sense for those who held reverence in the gods. And she couldn't deny she was a bit curious about this claimed god walking amongst humans.

Jude was most likely waiting for Mila. She sighed, settling on a bench and rubbing her sore ribs, wanting a moment of solidarity before joining the crowd. It was strange not seeing Seren after spending so many days together. She hoped Jude was right, and he was at the celebration. As much as she wanted to erase the memories of the Sanguine Kingdom, she couldn't escape the recollections of everything they'd been through together.

Seren had started out as a confused stranger, an inconvenience that had caused her trouble, but the desperation in his face had haunted her the day they'd met in Vavilon. Then, he and Jude had gotten themselves kidnapped in hopes to help her. It was stupid. Idiotic. Yet, Seren had done it. If he had never shown up, Mila would have never escaped her fate. She hadn't understood it. Why had he gone to such lengths to save her, even when she'd pressed a blade against his throat and called him a murderer?

Mila shifted her weight, her boot catching on something sharp. A brief sting pricked her ankle, faint enough to dismiss as a snag on a thorn. The sensation lingered, though, an unusual warmth spreading up her leg. She brushed it off.

She needed to get back to Jude and not keep him waiting, but...why couldn't she stop thinking about Seren?

There was so much she didn't know. He'd never explained how he had gotten them out of the kingdom. And she couldn't shake the fear she'd seen in Eden's face when the serpents disobeyed her, refusing to harm Seren.

"Who are you really?"

"I'm afraid to tell you."

A part of Mila thought she should demand the truth from him. Seren had been determined to return to his homeland, but his hesitation had been obvious every step of the way. He was hiding something, and she wanted to know what. During the Trial of Nightmares, he had seen something that almost destroyed him. She would never forget the way his face had gone empty, as if nothing of him remained. Then, he'd been angry. Then, broken.

It wasn't her business. But he knew exactly who she was. Why wouldn't he just tell her? And... Why did she even care? This would probably be the last time she saw Seren now that he was home. Mila stared at her black-laced hands, overcome with the urge to rip the gloves off.

"You look dreadfully glum," a voice said.

Mila lifted her head, startled. Her hand instinctively flew to her dagger.

"Relax," Iris said, raising her hands. "I mean no harm."

Mila scanned her older sister, eyes narrowing as her grip on the dagger loosened. Iris wore a plain dress, her blonde hair tied back, and dark circles under her eyes hinted at sleepless nights. With a tired sigh, Iris settled on the bench beside Mila, adjusting the leather bag slung over her shoulder.

"What're you doing here?" Mila hissed, a surge of heat rising in her chest. "Did mother send you?"

"I came here on my own," Iris said. "Mother doesn't know I'm here."

"That doesn't answer my question."

Iris cleared her throat before meeting Mila's unwavering stare. "I just came to talk."

"To talk?" Mila scoffed. "Since when do *you* want to *talk*?"

Iris's pale green eyes closed for a second as she released a weary breath. "How does it feel? To be free of the binds of the Sanguine Kingdom?"

Mila shrank away, surprised by the tone in her sister's voice. Iris had always had nothing but cruel words and glares for her. Now, Iris's tone was somber, even defeated.

"I'm not free," Mila said.

"Yes, but the boy who took your name loves you." A warm breeze tousled Iris's straw-colored curls, and Mila glimpsed the pale yellow snake hidden around her neck. The sight unsettled her, more than it should have. "I only wonder how long that will last."

"Okay, we're done here." Mila jumped to her feet, but dizziness swept over her, as if the ground beneath her was tilting. For a moment, it was as if she had been yanked out of her own body, floating in a hollow, empty void. She swayed, her hand gripping the back of the bench as her breaths came shallow and uneven.

What the hell was going on?

"Feeling alright?" Iris asked, a hint of amusement in her voice.

"I'm fine," Mila said, the words feeling hollow in her throat. She settled back onto the bench, trying to ignore the heat prickling across her skin.

"You cannot outrun fate forever, Kamilah," Iris said. "You have to come back to the kingdom."

Mila laughed, but the sound came out wrong. "Why would I *ever* return to that wretched place?"

"Because it belongs to you," Iris said. "You're the heir to the Sanguine Kingdom, whether or not you like it. You *saw* what mother had become, didn't you?" Mila's heart skipped a beat. "The blood of both Adamus and Eden runs in your veins."

Mila yanked her hand away. "You *knew*?" she said. "This entire time, you knew everything?"

Iris sighed. "Please, sit. Just let me say my piece and I'll go."

"Fine," Mila grumbled as she slumped onto the bench, crossing her arms. A group of chattering women walked by, their dresses flowing around their ankles. "Make it quick." She rubbed her temples.

"I've been alive much longer than you," Iris began. "As Mother's first daughter, I once believed I would be the heir. But when Kamil and you were born, everything changed. I know you think Mother is wicked, but the years she's spent bound to a demon have not been kind to her. Believe it or not, she loved your father, Kamilah. When he was alive, she was...different."

Mila didn't believe that at all. Her mother had been nothing but cruel and cold her entire life.

"After your father died, the human parts of Mother died with him. She treated you and Kamil with a cruelty I'd never seen before, but she kept you tethered to each other, never allowing you to stray too far. At first, I didn't understand it. Mother claimed Lilith had expressed interest in you two. And when I learned you were both direct descendants of Adamus, it made even less sense. The Sanguine Sisters have been sacrificing the blood of Adamus for centuries. So why wouldn't you be the ultimate sacrifice?"

"Then I discovered the truth. Mother had shared her body, her soul, with a demon. The Sanguine teachings say Adamus cursed us all, blamed Eden, and that we must wipe his corrupted blood from existence."

Iris took a deep breath. "It took me years to piece it together. The demon had never been Lilith. It was Eden." She paused. "As Sisters, we're tethered to Eden, but our power does not belong to us. As a direct descendant of Adamus, the corruption of his blood lives inside you—a dark magic that's not borrowed but inherited through generations. They were cursed together because of his sin. And when you were born, that darkness merged with ours. The corruption combined."

Mila's brow furrowed. "What's your point? I'm not going to be queen," she grumbled. "I don't care about how powerful I 'could' be."

Iris grabbed Mila's hand, squeezing it tight.

"Listen to me," Iris hissed. "I've risked my life coming here to tell you this. You are the only one who can kill Eden. You're the only one who can break the curse and free us all. There's a reason Eden made you kill Kamil."

Iris pulled a parchment from her leather pouch, revealing a drawing of the twin serpents that sat behind the throne in the Sanguine chamber. Ancient writing, which Mila could not read, was inked along the sides. "Princess Ata and Prince Atsu, the twins born beneath the blood moon. Legend speaks of the twin snakes rising and ruling side by side with unprecedented power. Mother wanted you dead from the moment you were born." Iris's eyes traced the jagged scars on Mila's arms, causing her to recoil. "But Eden wouldn't allow it. She believed she could control you, starting with Kamil's death. He was your weakness. Your downfall. She let you be close to him, to love him, so you always had something to fear, something to lose. Then she used that fear against you, used you against yourself. When Kamil was sacrificed, all his dormant power became yours. It lives inside you; you just have to unlock it."

Bile rose in Mila's throat as a strange metallic taste filled her mouth. That couldn't be true. Could it? She had thought Kamil's sacrifice was meant for Eden, the power spread among the Sisters. And her entire life, she'd been told that Kamil had no magic inside of him.

Iris continued. "Eden couldn't allow Kamil's power to die with him, and she counted on you to be her next vessel. But this is where she went wrong. Her hunger for power drove her here. She underestimated you, and now, you're out of her grasp, and she wants you dead to prevent you from taking the throne and before you've realized your true potential."

"But I was weak," Mila said. "Seren took my name after Eden took control of me." Her fingers curled at her sides. "I'm not strong enough."

"That may be true," Iris said, rolling up the parchment. She looked past the street, watching giggling children run by. "But you felt the resistance, didn't you? It's always been inside of you, the ability to deny Eden's will. It helped that boy take your name, Kamilah. You're hungry for power too. It's in your blood. You can *become* strong enough."

Mila gritted her teeth. "Eden can keep her bloody kingdom," she scoffed. "She has nothing to fear. I plan on staying far away for the rest of my life." Her eyes met the ground. "I refuse to lose myself to the corruption in my blood."

She'd never spoken the words aloud until now. Mila turned away, refusing to meet her sister's stare. If Mila continued to delve too deep into her power, the words her mother had spoken could come to pass.

I understand you more than anyone. I know your true nature. You have an insatiable bloodlust that burns within you. You were born with it, Ata.

"Eden will not stop," Iris said. "She's set on becoming more powerful until she can find you and kill you." The orange hue of the setting sun caressed her pale skin. "The sacrifices are increasing and—"

"That is none of my concern—"

"They're taking *children*," Iris said, breathless. "Just yesterday, little boys who should have been sleeping in bed with their mothers were prepared for sacrifice." From her pocket, Iris pulled out a small stuffed rabbit, old blood spattered on its face. "I have always been weak. I have always been silent. You have always been strong. Always loud. It didn't matter what Mother did to you. No matter how she tortured you. You always fought for what you believed was right. Always."

Mila felt sick to her stomach as Iris pressed the rabbit into her face. The world around distorted, as if only Iris and she existed. A cold sweat broke out on her forehead, and her heart raced as dread pooled in her gut.

"If you kill Eden, we will be free from this curse. You could forge a new kingdom for us, one where we're allowed to love and live without fear. We could end the line of evil and start over. You could wash away the blood." Iris clutched the rabbit, tears welling in her eyes

"How can I wash it away when mine is stained?" Mila asked quietly.

Iris ignored her comment and sighed. "You know, I had a son once."

Mila's heart pounded in her ears. Her blood ran hot.

"I became pregnant," Iris whispered. "It was several years ago, long before you were born. When I found out it was a boy, I tried to keep it a secret and I told mother I lost the baby." Her hands shook. "I couldn't keep him safe, and I had to watch as mother tore him from my arms and set him on the altar to sacrifice his innocent soul to Eden."

"Iris..."

"You are our only chance," Iris said frantically. "All you need to do is to sever the bond between you and that boy, so you can get closer to tapping into your full power. We need you, princess. *Please*."

"I can't—"

"The blood of these children is on your hands, too," Iris said. "Eden will not stop until you're dead."

The words seared Mila's core. "I don't know how to sever the bond and neither does he," she said desperately.

"Yes, you do."

Mila's heart plummeted.

The pounding in Mila's head intensified as Iris's words settled in her mind. Something was off, but she couldn't quite place it—the throbbing in her skull, the tightening in her chest. She tried to shake it away, focusing on her sister's face, but the pressure only built.

"You're on your way to see him now, aren't you?" Iris's voice sounded distant, muffled, as if coming from the end of a tunnel.

Mila blinked hard, her breath coming in a sharp gasp. She should have said something, should have pushed back, but her mind felt thick, sluggish. "Yes," she said.

"You know what you have to do, sister." The world seemed to close in around Mila, and suddenly, her sister's next words felt like the only truth. "Kill Seren. Tonight. Break the bond and free us."

Mila's heart raced. An unnatural heat crept up her spine, seeping into her limbs. The words dug deep, flooding through her like a tide, drowning out everything else.

"You don't love him. It should be easy."

Mila traced the rabbit's face for a long moment, imagining small hands wrapped around it. Before speaking, she looked up, but her sister was gone.

Jude was waiting beneath the sculpture of Helios, the fading twilight catching on his silken white shirt, the golden buttons glinting faintly. He rolled up his sleeves and pushed his curls away from his face. Leaning against the calf of the marble god, he casually chewed on a mint leaf, his expression bored. Though he still looked a bit run down, the sickly tint in his lips had faded over the past few hours.

Mila stepped toward him and cleared her throat. Jude's face lit up, and he greeted her with a princely bow.

"Ah, there you are," Jude said, taking her hand. "You look lovely." He brought her knuckles to his lips, brushing them lightly.

Mila's face grew hot as he dropped her hand. "Thanks."

Jude studied her, his golden brows drawing together. "Are you feeling alright?" He lifted a finger, brushing it across her clammy forehead. "You're a bit pale."

Mila blinked, a knot tightening in her stomach. "What? Oh, no, I'm fine." She managed a smile, though it felt fragile on her lips. "Just nervous to be in a church, I suppose."

"Well, you'll be with me, so there's nothing to fear." Jude smiled and motioned toward the open doors of the Grand Cathedral. Citizens thronged around it, kept at bay by acolytes. It seemed everyone was hoping to catch a glimpse of the Mother. "And it looks like we arrived just in time."

He glanced at the crowd, then extended his arm to her. "Follow my lead. They're being very particular about who is allowed to enter."

Mila looped her arm with his, and Jude gave her an impish grin. "Lucky for us, I've got a knack for finding my way into places I don't belong."

Jude walked toward the doors like a peacock with its chest puffed out, weaving through the crowd with little effort. His usual mischievous smile had diminished, replaced by a serious demeanor. As they approached the doors, two priests stood on each side, wearing dark purple robes with golden suns, moons, and stars embroidered at the ends of their sleeves and hems.

"Family name?" the taller of the two asked, scrutinizing Jude as he pulled out a parchment with a list written on it.

"Gods." Jude's tone turned haughty and indignant as he continued, "My family's reputation precedes me. Surely you must recognize the esteemed lineage of House Ilvias. It would be an affront to the Mother herself to deny me entry after I've traveled such a long way. As the eldest son of House Ilvias, I assure you that your Grand Priest will hear of your absolutely *treacherous* behavior toward my bride and me." He lifted his chin, his expression taut as he extended his hand, revealing a gilded ring adorned with a family crest. "So, if you'll please let us through."

The priests exchanged glances, clearly stifling their reactions to Jude's snobby behavior. Mila was certain he took pleasure in intimidating others, her mind flashing back to his impersonation of a lieutenant when she had first met Seren.

The priests gestured toward the open doors, a silent invitation into the Grand Cathedral. As they walked past, Mila shot Jude a stern glare. "What did you do?"

"Oh, nothing too drastic. I had an unpleasant run-in with a snot-nosed noble earlier today," said Jude with a gleam in his eye. "Oh, don't look at me like that. It was part of a job. Besides, the brat deserved it. I simply borrowed his clothes and family crest while also delivering a message from a customer."

Mila let out an amused breath. "Being a mercenary means you can steal from noblemen and bully them?"

"No," Jude said with a smirk. "Being a mercenary means those who think they are untouchable get to understand what it feels like to be scum on the bottom of a shoe. Noble or commoner, when I'm the man with the gun, it doesn't matter who you are."

Mila pulled at her dress, the fabric suddenly feeling too tight. Jude seemed to notice, casting her a soft smile as they stepped through the towering doors. The Grand Cathedral was magnificent. Mila had never been inside a church before and wondered if they were all this beautiful.

Paintings adorned the vaulted ceilings, telling entire stories and leaving no space untouched. Her eyes widened at the sight of animals and humanoid creatures she had never seen before. Instead of the bone-chilling ugliness that most demons carried, these beings possessed a painstaking beauty: women with fishtails painted in iridescent colors, birds with feathers in impossible hues, elks with antlers that touched the sky, large serpent-like creatures with scales that glittered like diamonds.

Arched trusses stretched along the sides of the ceiling, ornament details carved into each one as if pulled from the gates of heaven. Floating white candles were suspended along the walls, lighting a path down the long corridor. As Mila took in the opulence, Jude's arm slipped away from hers as he hurried along the dark purple carpet, marked by the moon phases.

The two of them followed the flickering path of candles, their low glow guiding them into a grand chamber bustling with people. It resembled a ballroom though Mila assumed it was a room typically used for congregation.

A small ensemble of musicians, all donned in elegant pale blue robes, filled the air with tranquil tunes in a corner. Tables adorned with a wealth of culinary delights sprawled across the chamber—overflowing with a cornucopia of fruits, succulent meats, baked breads, and an array of cheeses. Handmaidens dressed in simple white gowns set bottles of wine and spirits upon the tables, arranging fine goblets in balancing towers.

On the northern dais sat a chair—or rather, a throne—carved from ivory, embellished with polished amethyst, and resting on golden legs. Behind it hung a tapestry depicting a woman with white hair holding out her hands as if to pluck a star from a star-ridden sky.

"I'm going to get us some drinks," Jude said. "I'll be right back."

Before Mila could protest, Jude slipped behind a woman and made his way toward a table. She grimaced, wringing her hands as she scanned the crowd for Seren. But there was no sign of a young man with black hair streaked with white. She needed to find him. She *had* to find him.

You don't love him. It should be easy.

Kill Seren tonight.

The words grew louder, echoing in her mind. The hilt of her dagger pressed heavily against her thigh, its weight almost unbearable.

"You."

A hand slammed onto Mila's shoulder, and she reeled around to meet a pair of dark eyes. The man towered over her, his face thin and his features sharp. He wore pristine, unwrinkled dark blue robes adorned with golden suns, stars, and moons.

Mila brushed off his hand and stepped back. "Can I help you?" she asked in a polite tone.

The man grabbed her arm, squeezing it roughly. Suddenly, it felt as if he could see through her, as though he was stripping her bare without a touch, peeling away the layers she kept hidden.

"Stop," she breathed.

Magic.

"I can see what you are," the man said, onyx eyes flickering. "It's time for you to leave."

Mila's heart stuttered. "I don't know what you're talking about," she said, remaining calm.

He squeezed Mila again, this time making her wince. "Why are you here?" the man demanded.

Mila held her head high, her eyes piercing into his. "I'm looking for my friend, Seren," she replied, voice bitter. "Perhaps, you know him?"

At these words, the man took a step back, his face paling. "Stay away from him," the man hissed. "I don't know what malicious intentions you have, but I sense nothing but corruption radiating from you. It's time for you to go, Sister."

Mila froze. What *could* the priest see? Could he see the bond between Seren and her? The corruption in Mila's blood? Was it possible that he'd read her thoughts and seen her grappling with her intentions toward Seren this evening?

"It's not polite to grab a lady without permission." Jude smiled at the priest from beside Mila, a silent threat lurking in his blue eyes. "I thought you would know better, Aiden."

Aiden?

"You're...alive?" the priest asked.

"Of course, I'm alive. You didn't think you'd get out of paying me, did you?" Jude raised an eyebrow. "That wouldn't be very priest-like of you, now, would it?" He took a deliberately slow sip of his wine as the music began to fade. "Now, I'd appreciate it if you left my date alone. After all, I've done you quite the service. It'd be a shame to cause a scene at such a lovely event." With both goblets balanced in one hand, he slid his other arm across Mila's waist, pulling her close. Heat rose to her cheeks.

"Are you threatening me?" Aiden asked, stepping forward.

Jude grinned. "Certainly not," he replied, though his expression said otherwise. He gave Mila's side a gentle squeeze. "She helped me save Seren and is a dear friend. And frankly, I'm a great judge of character. I'm merely asking you to let us enjoy the celebration. I'd hate to speak with whoever's in charge about the *lack* of payment I've received for my work with the Helios Legion—"

"Fine," Aiden interrupted, sweat forming on his upper lip. "You'll get what you're owed. Don't make me regret this."

"Cycris."

An acolyte in powder-blue robes tapped Aiden's shoulder. "I'm sorry to interrupt," the young man said. "Eldyir wishes to see you."

Aiden's gaze shifted between Jude and Mila for a moment. He clenched his jaw. "One wrong move, and you're both out." He turned, his robes dragging behind him as he weaved his way through the crowd.

Jude dropped his hand from Mila's waist with an exhale. "I'm not very fond of that man," he grumbled. "Anyways, would you like some?" He handed Mila a goblet filled to the brim with deep red liquid.

"No, thanks."

"More for me then. Hold this, will you?"

Mila held a goblet as Jude drank one, and then swapped them out, chugging the other. His face quickly became flushed. "Now that is *delicious*."

"Where is Seren?" Mila asked, rubbing her arm. "I haven't seen him."

"Not sure."

Mila watched Jude's unmoving expression as he snagged another drink. Why did she get the feeling that he was lying? But...

Kill him.

"I think I should leave, Jude," Mila said. "I have a bad feeling—"

"Wait, look," Jude interrupted. "Something's happening."

Everyone in the room had gone still, their attention fixed on the priest standing upon the dais. His robes, pale against his dark skin, shimmered with mesmerizing shades that shifted between night and day depending on the angle of the light. A medallion of gleaming white silver, etched with a star, hung around his neck.

"Welcome," boomed the man, his voice filling the room. "I extend my heartfelt thanks to everyone gathered here today. My condolences are with Wreiss for losing the young prince. And a special thank you to Princess Greta for braving the journey despite recent events."

A small, sickly girl in an ocean blue dress bowed, her sand-colored curls falling down her back. "Thank you, Eldyir."

Eldyir smiled in return. "And also, a thank you to Lord Ulysses of Durcova for your presence as well. We all mourn the loss of Calarinn," Eldyir continued. An elderly man dressed in a brown suit inclined his head in thanks. "Let us have a moment of silence for those lost to the Veil."

Mila awkwardly bowed her head along with the rest of the room. Jude shot her a glance and winked, as if sensing her discomfort.

After an interminable silence filled the room, Eldyir lifted his head and placed a hand on his heart. "We're facing dark times, and days are growing darker by the hour," he said. "The Veil is spreading, a virus is rampaging, and fear is growing. It's natural to feel fear; it keeps us alert and helps us survive. We must acknowledge it, understand it, and learn how to manage it. I commend everyone who has brought their fears here today. It's human to feel fear and doubt in the face of death and despair."

The priest smiled, deep lines forming around his eyes. Though he appeared young, his words carried wisdom beyond his years. "But there is something stronger than fear—faith. Today, we come together as allies, as friends, and as family, united in our search for hope. For years, we have been divided by our fractured gods, but today, that changes. Today, I ask you to set aside everything that separates us and remember the promise we were given: the promise of the Mother. It is said, 'In the darkest hour, a light will burn.' And now, we gather to celebrate the Mother's return and the light that will drive the darkness away."

Whispers erupted around the room.

"Please, silence," Eldyir said, holding up his hand. "I expected much doubt today. But tonight, I see among us the faithful, the true. I see those who have not let the whispering dissonance of the godless blind them from the truth I am pleased to reveal. The Mother has truly returned, and she is among us even now."

With those final words, Eldyir clapped his hands together, and everyone directed their attention as a figure stepped out from behind the tapestry.

The gasps were immediate.

"So young..."

"A boy..."

"His eyes...just like the paintings."

"His hair...like starlight..."

Seren's eyes glistened like stars trapped in purple gems, shimmering with an otherworldly light. He wore heavy, gossamer white robes that flowed across the dais like fresh milk, their silky fabric catching the light with every movement, embroidered with golden stars, suns, and moons that seemed to twinkle. Jewelry fit for royalty dangled from his ears. His silvery-white hair was mussed, as though he had just woken from sleep, strands catching the soft glow that surrounded him.

Mila knew what everyone was thinking—what she herself was think-ing. He looked beautiful, divine, like a holy being or an angel carved by the gods. Yet, beneath that beauty, he was just a boy, his face marked by doubt and fear.

Mila turned to Jude, her jaw hanging open. "Did you know?"

Jude didn't move, not tearing his eyes away from Seren. "Yes."

"For how long?" Mila whispered.

But he didn't answer. It was as if he were under a spell, his gaze locked.

The Mother was *Seren*? Mila's head reeled, sweat dampening her palms.

Seren cleared his throat, and even from the distance they were, Mila could see his lower lip trembling. "Welcome," he said, a hand clutching the arm of his chair.

From his left, Aiden locked eyes with him and nodded methodically.

Seren cleared his throat. "Thank you all for coming," he said, his words sounding hurried and rehearsed. "I welcome everyone who has traveled here to celebrate. Please accept my offerings of food and drink in honor of this occasion." He raised a silver goblet filled to the brim with deep red merlot. "I, reborn of Alernaea, Holy One of Light, have seen the future. It is bright."

He paused, and Mila's gaze flicked to Aiden, who had stiffened, his stare locked onto Seren. Seren's hands trembled on the stem of the goblet. "I promise you..." The room fell silent, all eyes fixed upon him. "I assure you that from this day forward, salvation has arrived. I solemnly swear that I will bring forth the Cleansing of the Veil and stop the Sundering. I will make any sacrifice necessary, just as the goddess once did, as fate would have it."

Mila's eyes widened, and Jude's face paled as Seren raised his goblet to toast. The crowd erupted in cheers, clapping their hands.

For a brief moment, Mila met Seren's gaze from across the room. It felt as if he was pleading with her.

Save me.

Thirteen

"Change cannot come without sacrifice, for a tree must shed its dead leaves before spring flowers may bloom."

—the Scribes of Wisdom

Seren had hardly slept since arriving in Lumina. There'd been nothing but fussing over the Mother and preparations for the Grand Celebration in the Grand Cathedral. It was historic, Aiden had told him, a moment that would be remembered and spoken of for hundreds, perhaps even thousands, of years. And Seren was the imposter, standing in the shadow of a goddess's ghost.

The last few days had been spent with Aiden, the priest coaching him on every response for all the questions that would come his way. Could he cure the virus? Seren was supposed to say, *'While my path is guided toward other duties at this moment, I carry hope that we may yet find healing for all who suffer. My heart is with them.'*

If asked what magic he could perform that the priests and saints could not, he was to say, *'There are forces I touch that lie beyond words and sight. Trust that they work in ways that are not always visible but no less present.'* The rehearsed words left a bitter taste in Seren's mouth.

Now, Seren's lips were pressed against outstretched hands. Heavy jewelry was draped around his neck, and gaudy rings slipped onto his fingers, all offerings to the Mother Goddess. Seren felt as though he was walking through a dreamlike haze as desperate fingers reached for his silky robes, and people flooded him with questions. The acolytes stationed at Seren's side worked to keep the grabbing hands away, scrutinizing each piece of jewelry, ensuring that no dark magic was embedded in the gifts people offered.

Eyes met Seren's, full of wonder and curiosity. It made his stomach twist and turn, tying itself into impossible knots. As gazes and whispers followed him, Seren wanted to scorn the people around him.

How could you put your faith in me? The question sat heavily on his tongue, but he didn't dare speak it. No. Instead, he smiled politely and repeated the memorized phrases. And he did not believe a word of it. Not a single one.

The only thing keeping him from becoming undone and unraveling was each rhythmic drink he took from his silver goblet. It was his seventh glass of red wine. And who had the authority to stop him? Was Seren not a goddess incarnate? The Holy One? Destined Cleanser of the Veil? According to the prevailing belief, nobody had the authority to stop him.

So, Seren drank another. And another. Until faces began to blur together, and he felt like he could breathe a little easier.

Aiden set a hand on Seren's shoulder, whispering in his ear, "You've had enough to drink, Seren. Remember, you need to keep your composure."

Seren ignored him and asked someone for their glass of wine. The man appeared shocked but handed Seren his silver goblet with a smile. Seren weaved in and out of the crowd, making his way back to the excessive chair on the dais. Waves of heat washed over him as the wine flooded his bloodstream. He was certain that if he could lay in bed, he'd have no trouble sleeping now. Perhaps he'd start requesting bottles of wine before bed. He couldn't help but smile at the thought.

"You haven't finished with your regards," Aiden warned. "You should accompany Eldyir while he speaks to the royal families."

Seren waved a hand, cutting Aiden off as he made his way up the polished steps. "Let the people celebrate," he said. "They seem pleased enough just to gawk."

"You are here to bring people together," Aiden said sharply. "Do not forget your role tonight."

Seren rolled his eyes, fiddling with the dangling jewelry in his ears. "And what's your role tonight?" he asked. "To scold me like a child?" Seren's gaze traveled to the acolyte stationed to his left, a younger man with red hair and deep brown eyes. "I don't need to be babysat, despite what Aiden may tell you. Are gods not the ones that do the protecting?" The man's lips twitched, threatening to turn into a smile.

Aiden's voice lowered as he leaned in. "Do not make a fool of yourself, Seren."

Seren scowled, slumping into the chair. He searched the crowd for Mila, scanning the faces. The wine was truly running its course, as were the sleepless nights. Earlier, he could have sworn he saw Mila standing at the far side of the room, her eyes meeting his. But the moment passed quickly, and when he blinked, she was gone. A small part of Seren feared she'd never been there at all. That he'd been missing her so deeply, he'd conjured her in his mind, and she had appeared for a second, only to slip away from him.

Despite Seren's requests, Aiden had relayed none of the letters he'd written to Mila. Though, truthfully, maybe that was for the best. Several of them had ended up crumpled in the trash, their sleep-deprived scrawl and half-formed confessions discarded before they could see the light of day.

Seren sipped on the wine, staring at the remaining merlot liquid for a moment before letting out a heavy sigh. He lifted his gaze to Aiden. "Can I leave now? I'm not feeling well."

"No," Aiden hissed. "You are to sit here and greet the daughters and sons of the noble families that have made a great deal of effort to see you. There is still doubt here. I sense it."

Seren felt a laugh rising in his throat, his face growing warmer by the second. "And what am I supposed to do about it?" he said. "I cannot blame them in the slightest."

The acolytes at Seren's side exchanged glances but remained silent. Aiden rubbed his temples with an exhale. Several minutes passed as Seren watched the dancers twirl across the floor. Colors blurred together, waves of blue, blooms of pink and purple bleeding into each other. The music wove through the air, and Seren's gaze drifted to the harpist. The acolyte, dressed in powder blue, had short blonde hair framing her face as she delicately plucked the strings, her eyes closed in concentration.

Seren's hands twitched beside him, following each careful movement. The harp's sound was subtle, almost drowned by the melody of the flutes winding through the chamber. Seren looked away, his hands tightening on the armrests of his chair.

Acolytes lined the base of the stairs, another layer of protection from those who gravitated toward Seren. He was acutely aware of the young women who couldn't seem to tear their stares away from him, as if he were an otherworldly creature. It made his skin crawl.

Seren rose from the chair. He wasn't about to sit here like some ornamental figure. If he was going to be trapped at this stupid party, then at least he'd make the most of it. He would find Mila and prove to himself that his mind wasn't playing tricks. He turned to Aiden, but the man's focus was elsewhere, locked on something in the distance.

"Get your hands off me!"

Seren's eyes snapped down to a man roughly yanking his arms away from an acolyte at the base of the stairs. The man was dressed in a flowing lavender robe with wide sleeves and a sash around the waist, the fabric adorned with patterns of snowdrops.

"Your Highness, please, calm down," the acolyte urged, his voice strained. "You will have your time to speak to the Mother—"

"The *Mother*," the man drawled, his dark brows furrowing in derision. "And how do we know it's true?" His voice rose, slicing through the music. "You dance and celebrate like fools. How are we so sure this is not a trick to instill false hope? The priests and saints are nothing without their magic. Who's to say they wouldn't go this far for faith? Who's to say they wouldn't drag kings and queens across the country to lie to their faces?"

Seren stilled at the top of the stairs, watching as the man turned toward the crowd. The music paused, the room stilling around them, all eyes watching.

"My people are dying from the Blue Inferno. And every moment that passes, the demons of the Veil grow with power. And you all dance and laugh while your savior sits on a throne and drinks wine?" The man scoffed, turning to Seren, his dark eyes burning. "I don't believe a word of it."

A hand sat on the man's shoulder, a young woman with long black hair and skin as white as snow. "Father, please," she whispered. "Let us ask for an audience and—"

"No," the man snapped. "I think he should prove it to us. Right here, right now. Prove you are the goddess reborn."

Seren's heart stuttered, and his hand tightened around the stem of his goblet. Aiden stepped closer, his shoulder brushing Seren's.

"Your Highness, please," Aiden said, inclining his head. "I understand your doubts, but I assure you—"

"Can you not speak for yourself?" the man interrupted, cutting through Aiden's words.

Aiden's face paled.

The world pressed in around Seren, too still, too quiet. Every eye in the room was fixed on him, waiting for his response.

Seren cleared his throat. "You are right to doubt," he said, surprised at the calmness in his own voice. He took a steady breath, then sipped from the goblet, the bittersweet taste lingering on his tongue. The man's mouth twitched, surprise dawning on his face at Seren's composed response.

Seren rose to his feet, a flush spreading from within, filling his chest. "It would be foolish not to question my presence," he continued, stepping down the stairs, heat unfurling through his limbs, seeping into his mind. "I know how deeply you've all suffered." He raised his goblet, his tone shifting, no longer calm but tinged with something he might regret later. "I know my promises mean nothing."

Something stirred inside him—anger? Resentment? Bitterness? He wasn't sure, but he felt it clawing at his insides, threatening to break free. How could they be so credulous, so willing to accept empty words? There were a hundred things he wanted to say.

You're right. I'm a fake. A liar. And you are all fools.

The words pressed at his lips, the very words Aiden feared he might speak, threatening to spill over. But they didn't come.

Something shifted in the air. An electric crackle ran down Seren's spine, and his body went rigid. Starbursts flared behind his eyes, disorienting him for a brief moment, just long enough to make him stagger inwardly but not enough for anyone to notice.

"*Seren,*" she spoke. Her voice was soothing yet startling, a paradox threading through his very being. "*Calm yourself.*"

Seren nearly scoffed. Calm? But then he took another step and froze. A numbness flooded his legs, spreading through his torso, traveling to his arms, reaching his fingers. And then, a warmth, strong and unwarranted. Seren felt a smile, one he hadn't meant to offer, curl his lips, as his body straightened and his head inclined as though on its own accord. A calmness settled over him, shifting the very core of who he was.

"You have traveled a long way, and your skepticism is justified," Seren said, his voice now softened, almost distant. The man's eyes widened, and all the world seemed to hold its breath. Seren did not react, though he, too, heard it—the tone of a woman's voice, soothing and ethereal, entwining with his own. "You do not have to believe my promises, your Highness." Seren smiled. "You hail from the land of eternal winter, a devout follower of Ryu, God of Wisdom. It is wise of you to doubt and brave of you to speak on behalf of your people. I am certain Ryu smiles upon you now."

Seren took another step. "I am only a vessel bearing a fragment of an ancient promise. I cannot mend this world's wounds with a single word, for I know it is broken." He paused. "You ask why we are gathered here, and I will tell you: we are here to stand united in faith. True faith is never blind; it is forged in the fires of doubt, tempered by the struggles within."

His voice grew quieter, almost a whisper. "Today, I ask you to believe, to trust. To let your fears rest, even if only for a moment. Proof, I cannot offer. True faith is not given, but born."

Seren was at the bottom of the steps now, face to face with the man. His dark eyes shone with reluctance.

"I would like to offer you a gift," Seren said, his voice unwavering and melodic. "A small promise that you can watch unfold. Your wife, she is with child."

The man's face blanched.

"She is sick," Seren continued. "The pregnancy has been difficult for her."

The man nodded. "Yes," he managed.

"I can offer you a promise of life," Seren said. "And in return, I ask for your prayer, for your belief, and for you to spread it amongst your people."

A familiar tingle coursed down Seren's back, gathering within him in a more controlled manner, like a feather floating in a breeze. Seren lifted his empty hand and opened his palm, a brilliant light bursting forth. Gasps filled the chamber as the light swirled and gathered. It merged, forming into a crystal shaped like a lotus. The room was bathed in its radiant glow, and Seren, transfixed by the shimmering colors dancing within, held it aloft, feeling the warmth of its light on his face.

As the crystal lotus floated above his hand, a sense of awe washed over Seren. It was unlike anything he had ever seen before. The vibrant hues of blue, purple, and pink shifted and blended, creating an ethereal display of beauty. Whispers of wonder replaced the gasps in the chamber as everyone marveled at the mesmerizing light, as if the crystal lotus held within it the essence of pure magic. Energy pulsed through Seren's fingertips.

Seren lowered the crystal lotus. The chamber remained hushed.

"A gift," Seren said, "for your daughter. May light always guide her. She will do great things."

The man stumbled back with a gasp, staring at the crystal in his hand. "This...this is my wife's favorite flower," he stammered. "She always said it brought her peace and hope." Tears streamed down his face. "This pregnancy has taken a toll on her body. I feared she would not survive."

Seren nodded. "Just as the lotus blooms from muddy waters, your wife and child will prevail. Upon her birth, this crystal lotus will offer protection. She will survive."

He placed the lotus-shaped crystal into the man's hand. Instantly, a warm glow enveloped the man's palm, spreading a sense of calm throughout the room. The man fell to his knees, bowing his head. "Thank you. Please, forgive me for my doubt."

Cold flooded through Seren's limbs, seeping out from his chest. The warmth, that calm certainty, faded all at once. He nearly staggered, the emptiness hitting him like a wave. He blinked, staring back at the man bowing before him, as if waking from a dream.

"Please, get up," Seren said hoarsely.

Without waiting to watch the man rise, Seren turned his back to the whispering crowd, meeting Aiden's gaze. The priest's face was drained of color, a question lurking in his eyes. Seren steadied himself, determined not to let his features betray his own shock. He settled back in his chair just as the music resumed, and the celebration came alive once more.

The man held his lotus for all to see, drawing the crowd's attention as they gathered around, eager to touch it. The focus had shifted to the miraculous item, letting Seren fade quietly into the background.

He leaned toward the red-haired acolyte beside him. "Fetch me a bottle of the finest wine in this place, will you?"

The young man cast a nervous glance at Aiden before nodding and hurrying off the dais. Aiden, meanwhile, stood rigid, his face still pale and his jaw clenched.

"Are you satisfied now?" Seren asked. "May I go?"

"You still have wine in your hand," Aiden replied stiffly.

Seren looked down at his goblet. "Ah, I do." With a sigh, he drained it and handed the empty goblet to Aiden. "All the more reason I need more."

Aiden strode to Seren's right, lowering his voice to the acolyte. "Fetch Eldyir for me." The young woman nodded and hurried away, leaving Aiden and Seren alone on the dais.

"How are you feeling, Seren?"

The question made Seren pause. "I'm...fine," he said, his voice guarded.

"The Mother spoke through you. Last time, you were nearly overwhelmed."

Seren blinked, feeling a prickle of uncertainty. "Last time?"

Aiden's brows knitted, his expression cautious. "Yes, I thought you'd recall." Then, his features softened. "I suppose you were quite young."

Seren swallowed the lump in his throat. "It's far too warm in this place." He peeled open his heavy robes to reveal a silken white shirt underneath. As he lounged back with a sigh, the shirt fell open down the center of his chest.

He tried not to smirk at the discontent on Aiden's face as a few women giggled in Seren's direction. But Seren didn't care at all; he was busy scanning the room. Laughter filled the air as rosy-cheeked guests exchanged drunken words, their eyes glinting with interest. Perhaps, he'd done enough.

The Grand Priest ascended the steps, returning from his formal greetings, and whispered something in Aiden's ear. He and Aiden moved behind the tapestry, exchanging hushed words on a topic Seren had no interest in. And then, he saw her. Through the blur of colors and faces, she was solid. Real.

Seren threw a look over his shoulder. Aiden and Eldyir were deep in conversation, and the acolytes had yet to return to stand at Seren's side. Neither priest took notice as Seren slipped from his seat, his open robes trailing behind him. The acolytes at the bottom of the steps stayed in place, as they'd been instructed to. Seren quickly wove through the crowd, passing over faces, searching for familiar brown eyes. He felt hands reaching out, brushing against his clothes.

"I touched him."

"He's so beautiful."

"He looks just like her."

Seren didn't care. His thoughts were heavy with wine and exhaustion. All he wanted to do was see Mila. She was all that mattered right now.

Maybe I should have told her.

Except he hadn't wanted to then. Now, he had a thousand things he wanted to tell her. He wanted to tell her how beautiful she looked, like the starflowers that twinkled in the fields. He wanted to tell her that she was the strongest person he'd ever met. He wanted to tell her that he would have died for her, over and over again. But most of all—he wanted to tell her that love was a word he longed to taste on his tongue with her name next to it.

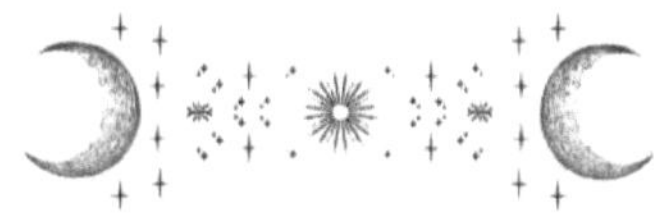

Jude had disappeared again, claiming he was getting more wine. Mila wove her way through the crowd, her heart thundering in her chest. She spotted Seren approaching, but the watchful eyes surrounding him made her uneasy. He was heavily guarded, even in the shadows. Acolytes stationed along the walls kept their eyes fixed on him. If she wanted to get him alone, she would need a distraction.

Nearby, a couple of men laughed, reaching for wine from a tower of glasses on one of the tables. Mila smirked. Perfect. She flexed her hand, a burst of heat flooding through her veins. One man yelped, twitching as she took control, falling forward at her command. Red wine spilled across the marble floor like fresh blood. Glass shattered, and all attention turned to the mess she'd created. Seren seemed to take the moment as a cue; their eyes met for a fleeting moment before she turned the corner, slipping through an archway.

Follow me, she thought, as if he could hear her.

Mila's mind raced, thoughts tangling into a chaotic mess. All this fuss, all the preparations for a Grand Celebration—and it was all for Seren? Her shoes echoed against the marble floors as she hurried down the hall.

Seren, the one everyone believed would cleanse the Veil? Not only the son of a god, but a reborn *goddess*? She shook her head, fidgeting with her gloves. No, it changed nothing. Did it? Mila knew better—didn't she?

Kill Seren tonight.

That's right. The words pierced her like a blade laced with poison.

You don't love him.

Mila threw a glance over her shoulder as she exited through an open archway. It led to a magnificent garden courtyard, a maze of white roses climbing over the cobblestone walls. She reached down her thigh, pulling her dagger from its sheath. She wound deeper into the gardens, hoping Seren was alone and close behind.

Once Mila felt she was far enough, she leaned against the garden wall.

"Shit," she whispered. "Shit. Shit. Shit."

Mila weighed her dagger in her hands, the opalescent blade shimmering like fallen stars. Sometimes, Mila wondered if it was strange that she had held onto it. After her brother's death, shouldn't she have cast it aside, not able to bear to even look at it? She'd killed somebody she'd loved with it.

The blood of these children is on your hands, too, Kamilah.

Mila hit the back of her head against the wall as if it would rid Iris's incessant words from her brain. Her breathing quickened. Iris was right, though, wasn't she? If Eden was sacrificing children to obtain power and eventually reach Mila, then her hands were soiled. With a sigh, Mila pressed her temple against the cool stone.

Even if Seren was a reborn goddess, Mila had never held faith in the divine. The people of the Sanguine Kingdom had always deemed the gods unimportant. Useless, her mother had once called them. The time of the gods ended long ago. Even if she wanted to use it as an excuse, did she even believe it herself? Hadn't she learned at a young age that small sacrifices can bring the greatest rewards, no matter how cruel? The end of one life could free hundreds of women from a bloodthirsty demon and save innocent boys from death. And Mila would be entirely free.

What did Seren even mean to her? The more she thought about it, the more her head throbbed with an ache that pulsed behind her eyes.

Mila twirled the dagger between her fingers.

I care about you, Seren.

Hadn't she meant those words?

You don't love him.

Again, those words sliced through her. Mila winced, pressing her entire forehead against the wall. She tucked the dagger behind her back, her breath coming in shallow breaths. That's right. She didn't love him.

Mila's skin prickled and she turned just as Seren rounded the corner. He stayed in the shadows for a long stretch of seconds, murmuring unintelligibly under his breath. He stumbled forward, hand grasping the wall with a grumble as if he was attempting to turn around.

"It's not polite to spy on ladies," Mila finally said.

"I'm not spying," he said. "My stupid robes were caught on the thorns."

Seren stepped into the moonlight, silvery hair disheveled. His white robes were parted, revealing an unbuttoned silken shirt that exposed the fair skin of his chest. He really was beautiful, his amethyst eyes glistening with the guilt of a troublesome child. With a sloppy smile, he stepped toward Mila, only to have an unopened bottle of wine fall from under his arm, rolling out on the cobblestone. He frowned, reaching for it with heavy-limbed movements.

"I hope you're not planning to drink that," Mila said with a forced chuckle.

Seren stood unsteadily on his feet, dusting himself off. "And why wouldn't I?"

Mila rolled her eyes. "You're drunk, Seren."

Seren brows drew together. "I am certainly not drunk."

"You most certainly are."

His expression showed offense despite the undeniable truth of the notion. He parted his lips as if to argue but stumbled instead. Catching himself on the wall, he lurched so close that his hair brushed against Mila's skin. Their faces were inches apart, his wine-laden breath cascading over her. She caught scents of jasmine and lavender on his skin.

"Sorry," Seren said, eyes wide. "I'll admit it, maybe I did have too much wine. The world won't hold still."

Mila tensed as he reached behind her, plucking a white rose from the entanglement of thorns on the wall, and carefully placed it in her hair.

Then, Seren pushed off the stone, clearing his throat. He leaned down, grasped the neck of the wine bottle, and lifted it, staring at the cork with narrowed eyes. He looked around the garden, leaning to grab a small rock. "Here goes nothing," he murmured, placing the bottle on the ground and striking the cork with the rock. After a few forceful taps, the cork popped out.

Seren took a long drink, merlot liquid running down the curve of his throat, past the swoops of his collarbones, staining his shirt like blood.

"Why didn't you come see me?" Mila asked. "I waited for you."

Seren wiped his mouth on his sleeve. "I tried," he said. "Aiden was..." He trailed off.

"Keeping you a hostage?" she finished.

Seren raked a hand through his hair. "You could say that. I've been looking for an opportunity to sneak away for days, but..." He frowned.

A soft breeze blew across the garden, chilling Mila to the bone. "Let me guess," she said. "It's for your protection." She scoffed. "Do you listen to everything Aiden tells you to do?"

Seren's brow furrowed, clearly bothered by the question. "Well, he's the only one who cared enough to get me out of the Godless City, wasn't he?" There was bitterness in his tone, as if he didn't quite believe it himself. He took another long drink.

"Sure, and he took four long years to do it. I don't see why he should be telling you where you can and can't go," Mila said. She rubbed her arm where the High Priest had grabbed her earlier. "Or why you listen to him."

Seren's frown deepened. "It's not that simple," he said. "He's always believed I would change the world. Now, I have to make *everyone* believe the Mother has returned to save them all." He slurred the last words, as if they left a bitter taste in his mouth. "And so, I have a 'reputation' to uphold."

Mila's hand tightened on the dagger. "Do you believe that? Did you mean all those words you said in your little display?"

Seren inched closer, his lips blushed with wine. "I don't think I have a choice," he murmured.

"There is *always* a choice."

Seren ran his fingers through his silvery hair. "And what is my choice?" he said, voice low. "Tell everyone that I'm not the Mother and that we're all doomed to die in the Veil? I *am* the Mother, Mila. As much as I hate it... I don't think I can deny it any longer."

His words filled Mila with guilt. Different worlds, but they felt the same. Trapped. However, when she looked at Seren, she didn't see a savior who could change the world. She saw a self-loathing boy with a hundred unbreakable walls. With each admission, another truth was frozen beneath the surface. Mila bit the inside of her cheek as a jolt of pain sparked in her head.

"You remembered in the Trial of Nightmares," Mila said. "That you were the Mother. Didn't you?"

Seren's jaw tightened, his fingers curling. "And now I wish to forget." He sipped on the wine. "At least for tonight."

Mila swiftly snatched the bottle from Seren's hand, and his eyes widened in surprise. She guzzled the wine, hoping it would dull the pain in her head, blur Seren's face until she no longer knew who he was.

Kill him tonight.

The words were a steady pulse, thrumming beneath her skin.

"Don't drink it all, I wasn't done," Seren complained.

"As if you need more," she said. Wine dripped from the corner of her mouth. Seren's thumb came up, softly brushing it away. They stood in silence, his touch lingering on her skin, his long lashes casting shadows on his cheek under the moonlight.

"What're you thinking?" Seren whispered.

"I'm thinking that you're a drunken fool," Mila breathed.

"Is that all?"

Mila hesitated. "I'm thinking that you should go back inside," she replied, the words feeling like hot coals in her throat. The cool hilt of the dagger pressed against her back. "I'm thinking that you shouldn't be out here alone with me."

Something was wrong; she could feel it.

"And yet, that still doesn't tell me what you're thinking," Seren drunkenly mused.

"Tell me what *you're* thinking," Mila challenged.

"Isn't it obvious?" he said. "I'm thinking of how badly I want to kiss you."

Mila's heart pounded as her eyes traced the curve of his jaw, the softness of his mouth. "You're not being yourself, Seren."

"That's alright," he said, his lips drawing closer to hers. "I don't like myself that much, anyway."

"Does self-deprecation charm every lady?" Mila asked, her voice unsteady.

Seren smiled. "Depends. Is it working on you?"

His hand brushed against the back of her neck. "I want to kiss you, Mila. If you'll let me."

Mila stilled. Had he truly said those words?

You don't love him.

It didn't matter. She found herself speaking anyway. "You can kiss me," she whispered.

Seren leaned in close, the silken strands of his pale hair filling Mila's periphery. A small sigh escaped him, carrying the weight of a hundred unsaid words into the space between them. Seren tilted his face and pressed his wine-stained lips to hers. He was warm. Soft. His hands slipped around the curve of her waist, holding her as though she might break if he held her too tight. Mila's eyes fluttered shut, a hand slipping behind his neck, the dagger still clutched behind her back, unnoticed.

She parted her lips against his. They had technically kissed twice before, but this—this was the first real one. The first one that had a chance of mattering. The first one with any truth in it.

One of Seren's hands drifted from her face to tangle in her short hair, gently pulling her closer to his warmth. His kiss was clumsy—desperate, even. His other hand moved from her waist, gliding over the smooth fabric of her dress, his fingers tracing along her bare collarbone before drifting up the curve of her throat. She shivered, leaning in, yearning for the kiss to deepen.

What am I doing?

Mila repositioned her right hand, the dagger's point hovering over his back. One swift, decisive movement, and it would pierce his heart, ending this once and for all.

Iris's voice flooded her mind again. *You don't love him.*

But Seren kissed her harder, his breaths uneven, as he pressed her backward until her shoulders met the cold stone wall. Desire flooded her as Seren's hands dropped to her hips, and when he pressed his body against hers, a low, pleased sound escaped from his throat.

Just do it.

But she hesitated. A sharp pain traveled up her spine.

Seren broke away from her lips, breathing hard, kissing her cheek before dipping his face to kiss her neck, her shoulder.

I...don't want to.

Heat seared through her mind as she resisted the idea. Mila's hand trembled on the weapon as her fingers started to burn as if hovering over a flame. "Seren, stop," she said, her eyelids fluttering.

Seren pulled away, his forehead leaning to rest upon hers. "*Ata*," he whispered, her true name slipping from his lips like honey.

Mila seized up, and the dagger clattered to the ground. Something inside her shattered. She gasped as the pain in her head disappeared, clarity flooding in. Seren's gaze flicked to the weapon, then back to her, his face unreadable.

"Seren—"

It happened so fast that Mila couldn't react. His hands pinned her wrists to the wall.

"Mila?" His brows furrowed, eyes wild. "What were you...?"

"Wait—"

"No, don't speak," Seren demanded. He'd already said her true name. Her mouth clamped shut, not a word able to escape. "Were you trying to *kill* me?"

He waited for a response, but Mila could form none beneath the command he'd given. Desperation clawed at her insides. But Seren took her silence as his answer, his mouth turning into a grim line. "Was any of this real, Kamilah?" His voice shook. "Do you feel anything for me in return?"

Mila's heart jumped into her throat.

"Just give me an answer and I'll let you go."

She couldn't.

"*Answer me, Ata!*"

Mila froze as Seren's voice rang out, a chill rolling up her spine. This time, the poison had no hold onto her. No, this time, Mila was left with nothing but the truth and Seren's demand.

She thought of his careful hands on the small of her back, the way he dipped into her when they danced. His smile, almost heartbreaking, never reached his eyes. His determination to save her from her fate, even after she had held a knife to his throat. And what of the promises he had kept? Or the feeling that had encompassed her when she'd stirred in his grasp, half alive, thinking how comfortable it would be to die in his arms?

Was it real?

The question thundered in her ears, roared in her blood. Every cell in her body vibrated with the anticipation of the truth.

Was it real?

And if it was? Did it even matter?

Mila's feelings, no matter how raw or real they could be, could not bury the truth. Everything was bigger than the turmoil within her. She'd been told her entire life that she would rule a kingdom of her own, and she had denied it. But what if she *could* take her rightful place and change everything for the Sisters? Free them and forge a path of her own. Everyone had tried to forge a path for Mila, always telling her what needed to be done. It'd been that way since the moment she'd been born. And she didn't want any of it.

"Tell me," Seren begged—the words coming out more like a whimper.

Little did he know, she had no choice but to answer.

What had the truth ever done for her? What had love ever done for her? It had been her weakness and the source of all her pain. Looking into Seren's beautiful eyes, seeing the hurt painted across his face, Mila wondered what he would say if she revealed her true feelings to him. But what would it do to her?

Did she have room for more heartache? Did she have room for more fear? What if it was better this way? She had almost killed Seren twice already under compulsion. If she wasn't careful, she could lose Seren, just like she lost Kamil.

Seren had said her true name, but he had not asked for her to tell the truth. All he asked for was an answer.

"No." Half a breath—that was all it took. "It was never real."

Seren released her and strode toward the dagger. Grasping it, he turned and shoved it into her hands. Before she could pull away, his fingers closed tightly around her wrist, guiding the blade to press against his chest. "Then, do it," he said, his words slurring, breath uneven. His eyes blazed with feral desperation, an unsteady vulnerability that lay utterly exposed.

Mila's breath hitched. "You don't understand—"

"You're right, I don't understand," he interrupted. "I don't understand why you've waited this long. Or why you let me kiss you and confess how I felt?" He forced the tip of the dagger into his chest, wincing. "I don't understand why you don't just get it over with if this is what you came here to do. Kill me."

"You're not listening to me, Seren."

"I don't want to listen."

"You're drunk—"

"Do it!"

A surge of rage flooded Mila as she flicked her wrist beneath his hold. The blood dripping down Seren's front wrapped around his wrists and pulled him back, the dagger falling to the ground.

"*Listen* to me, you drunk idiot," she demanded. "The Sisters want you dead and whether it's for my benefit or not, I don't know. Iris came to see me, and she wants the bond broken. I don't want to kill you. I *never* wanted to kill you."

She leaned down, hitching her dress upward, and sure enough, two sharp points sat on her ankle, just like she thought. That damn snake had bit her.

Mila met Seren's gaze. "Are you done?" she asked. "Or do you want to use my name against me again?"

Seren's eyes narrowed, trying to focus on the tiny teeth marks on Mila's ankle. He was silent, and still, not a word escaping him. Mila sighed, and the blood bonds fell away. Seren took a step back, his hands shaking at his sides.

"I'm sorry," he breathed. "I didn't..."

"You couldn't have known."

There was a drawn-out silence. A gust of wind rippled through the courtyard, tossing Seren's pale robes about him like fluttering wings.

"Did you mean what you said?" he finally spoke. "That none of it was real?"

Mila closed her eyes. "Yes."

"But we..."

"It was just a kiss, Seren," Mila whispered.

"Mila, I—"

"Don't say it," she said, eyes flashing open, tears pricking the corners. "Please."

"Leave. if you don't want to hear it," Seren said quietly. He turned his back to her. "I want to be alone."

"Seren—"

"*Leave*, Mila!"

His voice echoed through the courtyard, and even the roses shuddered. Mila stood there for a moment, grappling with the desire to find the perfect words.

Love is a weakness, Kamilah.

"I'm sorry, Seren." Two useless and insignificant words that made no difference. She stood there in silence, unable to read Seren with his back turned. She strode across the courtyard, resisting the temptation to turn around—to tell him she was a liar.

Mila plucked the rose from her hair and crumpled it in her palm.

FOURTEEN

"The skies fall silent, death stirs among the divine; it is the triumvirate that will bring forth the light."

—Book of Disruption

Black and white swans rested upon the star-speckled pond, their long necks elegantly curled downwards. Wind rustled the white jasmine that climbed along the marbled archway of the open courtyard. Seren slumped against the wall, sliding down to the ground, bottle of wine in hand.

As he leaned back, a thorn snagged the back of his neck. Reaching behind, Seren plucked a rose from the wall, examining it between his fingers. The roses here were white, unlike the yellow ones that grew in abundance at the church in Stellaris. Seren sighed, stripping the rose of its petals one by one, watching them fall into his lap like fallen snow.

Raising the bottle to his lips, Seren took a long gulp, hoping the wine might fill the hollow ache in his chest. Water droplets hit his skin. He blinked, bleary-eyed, as another bead of water landed on the back of his hand. He looked up, expecting rain, but instead felt wetness running down his cheeks. Not rain. Tears.

Pathetic, he thought. He groaned, digging his fingers into his scalp.

Somehow, he'd made something already broken, so much worse. He was a fool. An idiot. A drunken moron who was losing his mind.

"You're missing your party," came a voice. "Lucky for you, I pointed those pesky acolytes in the wrong direction. You can thank me later."

Seren quickly wiped his tears and looked up. He pushed himself to his feet, swaying like a branch in a storm. It was Jude—real, present, alive, standing right before him. His white shirt took on a pale blue hue in the moonlight, and Seren traced the familiar lines of his face in disbelief.

Where had he come from? A stupid, wine-addled thought flitted through Seren's mind: had Jude walked out of the water, following the path of moonlight on the surface?

Jude dipped into a bow, smiling. His usually golden skin looked ashen, with dark rings shadowing his eyes, yet he remained as charming as ever. "Did you miss me?"

Without a second thought, Seren stumbled forward and wrapped his arms around Jude like a child. He buried his face in Jude's chest, hiding the tears still falling. *Jude smells nice,* Seren thought—*like orange peels and mint.* It wasn't until Jude rested his chin comfortably on top of Seren's head that Seren realized just how much taller Jude was.

"Ah, I'll take that as a yes," Jude murmured, his voice soft and amused. "You reek of wine, Seren. And Aiden is looking everywhere for you." He chuckled. "Are you causing trouble?"

Seren said nothing for a moment, his face still buried in Jude's chest. "I think I may vomit," he said, his voice muffled.

"Please, don't," Jude responded, gently pulling Seren back to hold him at arm's length. "I rather like these clothes."

Heat filled Seren's cheeks; he wasn't sure what had come over him. "Sorry," he mumbled. "I was afraid I'd never see you again."

Jude put his hands on his hips, grinning from ear to ear. "As if you could get rid of me that easily," he said. "I always finish a job. And besides, did you really think I would ever leave without saying goodbye? You'd think you know me better than that by now." He scanned over Seren's silvery-white hair, traveling to his eyes and lingering on his exposed chest. "Something's different about you. Can't quite put my finger on it."

"Very funny."

Jude lowered himself to the ground, patting the stone and beckoning Seren to sit beside him. Seren obliged and handed Jude the half-empty bottle of wine. "You brought me a gift? How thoughtful," Jude smirked, taking a swig of the wine. He wrinkled his nose and stifled a cough. "Quite strong, though." Seren held out his hand, and Jude shook his head. "I'd say you've had enough."

"Not nearly," Seren grumbled. As if to betray him, his body let out a small hiccup. "So... Where have you been?"

Jude shrugged. "Had a couple of jobs in Stellaris that I took care of after I got out of the Sanguine Kingdom."

Seren eyed Jude as he sipped his wine. Why did he get the feeling Jude was lying?

"You were clearly successful in your princess rescue," Jude added with a grin. "Never doubted you for a moment."

Seren didn't respond, only sighed.

"Just as quiet and mysterious as ever," Jude said. His tone was light and playful even, but Seren could have sworn he heard disappointment. "You can talk to me, Seren. You know that, don't you?"

Seren gazed down at himself, his stomach churning at the sight of the jewelry draping his neck and adorning his fingers. It was ridiculous. Yet, he couldn't deny the transformation; he certainly looked the part—the handmaidens had made sure of that.

He had refused to let them dress him, fearing they would see the scars on his back. When they presented him with the elegant ivory robes, they explained that they symbolized his embodiment of light, akin to the goddess. He had been terrified to show the people at the celebration that this was what he was supposed to be: the incarnation of self-sacrifice and light—resplendent, beloved, and revered.

It was all untrue.

"Do you think I'm anything like her?" Seren said.

"A goddess who sacrificed her well-being for the fate of others?" Jude asked, smiling affectionately. "I think so."

Seren groaned, face-planting into his palms. "You're wrong."

"I'm never wrong," Jude replied.

"I almost wish I never came back," Seren slurred, his words tumbling out too freely. "Aiden can hardly bear to look at me. Mila…" He hiccuped and cut himself off. "It doesn't matter. I hate being looked at like that. Like I'm…" He paused, rubbing his temples as his head throbbed. "I played the harp, I drank the tears, I even look like her… Despite that, I can't shake this horrible feeling. What if I can't do this? What if I can't reach my fate?"

"You can, Seren. You must reach for the stars," Jude said theatrically.

Seren lifted his head, his eyes glistening with tears. "What if they're beyond my reach?"

Jude rested his cheek on Seren's shoulder, his voice softer. "Then I will put you on my shoulders, and we will reach them together."

"You always say such ridiculous things," Seren whispered. Though, his heart swelled with warmth at Jude's words. He'd truly missed him.

"You never believe a word I say, do you?"

"Definitely not."

Seren sat silently, his gaze tracing the contours of Jude's face, noting how much thinner he seemed than Seren remembered.

Jude was always smiling, as if it were the most natural thing in the world. Even now, the faint ghost of a smile lingered on his lips. How did he make it look so easy? Why couldn't Seren be like that?

If Jude were in Seren's place, it'd be easy to believe someone like him could save the world. Jude made life feel lighter, less heavy, less sorrowful, like the sun breaking through clouds on an ugly day. He was the blue of the sky. That's what Seren should have been. Instead, he felt like the opposite: the gloaming, unable to hold onto the light.

"You're staring," Jude said, breaking the silence.

"Am I?" Seren murmured.

"You stared at me like that when we first met, you know?"

"Like what?"

Jude lifted his head, grinning. "Oh, you know," he said. "Like I was your knight in shining armor."

"I did not," Seren argued.

Jude smirked. "We should find something to distract you."

"And what did you have in mind?"

Jude playfully traced his finger over his lips. "I have a few ideas."

A crease formed between Seren's brows. "There's not anything that could get these thoughts off my mind. Oh, wait—perhaps another trip to the Godless City. If I can get a hold of some Somnia, maybe I can forget this ordeal."

With a tender touch, Jude lifted Seren's face by the chin, his eyes sparkling with mischief. "Listen to you, making jokes at last. Are you sure you can't think of *anything* else that could take your mind off things?"

"Knock it off," Seren said, half-heartedly pushing him away. He turned, clearing his throat as heat filled his face.

Jude chuckled and stood up. "What's got you so flustered?"

Before Seren could answer, Jude peeled off his shirt, threw it aside, and then stripped his pants.

"Jude, what the hell are you doing?"

"You can swim, can't you?" Jude asked, stepping out of his pants, his copper leg gleaming under the moonlight.

Seren stared at the pond ahead of them, where stars shimmered on the surface, fractured only by weak ripples from the sleeping swans. "Of course I can swim," he said. "But you're out of your mind if you think—"

Before he could finish, Jude crouched down, his face inches from Seren's. A beat passed, and Seren froze. Jude's breath brushed against his skin. Seren's lips parted, searching for something clever to say, but the words died before they formed. Instead, Jude slipped his hands beneath Seren's arms and slung him over his shoulder as if he were a sack of flour.

"What are you doing?" Seren cried out. He pressed his hands against Jude's back, fingers meeting with bare skin.

Jude rose to his feet, muscles flexing beneath Seren, his laughter warm and unbothered. "Just as I remember. You're light as a feather. Are you ready to go for a swim?"

"Jude," Seren warned. "Put me down."

"I will," Jude replied, his steps steady as he strode across the courtyard, "in a second."

"Wait, don't—" Seren's words were cut off as Jude tossed him effortlessly into the air.

For a moment, Seren was midair, untethered, and weightless. Black and white wings unfurled behind him as the swans woke from their slumber. Time seemed to slow as Seren met Jude's vivid blue eyes, bright with amusement. Their fingertips grazed—a fleeting touch—before Seren plunged into the water.

The cold stole his breath. Seren's robes whirled and twisted around him, their weight pulling him downward. He didn't fight the drag of the fabric or the ice filling his lungs. He let it take him until his back met the bottom. Bubbles escaped Seren's mouth and floated upwards, carrying his unfinished words.

It was quiet. Comfortable. Easier. Seren wondered if given enough time if his thoughts would dissolve into the water and vanish forever. His vision blurred, and his lungs burned, but he didn't move. His limbs remained limp as the world grew darker. Colder. Seren smiled, his eyelids fluttering shut.

I should...stay here.

Here, he could forget the pain of memories that clung to him like shadows, the expectations of a life he felt unworthy to lead.

The water pulsed around him, alive. Seren's eyes shot open beneath the water. Something stirred beneath him, slithering into view. Shadows curled between the folds of his robes, staining their whiteness with inky wisps.

"We'll stay with you."

A tendril coiled around his wrist. He was imagining it. He had to be...

"We will never leave you."

There was no fight within Seren as the shadows grazed the back of his neck, the sensation like fingers brushing his skin. It was all too familiar. He leaned into them, lips parting, water flooding in. This time, it didn't burn. He was fading, becoming the darkness all around him.

Yes, this is what he wanted.

This is where he was supposed to be.

He was sure of it.

And then the surface of the water broke, and the stars shattered. A hand plunged through the dark, gripping the front of his robes and pulling him upward.

Seren emerged with a ragged gasp, water streaming down his skin. Jude's frantic eyes locked onto his, piercing through the chill and darkness. Jude's warm hands gripped Seren's face.

"You should've told me you couldn't swim," he said, panicked. "Shit, Seren. Are you okay?"

It took Seren a moment to steady himself, the air burning in his throat like embers. Jude's hands didn't leave him, and Seren realized how warm he was growing despite the cold water. He cleared his throat, and Jude pulled away.

Seren stared down at his robes. No blackness stained the fabric, no wisps clung to his skin. The white robes had turned translucent, billowing atop the water like a delicate veil.

"I'm fine, I can swim, and the water isn't deep," Seren said, voice unsteady. "My robes were just heavy. No need to be so dramatic."

Jude raked a hand through his curls with an exasperated sigh. "I should've thought about that. I'm sorry."

Seren's eyes flicked to the water. Was he losing his mind? He lifted his chin and traced the stars flecking the sky, an expanse of tiny crystals.

"The sky is beautiful tonight. You can't see the stars like this in Vavilon," Jude said. He paused. "You didn't deserve to have the sky taken from you."

Seren turned to Jude in surprise as their shoulders brushed, a spark of warmth flaring within him. *I have this terrible feeling that everything I loved was taken from me. Even the sky.* He had said those words to Jude not too long ago.

"You remember that?"

"Of course I do," Jude said.

A knot tightened in Seren's stomach, the urge to share the ultimate truth rising in him. The scars on his back throbbed at the thought. Seren bit his tongue; the admissions lodged like stones in his throat.

"Are you going to go back to the Godless City?" Seren whispered. "Are you...leaving?"

Jude scooped water into his palms, splashing his face. Droplets glistened as they dripped from his chin. "That was the plan. Mila already asked if she could come with me," he said. "I have a couple of jobs here, so I'll most likely stay for a month or two to take care of them. I have to say, I like it here though. The green hills and endless sky are something I could grow used to."

"Yeah."

Another beat of silence.

"Are you happy to be home?" Jude asked.

"Not really, but I'm happy you're here."

Jude grinned, his eyes lighting up. "Truly?"

"I wish you didn't have to go." The confession was barely a whisper in the night. Seren bit the inside of his cheek, his stomach fluttering.

Jude cleared his throat, his cheeks redder than Seren had ever seen. He looked away, hand drawing against his chest. "You know, Seren," he began, voice quieter now, "I don't have a family. I've had one goal for years, but I've never known how to reach it. When I met you, I finally felt like I had a grander purpose, as silly as that may seem. I felt...important."

He chuckled unevenly, then let his hand drop to his side. "But now that you're home, moving on to pursue your destiny, I keep wondering—what is mine?" His features slackened with an unfamiliar sadness. "I'm only really good at a few things, and they're not things that I'm proud of."

Seren's gaze flickered to Jude's hands, where water still dripped between his fingers. The strange idea crossed his mind to grab Jude's hand, but he didn't.

"I know you hate all of this," Jude sighed. "Everyone telling you what your destiny is and the expectations that you're meant to fill." His honeyed brows drew together. "And I understand why. You have every right to feel the way you do. So, don't be angry when I say this, but a piece of me is...jealous." He winced as the words came out.

"What? Why?"

"Because at least you have a place in this world," Jude said. "I can't seem to figure out where I belong."

Seren blinked, caught off guard by the honesty in Jude's voice. The fluttering in his stomach became a knot, a mix of guilt and something else he couldn't name.

Jude laughed, though it carried no joy. "Maybe that's why the Godless City felt right," he admitted. "There's no purpose there, no expectations. Just surviving day by day. Get the bad guys and make money. And for a while, that felt like enough. But now...now I'm not so sure."

"What if you belong with me?" The words tumbled out of Seren before he could stop them. He turned away and cursed under his breath, heat rushing to his cheeks. Gods, he sounded ridiculous, didn't he? Desperate and pathetic.

Jude didn't respond.

The quiet stretched between them, heavy and unforgiving.

"What...would you say if I asked you to stay?" Seren finally whispered. "Maybe it's silly to ask, and I understand if you don't want to. I know all of this was only a job. But I just..." He took a deep breath, and turned to face Jude, back straight. "I don't want to say goodbye."

Jude ran his fingers through his tangled curls, casting his eyes skyward. "If you asked me to stay, I'd ask you for how long. If you asked me to stay until morning, then I would leave when the sun rose. If you said until you grew tired of me, then I'd leave quietly in the night as you slept. But if you asked me to stay until the end..." He turned to Seren, his blue eyes gleaming with something unspoken. "Well, then, I would never leave your side."

Seren's heart pounded in his chest, and he failed to find the right words. Instead, he stared at Jude with a vacant expression—willing himself to say something—anything.

"I mean it, Seren. I will help you reach the stars if you'll have me." Jude smiled, as bright as morning. "Maybe I'll get lucky, and *you'll* be my destiny."

Seren couldn't stop the pathetic words from leaving him. "And we'd never have to say goodbye?"

Jude smiled. "Never."

"Then, I'm asking."

Jude took a step closer. "For how long?"

"Till the end."

The air shifted between them in a way Seren couldn't explain, and he found himself looking at Jude in a way he never had before. Beneath the moon and starlit sky, with his messy curls and that devilish smile, Jude seemed to shine, radiant as the sun itself. Seren drank in the moment, captivated by how Jude's golden skin glistened in the faint light.

Why was Seren's heart racing?

Had Jude always looked like that?

"I just wonder what the end means for us," Jude said, head tilting.

"Who knows," Seren said, shrugging nonchalantly. "Want to find out?"

Jude drew closer and Seren's heart betrayed him, startling against his ribs. An arm swung around Seren pulling him in close, ruffling his hair. "You're not just saying that because you're a sappy drunk, are you?"

Seren flushed. Truthfully, the alcohol wore off much too fast on him and his head had cleared since he was pulled from the water. And the truth had not changed. He'd woken up in a world with Jude in it, and for them to part ways... Well, that thought bloomed into an ache across Seren's chest. It was almost worse than the sting he had felt from Mila's words.

Was it naïve of Seren to still hope, after everything, that this could be real? Maybe Jude would stay with Seren? That he wouldn't have to face his fears alone? He didn't want to be alone anymore. But what Seren was asking was selfish. This was his fate to carry, it wasn't meant for anyone else. That's what he'd been told. It was too much to ask, too much of a burden.

It wouldn't be long until the celebrations ended, and the comfortable smells and sights were far behind Seren. He couldn't deny the fear that lurked beneath the surface. And he couldn't bear to tell Jude that, if he stayed, they would have to journey through Andanova in search of the harp. But right now, it was not the time. Seren would enjoy this moment, the closeness. Jude by his side making promises. It drowned out everything else.

It was enough.

Jude cleared his throat and released Seren. "You know…" He trailed off. "There's something I want to say, but I don't want it to change anything between us."

Seren blinked, caught off guard by the sudden seriousness in Jude's tone. "What is it?"

"Well," Jude started, then hesitated. "It's just that…" He paused again. Was it the lighting, or were his ears turning pink beneath his curls?

"Seren, I—"

"Seren!" a voice boomed.

Aiden strode across the courtyard, dark hair plastered to his forehead and sweat trickling down his temples.

"Oh, shit," Seren grumbled.

Aiden approached the edge of the pond. "I've been looking all over for you," he hissed. "There are significant matters at hand here, and what're you doing? Splashing in the water like a *child*. Get out of the water, Seren."

Seren flinched. Without a word, he trudged out of the water, Jude following behind.

"Sir, it really was my fault," Jude began. "I shouldn't have—"

"Enough!" Aiden snapped, cutting him off. "I'm done with your sneaking and lies. Leave the cathedral at once. You're no longer welcome here."

Seren wrapped his soaked robes closer to his body. "Leave Jude out of this," he demanded. "This has nothing to do with him."

Jude placed a hand on Seren's shoulder. "It's alright," he said. "I don't want to cause any more trouble for you. I should go." His voice dropped to a whisper, his head bowed. "We'll see each other again soon. I promise."

Seren took a deep breath, his tense shoulders relaxing. He shot a glare at Aiden. "Okay," he said with a hint of defeat. "I'll see you later, then."

Jude nodded and moved to gather his clothes.

"Come, Seren," Aiden said. "*Now.*"

Seren scowled and crossed his arms over his chest as he followed Aiden. A familiar weight of disappointment settled in his belly. Aiden remained silent as they walked through the echoing halls. It was empty and quiet, and Seren assumed the celebration had come to an end after his disappearance. Upon reaching the stairs to Seren's chamber, Aiden halted.

"I'm disappointed in you," Aiden said, his back still turned to him.

"What's new?" Seren spat. Water dripped from his robes, pooling on the creamy marble floor. "I've always disappointed you."

Aiden reeled around, dark eyes flashing with anger. "You're an adult, Seren. It's time you start acting like one. You ran off from a very important event to behave like a *child*."

There it was again. Aiden said the word with such disdain.

"When was I ever allowed to *be* a child?" Seren's voice echoed down the corridor. He took a step toward Aiden, his fists balling at his side. Once, Seren had been smaller, looking up at Aiden. But somehow, in the years that had passed, it was now Aiden who had to look up at him. "I had no friends. I had no freedom. And no matter how hard I tried, I still failed to fit your perfect image." But Seren didn't stop. The anger was unrelenting, something he had buried for too long. "I'm sorry that I'm not who you want me to be. I'm sorry that I am a disappointment. If you have an issue with that, maybe you should take it up with your gods."

Before Aiden could respond, Seren stormed past him and ascended the winding staircase. His skin itched, the rage writhing beneath the surface almost too much to bear. He left Aiden behind. Tried to leave his anger behind. As he climbed, one thought pulsed through his mind, like a steady heartbeat: *Till the end.*

Fifteen

"If the devil was born from the malice of humankind, where was malice born? Where does darkness live if not in our hearts and in our bones? I see only darkness. Darkness. It calls and awaits to be answered."

—the Personal Diaries of Felix Amos

Nine years ago

The creature nuzzled the woman's neck, its sapphire eyes glistening in the sunlight filtering through the golden leaves. She ran her hand along the bridge of its nose, careful to avoid the sacred horn in the center of its forehead. With a long sigh, she leaned against the tree as a breeze stirred her red tresses.

Any minute now, he would be here. She was always waiting for him, and he never failed to come. She sensed him before she saw him—a subtle prickle traveling across her skin, raising the hair on her arms.

"Do you make it a habit to stare?" she asked with a smile, peeking behind the tree to meet his amber eyes.

With a chuckle, he strode past her, his dark hair curling around his ears like tamed waves. He was always breathtaking. She had once told him under a clear sky that he was a cruel beauty—not quite like the sun, dangerous and blinding, nor like the moon, soft and subtle. He smiled, a faint glow emanating from his skin.

"A god can do as he pleases," he said, his voice a warm caress.

She raised an eyebrow. "And what does my god bid to do today?"

"Your god?" he purred. He moved in circles around her, his thin white robes fluttering even though there was no breeze.

She stood, bare feet meeting the plush moss beneath her. He was taller, stronger, and far more beautiful. She wondered what would happen if she touched him. Would her fingers turn to ash? Would she cease to exist, becoming stardust?

"Well, you must be my god," she said. "For you are the only god who visits the garden, the only god I pray to, the only god I wait for."

"Blasphemous," he said, though he was still smiling.

She took a step forward, the urge to reach out almost unbearable. He drew back, smile fading, and her hand faltered, disappointment settling in her belly. He looked away, his mouth a tight line.

"Is it possible for a god to look so defeated?" she whispered.

A muscle twitched in his throat. "Gods can be many things."

"Joyous?" She tilted her head, her voice soft but pressing.

"Sometimes." His gaze flickered away, just for a moment.

She took a step forward, eyes narrowing. "Wrathful?"

"Often." His jaw tightened as if bracing for her next question.

"Covetous?" Her voice dropped to a whisper, the tension between them thickening.

He remained unresponsive, his body rigid.

She smiled carefully. "Gods have many secrets as well. Do they not?"

"You test me," he said in a monotone. "It is unwise."

The woman twirled a piece of red hair between her fingers. "And yet, here you are again. Why is that?" The white creature whinnied, nudging her in the back. She stumbled into him, her eyes meeting that golden gaze. There was no burst of flames, no burning at his touch. He was warm—soft—human. The scent of a midnight summer sky washed over her.

He peeled her hands away, his face expressionless. "I am a god; I can do what I desire."

"And what is it that you desire?" she breathed.

Amber eyes blazed, but he spoke no words.

"I only belong to him because the other gods bid it." She bit her tongue. "Do you bid it as well?"

He stepped closer, sunlight cradling the curves of his face. "You speak dangerous words."

"I am unafraid."

"You're curious," he said. "I have never met a mortal who did not fear the gods until you."

"Should I fear you?" she whispered.

"Perhaps," he mused, his hand brushing beneath her chin. "Or perhaps it is I who should fear you."

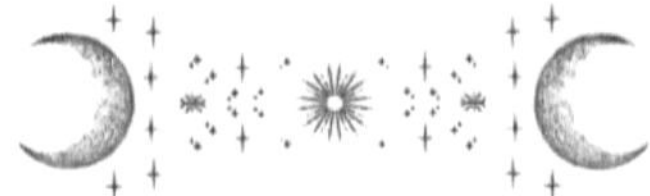

Emeryn's head smacked against the wooden desk. With a curse, she rubbed the bump on her forehead. She had fallen asleep again. She rubbed her eyes, peering out the window. The wind howled and tore through the limbs of the trees without mercy. Zephyr, God of the Wind, must've been in a foul mood.

Emeryn sighed and closed the book in front of her, pushing it aside. Her head ached with fatigue, and a yawn escaped her. The endless scriptures, filled with metaphors and riddles, were tiring to get through. No wonder Aiden was always so worn out.

"Still here?"

Under the flickering candlelight, eyes as dark as a bottomless lake locked onto Emeryn's. His torso bore sluggishly bleeding claw marks, and a fresh cut marred his squared, stubbled jaw. His bronzed skin was smeared with blood and dirt.

"Damian, you're hurt."

Without hesitation, Emeryn stood and walked to the washroom. She grabbed a cloth and wet it before returning. She beckoned Damian over and dabbed his face, grimacing at his wounds. He peered intensely into her eyes, not moving a muscle.

"There was a nasty demon loose in Larimar," he said with a tired sigh. His dark brows came together as he leaned against a bookcase. "Why are you still here? You were supposed to go home."

"I'm not ready to go home," she murmured, pressing the cloth into his cut. Damian flinched. "You should rest. I can wrap your wounds." She reached for the slashes on his chest, but he seized her fingers. Darkness spread over his hand like soot up to his knuckles.

"What're we doing, Em?" he said, exhaustion weighing his voice down. "Do you want something more from me?"

Emeryn was silent and lifted his torn shirt over his head. She ran her fingers across his shoulders, feeling him shiver under her touch. Her hands grazed up his skin finding the edge of his jaw. His expression shifted, a deep yearning evident.

Emeryn pressed her lips to Damian's, the taste of iron on her tongue. Damian was never gentle. His kisses were hungry, rough, and his callused hands quick to find their place over her hips. Emeryn turned off every thought racing inside her and focused on the feel of his hands on her body.

Help me forget, she wanted to beg.

The dreams were haunting her.

Thoughts consuming her.

Her blood. All of her deaths. And those amber eyes that never forgot her.

Damian sat up in bed, his scarred chest cloaked in shadows by the wavering candlelight. Though shallow, his wounds had been carefully cleaned and wrapped by Emeryn. He looked at her, a boyish grin spreading across his face. She lay across from him, her body covered by satin sheets. Blue smoke curled into the air as he brought a glass pipe filled with a sweet-smelling substance to his lips. He sucked the smoke between his teeth, his pupils widening before he set the pipe down.

"Somnia can make you go mad if you're not careful," Emeryn scolded. "I really wish you'd stop smoking it."

It was a common drug within Vavilon because of the way it blurred dreams and reality together. Some people had sweeter dreams than others, and some got so lost inside them that they couldn't find their way back to themselves.

Damian cocked an eyebrow. "It's only a bit," he replied defensively. "I like the dreams it gives me. Besides..." He wiggled his blackened fingers. "It doesn't matter anyway—I'll be dead soon enough."

"Are all exorcists so eager for their death?" she sighed.

"Do all holy women barter their body for favors?"

Emeryn clenched her jaw. "I am no holy woman," she said stiffly. "Must you always be so brutish?"

"I am just as brutish as you are beautiful," he replied, a wry smile playing on his lips, "and I think both have served us well." He reached toward the bedside table, his fingers closing around a glass vial filled with shimmering blue powder. "So, tell me the truth, Em. What do you truly want?"

Emeryn sat up, the blankets pulling taut as she drew them to her throat. "Nothing more than what I've already asked for. I just wanted company tonight." And she spoke the truth. Loneliness had long settled into her, a weight that refused to relinquish its hold. Sometimes, Emeryn liked to pretend her heart was free to give, but the illusion never lasted.

Damian rolled his neck on his scarred shoulders, a weary sigh escaping his lips as he filled the pipe with blue dust. "I'll never trust a woman who is as clever as she is charming, but I suppose it's too late for that. This trinket must be important." He closed the vial, setting it on the table.

"Very."

"Alright then." Damian's eyelids grew heavy as the Somnia began to claim him. A sideways smile lifted his cheek. His hands fell to his side, powder spilling onto the blankets. "I'll do my best to bring it back. If I come back alive, that is."

Emeryn's frown deepened as Damian twitched and slipped into a Somnia-induced sleep. She reached for the pipe, setting it back on the table. With a resigned sigh, she snatched the blankets from the bed, wrapped them around herself, and crossed the room. Emeryn stared out the window, watching the storm rage on.

Damian had promised to retrieve the lullabox but worry gnawed at her. She would pray for Damian's safety, and for his success, but she didn't dare speak to the gods. They wouldn't listen anyway. Instead, she released her hope into the air, as if fate was a living, breathing thing that would hear her.

Exorcists never lived long, whether it was at the death of their curses or the hands of a demon. The Order of Azazel had entrusted Damian with this dangerous mission not only because he was one of their strongest exorcists, but because his curse was closing in. His journey would take him to Andanova, where he would confront a fearsome demon sorcerer known among exorcists as the Withered One.

Emeryn pulled on her faded green dress and tied her hair back. She didn't bother to be quiet, knowing Damian would be asleep for hours. She closed the door as she slipped out of the room. It wasn't that Emeryn didn't care for Damian, but she had no desire to sleep next to him. She had always done the same with Aiden, sneaking from his bed in the dead of night.

As Emeryn made her way through the dimly lit hallways, the licking flames of the melting candles danced before her. Eventually, she reached the main chamber of the manor, which was bathed in a feeble glow emanating from an oil lamp on the verge of burning out.

Towering bookshelves draped in cobwebs lined the walls of the room. The Silver Manor had fallen into neglect, dust blanketing every surface.

After inheriting the manor from his late mentor, Damian dismissed all the servants. He had kindly offered it to Emeryn as a temporary residence during her stay in Aestus. However, soon she would depart for the capital of Wreiss in search of a Seer. And hopefully, after that, she could finally go home.

Emeryn sat at a dusty desk, reaching for a quill and ink. She grabbed a stained piece of parchment. But she could not find the words to write. Her hand hovered above the empty page. Ink droplets spattered the paper as she stared at it through bleary eyes.

"Oh, Seren," she whispered as the quill slipped from her grasp. She buried her face in her hands. "I hope you can forgive me."

Emeryn longed to return to Stellaris, to cradle her son in her arms. But Aiden had been caring for him, imparting the teachings of the Trinity, which took precedence over everything else. Someday, Seren would understand that she had only done what she thought was best—that everything was to protect him and his destiny.

A shiver raced down Emeryn's spine as she lifted her head and came face to face with a pair of penetrating amber eyes staring at her from the shadows of the chamber's entrance.

"Ah, forgiveness," he said, his voice carrying a wintry edge. "One can't expect it to be given as freely as they hope, can they?"

Emeryn's heart skipped a beat.

"I always thought forgiveness was such an interesting concept," he continued. He stepped into the light and ran long fingers through his dark hair, the white streak starker than ever. "It's like biting into a crisp apple, only to find maggots crawling into your throat. *Deceptive*."

Samael wore a long coat as black as night, moving like a shadow through the study toward her. Emeryn froze as he hovered behind, pressing his finger into the wet ink. Samael's hot breath engulfed the back of her neck as he leaned closer, his lips barely grazing her cheek.

"You've been busy," he whispered. "A High Priest, a famed exorcist, a god? What's next, a demon?"

Emeryn jumped to her feet, the chair toppling to the floor behind her. She barreled past Samael. "It's none of your business."

Samael blocked her, his movement like lightning, appearing in her path in a blink. Emeryn's back collided with the bookshelf as he pressed himself against her, cobwebs sticking to her hair.

"Perhaps not," Samael said. He reached out, grabbing a loose tendril of red. "But can you blame me for my jealousy?"

Emeryn turned her face away. "What do you want?"

"What do you think I want?" Samael asked, laughing bitterly. "The same thing I've always wanted. You." His fingers brushed under her chin, bringing her eyes to meet his. "Do you truly think this would make me hate you?"

Emeryn's face burned with humiliation.

"It doesn't matter how many men you sway," Samael crooned. "It doesn't matter how many times you say you hate me if it is my name on your lips and nobody else's." His stare burned right through her. "We've done this dance many times, and I would dance with you for eternity."

"I'm done dancing," Emeryn said, pushing his hands away. "You're nothing but a stranger to me."

A low growl rumbled in Samael's throat as he neared her, his lips inches from hers. "I am no stranger; I have always known you."

"You know nothing," Emeryn spat.

Samael brushed a thumb across her lip, and Emeryn's heart betrayed her, beating like a caged bird against her ribs.

"If I do not know you, then why, when you kiss another, does jealousy burn within me, and there is no quelling it? The more you tell me to stay away, the hungrier I become for even a moment of your attention. Even if you hate me, at least I am on your mind. Even if you curse me, at least you speak my name upon your lips. Even if I have become your nightmare, at least you still dream of me. That has always been enough because I have always been yours, and you have always been mine. We are anything but strangers."

Samael crushed his lips against Emeryn's. She should have pushed him away. She should have made him stop. But the intense familiarity stirred uncontrollable emotions within her, and the desire was stronger than anything else.

As Samael kissed her deeper, his hands cradled her face, fingertips brushing against her skin with a tenderness that made her ache. Emeryn felt the world around them blur; the storm outside faded into a distant murmur, leaving only the pounding of her heart echoing in her ears. Every fiber of her being screamed to respond, to surrender to the fire that blazed between them. She knew if she didn't pull away, she would burn.

Emeryn pushed against Samael's chest. He pulled away ever so slightly.

"We can't keep doing this," she whispered.

"Why?" Samael asked softly. "Come back to me, Emeryn. I will keep you safe. I'll keep Seren safe."

Emeryn was still. "He'll never be safe with you. You know that."

Darkness flickered in Samael's gaze. "You don't trust me."

"And should I?"

Samael was silent.

"You have to stop," she said, voice breaking. "You have to let me go."

Samael stiffened.

"I once asked you if gods dream," she said. "Long ago you said, 'Gods seldom dream, for gods do not sleep. And yet, I have dreamt of you with every breath and every beat of my immortal heart.'"

Samael's eyes widened. "How do you...?"

His face had never changed, an immortal beauty that had remained frozen in every lifetime.

"I remember everything."

Samael grew rigid, not daring to move as Emeryn leaned closer, lips brushing his ear. The name rolled off her tongue—a memory—a past unearthed from over a hundred lives and deaths. When she spoke his true name, the breath in Samael's throat hitched.

"That's impossible," he breathed.

Emeryn's hands wrapped around his clenched fists. "Gods should not dream." She pressed his palm to her cheek. "Look at what it has done to you."

"No, look at what *they* have done to *us*," Samael said, gripping her wrists, amber eyes fevered. His face distorted, somewhere between pain and shock.

"And you allow it," Emeryn replied, tears clinging to her eyes. "You never let me go. In every life you find me, and in every life, we fall deeper into a love that drowns us."

"It is hard for me too," Samael said fiercely, "to see you suffer so. I will end it. I have always found a way for us, and I will find one again. I love you. With everything I am, I love you. Is that not enough?"

Emeryn remained quiet.

"Of course," he said, clicking his tongue. He took a step back, raking a hand through his dark hair. "It was enough until he was born. You changed. Your blessing is but another curse for me." Samael didn't appear bitter, though; his visage held a particular apathy.

"He's your son."

"And *you* were *mine*!" The candles extinguished as Samael's voice rattled the chamber.

Emeryn sucked in a breath. When she looked into Samael's beautiful, immortal face, she saw the same anger that brewed beneath the surface in Seren.

"I was never yours," Emeryn whispered. She closed the space between them, her lips so close that she could feel his hot breath upon her skin. "I belong to no one. Or is that something you have forgotten?"

Sixteen

"The Great War raged day and night until the years bled together, staining the realms with the color of hate."

—Histories of Aerithium

The many eyes of the painted gods followed Seren as he soaked in the hot water. Their gazes glinted with molten gold and silvery starlight, unblinking and all-seeing through the steam curling toward the vaulted ceiling. Seren turned his head with a sigh, muttering under his breath about whose brilliant idea it had been to paint the gods on the bathhouse walls.

The gods certainly didn't need to see *everything*.

Seren had lost track of how many days had passed since the celebration. Three? Four? He wasn't sure. Word of his identity had spread quickly. The eldest prince of Kogarashi was blessed with another healthy daughter. His wife had survived childbirth despite the midwives believing neither of them would make it. The Mother's promise fulfilled had swept across the country, and now the King of Kogarashi himself had built a shrine in the Mother's honor.

It was strange, knowing Seren was responsible for so much...hope. Duty had settled on his shoulders, and there was no removing it.

Everything had changed.

Seren hadn't seen anyone besides Aiden and acolytes for days. The Grand Priest had been busy with his own duties. Most of Seren's time had been spent confined to his room, guarded by acolytes who rotated shifts outside his door.

Sleep was still a struggle; his nights were plagued by blood-soaked dreams of his mother—and of Anna. Dreams filled with all the things he desperately wanted to forget. Sometimes, he dreamed of driving his sword into Lord Glynn's chest, only for Anna to appear in his place, lifeless at his feet. He would wake shouting, drenched in sweat, as panicked acolytes burst into his room.

Maybe it was the lack of sleep or the nightmares, but Aiden had become increasingly irritating. Seren had begged him to dismiss the acolytes. It was humiliating. "It's just until the excitement dies down," Aiden had replied, though Seren wasn't sure he believed him.

Even the acolytes and handmaidens didn't act normal around Seren. Their nervous stares and awkward attempts at conversation betrayed their fascination. They stumbled over their words while delivering meals or escorting him to the bathhouse. Seren hated every second of it.

But Aiden's behavior had also been...off. He was too watchful, too careful with his words. When they spoke, his gaze lingered on Seren's face, and more than once, Seren had caught him glancing at his dark circles or the exhaustion that pulled at his features. He was trying not to notice, but it was there, Aiden's quiet observation.

Even the meal earlier had been an obvious attempt from Aiden, a meal that had sparked a memory of Seren's days in Stellaris. A warm loaf of bread with an array of cheeses and sweet berries, summer foods he had favored as a child. The gesture was kind enough, but Seren couldn't shake the feeling that Aiden was trying too hard. Was it genuine kindness or just an attempt to ease the tension between them? Seren couldn't tell nor did he care.

Seren leaned his head back, eyes closing for a moment. He should've been grateful. But it was all too much, too soon. He gripped the side of the tub, the cool stone grounding him. He just needed to escape for a moment. He needed away from Aiden's pity, away from his own mind, from the prying eyes of acolytes. Away from it all. The bathhouse was the closest thing to escape, and even still, the acolytes stood guard outside the doors.

If anything, Seren wanted to see Jude and Mila, but at this rate, it would be impossible.

Seren sighed, staring at the water's surface. The thought tightened his chest, and guilt rose like a lump in his throat. He'd made such a fool of himself with Mila. His sleep-deprived, wine-addled mind had ruined everything, and now he was left with nothing but regret. At least now, he knew the truth. Mila did not love him, and he'd been an idiot for thinking she might. Maybe it was better this way.

And Jude...

Seren missed him terribly. His stupid jokes and his ridiculous smile. However, Seren wondered what it was that Jude had wanted to tell him that night before Aiden's interruption. Jude had looked so serious, nervous even. It was strange.

Seren's hands skimmed over his ribs, the touch feather-light, before faltering. His fingers hovered over the hideous scars on his back. He clenched them into fists instead, sinking deeper into the water.

A knock echoed on the doors of the chamber, startling Seren. His breath hitched, and he sank deeper into the water, quickly tugging his arms back to hide the scars. "Yes?"

The engraved doors cracked open. "Your Grace..."

Seren cringed at the title, one he'd repeatedly asked not to be called over the past few days.

"Night is falling, and the Grand Priest requests your presence early in the morning. Perhaps, it's time to head back to your chambers?" the acolyte asked.

Seren gritted his teeth. Surely, Aiden was responsible for this too.

"Alright," he said, defeated. "Just let me get dressed."

The door closed, and Seren pulled himself out of the water, shaking his head like a dog, droplets spattering across the quartz tiles. Wrapping a towel around his waist, he reached for his clothes. Much to Aiden's dismay, Seren refused to parade around in heavy, white robes. Instead, he tugged on black trousers and a simple shirt with a sigh before leaving the bathhouse.

The acolyte led Seren through the cathedral's silent halls, where the light of candles reflected off the polished stone. By the time they reached Seren's chamber, night had fully fallen. Inside, a kettle of tea waited on his bedside table, the scent of lavender and lemon wafting through the room. *My favorite*, Seren realized, another memory revealed. Aiden must have had it sent up. Beside the teapot sat a dark green glass vial along with a note, undeniably Aiden's handwriting.

I know you haven't been sleeping. This should help you. Take a drop or two in your tea for restful sleep. Tomorrow is an important day. —Aiden

Seren scoffed, rolling his eyes as he poured himself a cup of hot tea. Drifting to the window, he paused, drawn by the sight outside. The crescent moon hung high, its silver glow washing over the garden below. He ached to be out there, beneath that sky. Alone. His gaze flicked from the draught to the tea in his hand.

Seren opened the vial, the scent of herbs filling his nose.

Just a few drops... he thought as he tipped it over the cup's edge. Then, Seren poured the entire vial into the cup, stirring slowly.

Seren strode to the door and opened it. The acolyte standing at his door straightened his posture. "Are you alright, Your Grace?"

Seren held the teacup out, wrinkling his nose. "This tea doesn't taste right," he said, offering it to the acolyte.

The man hesitated. "It smells fine to me, Your Grace."

Seren frowned, his voice laced with feigned concern. "Perhaps, but with all the strange herbs they use, it's hard to tell. It wouldn't hurt to be certain, would it? Just a sip to set my mind at ease."

The acolyte shifted on his feet, then nodded. "Of course." He raised the cup to his lips and took a drink. "Hmm, you're right. It does taste a little odd, but I don't believe it's anything dangerous."

Seren's lips quirked into a faint smile. "Ah, well. I guess it just isn't the best blend tonight."

The acolyte handed the cup back. Seren thanked him, shut the door, and leaned against it, his heart pounding as he waited for the draught to take effect. Had the man drank enough? The moments stretched until an hour, perhaps even two passed by. And just when he thought he might have miscalculated, a soft thud echoed from the hallway.

Seren cracked the door open. The acolyte was slumped against the wall, his chest rising and falling in a steady rhythm. Seren smirked.

Finally.

He moved quickly, grabbing his charcoal-grey cloak and pulling the hood low over his face. A pang of guilt flickered in his chest as he slipped out and down the stairwell. The dim light from dying candles cast the steps in a wavering glow, the ivory wax pooling in uneven rivulets.

Seren emerged into the darkened hallway. His steps were slow, measured, in case any other priests or acolytes were wandering about. But the corridor was empty, the stillness of the night pressing down like a heavy blanket. As long as he stayed away from the guarded entrance, he could avoid getting caught.

Seren wasn't sure where he was going; he only knew he needed to be alone. No acolytes stationed outside his door. No painted gods staring down from the ceiling or on bathhouse walls. No Aiden with his watchful eyes and constant reminders. Just a moment to breathe, to exist, without anyone or anything weighing on him.

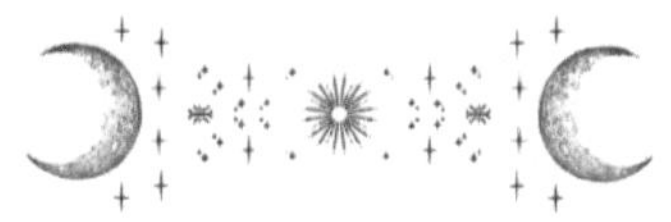

The first door Seren found led outside to one of the holy gardens. He breathed in the perfumed night air with relief, striding across the stones that wound deeper into the garden. There was no shortage of gardens around the cathedral, some for medicinal herbs, others for prayer, and a few that seemed to exist solely for their beauty. Seren hadn't been in this particular one before, but it was mesmerizing. Unlike the others, the flowers here hadn't been trimmed back. They were wild and overgrown, threading through the cracks in the stone and climbing the terraces of the cathedral.

Fountains glimmered in the moonlight, carved from marble with impossible intricacy. They formed a nearly perfect circle, each spaced evenly and portraying a figure, each a strikingly beautiful man, naked with wings arching from their backs. *Angels*, Seren noted as he scanned them, mentally counting. Seven. They had to be the seven angels who fell to cleanse the Veil, now remembered only as the Fallen. Their hands were outstretched, water trickling down their stone arms into the reservoirs below. Seren weaved toward them, his fingertips brushing against foxgloves and lavender.

Seren halted, his gaze drawn to the fountain in the center. It was cloaked in climbing roses, nearly camouflaged against the greenery of the garden. The blood-red flowers wound around the angel's calves and torso, trailing over his immense wings, their tips seeming to scrape the stars.

Seren approached the statue, fingers grazing the petals. The flower beneath his touch browned and crumbled into his palm. His breath hitched as one by one, all the flowers began to wither, as if the life had been sucked from them. He blinked, heart racing. The flowers were whole again—blood red, alive. He was seeing things.

Seren sat on the garden bench. It was nice here. Quiet. He let his nerves settle. He wasn't sure how much time had passed, but he stayed for what felt like hours, letting the stillness settle around him. At some point, his head grew heavy, and he rested against the garden wall. Darkness greeted him behind his eyelids, cold and welcoming.

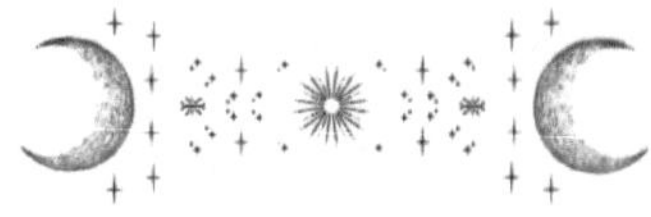

A faint scuff of a shoe against stone jolted Seren awake, followed by the echo of footsteps. He blinked through the haze, trying to shake off his drowsiness.

How long had he been asleep?

From the shadows of the garden, a boy emerged, no older than fifteen. Russet ringlets tumbled across his forehead, falling into eyes of an unusual milky green hue. Freckles, only a few shades darker than his deep bronze skin, scattered over his nose and cheeks. The boy's gaze fixed on Seren, yet it was distant, detached as if he was looking through him rather than at him.

He's blind, Seren realized.

A sleek weasel was perched on the boy's shoulder, its long brown body draped comfortably around his neck like a living scarf. Its black-tipped tail flicked as its deep brown eyes briefly met Seren's, and a glimpse of its cream underside showed as it shifted, curling closer.

"Alright, Theo, playtime," the boy said with a grin. He grasped the weasel, setting it on the ground. The creature jumped into a sea of flowers, disappearing in an instant.

Unlike the acolytes, who wore powder-blue robes, the boy was clad in a dark green cloak that swamped his small frame. Seren had never seen him before. Maybe he was a resident of the estate and was out for a nighttime stroll. Either way, he hadn't acknowledged Seren's presence, or perhaps he hadn't taken any notice of him yet. Seren stood still for a moment before quietly walking across the stone path, preparing to head inside.

"Admiring the fountains?" the boy chimed.

Seren froze and turned in surprise to meet the boy's amused smile.

"Yeah...I was just leaving."

"I've heard they're quite something," the boy said. He motioned toward his eyes. "Not that I would know. Can you explain them to me?"

Seren cleared his throat and strode back toward the fountains. He raked a hand through his hair with a sigh. "Uh, well, they're angels made from stone. The one in the middle is covered in red roses..." He winced, trailing off. "I'm sorry, I'm not very good at this."

The boy chuckled and adjusted the cloak around his shoulders. "It's alright. I should introduce myself anyway. My name is Felix."

"Nice to meet you," Seren said slowly. "I'm—"

"Seren," the boy finished. "I know who you are."

Seren blinked, unsure what to say. "Oh."

"The one with the roses is Lucifer, isn't it? Is that the one you're admiring?" The boy's milky-green eyes shone curiously.

Seren's eyes wandered back to the angel's face. "I was, yeah," he said quietly. There was a long moment of silence as Seren traced the wings of the angel. "It's a little strange though, isn't it? To keep it? Even though he became the Devil."

"Not really," Felix said, settling on the garden bench. The weasel momentarily popped its head out of the flowers, its nose twitching before diving back into the greenery. Felix reached for a flower, his fingers delicately tracing the petals of a blue cornflower. "It's good to have reminders of what was, and what could be. That's what my grandfather taught me anyways."

Seren sighed and found himself settling on the bench beside Felix. He supposed it was better than going back to his room and waiting for the sun to rise.

"Do you ever wonder...if he regrets it? Falling from grace to become what he was?" The question slipped out before Seren could stop it, an unguarded thought from a place of quiet loneliness.

Felix smiled faintly. "Not really," he said. "It is said that he wanted to be a god. When the gods refused him, he was cast out. All that bitterness and all that wanting...turned him into what he is now." He paused, as if lost in thought. "But I imagine it must be lonely to have made enemies of all those you'd once followed. Still, it's a very human thing, isn't it? To want what you can't have."

An unfamiliar pang echoed in Seren's chest. His gaze swept across the fountain statues again, their immortalized forms, water trickling from their outstretched hands. The Fallen, he knew, had tried to cleanse the Veil after the corruption, to undo what Lucifer, the most powerful angel, had done. And for that, they'd been twisted alongside him, just like the very thing they'd sought to fix.

"I suppose he's my enemy now," Seren said, voice soft. "Isn't he?"

Something skittered across Seren's boots, and he glanced down at the weasel tugging at his pant legs. Seren moved hesitantly, pleased when the creature allowed him to scratch between its ears.

"I think a true enemy is someone you hate with all your being," Felix said, tilting his head. "Do you hate him?"

It was a strange question. Did Seren hate the Devil? He was the one responsible for cursing their world, wasn't he? But wasn't their world already cursed, whether by demons or the Veil? It hadn't been the Devil who killed Seren's mother. It hadn't been the Veil that killed Anna; it had been the hands of a mortal man. It wasn't a demon who tore the wings from Seren's back or pumped him full of Somnia, it had been a scientist in a city of forbidden technology.

And he hated them. Didn't he?

He'd killed Lord Glynn because in that moment, he'd felt an unprecedented hatred that he had no control over. Seren had believed the lord deserved death. And Lumen...

Something twisted inside Seren. He pictured those cat-like yellow eyes, that vulpine smile, his long pale hair and alabaster skin. Seren had hated Lumen too when he remembered what he'd done to him. And he still wanted to kill him. Right?

The sun was rising in the distance, coloring the sky blue and stealing the stars. And for some reason, a memory stirred within Seren. Something long buried, revealing itself for but a ghostly moment.

"Why do you hate the gods so much?"

Lumen's pale eyes flicked to the starless sky, his thin lips pressing into a tight line. "Because even when I called for them, in my deepest despair, they never answered. They left me completely and utterly alone."

Seren's hand drifted to his chest, resting above his heart. "I think... I think I hate them too."

Something flickered in Lumen's expression, an emotion Seren couldn't place.

"You do not," Lumen said, his voice cool and measured. "To hate is to know, not to think. When you truly hate someone, it consumes you, just like love. It burns through everything else until it is all you are. You do not hate Seren, even when you should."

Seren clenched his fists. Lumen was wrong. There was hate inside him, that much he knew. It was deep, dark, and something that terrified him. If he allowed himself to truly confront everything he had locked away, what would he become?

"You have a busy day tomorrow," Felix said, pulling Seren from his thoughts. He clicked his tongue, and the weasel scurried toward him. Felix scooped him up and rose to his feet. "Don't stay out too long." He turned to walk away. "Though that drought is going to last longer than you expected."

Seren's eyebrows drew together. "Wait, how do you know that?" he asked. "Who are you?"

The boy chuckled. "I told you, my name is Felix. And we're going to be great friends."

Felix said it like a promise.

Seventeen

"In all that I am, affection cannot be taken from me. In all that I was, love held me together. But now, I wonder—how much longer can I endure before I am truly gone? Am I nothing more than the knowledge I've absorbed, the words I've spoken, the actions I've taken? What is this void that consumes me? This despair? I cannot see you anymore. Have you forgotten me, or have I forgotten you?"

—the Personal Diaries of Felix Amos

"Drugging an acolyte, Seren? The herbalist said he'll be asleep until next nightfall and it would've been longer if not for the herbs we have at hand." Aiden ran a frantic hand through his hair. "I really do apologize, Eldyir, for his behavior. I—"

The Grand Priest raised a hand to silence Aiden. "Enough, Aiden. The boy's feeling suffocated and Owen will recover just fine. I understand." He smiled at Seren. "The cathedral is well-guarded. I don't think it's necessary to have acolytes shadowing his every step."

Seren let out a grateful sigh, though he could've sworn he saw a vein twitch in Aiden's forehead. He placed a hand on his chin, his gaze drifting outside the window.

Aiden and the Grand Priest resumed their conversation, outlining Seren's tasks for the upcoming weeks. A detailed map was unfolded across the library table and the two of them spoke in steady, hushed tones.

On the Summer Solstice, just two months away, Seren would leave Lumina. A group of volunteered priests, and saints would accompany him, along with an exorcist. In the meantime, Seren would undergo training in holy magic.

Though Seren's memories were still fuzzy, he knew that Kallista's Harp, Caelum's Sword, and Helios' Crown were crucial for the Cleansing. These artifacts were directly tied to the Mother's magic and essential for purifying the Veil. Seren held his tongue, refraining from asking questions even as his head throbbed at the thought. How many hours had he spent studying as a child, preparing to wield these sacred items? He couldn't remember. All he could do was hope and pray that everything would slowly trickle back into his memory.

"Seren, are you going to answer the Grand Priest or sit with your head in the clouds?"

Seren frowned, meeting Aiden's impatient glare.

"Oh, I'm sorry, I didn't realize I was included in this conversation," Seren said bitterly. "It seems you both have my entire destiny planned out for me."

Aiden's eyebrows furrowed. "If you're going to act like—"

The Grand Priest waved his hand to silence Aiden once again. "Cycris, I can only imagine the pressure Seren is under. The celebration overwhelmed everyone, and his life has changed within a matter of days. He's been fussed over with no privacy and is preparing for a very dangerous journey." He smiled at Seren. "Perhaps one more day of rest before we start your training?"

"Can I leave the cathedral?" asked Seren anxiously. "I have a friend I'd like to see."

"No," Aiden snapped. "You are to remain in the cathedral."

Seren turned to Eldyir, hoping for a different answer, but his eyes gleamed, almost looking sad. "It's for your safety, Seren. I'm sorry."

Seren slumped against his chair with a sigh.

"We'll begin training first thing in the morning," Eldyir continued. "I will answer any questions you may have."

"I can train him," Aiden argued. "In my opinion, it would be best—"

"*I* will be training him. As the Grand Priest it is my duty," Eldyir interrupted. "Have faith." He set a hand on Aiden's shoulders and held out his hand, where a small seed sat settled in the cracks of his palm. Seren watched in awe as a flower of flames sprang up, a blaze of orange and yellow. "You see, Aiden? You feel it, too, do you not? There was belief. There was faith, even amongst the sea of worries and doubts. The Prince of Kogarashi has already named his child in Seren's honor. Soon, word will spread, and our magic will regain strength, even if it is only a small flicker. It only takes a spark to start a fire, and soon, embers will burn."

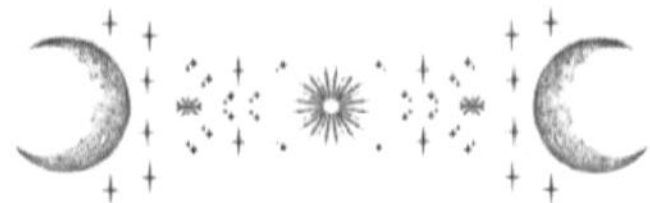

The next day arrived quickly. Seren rose from bed to find a note slipped under his door, instructing him to meet Eldyir in his private study on the western side of the cathedral. He dressed in a black button-up shirt, rolling the sleeves up to just below his elbows. Catching his reflection in the mirror, he frowned.

Running his fingers through his white hair, he wondered if there was a way to will it back to its dark color. Perhaps, after training with Eldyir, he could learn to control his Aura. He didn't want to resemble the Mother, and he missed the green of his mother's eyes. His thumb absently traced the ring on his finger.

When Seren left his room, there were no acolytes hovering outside his door this time. He hurried down the spiraling steps and collided with Aiden at the bottom of the staircase.

"Morning," Aiden said, impatiently adjusting the sleeves of his robes.

"Good morning."

"I'm being sent away to Sanctus for penance, and I may be gone for a day or two," Aiden said, sounding almost cold. "Good luck with Eldyir."

"Thanks."

Aiden turned, his navy-blue robes billowing behind him. Seren stood there until he disappeared down the hall, releasing the breath he was holding in his throat. A part of him was relieved that Aiden was leaving.

Seren walked through the corridors, brushing past priests and acolytes who walked by until he reached Eldyir's study. The doors were simple, carved from cherry wood with none of the intricacy that graced much of the cathedral. He supposed it made sense for a Grand Priest to choose an inconspicuous place to keep his private chamber.

Seren knocked on the door. It swung open at the touch of his knuckles. Stepping inside, he was surprised to find Eldyir nowhere in sight. In the corner of the room, a speckled white falcon perched silently, its sharp eyes flicking toward him before returning to some unseen point of interest, unimpressed by his presence.

The chamber exceeded Seren's expectations—filled with towering bookshelves, maps pinned to the walls, and paintings adorning everywhere the maps did not. Strange trinkets scattered the shelves and tables: compasses with crystal dials, white and blue rosaries dangling from ledges, and bundles of earth-colored incense sitting on painted porcelain plates.

Seren approached a large painting hanging on the leftmost wall. A massive mountain towered against an angry red sky with rings of clouds wrapped around the snowy peak like halos. The painting below showed many of the creatures Seren had seen in the church: a pale elk with a silver sword piercing its heart, a man between the jaws of an obsidian wyrm, and fire licking at the trees of the surrounding earth.

It's the Great War, Seren realized. His fingers brushed across the painting, a pang of sorrow entering his chest at the hatred depicted. So much death and destruction.

Eldyir's footsteps startled Seren as he approached from behind. "Quite the painting, isn't it? The Battle of Ethles, beneath the holy mountain."

"Terrible," Seren murmured, realizing his fingers were still touching the painting, resting on the wyrm. He pulled away.

Eldyir nodded. "Terrible indeed. War is the ugliest thing in this world. It swallows a man whole, strips the flesh from his bones, and spits him out, leaving no grave for him to lie in. It transforms men into monsters—and monsters back into men. It lays a man bare, leaving nothing but every hateful, writhing thought he's ever harbored."

"It seems pointless," Seren said. "So much...death."

"War is never without reason, whether good or ill," Eldyir said quietly. "But there is nothing fair or just about it." As Eldyir spoke, his brown eyes darkened as if the memories of bloodshed belonged to him.

Seren traced the rings of clouds around the mountain. "That's where Priests of the Trinity Etheles go to claim their magic, isn't it?"

Eldyir nodded, stepping forward, fingers running on the watery-inked edges of the painting. "Yes, at the peak of Etheles, there lies a pocket of purity," he said. "It is an untouched bridge between us and the gods that the corruption has not touched. There are very few of these places left in the world."

"You've truly spoken with the Gods of the Trinity?" Seren couldn't recall if he'd ever asked Aiden about his own journey to Etheles and found himself intrigued by the idea.

"Correct. Those deemed worthy receive a link to the borrowed magic of the gods, and the type of magic one receives depends on the god who grants it. For instance, the Saints of the Seas, blessed by Illiana, can manipulate water. The Priests of Harmony possess the ability to control emotions, dampening negative thoughts and feelings. The Saints of Zephyr can control the winds, while the Priests of Faunas have a special affinity with nature. The Priests of Kogarashi have mastered the ice and snow for Ryu, God of Wisdom. Disciples of Servius carry no magic but have always had a firm hand for justice and the law, and they are blessed accordingly."

Seren withheld his scoff.

"Priests of the Trinity are granted the power of light," Eldyir continued. "We are fortunate to have three gods who have remained united, never fractured by dissent or conflict. Others have not been so lucky."

Seren tilted his head. "But wasn't it different before? The seven noble families chose their gods and split apart, didn't they?"

Eldyir's expression softened. "Yes. Long ago, unity was fragile. When the noble families dedicated themselves to their chosen gods, they carved paths that shaped the world as we know it. But there were not seven, Seren, there were eight."

Seren blinked. "Eight?"

"We mustn't forget Jetharion Abjiviya, founder of the Godless City," Eldyir said. "Though he was of noble blood, he chose no god. There was a time when humans stood together, worshiping the gods as one. But war and death shattered that unity. Astrailis Lumina later founded the Trinity and built churches in their name hundreds of years ago. Her faith laid the foundation for all Priests and Priestesses of the Trinity."

Eldyir lifted his hand, releasing a careful stream of blue fire from his fingertips. "Despite corruption and evil, small purities have endured, keeping our connection to the gods alive. A priest or saint must dedicate their mind, body, and spirit to the gods before magic is granted to them. It is not given lightly."

Seren stared down at his palms, recalling the feeling of magic in his hand. Eldyir's hands wrapped around his. "You are different, Seren. You possess magic that is neither borrowed nor gifted. It belongs to you."

No, Seren thought. *It belongs to her.*

"I know I used magic at the celebration," Seren began, "but it doesn't come naturally to me. I've only used it in moments of desperation." He gulped, unsure why he was opening up to Eldyir. "I don't know how to do it on my own. She..."

"The Mother speaks through you from time to time," Eldyir said with a small smile. "It was a great pleasure to witness it."

"Yes," Seren said. "But it's sporadic. I don't... I was in the Godless City for some time and lost my way."

Eldyir rested his hand on Seren's shoulder. "You were grieving, Seren. The Unveiling of Stellaris was a tragic event, and you were only a child. Grief does not wait for anyone, and we will turn to any means necessary to forget the things that have hurt us."

Forget.

Seren searched Eldyir's face for a moment, wondering if he was somehow reading his thoughts, but the Grand Priest's expression gave nothing away.

The Grand Priest turned toward the painting of the mountain. "Aiden," he said, "speaks of you as if he expects you to perform miracles by tomorrow." Seren frowned. "That's why I didn't want him to train you. I could sense it in him from the beginning. Tell me, Seren, do you have any memories of your past life?"

Seren's cheeks burned. "No."

"Then, one cannot expect magic to come easily," Eldyir said. "You may be the reborn goddess, but you are still inexperienced." He smiled, shaking his head. "I remember when Aiden climbed Etheles with his younger brother. He was naïve and overconfident back then. When the gods gifted Aiden with magic and denied it to his brother, they gave upon him a higher form of magic, just as they once did with me. At first, he did not know how to control it or use it effectively. He, too, was reckless, though he would never admit it. After all, we are only human."

Human. The word plunged deep into Seren. Is this how the Grand Priest saw him? Not as a walking deity, but merely a boy with the power of a goddess living within him.

"I didn't realize Aiden had a brother," Seren managed.

"Ah yes," Eldyir said. "He left for Vavilon shortly after, embittered. If only I could've told him, the gods work in mysterious ways. I am certain they have unique plans for him. He is far too gifted to go unnoticed." He straightened his robes. "Now, tell me, has Aiden taught you any spells?"

"No," Seren began. "Well, yes. Just not...directly. I've seen him cast spells many times, but I never imagined I'd be casting them, too." He rubbed the back of his neck. "But I also never imagined I'd be journeying to Andanova, either."

"Ah yes, it's normal to be afraid, but faith is stronger than fear."

"Faith in the gods?"

Eldyir smiled. "In oneself. Your magic lives inside of you, an everlasting light that cannot burn out. You must feel it deep within yourself and accept it as part of who you are. It will come to you in times of need because it is a part of you. And if you call on it, it will answer." His smile grew. "And the more belief *others* have in you, the more you will become capable of great power."

"The Mother..." Seren trailed off. "What magic was she capable of?"

"A very powerful magic," Eldyir said. "She had the abilities of light, protection, healing, and creation. Above all, she had a love that encompassed everything. Creation is something priests and saints can't do; it's a power reserved for the gods. All energy is borrowed and must be returned."

Seren thought of the glass lotus he had somehow manifested from light, and the magic that pulsated through it that had protected two lives. Eldyir moved toward the window, looking toward the sun, his dark skin glistening.

"What a priest or saint can do has severe limitations," Eldyir continued. "There was once a time when we were capable of much more. Long ago, one could even choose to dedicate themselves to all the gods, wielding the borrowed power of every god. But those times are far behind us. Even with three gods siphoning power to the Trinity, we are still no stronger than those who worship one god. A human body can only withstand so much magic." He turned back to Seren. "Do you still remember the basic spells from your studies in Stellaris?"

Seren stiffened as Eldyir's hazel gaze burned into him. Was this a trick? Did the priest somehow know that Seren had forgotten much of his life? He hadn't told Aiden and didn't plan on telling him anytime soon.

"Yes," Seren lied.

"Good, then perhaps you can show me some?" The lines in Eldyir's smile deepened. "Most spells require verbal cues—but I have no doubts that with proper training, you will not need to speak them into existence."

"Sure."

Damn.

Seren gritted his teeth, his fingers curling. He didn't want to give away the gaps in his memory. He closed his eyes, trying to recall even just a glimpse of spells. Closed doors, harps, books, and more books. Then, a flicker of memory played behind his eyes. Aiden's white hands moving swiftly, his lips murmuring a spell, and the sensation of fire coursing through Seren's body. Seren had no idea what it did, but he didn't want to appear foolish by admitting to Eldyir that he had no clue how to perform magic.

Seren ran a finger over his forehead, crossed his heart, and felt a hum of magic within him. It flowed effortlessly. And when he opened his eyes, the Grand Priest had backed into the wall, his face ashen.

"A powerful spell used to seal away dark magic," Eldyir said quietly. "Not what I expected."

Seren's throat tightened as he stared down at the marks scorched into the floor—the very ones he had just burned with his magic, marks that had once been seared into his own skin.

"I'm sorry," he breathed. "I must have done the wrong one."

"It's alright," Eldyir said, his voice catching briefly. "Let's start with the basics, shall we?"

With a simple incantation, he removed the mark from the floor and made no more remarks on the spell. Eldyir pulled books from the shelves and began to recite spells to Seren.

Two hours went by, and with each lesson, familiarity rose in Seren, and he answered Eldyir's questions with ease. It was strange, knowing he had learned all the information before, and having it resurface. He'd been a stranger to himself for weeks. With each memory of knowledge, Seren found his confidence growing.

The first spell had come naturally to Seren, but he struggled to perform the new simple spells with control. When Eldyir asked him to conjure fire into his hand, Seren had produced measly sparks out of his fingertips the first time, and the second time, he'd almost set the entire study ablaze. And when asked to summon light, he was certain he'd blinded Eldyir before the Grand Priest had finally recovered. However, Seren did manage to create a small crystal and chose the shape of a falcon.

Sweat dripped down Seren's neck as he fell against the wall, huffing. "I can't get it right," he groaned. He slammed his fist onto the table, dangling rosaries falling to the floor.

"It'll take practice," Eldyir said. "Wielding magic comes from a place deep within. Think of it as a flame in the pit of your belly. You must draw out the warmth, willing the flame to grow until it's yours to command, without letting it burn you. But at the core of your magic, you hold the power of a deity, Seren. It could take years before you learn to control such power."

"Years?" Seren snapped. "The fate of the world depends on me, and you're telling me it could be *years* before I can access my full potential?" He rubbed his temples, a headache throbbing behind his eyes.

Eldyir sighed. "Let's take a break. You've done well today, despite what you may think."

Seren scoffed, pacing. "I'll be thrust into Andanova blindly, searching for the harp in just a matter of weeks. I need to do better than this."

Eldyir walked to his desk and retrieved a rolled-up parchment. With care, he unrolled it onto the table. Seren stepped closer, glancing over Eldyir's shoulder to see a detailed map.

"You will not go blindly," the priest assured him. "The Andanovan castle remains untouched by the demons that roam the land. The creature that rules the castle forbids them from entering. Many have ventured into its depths—exorcists, priests—but none have succeeded in finding the creature's chamber of stolen items."

Seren frowned. "But how will we be safe from this...creature?"

"It resides in the temple," Eldyir said, his tone measured. "Corruption runs deep in a holy sanctuary that has been caught in the Veil and it feeds off the power there. If all goes well, you should be able to avoid the creature itself as long as you remain undetected. Find the chamber of stolen items, and you will find the harp."

"And if it's not there?" Seren pressed. "How do we know for sure?"

Eldyir's smile was calm, almost knowing. "Faith has grown since your arrival, Seren. The Seers' visions have cleared, and they've confirmed that the harp is indeed in Andanova. You may not see it, but already, you've begun to change the world."

Seren swallowed hard, his throat dry.

"You must understand," Eldyir continued gently, "this journey carries great risk, but Kallista's harp is essential for the Cleansing. Frightening as it may seem, do not let it weigh too heavily on you. The gods will guide you. Whether it takes months or years, they will not lead you astray."

I can't do this, Seren wanted to say. Instead, he nodded, straightening his posture. "I'll do my best."

Eighteen

"Magic is a gift of the gods, and in turn, it may be taken. All that is borrowed must be returned."

—Compendium of Magic

Seren's muscles ached as he swung the sword. With a sigh, he wiped the hair out of his eyes before thrusting the weapon into the dirt. Another week had passed in the blink of an eye. Days blurred together in endless magic training sessions, each leaving him ragged. It was an unusual exhaustion, one that penetrated his soul and weighed heavily on his core.

You will find balance, Seren.

Seren yanked the sword out of the ground and ran a finger down the blade, controlling his breathing as he adjusted his stance. In the Behethium Forest, the sword had felt like a heavy weight he could barely wield. His body remembered before his mind did, and the memories continued to flood back. He knew how to block and plant his feet because of his training. Seren had been skilled with a sword, more so than with his studies or learning to play the harp. Yet, that boy who had once been so adept still felt like a stranger to him.

Seren raised the sword.

The day before, Aiden had returned to the cathedral. Seren had thought about confronting him about the seal on his back, wondering if Aiden had been responsible. However, he decided he didn't want an answer. Seren was certain Aiden was avoiding him. They had exchanged only a few words upon Aiden's return, which had dampened Seren's mood. Seren had asked Aiden about seeing Jude, but Aiden barely paid attention and waved him away.

You have no time for friendships, Seren. And that mercenary is nothing but trouble.

Seren slashed the tree.

You need to focus all your energy on your training. Do not even think about bothering Eldyir with these notions.

He severed a branch.

You need to make up for the lost time.

Seren cried out, plunging his sword toward the tree. It stuck through the center, splintering the surrounding wood.

"Ah, damn." Seren panted, wiping sweat from his brow. The calluses on his hands had ripped, bleeding down his palms. He wiped the blood on his white shirt, knowing his hands would heal within a matter of seconds. With a grunt, he pulled the sword from the tree, stumbling back, and realized he'd shattered the damn thing.

"Now that's something I haven't seen before."

Seren reeled around to see a tall young woman leaning against the carved ivory archway of the church's garden. Her kohl-lined hazel eyes, like those of a predatory cat, pierced Seren as if he were a mouse about to meet her jaws. He felt a twinge of discomfort under her lingering gaze. Strapped to each hip were copper pistols, glinting in the light, and a number of melee weapons.

"You may want to wipe the drool," the woman said. Her thin lips curled into a smirk, highlighting a jagged scar that ran from the corner of her mouth to just below her cheekbone.

Seren ignored her, focusing on the broken sword pieces at his feet. He cursed when one of the shards sliced through his finger. He brought it up to his lips to suck the blood, but he was happy to see it heal right away.

The woman shifted, stepping forward with a quiet grace, her raven-black hair falling to her pointed chin as she moved. A red sash encircled her waist and twin crimson-handled swords sat crossed on her back. Her blackened steel breastplate, scratched and stained with what he assumed was old blood, gleamed beneath the twilight.

She stopped a few feet away, her eyes never leaving him. Seren instantly noticed how quietly she moved, her footfalls barely making a sound. He wondered how long she had been watching him before he had noticed.

"Are you lost?" Seren asked, growing annoyed by her gaze.

She shrugged as if she were bored. "Nah, just watching a moron fight a tree."

Seren gritted his teeth. "Pretty sure you aren't supposed to be here," he retorted. "You don't look like a priest or saint."

She made a gagging motion, then walked past him. "I would hope so." She removed a sword from her back and threw it in his direction. He seized it midair.

"What's your deal?"

The young woman grinned. "The name is Cin Silver," she said. "It looks like you and I are going to be working together. I wanted to see the 'chosen one' for myself." Cin raised her thin brows. "And it looks like I found him fighting a tree." She rolled her shoulders, muscles rippling in her lean arms.

Seren raised an eyebrow. "You're an exorcist?"

"Yep." Cin unsheathed the second sword from her back. "Show me how you fight. I don't imagine you'll be battling many *trees* in Andanova."

Seren jerked his arm up as she slashed the sword toward him. "I never said I wanted to—"

Clang.

"Too slow."

Seren growled as her sword cut across his shoulder. Blood ran down his arm. He twisted his body and brought his sword toward her. She deflected him, a disinterested expression on her face. Frustration grew and Seren swung again. He gasped as his sword hit nothing but air and felt the cold tip of steel on the back of his neck.

"I didn't even see you move," Seren gasped.

"Don't blink."

"What—"

Cin was a blur, her feet meeting with his knees, knocking Seren to the ground. "You're pathetically slow."

Seren ground his teeth. "I'm just tired, and you're ridiculously fast."

Cin kneeled, face inches from his. Seren noted an additional scar splitting from her left eyebrow. "And what happens if you become tired in Andanova? There are monsters quicker than me. Everyone will die protecting you if you cannot defend yourself. Some chosen one you are."

Seren was quick. He jumped to his feet, a foot meeting her chest, as he had watched Jude do once. In surprise, she stumbled back but didn't release the sword from her grip. She grinned as Seren came at her, sword in hand, slashing quicker than before. She ducked, missing each slash.

"Is that all you've got?"

Seren's anger rose. Cin was on his left, beckoning him with her finger to tease him. She moved again, and Seren saw her in a blur reach his right side.

Her footsteps truly make no sound at all, Seren thought.

If Cin wanted to, she could have him by his throat again. She was enjoying mocking him. Seren growled. The sword hit nothing but air once again. He whirled around, realizing she was gone. How, in the time it took him to blink, had she disappeared?

A whistle sounded from behind him. Cin's feet dangled above him as she stretched out languorously like a lazy cat on the branches of the tree, a grin spread across her face.

"I give up," Seren said, thrusting his sword onto the dirt. "I'm done with your little game."

Cin cackled, jumping down from the tree and landing on her feet. "We've only just started."

The next day, Seren sat in the clawed chair of Eldyir's study, sprawled across the purple velvet cushions. It had been a pleasant day. Eldyir had invited him for lunch and the two of them had enjoyed roasted chicken sandwiches with garden tomatoes.

Seren sipped on warm tea, the morning sun streaming in through the open window. He watched as two starlings danced around each other in the blue sky for a moment before disappearing out of sight. Mila and Jude crept into his mind. His heart sank into his belly, no longer in the mood for tea. He shoved the porcelain cup onto the table, sighing.

Eldyir also sighed for what Seren had counted as the fifth time. He stood over his desk, his robes ruffling as a gust of early summer wind blew through the window.

"What's wrong?" Seren propped himself onto his elbows.

"Several young boys have gone missing in the surrounding towns," Eldyir said solemnly. "It's the work of the Sanguine Sisters, no doubt. As the Devil grows stronger, so does their magic."

Seren bit his tongue, refraining from telling Eldyir of his own knowledge of the Sanguine Sisters. If Mila was still anywhere in Aurelius, it would be a danger to her life.

"The Devil certainly is making progress," Seren grumbled.

Eldyir lifted his head. "Do you recall the origin of the Devil, Seren?"

Seren hesitated. "He was once the gods' favored angel," he began. "And he wished to be a god himself, and for that, he was punished."

Eldyir observed him keenly, sensing his uncertainty. "Yes, he once stood alongside the gods, a valiant and loyal overseer of humanity. He was a wise and powerful leader among the greatest of angels—"

"He dared to challenge the gods."

"Ah, if only it were so simple," Eldyir mused, his eyes distant. "He defied the Mother, the Father, and the Creator, and for that, he was cast from Aetheria. Then, he deceived Eden and Adamus, leading to their expulsion from Aetheria, nourishing himself on their malice, their sins, spreading his corruption across the world, amassing power."

"And then he corrupted the Veil...?"

"Yes," Eldyir replied, brows furrowed. "Several hundred years after the Great War, a terrible evil spread, tainting those within the Veil." His hand hovered over the painting that hung above his desk. Eldyir had called the horned horse a unicorn. "The world was a much different place."

"And soon the Devil will start the Sundering," Seren said slowly.

Eldyir licked his dry lips. "Ah, the Devil has already started it, Seren. He is the cog in the machine that turns all the wheels with the flick of his wrist. This virus that ravages the west is no doubt his work, and it will only worsen. The fish are disappearing from the seas and soon they will be empty."

"Aiden talked little about the Sundering," Seren admitted.

Aiden had wanted to wait until Seren was older—more prepared for the darkness he would have to face.

On your sixteenth birthday, I will tell you everything you need and want to know, and give you earnest answers.

But that day had never come because Seren had been in Vavilon.

"Here." Eldyir grabbed a book from the shelf, beckoning Seren over. After he found what he was looking for, he pushed a red leather book into Seren's palm. "This is the Book of Disruption. It is a collection of the scriptures and prophecies that speak of the Sundering."

Seren ran his hands over the bound spine. He'd never heard of this book before nor seen it in Aiden's library in Stellaris. He flipped it open to a random page, skimming the surface. There were handwritten words scrawled all over the pages.

Eldyir's fingers ran over the words. "Curious that you opened this page," he murmured. "I recognize this handwriting. These are words written by the greatest Seer of our time, Felix Amos..."

Seren could have sworn his fingers shook momentarily as they hovered over the text.

Balance falters in the depths of good and evil. No true beginning, no lasting end. Should the light consume the dark, all will fall. Should the dark drown the light, all will be lost.

A chill crept up Seren's spine. "What does it mean?"

Eldyir was silent for a long moment. "Evil will never truly have an end," he said. "Even after your will is done. You know this, though, don't you?"

Seren swallowed. Of course, he knew that. He shut the book, setting it on the desk.

"If I can truly cleanse the Veil...the demons will return to their original forms, won't they?"

As Seren posed the question, he couldn't help but imagine creatures of pure magic roaming once more. A world without the fear of demons and the Veil. A world of boundless magic and wonder.

"They will exist as they once were," Eldyir said. "It is what we were promised." He set a hand on Seren's shoulders. "Trust yourself. All will be well, no matter the roads you take to your fate."

Eldyir differed from Aiden in so many ways. He didn't pile his expectations and put them upon Seren's shoulder to carry. He only guided him. Seren sighed, watching as Eldyir flipped through a blue book, most likely finding spells for Seren to study. A prickle traveled down Seren's spine, across the scars on his back.

I could tell him.

Eldyir lifted his head, eyes meeting his. "Something else on your mind?"

Seren shook his head. "No."

Eldyir raised an eyebrow. "Has anyone told you that you are a very poor liar?"

Seren scowled.

"I have something new for you to try today regarding your magic," he said, setting the book down. "I'd say you've nearly perfected concealing your Aura. We can move on to something else." He smiled.

At these words, Seren perked up. Eldyir had been teaching him about Aura and how to control it, just as Seren had hoped. Though it was difficult and draining, he had at least gained the ability to appear as he once did with concentration—green eyes and dark hair. Though Seren hadn't been wasting energy on concealing his Aura, there was no point within the cathedral.

Eldyir had also taught him how to sense the Aura of others. It made him think of his time in the Underbelly, when Kitsune had accused him of seeing through her Aura. But some Auras were stronger than others. If he had truly seen past Eden's Aura, then he would have known she lived inside Mila's mother.

When Seren had asked why it came so naturally to him before—so effortless that he hadn't even realized he was doing it, even as a child—Eldyir explained that the Mother had always been with him, safeguarding him since the day he was born. But, like all children, it was time for Seren to learn on his own. For some reason, the words stung.

Every day brought Seren closer to the Summer Solstice, and every day reminded him of it. He had to hone his abilities with skill and full control before he went to Andanova. Even a few words of encouragement from the goddess in his head would've been helpful.

Eldyir led Seren out of the study and through the halls of the cathedral, their footsteps echoing off the walls.

The two of them emerged outside. Eldyir continued to the outer eastern edge of the gardens, where a patch of sunflowers grew as tall as Seren. Winding through the garden paths, Seren followed closely behind. The flowers towered over him, resembling golden suns sparkling under the baby-blue sky.

The two of them reached a gilded gate with crests shaped like suns. The Northern Estate of the Grand Cathedral was dedicated to Helios, the Southern to Kallista, and the Eastern to Caelum. For those who had ties to the church but needed help and refuge, the Western Estate served as the community shelter.

Eldyir opened the gate with a wave of his hand. As they approached, Seren couldn't shake the sensation of being watched, feeling the weight of curious eyes following their every move. Brown chickens roamed freely, plucking bugs from the green grass. A group of children chased each other across the yard, pretending to be priests banishing demons back into the Veil. Orange-tipped butterflies gathered around the sunflowers. Eldyir moved toward a modest oak building tucked in the corner, its windows draped with blue curtains.

Eldyir lightly rapped on the oak door. It creaked open, revealing a woman on the other side, her features obscured by a cloth draped over her face.

"Father Eldyir," the woman greeted, her head bowed.

Eldyir returned the gesture. "Afternoon, Merida. How is he?"

Merida shook her head, sadness visible in her eyes. "He's remained lucid for the last hour, but I don't think he has much time left. He's gotten drastically worse since this morning. I was just about to send for you."

For the first time, Seren saw a worry flash over Eldyir.

Merida's curious gaze wandered to Seren. Eldyir glanced between the two of them, his shoulders loosening. "Pardon my manners, this is Seren."

Merida dipped her head, red hair falling past her elbows. "May I just say the resemblance is uncanny?" she said. "Rumors do not give your beauty justice."

Seren offered a nervous smile but said nothing in return.

"May we come in?" Eldyir said.

The woman moved to the side, allowing them to pass. Seren fought the urge to throw his hands over his nose. The room reeked of sickness. An assortment of medicinal herbs and supplies were strewn across the wooden tables. It dawned on Seren that Merida was a Moon Maiden, entrusted with the care of the sick and injured on estate grounds. The building was full of empty beds, except for one in the far-right corner. The blankets were wrapped around a shivering figure by the bedside, where a single candle cast a flickering light.

"Wait outside for me, will you, Merida?" Eldyir said.

"Of course—oh, and don't mind Theo, he won't leave the boy's side." With another glance at Seren, she closed the door behind her.

Eldyir placed a reassuring hand on Seren's shoulder. "No priest or saint has the power to cure this virus," he murmured. "It is beyond our abilities but not beyond yours."

Seren's face blanched as he stared at Eldyir in disbelief. "What?"

"This boy means a lot to me," Eldyir said, his hazel gaze unwavering. "He is the grandson of my dearest friend, and I have vowed to protect him. But I am powerless against this virus." He pressed his fingers against Seren's chest. "I know you have the ability to save him, Seren. Let go of your doubt, let go of your fears. Allow the Mother to guide you."

Was Eldyir going mad? The most powerful of holy magic users had deemed this virus incurable. Seren was still learning and hadn't even come close to mastering his abilities. He automatically took a step back.

"I don't know how," he said desperately. "I can't..."

Eldyir dropped his hands. "I have the deepest faith in you, Seren. You must trust in yourself."

Eldyir strode to the door, his stare lingering on the shivering figure. His hands clenched at his sides, but he didn't say a word. Instead, he disappeared behind the door, leaving Seren alone.

Seren hesitated for a moment before stepping toward the bed. The figure turned, lowering the blankets, and light hit his russet ringlets. His milky eyes locked onto Seren's. Freckles scattered across his nose and cheeks like constellations, and his lips carried the faint blue tinge that matched the color of his fingernails.

Felix, the boy from the garden.

He clicked his tongue and patted his lap, his movements feeble. A small mound under the blankets shifted, revealing a flash of reddish-brown fur. His weasel emerged and climbed up onto the boy's chest.

"Who's there?" Felix wheezed. "Come closer."

Plumes of frosty breath filled the air between Seren and the boy. Felix reached out a trembling hand. Seren hesitated for a moment before mirroring the movement. As their fingertips met, a strange sensation coursed through Seren's body, sending a shiver down his spine. Startled, Seren recoiled, withdrawing his hand and taking a step back.

"It's you," Felix whispered. His blue lips curved into a relaxed smile. "Seren."

"You're sick," Seren said. "You're...dying."

"And Eldyir wants you to...save me. Doesn't he?"

Before Seren could respond, the boy coughed, dark droplets spraying on the blankets.

"I told you, we were going to be friends," he said, voice faint. "We can't be friends if I'm...dead."

"I can't help you," Seren said, panic creeping into his voice.

"I don't know how."

"Yes, you do," Felix whispered. "I saw it. I saw you. Us."

"What are you talking about?" Seren demanded. "I don't under-stand—"

The boy's cold hands reached out and clasped Seren's. An electric feeling coursed through Seren and froze him into place. And then, the room changed. It was flooded with warm light coming in through a frosted window. Outside, snowflakes fell, fast and hurried. Across the table, Felix sat laughing—he was older, not by much, but he had grown into himself more. His green cloak no longer swallowed him whole.

"Do you remember when we met, Seren?" Felix asked, his voice sounding as if it was something from a distant dream. "I told you we'd be great friends."

And just as quickly, it was gone. Seren was back in the room, his breath shallow and uneven.

Felix's hands dropped from his own, limp and cold. The weasel, its twitching nose nudging Felix's face, let out a squeak before scratching his shoulder with sharp claws, drawing blood.

"Felix?"

The smile on Felix's lips vanished. His features went still, his chest barely rising and falling. Slowly, he collapsed onto the bed in a heap, his eyes rolling into the back of his head.

"No, no—wait."

Seren panicked. No. He was going to die before Seren could even get the chance to try. And he was going to ruin fate all over again, wasn't he?

Fear rose inside of him as he grasped the boy's icy wrist, his pulse fading beneath his fingertips.

Seren murmured a simple healing spell, hoping that it would work. Nothing happened. The weasel crawled down and nudged Seren's hands, chittering noisily.

"I don't know how to save him," he whispered. "He was wrong... I...I can't."

Seren gripped Felix's wrist, his heart plummeting as the pulse faded. *Thump. Thump. Thump.* And then it stopped.

Seren hung his head in shame. How was he supposed to cleanse the Veil? How was he to survive Andanova? He couldn't even cure a boy from a virus. The gods had chosen wrong.

The weasel continued to scratch at Felix, even going so far to sink its little teeth into the flesh of his forearm.

"He's gone," Seren told the creature. It turned to him as if understanding his words, its small teeth bared. It lunged, latching its sharp teeth into Seren's hand. He cried out, pulling away with a growl.

"I'm sorry," he said fiercely. "There's nothing I can do."

The weasel snarled at Seren before it curled onto Felix's chest. It nudged him with a distressed whimper.

Seren sank to his knees, his face falling into his hands. How many lives would be lost that he could not save?

A warm hand pressed against Seren's shoulder. He lifted his head. "I'm sorry, Eldyir. I couldn't save him." He turned around, expecting to see his mentor's disappointed expression, but there was nothing behind him. He stood and looked around the room but saw nobody.

Then, Seren felt as if arms had wrapped around him, warm and comforting. A gentle bloom unfurled in his chest, and his heart steadied.

"I am with you, and I am all around you, Seren. Even when you fear you are alone, I am here."

Without thinking, Seren grasped Felix's cold hands in his own, the chill seeping into his skin. He could see it—a faint pulse of orange, like a flickering ember, that he knew without question was the boy's soul clinging to his body. He could still save him. A familiar tingle raced down Seren's spine and flooded his veins, a sensation like a gentle current. In the past, he hadn't understood this feeling, but his training with Eldyir had revealed its source as magic. He allowed it to rise, digging deep into his core and drawing forth his power.

As Seren focused, he saw dark tendrils coiling around Felix's soul, their relentless grip threatening to shatter it. Seren willed his magic to counteract it, envisioning a warm, radiant light to drive out the cold darkness. Invisible threads of light emerged from his palms, glowing, intertwining around the boy and coaxing the dark tendrils away with their brilliance.

Get out.

Seren strained, sweat forming on his brow.

Get. Out.

Pain exploded behind Seren's temple. Felix's mouth opened, and a wispy miasma of darkness seeped out. The windows rattled as the darkness screeched, a sound of anger, rage at something that had been stolen. The candle's flame died.

And then they flowed toward Seren.

The darkness coiled around Seren's throat and crept into his nose. His eyes watered as he stumbled back, clutching his face.

"We've been searching for you."

"Share your flesh and share your bones."

Seren felt his magic building and with a cry, bright light burst across the room, expelling the darkness. The candle flickered back to life. The darkness was gone as soon as it had come. Seren fell into the wall behind, sweat pasted on his forehead, panting.

Felix sat up in bed, his eyes wide. His hands flew to his throat, and for a moment, panic flashed across his face. But then, his lips returned to their natural color, and the flush of life crept into his cheeks. The weasel chittered happily, nudging Felix's fingers.

"I'm alright, Theo," Felix giggled. "I told you Seren could do it."

"You're a Seer—" Seren began, but Felix pressed a finger to his lips.

"We're friends now," he said softly. "So, you have to promise me something."

Seren remained silent.

"You can't tell anyone," Felix continued. "Do you swear it?"

Seren hesitated. "But...why?"

A shadow passed over Felix's face, his expression shifting into something almost vulnerable. "Just...trust me. Please."

And though Seren couldn't explain why, he did. He trusted this strange boy in a way that was both unsettling and comforting all at once. What was one more secret to carry?

Nineteen

*"The Great Guardians, entrusted with protecting the gates of
Aetheria, bestow entry only upon the deserving. However, as the
corruption spread, it took root within them. What implications
does this hold for our souls? Is it possible that we are already
condemned? Is it possible that we have already descended into
hell?"*

—the Scribes of Wisdom

For weeks, Jude had enveloped himself in palpable sulkiness. Mila watched as he exchanged coins with a woman, marking the end of his last job in Lumina. His smile, though courteous, faded as he turned away. Recently, his behavior had become increasingly odd. Today, he was particularly sullen after being told for the umpteenth time to stay away from the Grand Cathedral grounds. The acolytes had made it clear that if he needed help, he should seek assistance at churches within the city. When Jude claimed he was a friend of the Mother, the acolytes had laughed in his face.

The sight of numerous acolytes congregating in a single location had sent shivers cascading down Mila's spine. Aiden's knowledge of her identity had left her eager to depart for Vavilon. But Jude was insistent he finished his odd jobs, and he had seemed particularly stressed finishing his final one. She'd seen him catching longing glances at the cathedral and although neither of them said it—he was thinking about Seren.

Jude settled on the park bench with Mila, exhaustion etched into his face. He dusted the dirt from his white shirt and silently rolled up his sleeves. He heaved a sigh, wiping sweat from his brow. Delving into his pocket, he retrieved a piece of dried meat. He ripped off a piece with his teeth and chewed violently.

"Are you alright?" Mila asked.

"Just dandy."

Mila flinched at his abrupt response, so unlike his usual warmth. She had busied herself over the past several weeks by helping Luna at her shop and saving money of her own, maintaining a distance as Jude completed his tasks. Initially, she had joined him out of boredom, but now regret crept in.

"It certainly doesn't seem that way," she retorted.

"They treat him like a prisoner," Jude said, his mouth still full. "He's been demoted from lab rat to a princess secluded in a tower, for heaven's sake." He took another bite, his brows knitting together. "They act like I'm going to walk in the cathedral and shoot him between the eyes."

Mila fixed her gaze on her hands, at a loss for words. Witnessing Jude in a state of genuine anger was uncharted territory. "They're getting him ready for something," she murmured. "There are rumors around town about a going-away ceremony for the Summer Solstice."

Jude seemed to ignore her comment, stuffing a piece of bread into his mouth—likely pulled from his pocket. "It's been nearly two months," he whined. "It was easy when I had jobs to worry about, but there's nothing else to do in this city. I want to see him. I *promised.*"

"I understand," Mila said. "It's already been this long, Jude. I don't think he would blame you if you left without saying goodbye."

"I'm not saying goodbye," Jude said. He crossed his legs, picking a piece of grass off his midnight-blue pants. "Seren asked me to stay with him."

Mila blinked, a sense of dread washing over her. "What?"

"He asked me to stay," Jude repeated. He rubbed his chin, lost in thought. "And I said yes." Mila thought she saw a fond smile curve on his lips, but it quickly disappeared. He bit another piece of bread off. "He didn't ask you to stay too?"

Mila turned away, not wanting Jude to see her face. "No, he didn't."

Why would he?

Mila clenched the fabric of her pants, her knuckles whitening. Familiar irritation rose inside of her. "So, what? You're going to stay with him? Here? I thought we were going back to Vavilon together. Seren was just a job, and you finished it."

Besides, Mila had planned to go to the Underbelly of the city and seek Kitsune again. If anyone could instruct her on an alternate method of breaking the bond, it would be that demon.

Jude stuffed more pieces of bread into his mouth with a frown. "Sure, it started that way," he murmured, "but things changed." He looked into the distance, sapphire eyes sparkling. "There is nothing for me in Vavilon."

"I don't understand."

Jude smiled. "I don't exactly understand it either."

Mila was sure Jude wasn't going to elaborate. She sighed, staring down at her hands, thinking of the dagger pressed against Seren's back. Truthfully, there was nothing for her in Vavilon either.

Crickets chirped outside the cracked window. The silvery glow of the crescent moon seeped into the room, its faint light casting delicate shadows across the furniture and walls.

Mila tossed and turned in bed, flinging the cotton blankets off her bare legs. If she could only turn off her endless stream of thoughts. It had been almost two months since she and Seren had arrived in Lumina. Knowing that Jude wanted to remain by Seren's side meant she would have to go back to Vavilon on her own.

Mila didn't belong with Seren. She threw her arms over her face, stifling out her groan. She could go to Vavilon on her own, still seek Kitsune like she'd planned.

Every night since the celebration, her sister's words plagued her. She went through the motions, wondering if Iris had tricked her into killing Seren because of his importance. Then she heard the townsfolk talking about the boys who had gone missing. Three days earlier, a distraught mother had approached Mila in tears, describing her four-year-old son and asking if she had seen him. Mila had run to the inn and vomited.

One thing was for certain—Mila needed to break the bond between her and Seren. She needed to end Eden's reign. And although she wasn't sure how much belief she held in Seren's appointed title, Mila couldn't help but hope it was true. A world without demons would change everything.

A rustle outside the window broke Mila's thoughts, and she sat up. She slipped out of bed, peering through the corner of the glass.

"Jude?"

The two of them had been staying in the same inn, with their rooms across from one another. He should not have been out of bed at such an unusual hour. Mila hurriedly dressed in a pair of black trousers and a matching blouse with sheer sleeves for the summer's warmth. Finding suitable pants had proven troublesome, given that most women outside the Godless City favored dresses. She draped a cloak over her shoulders and stealthily opened the door, catching sight of Jude a few paces away. She slunk into the shadows and trailed him, curious about what he was doing. It didn't take her long to realize exactly where he was going.

"Damn it, Jude," she whispered under her breath.

Mila darted between the buildings, careful to stay undetected. When he approached the Grand Cathedral, she lost sight of him for a moment. Lanterns were lit outside the cathedral, lighting the walkway to the entrance. Mila pressed herself behind the statue of Kallista as two acolytes walked by, talking to each other.

"Eight more days," a young male acolyte said. "They say the Mother will begin the quest to cleanse the Veil."

"Thank the gods. I'm so over babysitting duty," said the woman acolyte. "Nobody is dumb enough to try to assassinate a reborn goddess."

"I wouldn't hold your breath on that."

Mila darted through the shadows, pinning herself against the next statue. The acolytes rounded the corner of the cathedral. She scanned the area. Where the hell was Jude? She crept toward the entrance, staying hidden. Mila lost sight of the acolytes as she hurried forward.

"Jude?" Mila whispered. "Where are you?"

After receiving no response, Mila hid behind a rose bush for several minutes, listening for footsteps. Suddenly, a yelp sounded near the cathedral doors. As soon as it came, it was gone. Shuffling. Then it was quiet. Mila peered around the corner, eyes wide.

"Jude, what're you doing?" Mila hissed.

Caught in the act, he only offered a conspiratorial smile. The two acolytes lay unconscious against the wall, one of them stripped down to nothing but his undergarments. Jude pulled on the stolen plain blue robes. "I'm going to visit Seren, of course."

"You're crazy," she said.

"What's crazy is that I didn't do this sooner," Jude said. Boyish excitement shone on his face as he eagerly adjusted the robes. "Don't just stand there. Get dressed if you're coming with me."

Mila groaned inwardly, moving closer to the unconscious acolytes. "Jude, we shouldn't be doing this."

"First of all, you followed me," Jude said, adjusting his mussed hair. "And you know how much I *loathe* rules. Now, how do I look?" He spun around and clasped his hands as if to pray. "I could get used to these. Very breezy. Meet me inside?"

Before Mila could get a word in, Jude slunk onto the pathway, straightening his back, preparing to enter the cathedral.

"Damn it," Mila whispered. With a scowl, she stripped the robes off the other acolyte and pulled them over her clothes.

Seren didn't want to see her, Mila knew that. And even though she ached to see him, to tell him she was sorry, the thought of doing so made her want to turn tail and run.

Seren woke to banging on his door. He jolted up, his hair sticking up in several places. He grumbled to himself, peeling the blankets from his naked torso. Without bothering to put a shirt on, Seren climbed out of bed and answered the door.

"Are you ready to train?"

Seren blinked. "The sun hasn't even risen yet," he grumbled. "We've been at this for weeks. The Summer Solstice is next week and I'm tired. Between Eldyir and this—"

Cin hit him on the shoulder, almost knocking him down. "But you've improved so much already," she said with a smirk. Her eyes trailed down his exposed skin. "Besides, I'd say training has done you some good."

Seren's face flushed as he slammed the door shut. Grumbling under his breath, he approached the chest nestled beside his bed. He retrieved a snug black shirt without sleeves, a gift from Cin. The fabric was light and breathable, refusing to cling to his skin despite how much he sweated when they trained. Hastily yanking on his pants, he reached for the silver sword resting nearby—a gift from Eldyir.

Seren was exhausted. He had been working in the infirmary with Merida on the Helios Estate, healing those afflicted with the Blue Inferno. When he had told Eldyir about what he had seen with Felix, Eldyir's expression had darkened. "Corruption beyond the Veil," Eldyir had said. They agreed to keep Seren's observations a secret, with Merida sworn to silence. Seren only healed those brought to him, and afterward, he never saw them again. The Grand Priest had advised Seren that it would be prudent not to announce that he could cure the virus. If people knew, they would flock to him, and Seren couldn't spend all his days healing the sick.

Seren had asked Merida about Felix and was told that he lived on the Helios Estate with his sister. Their parents had died when they were young, and the Grand Priest had taken them under his wing after their grandfather had passed. It was strange to think that Felix, with his Seer abilities, was hiding it from Eldyir. Still, Seren had done what the boy asked and hadn't discussed it with anyone, not even Cin, though they'd been spending a considerable amount of time together.

Cin was waiting for him at the bottom of the steps. Seren followed her into their usual spot in the garden courtyard. He yawned and rubbed between his shoulders.

Cin turned toward him, gloved hand on her hip. "I heard a rumor," she said. "You're not going to like it."

Seren assumed his stance, his sword gripped in his hand. Cin lunged at him, her movements as agile as they were fierce. Having spent countless hours training with her, Seren came to understand the way she moved. Quick, lean, and tall, she possessed not only speed but also formidable strength. However, Seren also learned that he could be quick too—and he was strong. Metal against metal clashed under the lantern light, the sound echoing through the night.

"What kind of rumor?" Seren asked, effortlessly dodging her attack.

"Vavilon discovered a cure to the Blue Inferno," she said. "They healed thousands of people in their city over the last week. Durcova has allied with Vavilon and Wreiss is considering the same."

Seren flinched as the blade nicked his ribs. "What?" he said with a gasp, dodging her next attack. He thought of the darkness he had pulled straight from Felix. And somehow, he knew. He didn't know how, but deep down he did. It was impossible that Vavilon had completely cured this corruption. They were only stopping the death. The souls of those cured by the virus were still in danger.

"Can you blame them?" Cin asked. "Hundreds of people are dying from this virus, and it'll only get worse. Despite what people say about your identity, this situation is beyond your control. You can't heal thousands of people at once." Her sword grazed Seren's cheek and she rolled his eyes as he winced. "You're rusty today. It's like you're not even trying."

"I told you, I'm tired," he grumbled. He swung his sword toward her. "And believe it or not, I've got a lot on my shoulders."

"Yeah, like this damn suicide mission," she scoffed.

Their swords met again, faces about an inch apart. Cin's scarred eyebrow raised, her hazel eyes threatening.

"If you think that, why are you coming?" Seren challenged. "Why prepare me for Andanova?"

Cin's left hand dropped to her side, the weight of Seren's sword pressing against her own. With her pearly teeth, she ripped off her glove, revealing blackened fingers that appeared dirty with coal-dust grime up to her knuckles. Seren's eyes widened.

"I've nearly reached my limit," she said with a grimace. "But if there's even a chance that retrieving that silly musical instrument will change the world, then count me in. I'll kick some demon ass along the way." She paused, her gaze unwavering, as if there was another reason that she was refraining from speaking. "Plus, my Order assigned me to this mission when the Grand Priest sent for an exorcist, and I accepted willingly."

"What do you mean you've reached your limit?" Seren asked.

"My abilities do not come freely. Priests and saints have the gods, and I have the Fallen."

Seren jumped back, sword falling to his side. "The Fallen Angels?"

"Yeah, it's why the priests are always scowling at me," Cin said with a laugh. "I'm just another soul sold off to a demon to them—until they need me, of course. The Fallen are different, though. Regardless of how many souls they take, the Fallen are condemned to the Veil for eternity. They're powerful sons of bitches with a grudge against the gods. Exorcists have enough honor to not allow our deaths to have consequences."

The biggest taboo about making a deal with a demon was upon death, the willing soul allowed the demon access to the human realm. It made sense that an exorcist would avoid that at all costs. They lived to exterminate demons while priests and saints only banished them back into the Veil.

"How long do you have?"

She countered Seren's abrupt attack with surprise, smiling. "A year, maybe two."

"I'm sorry."

"Don't be. I made my choice, and I wouldn't change it."

Seren jumped back and straightened his spine, planting his feet firmly as he gripped his sword.

"So, what was it like meeting a Fallen?"

Cin stopped, planting her sword in the dirt. "Nobody's ever had the guts to ask me that."

Seren shrugged. "I'm curious."

"I was seventeen," Cin began. "I know I was young, but the Order of Azazel took me in when I was ten. When Andanova fell, a handful of demons slipped through the Veil. One of them slaughtered my family. It left me alive. Bastard found it amusing. It said, 'If I kill all my foes, who will be left to tell the tales of my horrors?'"

Cin's fingers traced the scars on her face. "It gave me these. A priestess came into the village and was able to banish it back into the Veil. I was angry at her. I believed the demon deserved to die for what it had done. All the priestess had done was ensure that the monster would find a way to come back into our realm. The priestess took me to a church in Rëima, and that's when I met an exorcist. It wasn't just me that was angry, others believed the demon deserved to be killed. It had slaughtered the entire village, excluding three children—me among them. The other children had extended family, but not me. And so, they gave me a choice: to stay in the church or join the Order, and I made my decision."

"You were brave," Seren murmured.

"No," Cin said. "I was angry." She shook her head. "The Order of Azazel takes in orphans who have lost their families to the Veil or a demon and shapes them into exorcists. If I had stayed in the church, handmaidens would've brushed my hair and told me I'd be safe if I prayed to the gods. A bunch of bullshit. In the Order, they placed a sword in my palm and told me that one day, I could defeat the monsters that I feared. The choice was easy to make. I wasn't going to rely on some bastards in the sky." Cin licked her lips. "It was my seventeenth birthday when my master said I was ready. They called it the Fallen of Wrath. Nasty creature—sinewy muscle, eyes like blood rubies, and wings of nothing but thin bone. My master said that the Fallen of Wrath used to be called the Angel of Mercy." A chill went through Seren at her words. "It asked me why I wanted power, and the answer was simple—to kill monsters and prevent them from killing. And so, it made *me* a monster."

Seren studied his reflection in the sword's edge. "And what makes a monster?" he asked quietly.

Cin flashed a smile, a feline glint sparking in her eyes. "It depends. For me, the monster is the one lurking in the dark, not the one who hides from it."

Seren chuckled weakly. "You act as though you have no fear."

"I have plenty of fear," Cin said. "I am just not stupid enough to show it."

"Did you get your revenge?"

"I did."

The garden was silent except for the rustle of white roses swaying in the cool summer breeze. "I'm terrified," Seren admitted. "I'm afraid I'll fail, or that others will die for me."

As she approached him, Cin's expression softened slightly, though her voice remained firm. "Only a fool has never felt fear. Fear isn't a sign of weakness. A weak man would have fled—yet here you stand."

"Yeah," Seren said, a lump forming in his throat. "But I've fled before. Who's to say I wouldn't again?"

Cin sighed, adjusting her stance. "Let me rephrase that," she said. "Strength is determined in many ways, Seren. Sometimes, it takes strength to walk or even run away. Other times, it takes strength to remain where you stand. Belief is power. So, believe in yourself, or believe in your gods—I couldn't care less what you believe in, but pick something. It's the only way to survive."

"What do you believe?"

"What I believe doesn't matter," she replied. "This is about you."

Cin stiffened suddenly.

"What's wrong?"

"Quiet," she demanded. Cin's nostrils flared. "There's no wind."

Seren paced around the gardens, his eyes scanning the maze of flowers. They made a rustling sound, but she was correct—there was no wind this time. He saw nothing, but he felt a pressure, as if eyes were watching him. Something was wrong. Seren lifted his sword off the ground.

A crack echoed through the air, followed by a burst of blue light that cascaded just inches above Cin's head, striking the tree behind and turning its core to ash. Seren whirled around, searching for the source, but saw nothing.

Then, as if materializing from thin air, a man appeared in the courtyard. Seren blinked, instantly recognizing the Enforcer gear. They fashioned their helmets in the likeness of eagles, with golden and copper feathers extending from the large chrome pauldrons. The Enforcer's chest showcased the symbol of the chained sun. Seren's gaze focused on the strange, pulsating crystal device attached to a belt at the Enforcer's waist. A jolt of memory surged through Seren. Cloaking devices—technology that allowed Enforcers to blend in with their surroundings.

A scream erupted from the cathedral, followed by the shattering of glass. Seren foolishly looked towards the sound and was zapped with a burst of energy from the Arc-Caster. He let out a yell as he was thrown backward, electricity surging through him, his heart pounding too fast in his chest. He gasped, amazed that he wasn't burnt to a crisp.

Cin wasted no time. She cried out, using the remaining tree to propel her weight towards the Enforcer. Though they wore impenetrable armor, Cin, an exorcist who battled demons for a living, knew there was always a weak spot. She had once told him so. Seren watched as she forced the sword into the Enforcer's neck, just under his helm, before he even had a second to counter. The Enforcer crumpled to his knees in a heap.

"Are you alright?" she asked Seren, helping him to his feet.

He winced, nodded, and picked up his sword. "Why are they here? I don't understand."

A thunderous boom shattered the air behind them. Seren spun around just in time to see a window burst apart, fragments of stained glass raining down the side of the building. An acolyte came crashing through, arms flailing wildly, before hitting the ground with a sickening thud. Seren rushed to the acolyte's side, turning his head away with a gasp. Her pale neck had snapped—the fall killed her.

The cathedral shook with another explosion. Seren took off running, past the garden's archways, bursting into the hall. Cin stayed right on his heels.

Enforcers were everywhere. The elder priest, Dane, hurled a ray of fire toward one, only to be flung backward by an Arc-Caster's counterstrike. Seren's stomach twisted as blood spilled across the marbled floors, blasts of light ricocheting off the vaulted ceiling, shattering glass and murals alike.

Acolytes, still unblessed with magic, their combat experience limited, recklessly threw themselves at the Enforcers, only to be struck down in seconds.

Why weren't they running?

And then Seren saw Mila dressed in the blue robes of an acolyte, spinning around with her dagger, piercing through an Enforcer's armor with her blade.

Another Enforcer emerged from behind her, aiming a pistol at the back of her head. Jude rushed around the corner, his cybernetic leg connecting with the Enforcer's arm, the force bringing the soldier to his knees. Jude snatched the pistol from the Enforcer, whipping around only to get a kick to the gut.

"Jude!" Seren called.

Cin was quick, wrenching the Enforcer back as if he weighed nothing and dug her blade into the weak spot of the armor.

Jude and Seren's gazes met, both huffing. "What are you two doing here?"

Before Jude could respond, a body slammed into Seren, pinning him against the wall, crushing the breath from his lungs. A blue light appeared from underneath the Enforcer's helmet, fanning out as it scanned Seren's face.

A robotic voice chimed. *"Subject Zero confirmed."*

The color drained from Seren's face. They were here for *him*. He gulped. Was this Lumen's doing?

Jude kicked the man away with his leg, then deftly pivoted, snatching the Arc-Caster from the Enforcer's hand while using the hilt of his pistol to brush hair from his eyes.

"You asked me to stay, so I never left," Jude said with a grin. "I always come back. Remember?"

Seren's heart swelled. But before he could get a word in, a bolt of blue lightning flew between them, causing them both to fall back, the Arc-Caster flinging out of Jude's grasp. Leaping to his feet, Seren used his sword to slash at the Enforcer, but the weapon clanged off his armor.

Find the weak spot.

Seren scanned the chaos as he dodged a bolt of lightning, and then he spotted it—the elbows covered by material that didn't shine, allowing for flexibility in movement. Seren slashed and the man cried out, dropping his Arc-Caster. But his moment of triumph didn't last long. Before Seren knew it, a different Enforcer had pinned him against the wall, plunging a syringe into Seren's chest.

Mila flew out of nowhere, her dagger piercing straight through the man's armor, cutting across his neck. He fell in a heap, blood pooling from his throat. Mila and Seren's eyes locked for a fleeting moment before she turned around to slash at another, killing him quickly.

Jude approached Seren. "Are you alright?"

Seren gasped for air, ripping the syringe from his chest. A heaviness started to settle in his bones, but he shook it off. "Fine, just a bit dizzy." He grimaced. "They came here for *me*."

Jude frowned. "Well, then, let's get the hell out of here."

A group of acolytes charged past them, with Aiden at their side. He stopped, locked on Cin. "Get Seren out of here!" Aiden demanded. And just like that, he was rounding the corner down the hall.

"I can't just run away," Seren argued. "I need to help."

"No," Cin said, grabbing his shoulder. "The priests and saints are fighting to protect you and this cathedral. If the Enforcers take you, it'll be for nothing."

Seren felt a tug on his pant leg and looked down. At his feet was a weasel, lifting its paw, revealing its creamy-white belly.

"*Pssst.*"

The three of them redirected their attention to a short figure huddled in the corner, a hood pulled over his head. The weasel scurried over to Felix, scrambling up his brown boots and draping across his shoulders. "Follow me."

They all pivoted as heavy footsteps approached, accompanied by more shattering of glass. More Enforcers were on their way and by the sound of it—too many to fight. Seren turned, following Felix down the hallway, gesturing for the others to come along. Cin grumbled as Seren urged them forward, all falling into step behind Felix.

The boy ran his hand along the wall, his fingers tracing the murals as he guided them. He sped, maneuvering through corridors and away from the chaos until they passed Eldyir's study. Seren had never explored further into the hallway where Eldyir's study was located, so Felix's halt at the top of a descending staircase caught him off guard. Seren glanced back at the others before following. Mila was all the way in the back with her head down.

The staircase was narrow, as if the walls were closing in around them. As they went down further, the light of the cathedral vanished, leaving them in darkness. Seren heard a door swing open and followed Felix through.

"Shut the door," Felix demanded. "And lock it."

"I can't see a damn thing," Cin complained.

Felix chuckled. "What a shame."

He rustled around until light bloomed in the room. Felix offered the oil lamp in his hands, and Cin grabbed it. As she lifted it up, Seren scanned the room. Dusty books were piled on unstable shelves and tables in the cramped cellar. Old barrels sat in corners, along with splintered wooden crates.

"Who the hell are you, and why did you lead us here?" Cin demanded. She turned to Seren. "And why did you *follow* him? For all you know, this could have been a trap." Then she addressed Mila and Jude. "You must be Jude and Mila."

Mila remained silent while Jude grinned with delight.

"It's no trap," Felix said calmly, stepping forward. "I saw this coming, and I came to help."

Cin looked at Seren with disbelief. "Did you hear that?" she scoffed. "He *saw*."

"He's a Seer," Seren replied.

Felix smiled.

"You foresaw the Godless City attack and said nothing?" Seren asked. "You should have told the Grand Priest."

Felix's dark brows pinched. "I'll explain everything later. We need to leave *now*. Unless Seren wants to be strapped to a metal table again." He pointed in Jude's direction. "And unless you want to lose your life to an Enforcer, we need to go."

Seren's breath caught in his throat.

"I know you don't have the luxury of looking around, kid," Cin interrupted. "But there's nowhere for us to go."

Unbothered, Felix straightened himself, the hood of his green cloak falling off his head, revealing his coppery ringlets of hair. "Seren will get us out of here with magic. Won't you? Eldyir's shown you basic teleportation spells by now, hasn't he?"

The walls trembled, and they all swore as books tumbled from the shelves.

"Are you crazy?" Seren asked. "I can't get us out of here, and even if I could, where would we go?"

"Andanova."

Seren's blood ran cold. He was supposed to have more time. He'd been so busy learning spells, healing the sick, and honing his combat skills that he'd only grazed the surface of Andanova. All he knew was that the harp was supposedly in the castle. He couldn't go to Andanova now.

After managing to heal the virus, Seren had been able to harness his magic, but *teleporting* all of them? That required an immense amount of energy and concentration, even for a skilled priest or saint. And whatever had been in that syringe had made Seren's head a bit heavy.

Felix took a step forward. "You take us to Andanova, Seren, I've seen it. If you don't take us now, we will never make it. Enforcers will catch you and take you to the Auguries before we even reach close to the border. This is the only way."

"You really are out of your mind," Mila said. "What is he talking about, Seren? Why the hell would we go to Andanova?"

Seren ignored her, eyes on Felix. "Okay," he breathed. "I'll try."

"This is dangerous," Cin warned. "Teleporting multiple people is already difficult for a powerful priest, Seren. This kid doesn't know what he's talking about. You've never been to Andanova, and we have no items from there to guide us. You could kill us or take us somewhere else by accident. And even if it does work, we might end up outside the castle and be dead in seconds. This is a bad idea all around. I say we take our chances of escaping and kill some Enforcers on the way out."

"Look around, Cin," Seren hissed. "There's no time for plans. No time for any of it. If you don't want to come, then stay here. I'm not risking the outcome of Jude's death and being taken back to Vavilon." He looked at Felix. "I can't explain it, but I trust him."

Jude cleared his throat. He rubbed the back of his neck and pulled at the white collar of his shirt beneath his robes. "What if you had a *person* from Andanova? Someone who lived in the castle?" he asked, his voice strained. "Would that work?"

"That's impossible," Cin growled. "You've all lost your damn minds."

"Jude, you're agreeing with Seren?" Mila asked in disbelief.

"I trust Seren with my life. Don't you?"

The surrounding walls trembled, bottles of ceremonial wine rolling across the floor. Heavy footsteps crashed down the stairs and everyone turned their heads at the sound.

"This was a mistake," Mila said. "We shouldn't have come down here."

"You're all idiots." Cin turned toward the door, her hand on the hilt of her sword.

"Everyone shut up!" Seren yelled. "Jude, give me your hand. Mila, give me your dagger." Seren put his sword in its sheath, and Cin reluctantly did the same as he glared at her. Nobody questioned him as he grabbed the knife and ran it across Jude's palm until blood was drawn. Seren instructed everyone to clasp hands, and obliged, all placing their hands over Jude's, his resting at the bottom.

A boot crashed into the door, splintering the wood. Seren studied Jude's firm features, a strange feeling brewing inside of him.

"I need you to focus on the castle, Jude. Picture it in your mind."

"I'll try."

Another kick rumbled through the walls.

"Are we really doing this?" Mila breathed.

"It's already happening," Felix said, certainly.

Seren closed his eyes, trying to calm himself. If they didn't leave now, the Enforcer barging his or her way in could be the one to take Jude's life and drag Seren to Vavilon. He couldn't afford to fail.

Seren took a deep, steadying breath, the air cool as it filled his lungs. Somewhere inside him, the magic stirred—faint at first, like the flicker of a distant flame. But it had grown stronger since he'd healed Felix, becoming more familiar with each use, more natural. Now it hummed under his skin, waiting.

A tingling sensation spread down his spine, like a thousand tiny sparks igniting, and he seized it, guiding the flow of energy toward Jude's palm. Heat surged through his fingertips, warm and electric, flowing into Jude's skin like water seeking a path. Jude let out a small gasp.

Seren focused harder, pushing through the rising haze dulling his senses. The slow creep of numbness dragged at his limbs, making them feel distant, disconnected, but he couldn't stop now. And the magic burned bright, fighting to break free despite the cold, liquid weight pressing against his veins.

Seren's heart pounded against his chest, the pulse loud in his ears as he struggled to focus on the distant image of Andanova, a place he had never known. It felt foolish. But then, a surge of power rushed through his veins, making the hair on his arms stand on end. The air around him shimmered as if the world itself was bending to his will. In his mind's eye, the vision flickered—vivid—golden fields stretching beneath a wide, sapphire sky, the silhouette of a grand castle rising on the horizon.

He gritted his teeth and pushed harder, channeling the magic that whispered under his skin. Nothing. The vision wavered, slipping from his grasp like smoke.

Then, a sudden thud. The jarring sound of the boot striking the door harder.

Seren cursed under his breath and shut his eyes again, trying to reclaim the image. This time, the scene twisted. The skies turned a deep, bruised red, and where the fields had been, there was only devastation—charred land and crumbling ruins, as far as he could see. The air was thick, suffocating, carrying the bitter scent of ash and blood.

Seren was thrust forward much too quickly. His hand clutched Jude's, as if he were being propelled through time and space. It felt like someone had torn off Seren's skin and then put it back together again.

A cacophony of grunts and gasps erupted as they crashed into solid ground. Seren's body slammed against stone, the impact jarring every bone. He blinked, his vision blurring. For a fleeting moment, he thought he'd succeeded. He thought they were safe.

But then the air refused to come. He gasped, chest heaving under an unbearable weight. Panic clawed at him as he stared ahead at a cracked wall, his breath rasping in the silence.

No. Something was wrong.

I can't breathe.

"I knew that spell was dangerous!" Cin's voice blared. "He phased straight into it, damn it!"

Seren's vision blurred as he slumped forward, his eyes landing on the broken sword piercing his ribcage. He fell backward, the sword coming along with him. He heaved, blood dribbling down his lips.

Jude hurried over to him, cursing furiously as he kneeled. His hands landed on Seren's chest, soaked in blood. "Oh, gods," he whispered. "No. No. Seren."

Seren tried to speak, to tell Jude it would be okay, but no words came out. Instead, blood poured from his mouth, his vision swimming around the edges.

Jude stood and grabbed Felix by the collar, dragging him to his feet. "Did you see this?" he demanded. "Did you bloody see *this*?"

Felix did not respond, his body swirling out of Seren's sight.

"Shit, shit." It was Mila. "It looks bad." She sounded afraid. Worried. Like she didn't want him to die.

Cin stepped forward, grabbing the hilt of the sword in his body. "You both need to calm down," she roared. "I'm pulling it out, and you both need to be ready. He's going to bleed a *lot*. If you guys don't get it together, he's going to die."

Fear coursed through Seren as he watched Cin's face harden. Her hands tightened on the hilt. Jude pressed himself into the wall, his eyes meeting Seren's. The safe color of the sky. Seren didn't want to look away.

"I'm pulling it out, Seren. Hold on."

Jude's face faded out of focus.

No.

No.

Just leave it.

And without a second to waste, Cin yanked the sword out of his ribs. Seren let out a horrible choking sound as blood filled his lungs, and the world faded to black.

Twenty

"In times of crumbling kingdoms and war, it is to the Grand Priest that those who wield holy magic must turn. His words carry the law of the gods, guiding them to righteousness."

—Compendium of Holy Magic

When Aiden was twelve, he knew he wanted to be just like his father—a stoic man favored by the gods and trusted by his people. Aiden listened intently to the stories of gods, magic, and the importance of faith, never doubting a single word his father spoke. Aiden believed with every ounce of his being. His father had always made it clear that there was no room for questions or uncertainty, and Aiden accepted that without hesitation.

His younger half-brother, Lumen, clung to Aiden like a pest, mimicking his every move and claiming the same dreams and aspirations. Lumen never left him alone, always a nuisance, asking endless questions: *Why would the gods do this? Why would they do that? Is it true that humans are cursed for the sin of Eden?* He didn't know when to keep his mouth shut or stay to himself.

Sometimes, a twinge stirred in Aiden's belly when their father slapped Lumen or dragged him to his bedroom, Lumen sobbing through apologies. But Aiden ignored it and shoved the feeling far away. Lumen shouldn't have been asking stupid questions, he would remind himself. He must follow the laws of the Trinity. Lumen was a bother, nothing more. And everyone thought so—their father, their mother, who could hardly stand to look at him. Even the handmaidens treated him with cold indifference. Lumen was a constant reminder of defilement and sin. So, was it really a surprise when the gods rejected him at Etheles?

Why was Aiden thinking about that day now? Why, as he gathered magic in his palm, the Grand Cathedral's broken stained glass scattering at his feet, did Lumen's face flash in his mind? The disappointment, the light that left his younger brother's yellow eyes, the child who had looked up to Aiden for so long, dying on the mountain.

Aiden huffed, sending a blade of light at an Enforcer to his left. He ducked, evading a cascade of electric-blue light aimed for his head, glass shattering behind him.

Then, from behind Aiden, the Grand Cathedral doors flew open, more Vavilon soldiers storming in, with one standing out amongst the rest. His helmet sat atop his head, fashioned with a prominent beak jutting from its center, resembling the visage of a bird. The back of his armor had copper-colored wings infused into it, acting as a spiked shield flanking each side. His gauntlets resembled the talons of eagles—sharp and edged.

Aiden knew without question: a Novem, a head of Vavilon's military. Aiden took a step forward, feeling his magic surging within him. The gods had blessed him today, or perhaps Eldyir was right, and Seren's revelation had indeed strengthened their magic.

"You have no place here!" Aiden boomed.

The man took a step forward, mismatched eyes peering at Aiden through his helmet. "Lumina is harboring a fugitive, *Subject Zero*, property of the Novem. I, General Akarian, have come to retrieve the Subject."

Aiden gritted his teeth, eyes locking on the younger acolytes who stood trembling in their robes. No words were exchanged, but they understood what he was asking through his look.

Check on Seren.

"Nothing belongs to you here," Aiden seethed.

The general stomped his armored foot on the marble floor, the sound echoing as he laughed. He reached up and pulled his helmet off with a cybernetic hand. One of his eyes was deep brown, while the other was a striking blue, both vivid against his olive skin. Corkscrew curls, with tips tinted blue, a strange fashion in the Godless City, sat atop his head.

"You and your people have already made this harder than it needs to be. You can thank your Grand Priest for not heeding the Auguries' warnings." He flashed a pearly smile at Aiden, a single golden tooth gleaming amongst the others. "But by the look on your face, he didn't tell you about that, did he?"

Before Aiden could manage a response, Eldyir emerged from behind one of the towering stone pillars near the altar. His gait was slow, deliberate, like every step strained the last reserves of strength in his body. The priest's shoulders sagged, as if they could no longer bear the weight of the robes he wore. Deep furrows now marred his skin, lines like spiderwebs threading across his cheeks and brow. The magic that had once sustained him seemed to be unraveling, leaving behind not just wrinkles but a hollowness in his eyes.

"The boy is no longer here," he announced, his voice cracking. "Search if you must. He has left. Now, please, I ask you to take your leave."

General Akarian stepped forward, raising his hand. At once, all of the soldiers froze. The clash of steel and the shouts of battle died instantly, leaving an eerie silence to settle over the destruction. Glowering at the priests, Akarian circled around Eldyir and Aiden like a hawk eyeing prey, his metallic wings shimmering in the first light of dawn. "I do not think I will," he said coldly. "Tell me where the boy has gone."

Aiden clenched his fist, but Eldyir swiftly caught his hand, his dark eyes flashing a silent warning.

The general continued circling, his helmet dangling in his hand. "Do you think cowering in your churches for your gods to save you will change anything? While you rely on a pathetic myth, hailing a helpless child to cleanse the Veil, Vavilon is working on technology to destroy it forever. While your 'chosen one' makes minor feats, Vavilon supersedes. We have found a cure for the virus. And soon the Veil will be a distant memory."

Aiden stepped forward. "You cannot," he demanded. "You fools will sever our connection with the gods themselves."

"Men need no gods," Akarian sneered.

"You're wrong," Aiden said.

"Am I?" the general said. "Have your gods cured the virus? Did they stop Andanova? When will you see the truth, priest? You cannot hide from it forever. Do you think you're special because the gods gave you magic?"

Aiden's lip curled.

"Times are changing, and people will leave the gods behind where they belong—buried away in books and dead kingdoms. Your magic will fade, just as your faith already has. You cower in fear and beg for salvation while the gods ignore you. When did the gods last answer your prayers? You can claim faith, spit your scriptures, and await your prophecies. But what will you do when war comes to your doorstep?"

Aiden stilled.

"Do you think the Auguries are going to wait around while rumors of war begin? The Godless City will start the war, and the Godless City will finish it." Akarian's voice was sharp as a knife. "We have allies everywhere, priest. Perhaps those you keep close aren't as faithful as you think. Not everyone is as eager for death as you are." The general took a step forward, towering above Aiden and Eldyir. "No one is safe until we destroy the Veil forever."

"If you have no belief, then what do you want with Seren?" Aiden demanded.

"It's none of your concern."

A soldier hurried to Akarian's side, clad in burnished copper armor. "General Akarian, sir, we've searched everywhere. The Subject has vanished. We followed him into a storage room, but when we opened the door...there was no sign of him."

"What do you mean he *vanished*?" Akarian demanded.

The soldier cleared his throat. "As I said, sir—"

"Get out of my sight!" the general spat.

Akarian unleashed a roar, pointing his Arc-Caster at the ceiling. The painting above shattered down the middle, splitting the once-beautiful depiction of the pure Veil and humans.

Sweat dripped down Aiden's back as the general released a string of curses. He pointed the Arc-Caster in Aiden's direction, vibrant sparks dancing around the tip. "You would be wise to forget your gods," he hissed between clenched teeth. "Save your people from the darkness that is to come."

"The gods will save us," Aiden said, straightening his shoulders.

Akarian's lips curved, his golden tooth peeking through his lips. "Mark my words, priest. You cannot have peace without first having war. And you cannot win a war on your knees."

General Akarian barked at the Enforcers, demanding they file out. The soldiers fled past Aiden, their feet crunching atop broken glass and fragments of the crumbling ceiling mural. Aiden's pulse quickened, fury flooding over him in waves.

How dare they come into a holy place and bring so much destruction? They had shown no mercy, killing acolytes who stood in their way. It was a chilling glimpse of what the future could hold if war raged across the country. Could Lumina remain idle if Vavilon attempted to destroy the Veil and turn the entire world godless?

When the last of the soldiers finally departed, Aiden collapsed onto his knees, hands flat against the stone, mercifully spared from a palm full of glass. But that even felt like too much. Perhaps his wrists could not even support him. He gasped for breath, his limbs trembling from exhaustion. He had pushed himself to the brink.

"Aiden…"

Eldyir's faint call came from beside him. Aiden staggered to his feet, pushing his dark hair out of his eyes. As he turned, he saw Eldyir collapsed and still on the stone floor, his face drained of color. Around him, glittering red and gold shards of stained glass scattered the light, a reminder of blood, of mortality.

"Eldyir!"

The Grand Priest's hand quivered as he reached underneath his robes, pulling out his medallion. Blood coated his fingers, running red down the whites of his garments.

"Take it," Eldyir said quietly.

"No," Aiden demanded. "No. No. I'll heal you—"

"No, you will not," Eldyir breathed. "My time has ended, as all things do."

Aiden stared at Eldyir's face in disbelief. Eldyir's features now betrayed his true age; his hair was stark white, wrinkles carved deep into his skin. It was as if the magic that had sustained him for so long had finally abandoned him. Eldyir wrapped his bloodied hand around Aiden's and set the necklace in his palm.

"This is the fate the gods have chosen for me. As it is yours."

Tears spilled from Aiden's cheeks.

"Protect those dear to you. Protect Lumina. Guide Seren. He needs you." Eldyir smiled faintly. "The boy is good, Aiden. The boy is…true. Do you understand? Do not let the darkness deceive you. Take care of him. I want you…to take my place as Grand Priest. You are strong enough…to carry these burdens…these truths."

Aiden had a thousand unanswered questions, questions he had been too afraid to ask. And now, he would never have the chance. He couldn't take Eldyir's place; none of the priests or saints respected him.

"I'm not worthy," Aiden choked. "I can't."

His mind flashed to Seren, the child he'd failed, to Emeryn, the woman he'd loved, and to Lumen, the brother he'd abandoned.

But Eldyir's hands had already fallen to his side, with his lifeless eyes lifted to the heavens. Aiden clasped the bloodied medallion and pressed it against his lips in a silent prayer.

TWENTY-ONE

"Do demons remember what they once were? This question has haunted me for many nights. But what haunts me most is the possibility that they do not. What if they are irreversibly twisted, remembering nothing else? And if so, how can we be certain that we ourselves have not twisted into corruption, yet are too blind to see it?"

—Exorcist Damian Silver

*S*eren had little memories of his life before Aiden and the Church of Caelestis. Sometimes, he thought he could imagine his father's face, but the more he tried, the further it became. He remembered being happy and feeling warm when his father held him up to the sky and pointed to the stars. He remembered his mother dancing and smiling. But it always ended in a blur of shadow. It blanketed everything, distorted his father's face, ripped his mother away from him.

And then there were the dreams—strange and unsettling, lurking at the edge of his consciousness. Dreams he dared not utter aloud. In them, he transcended his human form, becoming a shadow that stretched across the world, snuffing out every glimmer of light. And then there were the dreams *where he transformed into light, pushing back the darkness with an infinite brilliance.*

Seren never tried to make sense of these things. He considered himself well-behaved. He did what he was told. He kept his private thoughts to himself. He didn't ask about his father. He didn't ask his mother why she was always gone or what she was doing. He didn't ask why the High Priest was always forcing him to study magic or history. He didn't—until he did.

On Seren's tenth birthday, his mother had baked him an orange blossom cake with lavender frosting. He had licked the sweet cream from his fingers, savored every morsel. Aiden had gifted him a book—of course—and his mother gave him a strange pair of magnifying glasses for birdwatching.

Seren knew he was supposed to be happy, but it had been weeks since his mom had been home. Everything felt good, for now, but he couldn't help but wonder: How long until she's gone again?

His mother had found him later on the edges of the church, watching birds fly through his new glasses. Seren wondered if Vavilon had produced it, as the knobs were made from gleaming copper, enabling him to magnify what he saw. He had never seen anything like it before. Seren had spent the day filling a sketchbook with heavy-handed scribbles of birds. The wings were always his favorite part to illustrate, and he'd taken his time adding detailed feathers.

"Your father also liked birds," his mother had said gently, looking over his shoulder. As the words slipped from her, she brought a hand to her lips as though she regretted saying them.

His mother settled next to him in the grass, leaning forward, red hair tickling his hands as she watched him draw. "He once told me that birds were born straight from the heavens, blessed with the ability to fly so the angels would never be alone."

The tip of Seren's pencil broke as he pressed too hard. He sighed and set it aside, lifting his face to his mother. "You never talk about father," he'd said. "Why not?"

"Someday, I will tell you all about him." She brushed Seren's dark hair and cradled his cheek. "For now, I want you to keep doing what you're doing. Listen to Aiden and follow the laws of the Trinity."

"I don't want to."

"Seren—"

"I hate it here."

His mother was silent as the wind blew through the trees, rustling the autumn leaves and casting shadows on the grass.

Seren clenched his fists. "Why are you never home?"

He couldn't erase the look on his mother's face. She wrapped her hands around his. "It's hard to explain, but I promise you I'll always be with you. Right here." She poked his heart. "You're a good boy, right, Seren?"

"What if I am only good because you want me to be?" He slammed his notebook into the grass, tears pricking his eyes. "Because if you think I'm good and do everything you say, you'll finally come home. You'll stay with me, and I won't..." Seren sniffled. "I won't be alone."

His mother had embraced him, clutching him to her chest. "You will always have good in you, my little star, and that light will guide you through even the darkest nights. And I will always, and forever, love you. Even in the dark, I will love you. You will never be alone. I promise."

But...

Seren's mother had been wrong. As the years passed, nothing changed. The loneliness grew and grew until it became a part of him.

And he was in the darkness now, swallowed by it. He had seen everything he was and everything he would become. Seren was alone—not just now, but always, forever. Darkness surrounded him as if it had been his true mother all along, his caretaker, his protector. The only glimmer of light came from the harp in the distance, its glow beckoning to him, offering both refuge and torment. Seren reached it, his fingers running down its polished body.

"This is a holy instrument, Seren. You must never play it with anger and sin in your heart," Aiden had once cautioned. "It would be an insult to the gods themselves."

But anger was all Seren had left. He was tired of Aiden's incessant rules, of his mother's constant absences. His resentment bubbled over as his fingers plucked the strings with reckless force.

Dark tendrils sprang from his fingertips, weaving through the strings. The harp's melodic tones morphed into screams, echoing like glass shards grinding against metal, tearing through his mind. A hundred malicious whispers surrounded him as shadows coiled around the harp's neck.

"We are yours to command."

"Take us, use us."

"We can be your strength."

"Together, we are unstoppable."

Together?

The word rattled around in Seren's brain, a persuasive whisper promising release. He strummed the string once more, and as it snapped, Seren could've sworn something inside him snapped too. The shadows cradled him for a moment, held him close as if they would never let him go. And then, Seren opened his mouth and let the darkness in.

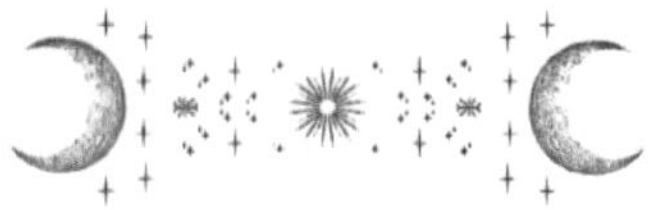

Seren woke with a gasp, sitting up, his hands clutching his bare chest. His fingertips ran over the large wound that was already scabbed over. It hadn't been a dream after all. His mouth felt dry, a faint bitterness lingering on his tongue. With a surprised exhale, he took in his surroundings, realizing he was in a massive bed covered in dusty, moth-eaten blankets.

"You're awake."

Seren almost jumped out of his skin at the sound of her voice.

Mila stood at the bedside, still wearing the blue acolyte robes, though they were soaked in blood. Her eyes were bloodshot, the skin beneath blotchy and raw. "I stopped the bleeding, and your body did the rest on its own." She let out a nervous laugh. "Cin nearly lost her mind when she realized I was a Sister, but Felix somehow convinced her I was harmless."

"Why are you here?" he said, his voice rough.

"I was waiting for you to wake up." Mila's eyes darted to the ground, her jaw tightening. Something flickered across her face, but Seren couldn't pin down the emotion. "I was really worried about you."

Seren glanced around and realized they were alone. The room was sparsely furnished. Only a bed and a rotting dresser remained, the latter holding a chamber stick with a wavering flame.

"Where is everyone?"

"Ensuring that we're safe for the time being," Mila answered. "We made it in the castle, but you can feel it, can't you? It's terrible."

"Yes," Seren replied. The weight of the Veil was exactly as he recalled, a dreadful, bone-chilling feeling that pressed down on him. "Did we...make it? Are we in the castle?"

"Yes, we are. " Mila settled on the bed beside Seren. "How are you feeling?"

Seren rested his head on the dirty pillow. "Exhausted," he mustered. "Dizzy."

"We all thought you were going to die," Mila whispered.

Seren squeezed his eyes shut for a moment, an unsteady breath escaping him. "Yeah, I thought so too."

A hollow ache settled in his chest where the sword had pierced him, a reminder of how close he had come to death. The aftershocks lingered, the weight in his bones like lead, dragging him down. If it hadn't been for his abilities, he would have died.

"Not even a minute in Andanova and you almost get yourself killed," Mila said softly. "We're really in for it."

"Yeah, no turning back now," Seren managed. He studied Mila's unreadable features. "I didn't think you'd be here with me."

"Me either," she said. "I understand if you...hate me. I know you don't want me here." Her fist clenched, gathering fabric in her hands.

"Hate you?" Seren repeated. "I could never hate you." The words left him more passionately than he intended, and he flushed. Turning toward the wall, he cleared his throat. "If anything, you should hate me. I made a fool of myself. I thought..." He stopped.

In the weeks they'd been apart, he had pushed away every thought of her. Realizing their connection had been superficial left him feeling vulnerable and naïve for confessing his feelings. And for that, he could neither blame her nor be angry.

"I never wanted to kill you," Mila said quietly. "Not in the Sanguine Kingdom. Not now. When you said my true name, it broke the hold the poison had on me."

Seren's heart thudded unsteadily in his chest, each beat feeling distant and faint. "I shouldn't have said your name. I was drunk, angry, and stupid—"

"Seren." When she said his name with such intensity, his gaze lifted. "I forgive you. Just don't do it again."

Silence stretched between them.

"So, the Sanguine Queen still wants me dead, I presume?" Seren sighed.

Mila smiled. "I'm sure she does, but..." She hesitated. "Iris came to me—she was desperate. Eden has been demanding younger sacrifices. The Sisters are kidnapping children, murdering them in cold blood. Iris thought killing you would free me—and that I could stop it."

Mila's gaze dropped, shame flickering across her face. "I never wanted to be queen. But if I could build a kingdom without bloodshed, maybe it would be worth it." She let out a shaky breath. "I'll find another way to break the bond—and I'll kill Eden. No matter what it takes."

Seren was quiet for a few moments. "I'll help you find a way to break it. If we get out of Andanova alive that is. I promise." He sank further into the bed, exhaustion pulling him deeper. He felt like he could sleep forever. Seren reached for Mila's hand, weakly squeezing it before pulling away.

"If there's one thing I've learned about you, it's that you keep your word," she said, amused.

"What else have you learned?" he murmured, eyelids growing heavier.

"That you're a terrible liar," Mila chuckled. "And a surprisingly great dancer."

Seren's eyes fluttered shut. "And?"

"And you're a good kisser."

His eyes snapped open, just in time to see Mila close the door behind her.

"I could never hate you," Seren whispered into the emptiness. "Even if you never love me back... I'll never hate you."

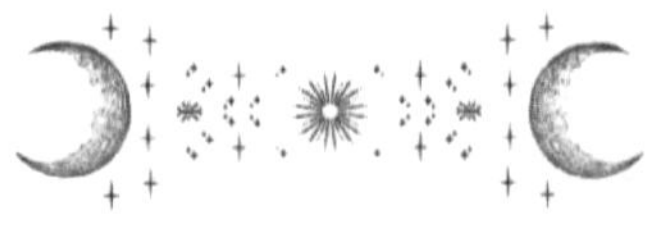

The door flung open, jolting Seren awake. Cin and Felix entered the room side by side. Cin's face was flushed red; her sharp eyebrows pointed downward. Mila followed behind and was no longer wearing robes. It seemed like she'd stumbled upon an item in the castle that the moths hadn't damaged—an ensemble of men's clothing that had a princely appearance. She wore a blue vest adorned with golden buttons and, underneath, a black blouse with sleeves that billowed out. Seren found it quite flattering and couldn't help but stare.

Cin's expression shifted to stern relief. "Good, you're awake. You can go talk some sense into that friend of yours."

As Felix stroked his weasel, a troubled look crossed his face. "Even Theo's worried about Jude."

Cin rolled her eyes. "That rat's brain is the size of a pea."

"Where's your heart?" Felix pouted.

"Don't have one."

Seren forced himself upright, swinging his legs off the bed. A wave of dizziness washed over him, and he gripped the mattress to balance himself before he could speak. Once steady, he pushed himself to his feet. "What's wrong with Jude?"

Mila leaned against the wall, arms crossed. "He stayed with you while you slept until Cin convinced him to take a break."

"More like bullied him," Felix grumbled.

"How long have I been out?" Seren asked.

"A couple of hours, give or take," Cin said. "Long enough for us to scour most of this floor."

Seren frowned. "And where is Jude?"

Mila sighed. "He locked himself in the music room down the hall and won't come out or talk to anyone."

Cin placed a hand on her hip. "Not everyone is strong enough to withstand the Veil," she scoffed.

"That can't be the only reason," Seren countered.

"Either way," Cin said, "this is no time for us to lose our heads. We have a harp to find, and we need to get out of here before the demon of this cursed castle realizes we're here. Go talk some sense into him."

Seren gave a firm nod.

"I'll come with you," Mila offered.

"No," Seren replied. "I'd like to go alone."

Cin sighed, flicking her gloved fingers dismissively. "No use arguing. Just go down the hall and make it quick."

Mila frowned. "We should stick together. What if the demon of the castle shows up?"

Felix rested a hand on Mila's shoulder. "He'll be okay."

Cin rolled her eyes. "Well, that makes me question everything. You almost got Seren killed. Your word means little to nothing."

"Leave him alone. I'm still alive, aren't I?" Seren scowled. "I'll be fine."

He walked toward the door, his stride uneven. His chest felt tight, but he shook it off. "Just wait here. I won't be long."

Before anyone could argue, Seren shut the door behind him.

The hallway was dark, and he immediately regretted not grabbing the chamber stick. As he walked, his footsteps unsettled the dust. He coughed, his chest burning, and braced himself against the wall, gritting his teeth through the pain. Rubbing his chest with a small sigh, he felt the raised skin of what was already forming into a scar beneath his fingertips.

Then, very faintly, he heard the sound of music—distant and soft, coming from directly ahead.

Seren paused, taking a deep breath. He held out a palm and closed his eyes. Though he felt weak after his injury, he was confident he could still use his magic. Warmth tingled in his fingertips, and a single purple flame erupted at the tip of his finger.

A layer of dust coated every surface, turning the once-grand castle into a ghostly relic. Oil lanterns, their glass clouded with grime, clung to the walls, cobwebs decorating their golden embellishments. Seren approached one, lighting the wick and smiling when it flickered to life. The oil had been protected, even after all these years. With a wave of his hand, all the lanterns ignited at once, their dancing violet flames illuminating the way. Seren grinned wider.

Eldyir had taught him something, after all.

The guttering light cast long shadows on the marbled walls, revealing intricate patterns in gold leaf, hidden beneath the accumulated filth. Seren's footsteps echoed, disturbing more dust that had settled for a decade.

At last, he reached the doors at the end of the hallway. The wood had rotted, and the golden handles—sculpted into the bowed heads of peacocks—bore recent fingerprints. Beyond the doors, the hushed sound of a piano drifted through. Seren tried the handles, only to discover they were locked.

Seren rapped his knuckles against the door.

"Jude?"

The piano's melody faded, swallowed by the stillness that followed.

"Will you let me in? Please?" Seren held his breath, awaiting a response, but only the quiet of the room greeted him. "Don't make me beg, Jude."

Although, I'm sure you'd love that.

Another tense pause followed, then the creak of floorboards echoed behind the door. The lock clicked, but the door didn't open. Jude's footsteps could be heard moving away. Seren cautiously pushed the door open, revealing a dimly lit room cluttered with various instruments. A brown mouse skittered out from a broken gittern, squeaking as it darted past Seren's feet. In the center of the room stood a grand ebony piano, its side adorned with hand-carved oak leaves, a half-melted candle resting in a golden chamber-stick. Jude sat at the piano, turned away from Seren. His shoulders tensed, his back arching slightly.

"Jude?"

Jude's fingertips, coated in thick dust, skimmed across the keys, producing a faint whispering sound. Seren stood quietly in the shadows, watching as Jude leaned back in the chair. He had shed the acolyte robes, now dressed in a pristine white long-sleeved shirt with cuffs slightly ruffled at the ends, paired with dark blue trousers that were now covered in dust. Strands of hair fell into Jude's eyes, casting shadows on his face, which were softened by the dim candlelight.

Then, with aching slowness, Jude began to play. Although the piano was out of tune, each note of the melancholic melody seemed to linger in the air, stirring a deep ache in Seren's chest. Jude's humming drifted through the room, his voice blending with the music. Seren closed his eyes, his fingers twitching involuntarily as if longing to join in and play alongside him.

"I have met Death, and She is kind,

Like waves that crash in a madman's mind.

A kingdom of gold,

To a devil, I sold,

My daughters, my sons, and my eternal soul."

Jude stopped singing. His head hung low, his hands quivering above the keys.

Seren stepped forward. "Practicing?"

"I guess so," Jude murmured, not turning to meet Seren. "I used to play this piano all the time. I always hated it." He laughed, shaking his head, hands running over the dusty top. "I can't believe it's still here. My mom used to tell me I had perfect pianist fingers—long and nimble." Jude waggled his fingers in front of his face. "Turns out I'm much better at pulling a trigger." Jude cocked his head to the side towards a dusty, cracked handheld harp sitting in the corner, the strings miraculously still intact. "Play with me."

"I don't know. I feel like we should get back to the others—"

"Play with me," Jude said again. He swiveled around in the creaking chair, his red-rimmed eyes meeting Seren's. The once bright sky blue in his eyes now appeared cloudy, as if a tempest had rolled in. He locked his gaze on Seren, his jaw clenched. "Rumor has it you can play the harp. Show me."

Compelled to listen with Jude's burning stare over him, Seren moved toward the harp, picking it up. He grimaced, wiping thick layers of dust from the body. His heart hammered in his chest as he cleared his throat, grabbing a chair. Seren plucked a string, cringing.

"It's terribly out of tune," he said.

"Do you know how to tune it?"

"I think so."

Seren's fingers delicately tweaked the pegs, moving on instinct. His stomach tightened, nerves rising with each silent second. He should have stopped this, told Jude to forget it, but something in Jude's expression made him uneasy. He wasn't acting like himself.

"Alright," Seren said. "I can't promise it's going to sound any good." He strummed a string again, surprised by its resilience. "These should've snapped after all this time."

"They're made of Andanovan gold," Jude said. "Now, play." He turned back around, his fingers waltzing across the keys.

With a deep breath, Seren's fingers strummed across the harp. He was afraid that memories would overwhelm him, that he'd want to cast the instrument aside. But he found his fingers moving from memory, beyond his control, plucking and weaving a tune he did not recognize.

Seren wasn't sure what he was playing, but his notes intertwined perfectly with Jude's piano, the sound like a thread pulling them together. Seren closed his eyes, letting the piano lead, his fingers dancing lightly over the strings. Perhaps it was because he had always played alone that now, with Jude, the music flowed freely—unfettered by fear. It was a desperate whisper, delicate as the wind beneath a wounded bird's wing.

Though their melodies came from different places—Seren's raw, untamed, Jude's measured, steady—in this moment, they fused, becoming a single, effortless breath. Jude's tempo quickened, and Seren's fingers followed, each note a swift, hungry pursuit. The strings thrummed beneath his touch, vibrating with a rising heat, a shared rhythm.

Then, with a final surge, Jude's hand struck the last chord, Seren's strings humming in his wake, a trembling echo. As the final note faded, Jude's fingers lingered over the strings, then lifted. With a deep breath, Jude rose to his feet.

Warmth flooded Seren's cheeks, his heart pounding. His blood felt hot, burning beneath his skin. He raked his fingers through his hair, strands falling into his eyes. Seren cleared his throat and set the harp on the floor.

Jude turned to Seren, his eyes widening. "You're glowing," he said.

Seren's face flushed further. "Well, now that you're back to making jokes, we should head back to the others—"

"No, you're *glowing*, Seren."

Seren looked down at his palms, sucking in a sharp breath. A glow emanated from his hands, but it was gradually diminishing.

Jude stood and stepped toward him, his hands reaching out. With a hesitant touch, he brushed the tips of his fingers against Seren's just as the light vanished.

"We should get back to the others," Seren repeated. He cleared his throat again, stood, and pulled his hands away. "I don't want to worry them."

Jude stayed motionless. "Worry them?" he echoed. "I thought you were going to die, Seren."

There was a strange tone to Jude's voice—not quite sadness, not quite anger, but something in between the two, almost like a betrayal.

"I'm okay," Seren said. "Still living and breathing."

Jude's head fell, resting against Seren's shoulder. "I thought I'd lost you. I thought you were going to die here. Just like they did. Just like I will."

Seren recoiled and gripped Jude's shoulders. When Jude's head remained limp, Seren reached beneath his chin, forcing him to meet his gaze. "You're not going to die here," he said, his voice firm. "And neither am I."

Jude was silent for several seconds before whispering, "The Andanovans had a saying: '*I fear not men with greed in their hearts, nor a man who is selfish. I fear the man with an emptiness inside him, vast and dark as the starless sky. Greed is neither thine enemy nor thy friend. Greed is thy returning lover, and all that is taken will return to an empty bed.*'"

Jude laughed ruefully. "And now, here I stand, returning to my empty bed."

His head lifted, tears streaking his face. "Why else would I have been brought here?" His voice trembled and his body followed. "What if my bed is also my grave? And what if it's yours too?"

Seren's mouth went dry, unable to find words.

"I can't lose you too, Seren. I can't lose everything again." A sob tore through Jude's words. "Is fate really this cruel?"

"Jude..."

Jude's fingers tangled in his curls, digging into his scalp. "It's not fair." He shuddered violently, gasping for air. "Why here? Why *now*? I thought I had more time." Staggering back a step, he lowered himself, curling into a ball as he muffled a cry.

"Jude." Seren knelt, gently pulling Jude's hands from his hair and clasping them in his own. "Look at me. I won't let you die here. I swear it, okay? And I won't die either."

Jude met Seren's eyes, his skin pale. "I'm so afraid, Seren," he sobbed. "Don't look at me like this—I can't—I just—"

Seren released Jude's hands, and he reached desperately at Jude's shirt. With a sharp tug, he pulled Jude closer, feeling the fragile weight of him sway. Jude stumbled into his arms, body shuddering as he buried his face against Seren's neck, the heat of his tears soaking through the fabric.

"I'm scared too," Seren whispered against Jude's hair. "I'm scared I won't find the harp, and all of this will have been for nothing. I'm scared I'll lead everyone down a path of false hope, only to fail them. I'm scared people will die trying to protect me..." He swallowed hard. "I'm scared of losing you."

Jude released a heart-wrenching sob into Seren's chest. "Your fears...they're not selfish," he gasped. "Mine are."

Seren's arms tightened around him. "That's alright," he murmured. "You're allowed to be selfish. I don't mind."

If the fear of death was truly selfish, then Seren would gladly let Jude be selfish—for as long as their lifetimes allowed.

Seren ran his fingers through Jude's tousled curls, letting him cry. He wasn't sure if he had ever witnessed such profound sorrow before—it was as though years of anguish had suddenly burst forth. Perhaps they had. Jude always seemed so happy, an everlasting light that never dimmed, but now Seren wondered if there was hidden brokenness within him, mirroring the cracks Seren felt in himself. As Jude's tears soaked his skin,

Seren couldn't help but think how exhausting it must be to hide behind a smile for so long.

Several minutes passed, each sob growing softer until Jude's breathing finally steadied. He melted into Seren's arms, his weight warm and heavy against him. They sat in silence for a while after that, Seren's hand threading through Jude's hair, the other firm against his back. A quiet fear lingered in Seren's chest—if he let go, Jude might fall apart again, and he wasn't sure he could hold him together.

"I'm sorry," Jude finally whispered, his voice hoarse. "I've turned into a blubbering baby. How embarrassing."

Seren continued to brush his fingers through Jude's hair. "*'Without rain, flowers cannot bloom under the sun.'*" His words were quiet, almost hesitant, but they felt right. Resting his cheek against Jude's head, he inhaled the comforting scent that was uniquely his. A strange ache bloomed in his chest—a deep, unplaceable twinge that made his grip on Jude tighten so hard that he felt Jude flinch.

"Are you reciting poetry now? What did they *do* to you in that cathedral?" Jude asked in his familiar teasing tone. He lifted his head to face Seren, his skin blotchy and his eyes swollen. And when Jude smiled, it was like the sun breaking through clouds, and Seren found himself leaning closer, irresistibly drawn to that light.

They were so close now, Seren's heart leapt in his chest. If he leaned in just a little more, their lips would touch. Only then did he realize his hand was still tangled in Jude's hair. He sucked in a sharp breath, his fingers slipping away as he drew back.

Seren turned his gaze away for a moment, his cheeks flushing. "It's from the *Book of Metanoia*," he grumbled. "Something my mother used to say."

There was a beat of silence, the two of them sitting close, legs touching.

"You never fail to surprise me, you know that?" Jude said. "I'm sorry for the dramatics. Can we just...keep this between us?" He smirked. "I'd hate to ruin my reputation."

"And what reputation is that?" Seren managed a smile.

"Oh, well, can't you tell? I'm very cavalier," Jude said with a dramatic flair. "Even in the darkest of times, I am unafraid, always."

"I seem to recall you turning very green the first time we were in the Veil together." Seren's smile widened. "But your secret is safe with me."

Jude let out a laugh, hollow at the edges, but it still sent warmth bubbling in Seren's belly. Then Jude sighed, pulling away from Seren entirely, raking his golden curls back. A part of Seren wished he hadn't.

"Thank you, Seren. I'm afraid I would have lost my mind if you hadn't been here."

Seren forced a laugh. "We can't have that. Are you...ready to head back?"

Jude tapped his chin with his index finger, mischief sparkling in his eyes. "Well, now I'm curious—if I amp up the dramatics, what else would you do for me?" A devilish grin overtook his features. "Would you truly have *begged* for me? Gotten down on your knees and everything?"

Seren rolled his eyes, the corners of his lips twitching upward. At least Jude was feeling better. "You like to push your luck, don't you?"

Jude smiled again and sighed, reaching forward. His slender finger traced the inside of Seren's palm, and a delicate shudder went through Seren's arm. He forced himself to look anywhere but at Jude, though he didn't pull away.

"Only when it comes to you," Jude murmured.

Twenty-Two

"Red is the sky when the sun bleeds, and eternal is the night when darkness plants its seeds."

—the Seer Diaries of Felix Amos

Mila sat on the cold floor, her back pressed against the wall. She watched the flickering flame of the candle by the bedside, its warm glow a small comfort after their less-than-ideal arrival in this terrible place.

Theo skittered across the floor, pushing his nose into every object he could find. He disappeared under the bed frame, followed by a squeak and a snarl. Moments later, he dragged a limp rat half his size by its neck, a triumphant sparkle in his eyes.

Felix sat on the bed, hands resting in his lap, his feet wiggling back and forth in his brown boots. Cin, meanwhile, sat in the corner on a rickety chair, sharpening her sword with a whetstone. They hadn't exchanged many words since Mila had used her blood magic to help Seren. Though Mila wasn't blind to the withering glares Cin cast her way from beneath thick lashes.

Mila sighed, unable to shake the discomfort gnawing at her. The silence since Seren's incident had been unbearable, and she kept finding herself replaying the moment.

It had been strange to see Jude like that. He had been ready to throttle Felix, as if Felix had been the one to pierce Seren with the blade. But the boy had remained calm. "He won't die, Jude," he'd promised.

The words had nearly broken Jude.

Even Mila hadn't believed Felix then. The sword had cleaved through Seren's ribs, and the amount of blood had been horrifying. Mila's blue robes had stained a lurid purple from the pool of red, the fabric soaked through to the clothes beneath.

Jude refused to tear himself away from Seren's side, his eyes glued to the steady rise and fall of Seren's ruined chest.

It was Cin who had gotten angry, demanding Jude take a moment to calm down, that he needed to pull himself together. Beneath her glowering gaze, Jude had listened—but instead of returning to the group, he'd locked himself away.

It had to be this place.

When Jude had said he had been in the castle, been to Andanova, Mila could hardly believe her ears. Why had he never told her? She had always been honest with him about where she was from, assuming he had been born and raised in Vavilon, never pressing the issue further. But *Andanova?* She had always thought his blue eyes were just a rare shade, unusually vibrant compared to most, never would it have occurred to her that Andanovan blood flowed in his veins.

"So, Felix," Cin said, breaking the silence. "If you're a Seer, where is your Scribe?" She raised her sharp eyebrows, sleek hair brushing her chin as she leaned forward.

Felix clicked his tongue and Theo looked up from his meal, licking his chops before climbing up the bedpost, onto the bed, and eventually settling on the boy's shoulders. "Can't you tell?" he asked. "I don't need one."

"You remember all of your visions," Cin murmured, as if not recognizing it before. "That's interesting." She set her sword against the wall behind, crossing her legs. "Okay, now, tell me this, what kind of lunatic are you to go willingly into Andanova with strangers?"

Theo nuzzled against Felix's cheek. "The adventurous kind, I suppose."

Mila cleared her throat. "Is it unusual for Seers to remember their visions?"

Cin answered before Felix could get a word in. "It's very unusual. Even more so because he's so young."

Felix looked offended at that. "I'm almost sixteen," he argued.

"Just a babe. I've got ten years on you, kid," Cin teased. "There's only one Seer documented to remember his visions and the two of you share a name. I'm assuming that isn't a coincidence."

"Yes," Felix answered. "He was my grandfather. Hence, my title, Felix Amos the Second." Felix folded his hands in his lap and turned to Mila. "My grandfather was one of the most revered Seers of his time," he said, a touch of pride in his voice.

Cin crossed her arms with a self-satisfied smile. "Are you as loony as your grandfather?"

Felix frowned. "My grandfather was a great man," he said calmly. "Yes, it's common knowledge that he lost grip on reality because of his visions, but that's only part of the story."

Cin let out a small *hmph*, her eyes gleaming with mischief like a cat about to pounce. "Now *that*, I've never heard."

Felix sighed, pulling his green cloak tighter around himself. "Of course you haven't. The Trinity has its secrets just like everyone else. You can't truly be that surprised."

When Cin didn't respond, Felix continued. "The priests and saints put faith above *everything*. Why do you think they were so quick to do a Grand Celebration for Seren's arrival? So quick to send him off to Andanova?"

Mila had already thought about that herself. It all happened so rapidly, and the church had paraded Seren around as if he were a prize. Rumors upon rumors had circulated through Aurelius during the two months of their stay. She'd heard a prince in Kogarashi had named his child in Seren's honor. Other rumors suggested that even the King of Oneriosa, who was allegedly busy plotting war on Vavilon had even taken an interest in Seren. If anything, he was hoping that Seren would help him lead the war against the Godless City. It had seemed reckless to draw so much attention to the proclaimed chosen one.

Cin laughed. "The priests and saints are selfish and send others to do their dirty work. That's never changed. They're a bunch of cowards. They shame exorcists for wielding dark magic to kill demons, yet all they do is banish demons back into the Veil. It's no surprise they'd send an eighteen-year-old boy to his death over a magical harp."

Mila couldn't argue with Cin. The priests and saints were supposed to be her natural enemy. Although they preached forgiveness and claimed to accept anyone into their sanctuaries without question, Mila knew that wasn't true. They would kill her without trial as a Sanguine Sister.

Felix scooped Theo off his shoulders, tickling his belly. "Since Seren is the Mother, then they believe he can't fail," he said, his voice light but serious. "To them, it's written in the stars—divine intervention. Those who follow the gods have clung to these beliefs for centuries. No matter which god one may hail, the Mother's return is the one truth written across time. She will return, and she will cleanse the Veil."

Mila wasn't sure she would ever grow used to words like that. Seren, savior of the world.

"So, why did they lie about your grandfather?" Cin demanded.

"I'm getting to that," Felix said. "As we all know, Seren's purpose is to stop the Sundering, to prevent the Veil overtaking the world."

"I don't understand all of this," Mila groaned. "And I certainly don't see how a *harp* is supposed to help with that."

Cin's gaze flitted toward Mila. "They didn't teach you this in the Sanguine Kingdom?" Her lip curled.

"No," Mila said sharply. "They were much too busy teaching me how to kill people who asked too many questions."

Cin grinned broadly, her canines sharp. "I like you."

Felix's milky eyes turned in Mila's direction. "I can explain if you'd like, while we wait for Seren and Jude."

Mila looked toward the door, sighing in defeat. "I suppose it'd be nice to know why we're all here."

"How much do you know about the gods?" Felix asked Mila.

Mila bit her lip, staring into the flickering flame. She had been raised to know the gods as nothing but worthless and weak. Mila didn't want to admit that she hardly even knew half of their names.

Felix took the silence as his cue. "The Mother, Alernaea, is one of the three primordial deities—the gods who created everything we know, and the gods who rule our realm. There's a lot of speculation about what happened to the Creator and the Father. Some believe that after our creation, they left the gods to their own devices, letting them rule the world as they saw fit. But the Mother remained—a steady constant, guiding the gods."

"She favored the gods of light because they were her solo creations—Kallista, Helios, and Caelum. Before the Great War, she gifted each of them a powerful artifact: a harp for Kallista, a crown for Helios, and a sword for Caelum. It's said these artifacts were lost during the conflict."

"Alernaea sacrificed herself to create the Veil from her very essence, a barrier to prevent humans and magical creatures from destroying each other. Legend says that when she flung herself into the ether, she shattered into fragments of light. Those nearby claimed they could hear her voice echoing in their minds—a promise that she would return to cleanse the corruption."

"I thought the corruption didn't happen until after the Great War?" Mila asked.

Felix shrugged. "They say the greatest of gods are not confined by time."

"Get on with it," Cin said, grinding her teeth. "I'd like to get out of the Veil sooner than later."

"I'm almost finished," Felix said, frowning. "After Alernaea's death, the gods fractured, and disagreements began brewing between them. The Mother had been the glue that held them together, and without her guidance, the gods fell into chaos. Not long after that, the Empyrean Crusade began, and people were torn over which gods to follow. Things got ugly, and many people died. But despite all that, Helios, Caelum, and Kallista remained side by side—hence the Trinity."

"As for the items, Alernaea created the Veil with her sacrifice, and these artifacts are pure, divine objects imbued with her essence. When priests and saints found Kallista's Harp in the ruins beneath Ethles, they tried to play it—and it killed them. It isn't meant for human hands. But Seren has already played it. He needs it to perform the Cleansing. All the items have a purpose. It is speculated that the sword serves as a key, the harp lowers the Veil's barriers to the Garden of Aetheria, and the crown heralds the ascension."

"What do you mean ascension?" Mila demanded.

Felix let out a sigh. "To cleanse the Veil, Seren must gather all the items of the Mother. In the end, after fulfilling the prophecies for each rite, he will become her again. He will sacrifice his human life and return to whence he came, uniting the gods again."

A long silence hung in the air until Mila finally whispered, "And what was your grandfather's response to all of this?"

Felix pet Theo, scratching between his rounded ears. "My grandfather said that the Cleansing would not come to pass. He was adamant that the Sundering was inevitable," he said. "And when he confided in the priests and the saints, they turned their backs on him. The Grand Priest, Eldyir stripped him of his title." A flicker of distant rage showed on Felix's features. "They were supposed to be friends."

"That's why you were in the cathedral," Cin murmured. "Isn't it? Eldyir kept you close in case you had visions."

"Yes," Felix said, his head hanging low, tight curls falling over his clouded eyes. "But why would I tell them? My grandfather...he dedicated his life to finding answers, even after being abandoned by his people. He pushed himself too hard, and..." Felix stopped, his hand clenching against his cloak. "He believed the Scribes were tampering with the prophecies of other Seers. Despite being told that his visions were corrupted and untrustworthy, he refused to let go. He ultimately disappeared without a trace."

"They probably had him killed," Cin mumbled.

Mila shot her a dirty look, to which she shrugged.

"Seer abilities run in families," Felix continued. "My grandfather warned my mother when I was born that the ecclesiarch would have interest, and they would want to ensure that I did not carry the same gift and 'corrupted' visions as my grandfather did. She wanted to protect me, no matter the cost." Felix's milky-green eyes stared vacantly ahead. "Mōkuras are rare flowers that only grow in Kogarashi at the base of volcanos. The red petals of the flower are used for inflammation and often turned into salves, but the roots of the flower are poisonous and cause blindness. My mother thought she was protecting me. How could I ever have visions if I did not have sight?" Theo pushed his nose against Felix's folded hands, as if sensing the weight of his words. "It obviously didn't work. When I was ten, I had my first vision and could *see* for the first time. Before she died, my mother made me swear I would never tell anyone."

Another brief period of silence ensued. Mila had no comforting words to offer the boy—what his mother had done was out of love and fear, and she had a feeling that Felix had made his peace with it long ago.

"Have you seen the Sundering?" Mila asked quietly.

Felix shook his head. "No, I can't see very far into the future, and my visions change—especially based on the decisions of those involved. Fate is a fickle thing. I swear I didn't know Seren would be injured when we teleported here. But it isn't always a vision; sometimes, it's just...a feeling. When Seren wanted to go see Jude alone, I could feel that it was safe, that they'd be fine. I've never been properly trained, so I have to choose to trust myself when certain feelings arise."

Cin snorted. "You mean a gut feeling? We've all got those."

Felix ignored her. "To be honest, my talents lie elsewhere. I see into the past more than I see into the future, but I have to be physically touching the object to see anything." He grimaced. "And unfortunately, dark memories manifest much stronger than happy ones."

"Are you going to tell Seren?" Mila murmured. "He's only here because everyone thinks he can cleanse the Veil and stop the Sundering. To think that it could be mistaken—"

"No," Cin said quickly, "and we don't tell him. For all we know, Felix Amos *was* crazy, and he was wrong. The last thing Seren needs is to think this is all for nothing and it's the last thing *I* need. Belief is power, and right now, Seren needs to believe he can do this. It'll keep him alive." She put her sword on her back and stood. Her armor shone beneath the light, revealing an array of dents and scuffs. "I put little belief in the priests, the saints, hell—even the gods, but if there's even a chance that finding these items will truly lead Seren to the Cleansing, I say we take our chances. I'm sick of death."

Mila stared at the stone floor, clenching her fist. "That's not fair. He deserves to know."

"And what good will it do to tell him now?" Cin challenged.

Felix frowned, lines of worry deepening in his face. "I have to agree with Cin. Doubt could destroy Seren..." he trailed off. "I just don't think now is the best time."

Mila crossed her arms over her chest. "I'm so over prophecies and destined fates," she muttered.

Felix laughed. "That's the problem with these things..." he said. "Avoid one fate, and you bring on another that might be worse than the last. The world has a way of balancing these things. At least... that's what my grandpa believed."

The flame in the room shuddered, and Mila could've sworn the shadows looked like serpents climbing the walls.

What had she brought into her life by avoiding her fate? Was there something else waiting for her entirely? She clenched her fists. Seren hadn't avoided his fate; she had seen his reluctance, his resentment toward a path he had been forced into. But the truth was there, buried beneath the lies they both told themselves.

Mila and Seren could control their actions, their choices—but they could not control the wind or the flow of a river. They could not stop the cycle of night and day. No. Wasn't that what fate was? A direction, a path, one that all walked upon. But didn't all paths eventually lead home?

TWENTY-THREE

"It is said that the royal family of Andanova possessed an unparalleled beauty, with hair like rubies and gold, and eyes reminiscent of the ocean and sky."

—Histories of Aerithium

There were many things Seren longed to ask Jude as they walked down the halls of the dead castle—once beautiful and grand, a place that Jude had known so well. Somehow, it made Seren feel...less alone. He had been selfish in his own way, obsessing over his loneliness, when, all along, Jude had been wandering the world like a ghost, a fragment of a realm left behind. To think that all this time, Jude had been drowning in his own fears, his own sense of emptiness, and Seren had been blind to it.

Yet, Seren couldn't seem to find the right words to say to Jude. They were almost back to the others now, but his feet dragged beneath him as he moved forward, eventually coming to a stop.

Jude slowed, turning to Seren. "Are you alright?"

"I shouldn't have asked you to stay," Seren said quietly. "It's my fault you're here."

"I still would have come, Seren. You have to know that, don't you?"

"But why?"

What reason had he ever given Jude? He had done nothing but put him in dangerous situations since the moment they'd met.

Jude shook his head with a smile. "Oh, Seren," he sighed. "Come on. The others are going to be worried sick if we take too long."

Jude was right. With that, they continued down the hall and into the room where Seren had been resting earlier. Cin, Mila, and Felix were gathered on the floor, whispering amongst themselves. Their heads turned as Seren and Jude entered. Cin rose to her feet, a sword held loosely in her left hand.

"Alright," she said, rolling her shoulders. "We can't waste any more time. I hope you've gotten yourself together, Andanovan."

Jude flinched. "Yes," he said. "I'm feeling much better."

"Good," Cin said with a grin. Her expression softened a touch, her gaze less sharp, a surprising change. "We're lucky we have you here. I can't say anyone's searched this castle with an Andanovan at their hip. Curious as I am, it's not my business to ask. But I'm counting on you to help us find the harp."

Jude gave her a princely bow. "I will do what I can."

Cin lifted one of her black combat boots to rest on the table's edge and reached inside of it. She pulled out a rolled-up piece of parchment and set it on the bed. Then, she set her other boot on the table and pulled out a curved dagger. She handed it to Felix.

"I hope you know how to use this," she said.

Felix frowned and handed it back to her before moving his cloak aside. He adjusted his cream shirt underneath, revealing a leather belt wrapped around his waist with a green pouch tucked inside. "I came prepared. I'm not an idiot."

Cin raised her eyebrows. "And what could possibly be in your tiny pouch that is better than this dagger?"

"Many things," was all he said with a waggle of his fingers.

Cin rolled her eyes. "Your burial." She stuffed the dagger back into her boot and beckoned Jude and Seren over to the parchment as she unrolled it.

Cin pointed to the second floor of the castle map. "This is where we are," she said with certainty. "The castle is massive, so it could take us hours to scour the floors completely."

Jude's golden eyebrows furrowed as he frowned, studying the map. "This is your map?"

"Yes," Cin answered impatiently. "Have a problem with it?"

"Well, yes," Jude said, finger running over the paper. "There's another floor below this one."

"Yes, the dungeons. As far as I know, they're empty."

"No, there's another place. It's where my fath—where the king would keep his greatest treasures, in the undercrofts. It's very well hidden and only..." Jude trailed off.

"Out with it," Cin said, brushing her dark hair back.

"Only a pure-blooded Andanovan can open the entrance," Jude sighed. "If it's down there, it's truly no wonder that nobody has retrieved the harp successfully."

A feline smile stretched across Cin's face. "Well, I say we check there first." Her smile faded as she turned to Seren. "This castle is safe from the demons of Andanova, but it is not safe from the demon king that reigns over it. We stick together, no exceptions. If even for a second, we think he's coming, we get the hell out of here."

"And go where?" Mila scoffed. "We're smack in the middle of the Veil. There is nowhere to go."

"There are many places to hide within these ruins," Cin said. "But I'd rather not have to resort to that." She sighed. "The days are different in the Veil—the sun dims enough for demons to be around, but most still prefer the night. We need to get out of here before nightfall."

Mila cleared her throat. "And how do you intend we leave once we find the harp?"

Cin's hazel eyes flitted to Seren. If things had gone as planned, they would have properly equipped themselves with magical items and had other magic users by their side. Seren could risk teleporting them all again but had a feeling that the others would be against the idea after his incident.

"Well, the harp, of course," Felix piped. "It lowers barriers, and Seren can play it to take us out of the Veil."

Seren bit the inside of his cheek. "Yeah," he managed. "I suppose that's true."

Cin nodded. "Alright then. We can check the armory on the way," she said. "You'll need a sword, preferably not one that ends up in your ribs. I'd rather not lend you mine unless I have to. I've seen you mistreat yours far too many times."

Seren frowned but held his tongue. He cleared his throat. "I think we should also have a plan in case we get separated," he said, his voice steady.

"And..." He hesitated, his gaze flicking between everyone. "The harp has to stay a priority. We can't let this be for nothing."

"Yeah, right," Mila shot back. "I'm not gambling any of your lives over a dumb musical instrument."

Seren exhaled sharply, raking his hair back. "That's not what I mean, Mila. You know that. But this is bigger than us—it's important."

"I have something that might help," Felix said, stepping forward. He reached into the pouch on his belt and pulled out five smooth gray stones, each etched with an embossed sigil that resembled a gust of wind. "If we get separated, these stones can bring us back together to a single location. They're bound by the sigil of Zephyr. When one is used, the sigil will glow on all of them, giving us a chance to reunite. However, they won't take us outside the Veil, and once one is activated, all of them trigger at the same time. All of us will be transported to the location chosen by the person who activates the first stone. So, we have to be careful."

Seren smiled as Felix set a stone in each of their palms. "You're a genius, Felix."

The boy beamed.

Each of them tucked their stones safely into their pockets. Then, Cin seized the dying candle by the bedside. The five of them filed out of the room, with her leading the way. Her black steel glinted under the candlelight as she beckoned them down the hallway, sword in hand. Jude was at Seren's side, with Mila and Felix close behind, speaking in hushed tones. Guilt gnawed at Seren. Had Mila known where he was going, would she have come?

Reaching the hallway, they began their descent down a darkened staircase. Shadows flickered along the walls, shifting with each step. Along the way, they passed a suit of armor displayed on a pedestal set into a recess, its surface cloaked in layers of grime. Seren couldn't help but imagine its former splendor—the gold gleaming under sunlight, its surcoat alive with deep greens, blues, and purples.

Cin groaned as the candlelight waned, weak and dying. Up ahead, the chamber was swallowed in darkness, the windows letting in only a dim, feeble glow that did little to guide the way.

"Damn," she muttered. "I should've known it wouldn't last."

"Here," Seren said. "Let me."

He took a steady breath, magic swelling in his belly. It grew, warmth spreading up his spine, like running water seeping into the crevices between his vertebrae.

Opening his palm, dozens of tiny luminescent birds burst forth. They swirled around him, their bright, delicate wings casting a shimmering light as they drifted through his hair and over his shoulders. Awe was etched onto his companions' faces as the creatures flitted past, illuminating the space with their white glow.

"They're lovely, Seren," Mila said, her eyes following one as it spun above her head.

"Your magic is strong," Cin added, sounding genuinely impressed. "It takes a great deal for a priest to summon magic in the Veil without breaking a sweat."

A bird landed lightly on the tip of Seren's index finger. He lifted it closer, studying the frosted feathering of its wings, the way its tiny chest pulsed with each breath of light.

"My magic is not borrowed from the gods," he said. "It belongs to me." He lifted the bird upwards, willing all the others to scatter.

At the bottom of the stairs, the birds lit up a long-abandoned drawing room. Once, it might have been a place of refinement, where nobles gathered for quiet discussion or private counsel. Now, its elegance lay in ruins. Furniture was scattered, tables overturned with legs snapped and splintered. A shattered chandelier hung precariously overhead, its remaining shards catching the light like scattered diamonds. Rust-colored stains marked the couches; their fabric faded to the pallor of rain-soaked parchment.

On the western side, remnants of a large stained-glass window remained, its broken pieces strewn everywhere. A cracked teapot, gilded with gold, clinked against Seren's toe before tumbling across the debris.

It occurred to Seren that the day of the Unveiling in Andanova must have been like any other. He could almost picture it: the gleam of white-oak furniture legs in the summer light streaming through vibrant yellow and blue stained-glass windows while women in satin gloves chatted, pouring chamomile tea into delicate cups.

Seren stepped over the wreckage, and Theo scurried ahead, squeaking as if leading the group. Cin trudged forward, the glass cracking beneath her boots, while Jude lagged, his movements slow and heavy.

"You two go on ahead of me," Seren said to Mila. She thanked him and guided Felix ahead, avoiding the wreckage.

Jude had halted, pulled toward the broken window, half his face cast in an orangish shadow from the filtered light. A bird fluttered near his shoulder as his hands gripped the ledge, knuckles blanching. Seren stepped over a broken vase, clearing his throat to announce his presence.

"It looks so much different from what I remember," Jude said, not turning to meet Seren. "In my mind, everything was dead. The endless fields of golden wheat were forever erased, the land scorched, and the trees blackened. But—it's here—pieces and ruins of what once was. If I were to go to the stables, the skeletons of the horses would greet me, but it would be the same earth I once walked upon."

Seren's shoulders brushed against Jude's as he peered out the window. He wasn't sure what he had expected. Perhaps the same, everything dead and left behind. During Seren's last visit to the Veil, it had been night; now, daylight revealed the sun hanging unusually dim in the sky. Its once vibrant light was reduced to an ugly, bloodied red, casting a dark crimson haze over the horizon and shrouding the world in eerie twilight. Strange, thorny ivy clung aggressively to the crumbling walls that had once guarded the castle while weeds sprawled unchecked across the land. They crept over ruined stones and scaled the trunks of lifeless trees. Shadows flickered between the trees. Demons.

"There used to be wisteria all around the castle," Jude said fondly. "The same pretty color as your eyes."

Seren flushed.

"There are no blooming flowers here," Jude continued. "The kingdom I once knew...it's gone." His shoulders stiffened. "It's the same place in a different world. *Stolen.*" He forced a smile, but it didn't drown the sadness his expression held. "I'm sorry, I'm just having a hard time pretending everything is okay when being here feels like this..." Jude's voice cracked. "I don't want to remember Andanova this way."

"You don't have to pretend around me," Seren whispered. "We're past that now, don't you think?"

"I suppose we are." Jude sighed wearily. "If anything...at least I'm here with you."

Jude's golden hair fell into his eyes, and Seren had the strange urge to brush it away. It wasn't until his fingers grazed against the warmth of Jude's skin that Seren realized he'd done it. This time, no heat crept into Seren's cheeks as Jude searched his face.

Amongst the decay and dust of the dead kingdom, Jude stood like a prince—golden as the sun, soft as the morning, with the sorrow of a hundred mourning angels painted on his face. And all Seren could think was that someone like Jude would have the brightness to bring all of Andanova to bloom again.

Jude was still, his blue eyes unreadable as Seren's hand lingered on him. Seren's heart pounded, slow and rhythmic, but a strange calmness washed over him. His fingers brushed Jude's neck as he took a step forward, the world around them fading into silence. No words were spoken—no silly banter or playful teasing—it was a steady silence, one that Seren wasn't afraid of.

Jude's long-lashed gaze drifted to Seren's mouth.

"We're falling behind," Seren murmured, his eyes lowering to trace Jude's jawline.

"Can we just stay here a moment longer?" Jude breathed, his voice barely above a whisper. He was so close Seren could feel the heat radiating from his body. "Please?"

The plea felt like something else entirely. Out of place. Like Jude was asking for so much more.

Seren met those ridiculously blue eyes, his mind flashing to the moments when the sword had plunged into him—just before he'd met the darkness. Safe. That's how it felt to look at Jude, as if he were Seren's personal sky, an endless blue that could carry him anywhere.

"Only a moment," Seren whispered.

Jude reached for Seren's hand, bringing it between them. Jude glanced down at their intertwined fingers, his expression unreadable. Then he brought Seren's knuckles upward, and for a fleeting instant, Seren had the absurd thought that Jude might kiss them.

"You've got that look again," Jude murmured, his lashes lowering. "I wish I knew what it meant."

Seren's fingers moved without thought, tracing Jude's jawline, the same gesture Jude had once done to him in the Sanguine Kingdom. His skin was soft beneath Seren's touch, impossibly so.

How am I looking at you? Seren wondered, but he didn't ask—because he knew. Instead, he leaned closer, his heart steady yet insistent in his chest. Before doubt could creep in or reason take hold, he pressed his mouth to Jude's.

Jude went rigid, and for one terrible moment, Seren thought he had made a mistake. Fear clawed at his chest. But then Jude's hands slid around him, pulling him closer, and his mouth opened against Seren's.

The kiss deepened, slow, achingly tender, and Seren's fingers threaded into Jude's messy curls—silken strands tangling between his hands.

This kiss was different from the one he had shared with Mila. That had been desperate, rushed—like trying to hold on to something slipping through his fingers. This one was unhurried, wanting, and growing deeper with every second.

Seren was losing himself in Jude—his touch, his scent. Jude's caress was like sunshine on his skin, his scent reminiscent of a summer morning, and his mouth as sweet as honey.

All Seren's thoughts left him; the questions and possibilities that haunted him seemed to grow wings and fly away. When Jude tilted Seren's head back, his kisses growing languid, more deliberate, Seren let him take the lead. He surrendered entirely, certain he could stay like this forever.

But Jude pulled away, breathless, and a sharp ache of disappointment pierced through Seren.

Reality crept back in—their surroundings, the others waiting, the weight of what came next. But Seren didn't want any of it. He wanted Jude to kiss him until everything else fell away, until the world faded, leaving only the shared breath between them.

A bird fluttered nearby, its faint glow accentuating the flush on Jude's skin. Jude didn't speak, his eyes lingering on Seren as though he was waiting for something. There was a silent question between them—one neither could answer. Instead of breaking the quiet, Jude grabbed Seren's hand, and they walked together.

Seren's heart raced, and he couldn't bring himself to glance at Jude, no matter how much he wanted to. All he could do was look at their intertwined hands.

The sound of voices ahead pulled him back to the present. The others were waiting at the end of the hall, their figures outlined by light. Cin stood with her arms crossed, an annoyed look fixed on her face. "You both need to stay close," she scolded. "What the hell were you doing?"

Seren couldn't stop the warmth creeping into his ears, no matter how hard he tried.

"Just a bit of sightseeing," Jude said with an easy shrug. "Don't spoil the fun." He clapped his hands together with an almost childlike enthusiasm. "The armory's just down the hall."

It didn't take them long to reach it either. The walk was silent. Everything they passed looked the same—ruined, empty, lifeless. Yet Seren couldn't focus on any of it.

All he could think about was how close Jude was standing next to him.

He was being a fool, wasn't he? They were in the Veil, surrounded by death and decay, and yet...his thoughts drifted to the kiss.

Seren's gaze shifted to Mila, walking beside Felix. A strange guilt coiled in his chest—unfamiliar and unwelcome. Was it guilt? Or something else? He didn't know.

"Hey, Seren. Are you with me?"

"What?" Seren's head snapped toward Jude, his heartbeat stuttering.

Jude smiled. "I asked if you were okay."

"Oh, yeah. I was just...thinking."

"Don't do too much of that. You might hurt yourself," Cin said with a grin.

She kicked the doors open to the armory, sending up a cloud of dust that had everyone bursting into fits of coughing. It was an unnecessarily dramatic entrance, to say the least, but Cin seemed pleased with herself.

They entered hesitantly. The armory had been gutted. Most of the walls were scarred and empty, the mounts torn away. Broken weapon racks littered the floor. In the corner, a few lonely, rusted blades sat, and dented helmets were propped against the stone walls.

Jude grimaced and leaned down to pick up the hilt of a broken sword, something that had once been regal, noble, now shattered. "Well, that's rotten luck." He tossed the weapon back onto the floor with a sigh.

Cin removed a sheathed sword from her back, handing it to Seren. "I suppose we can't have you unarmed."

Seren slung it on his back. "Thanks."

"I expect that back without dings in it, so be careful, idiot."

Without another word, they continued through the castle. Birds fluttered around them, occasionally drifting between the five of them. Jude had taken the lead now that they'd reached the first floor. He was unusually quiet as they passed through a grand arch, still standing distinct amidst the grime. Peacock feathers adorned the marble, each center filled with sapphires that twinkled beneath the light.

"It reeks of death," Felix whispered, tightening his green cloak around himself as he leaned closer to Mila.

When Seren passed through the arch, the air grew heavier—thick and cloying, pressing against his lungs with every step. The silence deepened, broken only by their footsteps and the faint flutter of small birds as they flickered ahead of him. Two fell, their light sputtering before their fragile bodies crumbled to dust. Seren exhaled, pushing more magic into the remaining birds. Their glow steadied, casting dancing halos across the walls as they spread into the chamber.

The throne room loomed ahead, a nightmare preserved in ruin. Time had not dulled the horrors within. The marble floor bore a sickly brown stain where a sea of blood had once pooled. A tapestry clung stubbornly to the wall, its once-vivid hues obliterated by dark, rust-colored streaks that split its fabric. The skeletal remains of knights were scattered throughout the room, their rusted armor barely clinging to disjointed limbs.

But it was the pile in the center that made Seren's breath hitch. Bones, hundreds of them, were neatly stacked into a mound. Skulls crowned the heap, their empty sockets facing the thrones that sat ahead on the dais. Jude stumbled back at the sight, his face blanching as his hand found Cin's arm. He doubled over and retched onto the floor.

To Seren's astonishment, the seven thrones remained untouched by the grime of the years. It should have been impossible, yet they gleamed with polished gold. The king and queen's thrones were a sight to behold, crowned with golden peacock feathers fanning from the tops of the chairs. Each throne was encrusted with sapphires and emeralds.

Jude released Cin's arm, wiping his mouth on his sleeve. He circled the pile of bones, his fists clenched at his sides. Silence hung in the air as he ascended the stairs, his footsteps echoing in the stillness. Jude's long fingers brushed over the king and queen's thrones with a delicate, almost reverent touch. His fingers continued to trace the tops of the thrones until he reached the far-left side. He paused, freezing for a moment. Then, he moved to the front and sat. His arms settled on the armrests as he tilted his chin upward, blue eyes dull.

"Just as uncomfortable as I remember," Jude said with a sigh.

Cin took a sharp breath, her gaze shifting to Seren. "You're not telling me that..." She paused, the answer glaringly obvious.

Nobody had asked Jude why he'd lived in the castle. He could have been a servant, a kitchen boy, but Seren knew that wasn't true. Why hadn't he seen it sooner? Piano lessons, Jude's effortless, honeyed words, the way he carried himself with both confidence and practicality...

Jude wasn't just the last Andanovan; he was a *prince*.

Images flooded Seren's mind without warning, blurring the present. The throne room materialized before him in all its splendor, bathed in golden light. Men and women, adorned in extravagant jewels and silks, glided across the floor to the distant tune of music. Servants filled golden goblets to the brim with frothing honey wine, while the scent of wisteria drifted in through the open windows.

Seated upon the throne were the king and queen. The queen's braided hair gleamed like spun gold, her eyes as blue as the sky. When she smiled at the king, all Seren saw was Jude.

The King of Andanova chuckled, kissing his wife on the cheek. His gray-blue eyes gleamed as she brushed a stray piece of fiery hair from his forehead. At the queen's side sat a young girl, a mirror image of her father, and beside her, a mischievous boy with a familiar smirk played with her hair. He was the spitting image of his mother. Three other boys sat on the remaining thrones—all golden hair and charm. And then, as suddenly as it came, the vision vanished.

"Once glorious," that familiar voice echoed in Seren's mind. *"Once beautiful. The darkness swallows the light."*

Cin's throat cleared, snapping Seren back to the present. A hundred questions lurked on her visage. "How do we access the undercrofts from here, Jude?"

Jude sighed, rising from the throne and descending the stairs with an unreadable expression. "Follow me." He waggled his fingers, beckoning them from the wreckage of the throne room into the hall. Seren's gaze drifted to the dirty paintings on the walls, wondering if, by studying them long enough, he might find a portrait of the young prince Jude once was.

Taking a sharp left, Jude led them down a set of stairs at the end of the hallway. Felix cursed, clinging to Mila as he stumbled on an uneven step. Theo skittered ahead, batting at the glowing birds that fluttered near his round ears.

"You're leading us to the wine cellar?" Cin asked. "Are you sure you know where you're going?"

Jude ignored her, and when they reached the bottom, he pushed the door open. The cellar was bathed in the birds' light. Beautiful oaken racks mounted to the walls were lined with bottles upon dusty bottles of wine. It was surprisingly intact, unlike the rest of the castle. Spiderwebs clung to the corks, and Seren caught sight of a fat-bottomed spider scurrying across the shelf.

Jude grabbed the nearest bottle, frowning at the cork. "Hmm..." His eyes scanned the racks for a moment before he let out a triumphant sound.

He snatched up a rusty corkscrew and set to work removing the cork. Without another word, he chugged.

"Please, tell me you didn't bring us down here just so you could get drunk," Cin demanded.

"Have you ever had Andanovan wine?" Jude asked, wiping his mouth. He held out the bottle to Cin, raising an eyebrow. "This might be your only chance."

"You're ridiculous," Cin muttered, but she took the bottle from his hands and pressed it to her lips. Her eyes widened. "Damn."

Jude grinned. "Delicious, isn't it? If only we could bring some back with us."

Before Seren knew it, they were passing the bottle around, each taking a drink. It was an absurd moment—trapped in the Veil, with the recent revelation that Jude was a *prince*, and yet here they were, passing a bottle of Andanovan wine as if the fate of the entire world didn't rest on this cursed mission. When the bottle reached Seren, he couldn't believe how sweet and smooth the wine tasted. The creeping thought of Jude's kiss bloomed in his mind once again.

"I hope this isn't why you brought us down here," Cin said, eyes narrowing.

"Leave him be." Felix removed his hood, curls tumbling across his forehead. "He'll find it."

"Find what?" Cin growled. "Do you get a kick out of being cryptic all the time?"

"I do, actually."

Jude finished a gulp of wine, having opened another bottle, a trail of deep red running down the curve of his neck. He wiped his mouth with the back of his hand and tossed the bottle aside with a grin. "Alright, now let's begin." He eagerly rubbed his hands together before reaching for the necks of the bottles and sliding them out of place.

"Not these ones," Jude muttered.

The others stood frozen, staring at him in bewilderment.

"What in the world is he doing?" Cin hissed.

Felix chuckled. "Just wait."

Confused and unsure of what to say, Seren and the others could only watch. Several minutes passed as Jude methodically removed bottle after bottle of wine. At last, his hand landed on one that wouldn't budge. The soft click released a hiss of air, and the leftmost wall shifted a fraction. Jude slipped his fingers into the gap, pulling the door open to reveal a hidden passage of stairs.

Jude grinned. "I knew I could find it," he said. Without waiting for the others, he disappeared down the steps, a pair of birds trailing after him.

Cin smirked. "I was beginning to think His Royal Highness had gone mad," she said before following Jude.

Mila unexpectedly pressed against Seren's side. "Are you sure Jude's alright?" she whispered. "I'm worried."

"I don't know," Seren admitted. "Did you know that he...?"

"Was a prince of a ruined kingdom?" Mila finished. "No, I didn't."

Seren frowned. "Let's just pray the harp is here, so we can get the hell out of here." He glanced down at the weasel, scratching his boot. "Have you seen anything with the harp, Felix?"

"No, but I'll tell you if I do."

The three of them descended the stairs in silence. At the bottom, Jude and Cin stopped before a golden door engraved with the intricate image of a peacock. Its long tail was adorned with seven shimmering blue stones, and its elegantly curved beak jutted out as the handle, untouched by the wear of time. Jude stepped forward, pressing his hand against the sharp edge of the beak. The metal sliced his flesh, and blood ran down his arm, staining the crisp white of his sleeves. Without hesitation, he smeared the blood across the seven stones, each one flaring to life with a deep crimson glow. The peacock's sapphire eyes lit up, and with a low creak, the door swung open.

Twenty-Four

"Lo and behold, the great steel beast rises from the ashes of forgotten sin. Chains tighten across the sun, and the land is scorched by the burning tears of the righteous."

—Book of Disruption

Seren had never seen so many treasures before. As the group entered the chamber, his eyes widened at the dazzling sight of jewels, gold, silver, books with gilded edges, long rolls of silk, and more. The room was massive, cluttered with draped curtains and giant mirrors, making the items feel like part of a surreal dream.

Seren caught his disheveled reflection in a giant silver platter, its edges engraved with tiny unicorns. If these treasures had gone untouched for ten years, it was impossible to tell. Everything was immaculately clean, with not a speck of dust in sight.

A beautiful tapestry hung from the ceiling, drawing Seren's gaze skyward. He was reminded of the image he had seen in Kitsune's den in the Underbelly. It was the same tree, the same burned sky and grass. But underneath the tree was a majestic peacock, his chest puffed up and feathers arranged flawlessly. Seren thought of the fox he'd seen in the other image, a mouthful of peacock feathers in its mouth. He shuddered.

"That stupid harp better be here somewhere," Cin sighed. "Let's split up and start looking. And be careful—there's no telling if anything here is enchanted."

"Oh, I'll get to looking right away," Felix said, a grin tugging at his lips. "I'll keep my eyes peeled."

"Why don't you stick with me, Felix?" Jude suggested. He held out his hand as one of Seren's birds landed on his palm.

"Alright." Felix clicked his tongue, and Theo promptly climbed his way up to Felix's shoulders.

The two of them circled around a table, disappearing behind a silk curtain. Seren tried not to let his disappointment show.

Mila appeared at Seren's side. "Guess that leaves us."

Cin had slipped away already, as silent as a wisp of smoke. Her ability to vanish without a sound was something Seren would never grow used to.

The two of them began strolling through the chamber together. A pair of birds followed each of them, lighting the way. It would be impossible to miss the harp if it was here. It stood about half as tall as Seren, its surface carved from a strange ivory that glowed with an ethereal light as though it pulsed with a life of its own.

"What happens after you find the harp?" Mila asked, her voice casual. Her gaze traveled to a dagger, its golden handle encrusted with sapphires.

"I take it to Lumina," Seren said with a sigh. "Eldyir will lock it away in a safe place until I've gathered all the items." He picked up a golden goblet, studying the leaves etched on the side.

"Why do *you* have to do it?" Mila scoffed.

Seren chuckled. "Destiny," he said in a dramatic tone. "Fate."

"How ridiculous," Mila muttered, glancing at him out of the corner of her eye. When Seren didn't respond, she cleared her throat. "So... What happens after you find all the items?"

Her fingers brushed across a blue book, avoiding his gaze.

Seren frowned, the question lingering as his thoughts drifted. Eldyir had warned him about what would happen during the Cleansing. His duty was clear: find the items, locate the gateway to the Garden of Aetheria, and end up exactly where fate intended.

Out of everything, the idea of sacrificing his human form hadn't scared him at first. He truthfully hadn't thought about it. Not until now. Eldyir and Aiden had made it clear they weren't exactly sure what would happen to him after the ascension. Would he become someone entirely different? Maybe.

Yet now, as his hand grazed Mila's and Jude's face flashed in his mind, a raw fear gripped him. He had pushed these thoughts aside before, opting to ignore them. But now he wondered... Would parts of himself remain? Or would everything he had ever been disappear, leaving nothing behind for them to remember?

"I'm not sure," Seren finally said. "I guess we'll find out."

"Yeah," Mila said. "I guess you will."

Several minutes of fruitless searching passed. The harp was nowhere to be found. They had scoured behind every curtain, peered into every shadowed corner, but if the instrument was in the castle, it wasn't in this chamber.

Cin groaned, collapsing into a clawed chair, her fingers pressing hard against her temples. Mila flipped through a red-leather book, slumped against the wall, her eyes scanning the pages without focus. Jude and Felix were elsewhere, but Seren imagined they had also held no success.

Eldyir had insisted the harp was in the castle. But why did Seren feel so certain Eldyir was wrong, that it wasn't here at all?

Seren sighed and pressed his forehead against the cool wall, squeezing his eyes shut.

Are you there? He thought desperately. *Can you help me?*

A warmth bloomed in the back of his mind, fleeting as an embrace, but it vanished before it could take hold. The silence stretched, deafening. Seren ground his teeth. He turned to Cin, ready to suggest they search elsewhere.

And then it hit him.

Seren stumbled into the wall, clutching his head as the world tilted around him. His hand pressed against the stone for support as his knees buckled. Breath fled his lungs, and his legs went numb. The darkness came fast, swallowing all sight and sound. He gasped, but no air came, his thoughts unraveling as he plunged into an infinite void.

Then, he was moving.

Weightless and formless, Seren was an orb of light gliding through the air. Shadows parted before him as he wove through dark trees, their skeletal branches clawing at the sky. He skimmed across ruins, the whispers of demons hissing on the edges of his awareness, their burning eyes retreating as he passed.

A domed temple rose from the desolation, a monument of bluish-gray marble draped in decay. Thorny vines and gnarled tree roots clung to its surface, fissures spreading through the stone-like veins. Chunks of rock lay scattered at its base. Seren pressed forward, his light reflecting off the statues flanking the entrance—mighty peacocks, their once-proud forms tangled in buds of wisteria that would never bloom.

The jeweled temple doors groaned open as his light surged inside. The chamber within was vast and desolate, the air heavy with silence. At its heart, an altar stood bathed in faint luminescence, and there, amidst the rubble, the harp glowed with ethereal brilliance.

"*There.*" Her voice flooded Seren's mind and he understood. She was showing him exactly where he needed to go.

A figure stepped out of the shadows, eclipsing the harp's glow. Long, tattered robes flared wildly in the rush of wind from the open doors. Its glowing blue eyes quivered in hollow sockets, unnatural and deadly. Half of its face was nothing but tarnished bone; the other stretched thin with sagging gray flesh. Its jaw unhinged with a creak like rusted hinges, snapping back together with a sound like shattering porcelain.

"*I see you,*" it hissed.

Seren jolted forward as if yanked by invisible strings, his knees colliding painfully with the castle wall. He gasped, the vision splintering apart.

"Seren! Seren!" Cin's voice broke through his daze, her fingers digging into his shoulders as she shook him hard. "What the hell is wrong with you?"

Seren pushed her off, huffing. "I know where the harp is," he said. "It's not here. It's in the Temple of Gala."

"What are you talking about?" Cin demanded.

Seren wiped the sweat from his forehead, meeting her kohled eyes. "I need you to trust me," he said. "We need to leave *now*."

The image of the demon burned in his mind, his stomach twisting. It had seen him. If it was in the temple with the harp, that could mean only one thing: it was the creature that ruled over this castle.

Seren weaved through the tables, pushing through silken drapes, his heart thundering. He parted an embroidered curtain, catching sight of Jude leaning over a table. His gaze was fixed on a necklace cradled in his palm. The deep blue gem sparkled on a thin golden chain, catching the light as birds flitted around him. Jude's fingers brushed the necklace's surface, his mouth set in a tight line.

"Jude."

Startled, Jude dropped the necklace onto the table. "Hey," he said, clearing his throat. "Any luck?"

Seren shook his head. "No, but I know where it is. We need to get out of here. Where's Felix?"

"Here." A blue and purple woven tapestry rippled as Felix popped out from behind, Theo licking his ear. "I was just sitting since I'm not much help at the moment."

Jude tucked his hands in his pockets, an uneasy smile on his lips. "Where to next?"

Before Seren could respond, the ground rumbled. Felix yelped, stumbling forward and clutching Seren for support as the floor trembled violently. Empty golden goblets clattered, rolling off the tables with metallic echoes that rang through the chamber. A silver mirror crashed to the ground, shattering into a cascade of glinting shards. The rumbling ceased just as Cin and Mila burst through the hanging drapes, weapons drawn.

"The demon of the castle must know we're here," Cin said, lip curling. "We need to leave, *now.*"

Seren turned to Jude. "Is there another way out of the castle from here?"

"Wouldn't it be better to take our chances with one demon than go out there?" Mila argued.

"We have to get the harp, Mila," Seren said, growing frustrated. "It's not here. We can survive the Veil. We've done it before."

A smile spread across Cin's features. "About time I heard you say something with confidence."

Jude rubbed the back of his neck. "I think we can get through the walls that way," he said, pointing behind him. "But I can't be certain." The room shook again, dust spilling from the cracks in the ceiling as more items rolled off the tables.

"Let's not waste time," Cin snapped.

Jude nodded, leading them through the chamber into a narrow, dark hallway lined with spiderwebs and broken stone. He beckoned them forward, and they cautiously ascended the stone steps. At the top, they emerged into a cramped space, the walls close and oppressive, with only a faint draft that hinted they were inside the castle's structure. Jude stayed in front, with Seren close behind, while Felix, Cin, and Mila followed.

Birds fluttered above Seren as the walls closed in. A musty smell filled his nose, and he bit down on the urge to cough. Without warning, another rumble shook the castle, prompting all of them to cover their heads as dust and dirt rained down. Seren couldn't contain the cough this time, his eyes watering. Startled, he stumbled forward and collided with Jude, who had come to a sudden stop.

"Jude, what're you—"

Jude's hand clasped over Seren's mouth. "Look," he whispered.

A hole roughly the size of Seren's fist punctured the wall. Seren peered through the opening, his cheek brushing against Jude's. He was looking into the throne room, bathed in greenish-blue light, every sconce lit with strange fire. A shadow moved across the wall. Tattered robes dragged across the stained floor, the ends resembling peacock feathers threaded with gold. Billowed sleeves hung from bone-thin arms, frayed at the edges. Upon its head rested a pristine golden crown adorned with blue and green gems encircling the rim—each reminiscent of the eye-like motifs found on peacock feathers.

When the creature turned, its face emerged from the dancing fire—half skeletal, a glowing blue eye in a hollow socket. The other half was loosely connected, its gray skin peeling like paper. Cracked and broken teeth were visible through translucent skin, while stringy strands of long, coppery hair hung from the intact portion of its head.

"*Little vermin have infested my castle,*" it said, voice raspy. It laughed, a rattling chill crawling across Seren's chest at the horrible sound. Jude froze in place beside him. "*I can hear all five of your frightened little hearts beating.*"

The creature hissed, snapping his robes before vanishing as if he'd never existed.

"Where did it go?" Jude whispered.

Seren pushed him. "Go, Jude. Now."

Jude rushed forward, the others close behind. Cin cursed, an unfamiliar fear creeping into her voice. Seren couldn't ignore his own rising terror; something about that creature stirred a dread too deep to explain.

Theo's shrill shrieks echoed down the narrow passage.

"Make that damn thing shut up!" Cin barked.

A piercing scream filled the air. *"Where is it!?"* the demon howled. *"Who took it!?"*

The temperature plummeted, and an ominous hum filled the air. From the other side of the wall came a crackling echo—followed by what sounded like clattering bones. The castle began to shake more violently than before.

The stone wall cracked open between Jude and Seren. A skull clattered, its jaw snapping as blue eyes flared, trying to force its way through. More followed suit, animated skulls slamming into the wall with deafening crashes, threatening to cave it in. Seren's blood turned cold as the walls around them began to crack, large sections of stone fracturing.

"Run!" Seren shouted, shoving Jude forward.

The castle shuddered, and Seren feared the walls might collapse on them. The five of them tumbled into each other like dominoes, limbs tangling in the cramped space. They scrambled to untangle themselves, each struggling to push to their feet as dust rained down from above. Seren pushed himself upright, reaching out to help Jude. There was hardly any room to move, but he managed to steady him just as another scream tore through the air.

"Where is it, filthy vermin!?"

"Go, go, go!" Cin shouted from behind.

Crashes thundered overhead. The ceiling was collapsing, showering marble that threatened to crush them. Seren's birds flickered and died, plunging them into darkness. He trailed behind Jude, the walls scraping against his shoulders, each breath a struggle in the thickening dust. With a sudden jerk, Seren collided with Jude's back. Amidst the chaos, Seren heard the distinct sound of Jude kicking something.

"Hurry!" Felix shouted from behind.

Jude let out a fierce cry as his boot slammed into something hard. A door burst open, red light flooding in. Jude tumbled outside, Seren right behind him, the others crowding close. They barely had time to brace themselves before the tunnel behind them roared. As they staggered to their feet, they looked back in horror. The ground shook, and chunks of stone rained down, filling the air with dust. Where they had just stood, only rubble remained.

"Is everyone alright?" Seren asked.

Felix staggered to his feet, his knees wobbly, and gave a shaky thumbs-up. Mila clutched her dagger, appearing unscathed, though flakes of dust clung to her disheveled hair. Cin wiped at a small gash above her lip, her armor decorated with a fresh dent.

Jude pressed his back against the castle wall, sweat trickling down his forehead. He squeezed his eyes shut, drew a gun, and placed his finger on the trigger. Cin's eyes widened as she glanced at her holster, realizing the weapon was missing—Jude must have stolen it sometime in the castle. The gun trembled in his grip as he leaned over, his face a sickly green.

Seren stepped forward, but Jude held up his hand. "I'm fine. Just give me a moment."

Their exit led them into what Seren presumed had once been the royal gardens. The dimming sun bled into the sky, casting everything in a crimson glow. Within the garden, untamed foliage ran wild, tangled with flower buds that would never bloom, while tree roots slithered up from the earth, twisting over the ground. At the garden's heart stood a fractured fountain, split in half, its basin brimming with a collection of bones.

"Jude, we need to move," Cin said, her voice tight.

The castle rumbled again, and half-broken windows shattered, sending shards raining down. Seren gripped Jude's shirt tightly, urging him to run. Mila grasped Felix's hand as they raced behind. Cin leapt over gnarled roots and broken stones, her movements fluid.

They came to a halt at the garden wall, thick with prickly vines.

"At this rate, the bastard's going to bring down the entire castle," Cin said, her hazel eyes flashing. "The fastest way out is to climb." She turned to them, brows set with determination. She sheathed her sword and flexed her gloved hands. "Quickly." She grasped a vine and hoisted herself effortlessly.

Mila frowned watching Cin's form disappear over the wall. "Can you climb, Felix?"

"Of course," he replied confidently. "My legs work perfectly fine." But as he approached the wall, he winced when his hand met the thorns. Determined, he lifted himself, his movements slow and deliberate as he searched for a secure grip. Before long, Felix disappeared over the wall, following Cin.

Mila climbed after him, throwing a look over her shoulder at Seren and Jude before hoisting herself over. "See you on the other side."

Jude remained silent, his face drained of color and his hand still gripping the gun. Seren gently placed a hand on the gun's barrel, guiding it downwards.

"Jude, we need to climb before that thing comes after us."

Jude let out a shaky breath as he tucked the gun into his waistband, his eyes meeting Seren's. "Okay," he breathed.

The two of them placed their hands on the wall, standing side by side, and began to climb. But as Jude reached for a divot to hold onto, his grip slipped, and he yelped, falling backward. He cried out as he scrambled on the ground, his hands digging into his pockets. Something blue flew from his grasp and landed in the dirt. Jude cursed, sucking on blistered fingers, before quickly snatching up the necklace, gripping it by the chain.

Seren jumped down beside him, his gaze snapping to the scintillating gemstone swinging in front of Jude's face, burning with that familiar blue glow.

A slow-dawning horror filled Seren's chest. "Damn it, Jude. Did you take that? You have to get rid—"

The wall between the castle and the garden exploded, sending rocks flying in every direction. A small chunk struck Seren squarely in the chest, flinging him backward. His back slammed into the dirt, the impact driving the breath from his lungs.

Dazed, Seren pushed himself to his knees, blood streaming down his arms. He blinked through the spots clouding his vision.

"Jude..."

Under the bloodied sun, shrouded in shadow, its head gleaming with gold, stood the monster of the castle. Jude trembled before it, the blue jewel clutched tightly in his left hand. His fingers were burning, but either he didn't notice or he simply did not care. His eyes were locked on the demon that stood before him. The creature extended a boy finger to Jude, brushing his cheek with a strange tenderness, its tattered robes billowing around its skeletal frame.

"Jude!" Seren's hand flew to the hilt of the sword strapped to his back. "Jude, run!"

The demon turned its head, its unnatural, glowing eyes locking onto Seren. Slowly, it lifted a withered hand. That was the last thing Seren saw before the earth split open beneath him and swallowed him whole.

Twenty-Five

"The sun turned black, the moon bled red, and stars rained down upon the earth as a war song echoed through the empty heavens."

—Book of Disruption

Felix must have seen it coming because before Mila knew it, he had yanked her back, his voice ringing in her ears as he shouted at Cin to get down. Then the garden wall sundered. Dust plumed into the air, and Mila struggled to make out the figures through the haze.

And then she saw it—the demon. There it stood in the middle of the garden courtyard crowned in gold. Despite its tall, skeletal frame, it moved with an eerie grace, gliding toward Jude, a hand outstretched.

Seren knelt on the ground, his hand gripping the hilt of his sword. He screamed Jude's name—and then he was gone. The earth cracked open beneath him, and Seren plummeted.

"No!" Mila screamed, scrambling to her feet.

The demon turned toward her shout, its one strange, glowing eye meeting hers. It raised its fleshless hands slowly, as if lifting strings from a puppet. From the dark corners of the garden, figures stalked forward.

Eyes as red as the Andanovan sun locked onto them as the demons neared, growls rumbling deep in their throats. Their black fur gleamed under the fractured light, the top halves of their faces stripped to nothing but bone. Pointed ears twitched as they snapped their frothing jaws.

"Hellhounds," Cin hissed from beside Mila, though Mila hadn't even known she was there.

"Suck their bones dry," the demon demanded. He swept his billowing robes around, a surge of dark wind swirling in his wake. In an instant, both he and Jude vanished.

Theo hissed and bristled against Felix's neck, his claws digging into Felix's cloak. Mila stepped in front of him. Cin and Mila exchanged a look, no words passing between them. Then Cin burst forward, her long, thin sword sliding from its sheath with incredible speed. A hellhound leapt at her, and she blocked its snapping jaws against the steel, her boot striking its stomach. The creature tumbled backward, its stomach momentarily exposed, and without hesitating, Cin drove the blade into its soft belly.

Mila's eyes scanned the scene, trying to count the number of rabid demons, but she couldn't react fast enough. Felix screamed behind her, and she whipped around. A monster clutched the back of his cloak, yanking him backward. Mila twisted, her feet leaving the ground as she launched herself at it. Her dagger plunged into its eye, and it released its grip. Hot blood splattered onto her elbow as she yanked the blade free, the beast exploding into viscera as if it had never existed.

Mila quickly helped Felix to his feet. "You should run," she said breathlessly. "Get out of here."

Cin battled four hounds at once, her sword flashing with every swing. Mila had never seen anyone move so fast. The hounds matched her pace as she swiveled.

Mila cursed under her breath as the remaining beasts turned toward her and Felix, their growls deepening with every step. Felix pressed his back against hers, his breaths fast and shallow.

"Run," Mila hissed, gripping her weapon tighter. "I'll hold them off."

There was a short pause, followed by Felix's exasperated voice. "Mila, where am I supposed to run?"

Mila blinked, feeling incredibly stupid. Of course—Felix was blind and the land around them was in ruins. Telling him to just "run" was about as useful as telling him to fly.

But there was no time for more words. A hound lunged, and Mila shoved Felix aside. She cried out as her dagger found the beast's hide. Before she could pull it free, the second hound slammed into her, driving her head into the fractured wall behind her. The dagger flew from her hand, and pain exploded in her skull, blood staining her hair. Her eyes widened in terror as the hound's jaws gaped, ready to take her head clean off.

Crack.

The demon yelped as a rock struck the back of its head. Felix stood over it, his face calm and determined, his hand gripping another stone.

"Use your magic!" he shouted.

Mila didn't hesitate. Magic surged through her veins, fiery and unrelenting. In an instant, an arrow of blood shot into the hound's eye. Mila willed it back, ripping the blood-forged weapon free as the beast collapsed, lifeless, onto its side.

With a flick of her wrist, a dagger of blood pierced another hound, charging toward them. Another gesture and she summoned a whip around the beast's neck, forcing it to the ground. It thrashed against her grip until Mila tightened her hold, and it took one last breath before succumbing to death.

"Good thing I didn't run," Felix said, voice trembling.

"Yeah, good thing."

Meanwhile, Cin finished off the last hound, her blade glinting in the crimson sunlight as it severed its head with a clean stroke. Wiping her blade, she strode toward the open chasm where Seren had fallen. Mila snatched her dagger, grabbed Felix's hand, and pulled him along.

Mila's stomach sank. The earth had split straight across the garden, exposing a jagged, dark abyss. The fall would have killed an ordinary person—but Seren wasn't ordinary. Mila clung to the belief that he was alive. If he wasn't... Surely, she would have felt their bond snap. Wouldn't she?

"Son of a bitch," Cin muttered, her jaw tight and knuckles white around her sword. "God damn it, Seren." She swiped a gloved hand across her bloodstained face, smearing grime across her cheek.

"He's alive," Mila said firmly.

Cin whipped around, her breath hot against Mila's face. "And how do you propose we get to him?" she snapped. "What's the plan? Jump into the abyss and hope for the best?" There was a feral look in her eyes, but beneath it, Mila caught the flicker of fear. Worry.

Mila dug into her pocket, her fingers brushing against smooth stone. She pulled it free, her hand trembling. "We can use this."

Cin's hand shot out, closing tightly over Mila's, the stone cool between their palms. "No. We need to get to the temple and find the harp before we even think about using these."

"This is ridiculous," Mila spat, yanking her hand back. "Forget the harp! That thing took Jude! Seren could be hurt and—"

Cin's lip curled in a slow, deliberate snarl, revealing unnervingly sharp teeth. "Not yet," she hissed. "*If* Seren's alive, he's no fool. He knows the stakes better than any of us. He knew what Andanova could cost and what the risks were. He'll find a way back. But if we leave the harp behind, we've already lost."

Mila turned to Felix. "You said the stones will glow if one is used, yes? They're all connected?"

Felix nodded. "Yeah, that's right."

Cin released her grip on Mila's hand. "If Jude has his stone, it might give him a chance—and it gives us a chance to help him. Do you understand? But first, we need to get the harp." Her expression softened, a rare change on her usually hardened visage. "I want us all to leave alive as much as you want to."

Mila clenched the stone, her chest aching at the thought of Seren lying injured, alone in the dark.

Felix set a hand on her shoulder. "Cin's right," he said. "Seren would want us to get the harp first, not waste the stone. Let's go to the temple and go from there."

Mila bit her lip, glancing between them. She clenched her fist around the stone before sliding it back into her pocket. "Fine," she muttered. "But if we're wrong—"

"We're not," Cin said, turning toward the chasm one last time before marching forward.

Mila sighed, looping her arm and Felix's and took a step forward. However, Felix remained rooted in place. Theo bristled around Felix's, whiskers quivering.

"Something's wrong," Felix said.

From the rubble and thick tangle of plants, movement stirred. Shadows shifted into focus near the castle walls. No—not shadows. Hellhounds. Too many to count. Their glowing eyes pierced the dim light as they stalked forward, low growls reverberating from their throats.

"Damn it," Cin cursed, her face paling.

Mila turned, her jaw set. "Run," she said. "Take Felix and run."

"Are you out of your mind—"

"Not only am I a Sanguine Sister," Mila cut her off, "but I am their future queen. I can kill them." She tossed her dagger in the air, and Cin caught it with a grin. "For Felix. I'll meet you two at the temple."

"Just head that way." Cin gestured right. "You can't miss it." She grasped Felix's wrist. "Don't you dare die, princess." Without another word, Cin and Felix fled.

Mila turned to the demons as they closed in, their snapping jaws and sharp teeth clattering together. She rolled her neck on her shoulders and flexed her fingers.

Seren had always promised never to take from Mila, and he had kept that promise. He didn't want her power—he believed it belonged to her. She had to believe that now. She had to believe she was strong enough to do this.

Mila's pulse roared in her ears. She forced a deep breath, steadying herself as the beasts charged. Closing her eyes, she blocked out the thunder of her heart and the rush of her blood and focused. She searched for their rhythm.

The world seemed to hush, each second stretching. And then she found it: the furious thrum of blood surging through veins, the frantic pounding of hot, angry hearts.

Mila's eyes snapped open, her arms sweeping upward. She felt the violent rupture as their hearts burst within their chests.

With a sharp thrust of her hands, the blood erupted, ripping free in riveting streams. Wicked blooms of crimson spread through their ribs, wild and rose-like, as the demons crumpled before her.

Mila moved as if she were dancing, the movements feeling so natural, so fluid. Blood encircled her wrists, taking the shape of serpents. Mila shot them forward and they wrapped around the necks of the nearest hellhound. She willed blood to rain down, shaped like crystallized arrows as they tore through their hides.

Snapping jaws lunged for her, and Mila dodged, her movements precise.

She lashed out again, the blood obeying her every will. It coalesced, twisting around her, a veil of red. It merged, forming a scythe. Mila didn't question the shape; it simply felt right. The scythe cleaved through the beasts. Their necks parted, blood spraying in violent arcs as their bodies collapsed.

Mila's heart thundered in her chest. Hot blood splattered on her face and clung to her skin, seeping down in rivulets. A laugh clawed its way up her throat, foreign and untamed, spilling free before she could stop it.

As Mila swiped her hand, the blood above her thrummed with life, a tempest of red. The sharp tang of iron burned her nose and throat. She let out a piercing scream, slamming her hand downward with unrelenting force. The hellhounds yelped as their limbs were severed. Again and again, she brought the weapon down, each strike more brutal than the last. Blood splattered across her, staining the blue fabric of her garments.

Mila flexed her fingers, and three hearts burst simultaneously. A grin tugged at her lips, unbidden, as she repeated the motion. A hound lunged from her left, but before she could react, another snapped at her heels, its jaws clamping onto her ankle. Pain shot through her, but she didn't make a sound. She drove the blade into the beast, pounding it into a crimson pulp on the ground.

The warm blood clinging to her skin, the sharp, visceral burst of their lives under her command...it felt good. Too good. Exhilaration coursed through her, urging her on. She wanted more.

She whirled, her blade slicing cleanly through another hound's neck. Its head hit the ground with a wet thud. A whip of blood lashed out, coiling around three more, slamming them into the earth. Amid the bloodbath and shattered bodies of the hounds, one remained.

This one was different. It was larger, with three snapping heads that snarled and lunged in unison. Mila didn't flinch. With a flick of her finger, all three heads flew, rolling to a stop at her feet.

She stood amidst the carnage, gasping for breath, blood dripping from her clothes and skin. That's when she saw it—a tether. Dark magic pulsed through the bond with unnatural energy. Mila froze, her blood-stained fingers trembling as she reached out. She had never seen it before. Not when her mother had control of her, not when Seren had taken her name. But now, there it was, right in front of her. The proof that Seren was alive.

When Mila touched the tether, it was real, solid. Her hand wrapped around it. Impossible. Power pulsed beneath her fingertips, steady like a heartbeat, the kind of power she had never been allowed to access. The magic writhed inside the bond, as if it recognized her touch. Seren was on the other side, and for the briefest of moments, Mila wondered if there was a way to speak to him, to see him, anything that might allow them to communicate.

She wasn't sure why she could see it or why she could feel it. And now...she wondered.

Mila raised the bloodied scythe above her head, her heart pounding. Her life flashed before her eyes: the dagger piercing her brother's heart, his blood spilling red. The nights she carved her own skin, desperate to bleed out the corruption, to rid herself of the disease her mother had gifted her. And Seren—Mila thought of Seren. Maybe, just maybe, she did love him. That he might be alone in the dark now, and this—this was the only thing that guaranteed he was alive. Without it, there would be no certainty, no security.

But she couldn't fall victim to the fear love brought, the doubts it caused. It would destroy her again and again.

Seren would understand. He'd seen the life she came from, glimpsed the pain she'd endured. And she understood him—what it felt like to be tethered to a fate you did not want, to a destiny you rejected. Seren thought himself unworthy; Mila knew that. And hadn't she, in some way, believed herself better than the Sanguine Sisters? But what if the fate they were both avoiding was the very thing causing them so much pain?

Fate could demand they walk their path, could try to bring them home—but Mila would claim that place for herself. She would build her own home. No, her own kingdom. She would not live in the castle her mother had built.

With a cry, Mila brought the scythe down, releasing everything buried deep inside her, channeling all the power she had denied. And then, with a final, primal scream, the tether snapped.

TWENTY-SIX

"When the wyrm deceived Adamus, he was cursed by the gods—his wings shorn, condemned to slither like a serpent upon the earth."

—the Chronicles of the Gods

*E*verything was red.

Seren blinked, his vision swimming. Blood lapped at his chest, the iron scent thick in his nose. It pulsed as if it had its own heartbeat.

Thump.

Thump.

Thump.

Seren took a step back, the blood sloshing around him. The surface rippled. From the crimson sea, a slender figure rose, running a hand through soaked hair before turning to him. Seren's heart skipped a beat.

Mila.

Her gaze was distant, unreadable. The blood stirred again. Another figure emerged beside her. Seren sucked in a breath.

Kamil.

Seren lurched forward, the thick blood dragging at his limbs. "Mila!"

Brown eyes met his—empty, cold. Kamil's hands lifted. "You don't belong here."

Seren was falling. Warm blood filled his mouth, his ears. He clawed at his throat, choking.

Then, all at once—air. He gasped, his back hitting solid ground. Rolling over, he heaved, his whole body trembling.

The blood was gone. Mila and Kamil were nowhere to be seen. Instead, Seren met a gaze shimmering like a cluster of stars, framed by strands of moonlit hair. He reached out, his hand trembling, and her slender fingers mirrored his movement. A rippling cut stretched across her features. He was staring into a mirror. No—a pool of opalescent water.

"Seren, you have to wake up."

"No." Seren's voice wavered as he plunged a hand into the water. It was terribly cold. "Not yet." His fists clenched at his sides. "You have to help me. You have to tell me what to do."

She was drifting farther away, sinking to the bottom. Beneath her, there was only darkness. So much darkness.

"I am always with you, Seren." Her voice filled him from the inside out. "In darkness and in light—I am with you."

Seren dove into the water, his hand grasping hers. She grabbed it tight, her fingers strong.

Dark veins spread over her porcelain skin. Seren tried to recoil, but her other hand reached for him, fingers digging harshly into his skin. Something shifted, her eyes dimming, the water growing almost too cold to bear.

Her voice transformed into a thousand whispers. "Wake up."

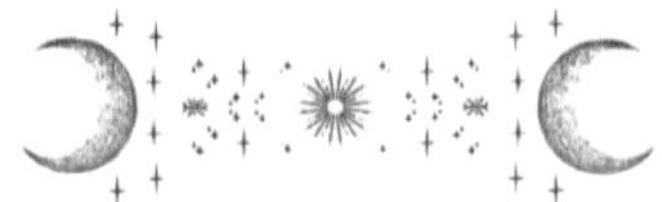

There was only darkness when Seren woke. A deep heaviness sat on his chest, and as he sat up, a wave of sharp pain shot through his ribs. He gritted his teeth, his breath shallow. His hands brushed over rough, jagged rocks as he felt around, trying to get a sense of his surroundings. Then, he looked up and caught sight of a faint sliver of red light far above him. That's right, he had fallen.

Seren clenched his fists and focused. Light erupted from his palm, and four glowing birds fluttered to life. He exhaled in relief as their bluish-white glow illuminated the chasm around him. The jagged walls stretched end-lessly upward, sharp and unforgiving. Seren was lucky to be alive, though it hadn't been without consequences—he was certain that he had broken a couple of ribs.

Climbing out was impossible from here. The walls were too rough, the height insurmountable. Behind him, solid rock sealed off any retreat. The only path lay ahead, deeper into the abyss. He willed the birds forward, their light guiding his way as he forced his aching body to move. His hand instinctively reached for his back. His sword was still there.

Seren's breathing was shallow, each movement sending spikes of pain through his chest. He could only hope his bones would mend quickly. As he ventured deeper into the chasm, a cool wind swept through the tunnel, whipping his hair back and sending the glowing birds flapping against its force. Instinctively, he tensed and drew his sword.

The wind howled again, a gust that seemed to scream like a tormented ghost, its echoes thick with anguish. Seren's skin prickled. The chasm veered to the left, and he followed the jagged path until it ended abruptly. Before him, a pair of sandstone stairs descended into darkness. He froze, uncertainty gnawing at him. Stairs—down here? Was his mind playing tricks?

No other path stretched before him. With a deep breath, Seren began his descent. Another rush of wind tore past, carrying a chorus of whispers, thin and hollow, like memories of forgotten souls. His heart skipped. He pressed his back against the cold stone wall, his muscles tensing, waiting for the sound to fade. When it finally did, he moved downward, step by hesitant step.

At the bottom of the stairs, a faint glimmer of warm light caught his eye, beckoning him forward. Seren stepped into a brightly lit chamber, where candlelight flickered, casting restless shadows across the limestone walls. Hundreds of ivory candles lined the ground and the edges of the walls, their flames swaying as he passed.

Seren stepped around the candles, his birds landing on his shoulders as he drew closer to the wall. His fingers brushed the cool surface of the stone. Ancient murals, etched with an unfamiliar language, covered every inch of the rock.

The first depicted three figures, their wings spread wide as they reached toward the heavens. Seren moved deeper into the strange underground corridor and froze at the sight of a giant tree. He traced the intricate branches with the tip of his finger, following their gentle ridges and curves, while his other hand rested on the dusty trunk. It had to be the Mother

Tree, portrayed countless times in various depictions. Beneath it stood smaller trees, all connected by the same roots.

"What...is this place?" Seren murmured.

A scratching noise echoed through the chamber. Seren whirled around, gripping his sword, but saw nothing. Someone had to be here—why else would all the candles be lit? He moved toward the flames, hovering his palm above one. He frowned, sensing a faint pulse of magic beneath his touch.

Seren turned back to the carvings and froze, his heart leaping to his throat. A cloaked figure now stood before the wall, hands pressed against the stone. He blinked, disbelief washing over him. He had been alone just moments ago. Tightening his grip, Seren raised his sword, pointing it toward the figure.

"Who are you?" Seren demanded. "Turn around."

The stranger's fingers traced the lines of the tree, slow and deliberate, unintelligible words spilling from his lips in a low murmur.

"I'm talking to you," Seren said sharply. "Answer me."

The figure froze. Then, very slowly, he turned, shock etched across his face. Seren's gaze locked with striking green eyes. The man before him looked utterly human—his deep auburn hair fell in unruly curls, his honeyed skin paled in the candlelight. Freckles smattered his weathered face like pinpricks of starlight.

"You... Can you see me?" the man whispered.

"Of course, I can see you."

The man stumbled forward, his green cloak dragging behind him. With callused fingers, he reached for Seren, recognition crossing his features.

"Seren?" he croaked. "Is that you?"

"Don't touch me," he demanded, grip tightening on the sword. "Tell me who you are. How do you know my name?"

The man bowed his head, his fingers withdrawing. "I feared fate had shifted again—that we would never cross paths. And yet, here you stand before me. How can this be?" He lifted his head, tears streaking his face. "I am the Seer Felix Amos."

Seren's mouth went dry. "What?" His sword lowered. "How is that...possible?"

Felix stepped to the wall, brushing his hands over the images. "I told your dear mother there would come a day when the two of us would meet, and you would learn the truths of this world. Though I never imagined it would be like this." His rheumy eyes filled with sorrow. "There isn't much time. I don't know how long we have, dear boy."

Felix beckoned Seren, and though hesitant, Seren followed him deeper into the strange underground ruins. Felix's wrinkled hands brushed against the wall, scraping away the dust.

"Time has been lost to me," Felix murmured. "I have been alone for a very long time."

"What is this place, and how did you get down here?" Seren asked.

Felix paused, his brow furrowing. "I...I do not remember how I came to be here." He resumed walking. "We stand in the ancient, buried Palace of Aethalis, long before the rise of Andanova. A forgotten past, buried beneath the lies of Gala, the Fallen of Greed."

Seren studied the man's hollowed face as Felix traced a hand over the image of a god or angel—Seren wasn't sure which. Four wings spread behind its back, and three halos hovered above its head.

"Gala was a Fallen?"

Felix nodded. "The Fallen are but servants to the Devil—searching for purpose in their cursed existence. Gala only assisted in burying the past, and what better way than to build a kingdom over it, hiding whatever truths had existed?" Shadows darkened Felix's face. "Even demons make deals with the one called the Devil. But the Devil does not keep his promises." His fingers curled against the stone. "Shadows in the light." His shoulders trembled. "Blood in the water. Shadows in the light."

"Are you alright?" Seren tentatively set a hand on Felix's shoulder. But when he tried to touch the man, his hand passed through him as if he were made of mist. Seren jerked back with a gasp.

Felix trembled, shaking his head. "Fine, fine," he muttered. "Where were we?"

"The Devil," Seren breathed.

Felix ran a palm over his face as if to ground himself. "What do you know of the Devil, Seren?"

"He was an angel."

Felix slammed his fist onto the wall. "Wrong," he boomed. He cleared his throat, turning back to Seren with a haunted look in his eyes.

"I don't understand," Seren whispered.

Felix pressed both hands against the stone. Seren blinked, his gaze narrowing. Surely his eyes were playing tricks on him this time. The longer he looked at Felix, the more it seemed as though...he wasn't actually there. The candlelight appeared to pass right through him, his body translucent. No. That couldn't be.

"An angel lives to serve their god," Felix said, his voice quiet. "Their power, their strength, comes from this singular purpose. They are ancient guardians, messengers, true believers. A god gains strength from prayer, from worship. Do you understand? Without prayers, a god would cease to exist—cease to be."

Felix paused, his gaze finding Seren's. "An angel without a god to follow has no purpose. But the Devil? The Devil is purposeful. He is strong, powerful, ever-growing in devotion and reverence—whether offered knowingly or born of fear or ignorance. He serves no one but himself, and yet countless serve him."

Seren held Felix's faltering stare, his chest tightening as his heart hammered in his ears.

"The Devil is no angel," Felix whispered. "He is a god."

It was as if someone had squeezed the breath from Seren's lungs. He stumbled backward, clenching the hilt of his sword. "That's impossible."

"It is the truth. Come."

Keeping a firm hold on his weapon, Seren followed the Seer deeper into the candlelit passage. Doubt gnawed at him, even as he sensed no malice in the man ahead. Was the Seer truly there at all? Questions clawed at Seren's mind, a hundred of them pressing against his tongue.

The Devil was a god? Could it be true? Not an angel who had fallen into corruption and betrayed the heavens, but a god who had once sat among the pantheon themselves?

No.

It had to be a trick.

A lie.

"Empty goblets, wallowing mothers... The end comes for my fallen brothers," Felix murmured, his fingers twitching at his sides.

The man was deranged—clearly, wasn't he? Or perhaps Seren had hit his head too hard when he'd fallen.

"I don't understand," Seren said again, his voice edged with frustration. "How can the Devil be a god? Why would a god do such a thing?"

Felix stopped in front of a carving, standing motionless. It was the Mother Tree again, but this time, beneath the sprawling canopy sat a woman. Unicorns reclined at her feet, etched with care.

"Do you know why it is forbidden for a human and a god to be together, Seren?"

Seren was silent.

"Love is powerful," Felix said softly. "Love is destructive. It brings war and death, and it births true hatred. Mothers will die for their children; lovers will kill for one another. Every human is born with an inherent desire for love—it cannot be helped."

"But a god does not love as a human does—a god should not love as a human does. Human hearts change over time while a god's does not. A god is not devoted to one but to all, bound to the universe itself. They cannot freely give themselves away in a sacred vow of true love. Our human lives are short and fleeting, snuffed out by the slightest breath, while a god is eternal, an ever-burning flame that even the strongest winds cannot extinguish."

"Humans are not meant to live forever. Mortals wage war against time, but it changes us in ways we cannot endure. And when the Devil fell in love with a mortal, it changed him too."

Seren traced the tree's trunk, his thoughts drifting to the tale from the Sanguine Kingdom—the story of the Devil and his love for Lilith. Their love had begun as pure devotion before their curse.

Lilith was created to belong to Adamus, but when she was no longer enough, he cast her aside and sought Eden instead. Seren couldn't deny the cruelty of it—the injustice. Her existence was shaped by tragedy, a tale of rejection and suffering—until the Devil fell in love with her.

"When the Devil saw Lilith's desire for freedom, her beautiful free will, he was drawn to her, Seren. He loved her so fiercely that hate festered in his immortal soul. Lilith was never meant to be his to love, and for that, the Devil paid the price and so did she."

"But that isn't fair," Seren found himself saying.

"We are created in the image of the gods," Felix replied. "Some would say even they are not without flaw."

Seren was at a loss for words as Felix continued walking. They came across another depiction of the Mother Tree, this time with a wyrm entwined around its colossal trunk. Though it was only a carving, Seren's mind filled in the colors from his memories. He could almost see the creature's fiery orange eyes, skillfully painted, its clawed arms clutching the tree, and its dark, serpentine body coiling around it. Beneath it stood a man and a woman, both naked, holding apples in their palms.

"It was not Eden who ate the apple," Seren said. "Was it? It was Adamus, just as the Sisters say."

"Yes," Felix answered without hesitation. "Adamus was a terrible man. Evil men crave what isn't theirs, and when he realized something in Lilith had changed—that she had grown fond of another—he forced her back. He kept her as a prisoner, claiming she'd never leave him, that she'd never belong to anyone else. And the Devil saw her misery and pain, and it became his."

"Why didn't the other gods do anything?" Seren demanded. "Why did they watch her suffer and let Adamus be cruel?"

The corners of Felix's lips twitched. "That is the very question the Devil asked, Seren. Why would the gods allow this evil to walk the earth? Why would they allow suffering to spread? It drove the Devil to defy their sacred vows. He saw Adamus's desire to be more, to want more, and tricked him into eating the forbidden apple, corrupting his blood. He was damned, never to know fulfillment again."

Felix's voice dropped lower as he continued. "The Mother Tree bears the fruit of the gods—fruit of good and evil, of knowledge, of power. A god need not eat, sleep, or dream. Adamus ate the apple, and he was weak; he was not worthy, and it ruined him. Never would a drink quench his thirst, never would food fill his belly, never would love satisfy his soul. As punishment, the gods cursed his entire bloodline to hunger for a power that can never be sated. And as for Eden, I believe you saw that for yourself, did you not?"

Seren had. Eden's hatred for men was buried deep within her. Her bloodlust, her desire to destroy the entire line of Adamus, and her belief that men were the wicked disease of the world.

"And the wyrm?" Seren whispered.

"It was part of the Devil's scheme," Felix said. "He used trickery, changing his shape into a form that would intimidate Adamus. And as punishment, his wings were shorn."

Seren grazed his hand across the portrait of the woman beneath the tree, using his palm to wipe the dust from her carved face. Sympathy flooded him.

"Who is he, then?" Seren breathed. "Do...I know this god?"

"Yes," Felix said. "He is a god that the Trinity follows and prays to every day."

Seren wanted to argue, but he couldn't find it in himself to say a word.

"The sun always burns," Felix said, his voice low. "The moon always shines. But stars? Stars die." His hand brushed over the wyrm. "Stars are born of both light and darkness, life and death."

Seren tensed, shaking his head. It couldn't be true. All the times Aiden had prayed to the Trinity, calling upon the God of the Stars, Caelum. All the paintings adorning the walls of churches and cathedrals. All those years Seren had believed the stars could hear his prayers.

"The gods wanted you to know the truth, Seren. Nothing is as it seems." Felix reached for Seren, and though his fingers pressed against his chest, Seren felt nothing. He stared at the Seer's hands. He could see through them. "Without truth, all will be lost."

"What am I supposed to do with this truth?" Seren demanded, his voice rising. "This changes everything."

Felix gripped Seren's shoulders. "Find the items," he commanded. "Destroy them." Though Seren could not feel it, Felix's grip was desperate, his eyes wild and unfocused. "Destroy them. Undo what is yet to come."

Seren staggered backward. Felix's face twisted into a state of confusion. His hands shot to his head, fingers tugging at his tangled curls.

"No, retrieve the items. Bring forth the light," he stammered. "No! Destroy them! End everything!"

Felix clutched his chest, collapsing to his knees. His figure flickered, fading in and out of focus, like a fragment of a dream.

"You're already dead, aren't you?" Seren whispered, the realization dawning on him. "I can only see you because you're condemned to the Veil."

Felix wheezed, shaking his head weakly. "You must find balance within yourself, Seren," he rasped. "Only then can you bring balance to the world."

Seren dropped to his knees, desperation clawing at his chest. "How?" he said, his voice trembling. "What am I supposed to do now?" He tried to steady his racing heart, but panic consumed him. Felix was fading, slipping away. "Please, tell me what to do."

Felix's trembling fingers reached for the ring on Seren's finger. "A song a mother sung, stars that can be undone, in death's grasp all is harmonious at last."

"What does that mean?"

"You have to go home, Seren."

Seren swallowed hard, his throat tight. "I can't go home," he said. "I have to get the harp before I go back to Lumina."

"No, not Lumina. The home where your father lifted you to the stars and your mother sang you lullabies. Where your father knew happiness." Felix's translucent fingers hovered near Seren's temple. "Where the truth was born."

Seren gasped, a surge of blurred images flooding his mind—his mother's green eyes, the roar of the ocean crashing against cliffs, amber eyes staring back at him, the faint hum of lullabies.

Felix's whisper was barely audible. "Go home and find what belongs to you." He pointed at the ring on Seren's finger. "Remember who you are, Seren."

Seren froze. "I know who I am."

Felix smiled, and sadness filled his eyes. "Tell young Felix to be wary of his visions. And tell Eldyir I never forgot. Even when the world went dark. His name is the one I will always remember."

Before Seren could ask anything more, Felix was gone, taking all the answers with him.

Seren forced his feet up the stairs that greeted him at the end of the chamber. He scraped his knuckles against the walls, letting blood flow down his hands. It healed instantly. Seren did it again. And again. Until he reached the top of the stairs. Red light flooded ahead, appearing closer than before. Seren headed for the chasm walls, his feet dragging.

How many times had he questioned the will of the gods, only for Aiden to lash out in anger? How often had he been silenced? Seren wanted to laugh. He wanted to scream. Most of all, he wanted to run—run until everything behind him was nothing but a distant memory, swallowed by the dark.

But the Seer's words refused to let go of Seren. He tried to deny them, to bury them beneath disbelief, but he couldn't. When Seren had stood in the throne room of the Andanovan castle, he had seen it for what it had once been. Except it hadn't been a vision at all. It was a memory.

Seren's mother had never told him about the home he'd had before Stellaris. Those memories had long faded into the background, something he had accepted as a lost part of his life. But now, he couldn't shake the vivid images that had resurfaced. Before the fall. Before Lumina.

Seren's thumb brushed over the ring on his hand, the gift from his father. A sharp pang filled his chest, and his knees hit the ground as his hand clutched the rock beneath him. He didn't want to return to this place he had once called home. He didn't want to think about his mother or his father. He wanted to retrieve the harp and leave Andanova for good. He wanted to reach Jude before something terrible happened—if it hadn't already. But Seren couldn't bring himself to even think that.

It was all too much.

Seren took a deep breath. He couldn't fall apart. Not now. He had to hold himself together. Rising to his feet, he slipped a hand into his pocket, searching for the stone Felix had given him. It wasn't there. His heart sank. It must have been lost in the fall.

Gritting his teeth, Seren turned toward the chasm wall, running his fingers over the rough, cold rock. He had hoped to avoid it, but the climb ahead was daunting, though not impossible. His ribs had healed. He could do this.

"Does the truth unsettle you, little godling?"

The voice was soft and cold, cutting through the stillness. Seren froze, his fingers tightening on the stone.

"Does it frighten you?"

A thin tendril of shadow coiled around his wrist, feather-light and icy.

"Does it anger you?"

"Leave me alone," Seren hissed.

"How long until it consumes you?"

The rock scraped beneath his hand as Seren clenched his fist. Slowly, he released his grip and turned around. "That's what you want, isn't it?" he spat, his voice rising. His eyes scanned the chasm. "For it to consume me. To turn me into a monster—just like you did in Calarinn."

A low, mocking laugh echoed around him, and another wisp of shadow grazed the line of his neck. *"We did nothing,"* the voice purred. *"We are only here to serve, godling."*

The shadows slithered closer, alive, their tendrils weaving together like threads in a loom. Seren opened his palm, and several birds burst forth, their wings bright in the dark. They flitted into the air, their light drawing the shadows back for a moment.

But only for a moment.

The darkness surged forward, swallowing the birds as the shadows began to writhe and pulse. They stretched upward, limbs taking shape, a torso solidifying. What emerged was neither whole nor broken, its edges flickering and rippling like smoke.

And then it moved.

The tilt of its head, the slight shift of its shoulders—it was uncanny, too familiar. Seren's stomach twisted. He took a step back, and the shadow mirrored him.

"*Why do you hide?*" it asked, its voice a chilling echo of Seren's own. "*Tell me, Half-Light, why do you run?*"

Seren's breath hitched, but he forced himself forward. "What do you want? Who are you?"

The shadow chuckled, lifting a hand to where its face should have been. The fingers curled like smoke, dissolving at the edges. "*We are you,*" it whispered, "*and you are us. Stardust woven into flesh, destined to return to the dark that birthed us.*" It stepped closer, its form distorting the air around it. "*We have always been with you.*" Its voice lowered, almost affectionate. "*And we will never leave.*"

Seren's hands trembled. "I don't want your help," he said. "Leave me alone."

The shadow tilted its head, a cruel smile forming in its words. "*Are you sure about that, little godling? Do you not crave your judgement? Did you not feel it when we killed the lord?*"

Seren flinched, his back pressing against the wall. "I shouldn't have done it. It wasn't my place," he whispered. "It was wrong."

The shadow leaned closer and it laughed. *"You and I both know you don't believe that. You're afraid—of who you truly are, of what you feel, of what you're capable of."*

"No—"

"Let us in again. Let us show you what you've forgotten," the voice whispered. It felt as if cold fingers had reached into Seren's mind, a pulling, a pressure that weighed him down. *"We can help you remember."*

A shadowy hand reached out, tendrils brushing against Seren's temple. His body froze.

"Let us in," it urged, its voice like a breath against his ear. *"You've forgotten. Let us remind you."*

Shadowy fingers stretched, grazing his skin. Seren couldn't move. Images flared in his mind: blazing birds plummeting from the sky, their scorched feathers turning to ash. Beautiful, humanlike creatures, their powder-blue skin and citrine eyes consumed as darkness crawled into their mouths, their eyes, their very souls.

Angels clad in white and gold, curling inward as their ivory feathers tore away to reveal raw, glistening bone. Fallen stars streaking across an empty sky, collapsing into themselves, sprouting teeth and shadows.

"Stop."

A sob tore through Seren's throat.

Then, he saw himself.

Wings of shadow erupted from his back—the color of a starless sky. The darkness stretched out to meet him, a hundred hands reaching toward him, beckoning. And it whispered, over and over again: *"Welcome home."*

Seren forced his eyes open, staring into the faceless entity that mirrored him. He reached out, his fingers slipping through the shadows. Time slowed. His heartbeat stilled, the blood in his veins freezing. And before him, there was nothing—just an endless stretch of void.

"We have seen everything—we have seen all," the shadow rasped. *"If you stay in the light too long, you will burn."*

Wings unfurled behind the figure, vast and endless, their edges curling with shadow. They folded around him, cradling Seren like a child held in the arms of a mother. Hands, cold and insistent, threaded through his white hair, tugging at the collar of his shirt. A hundred voices rose from the abyss, a murmur of whispers.

"You have been taught to fear the dark, to see it as unnatural, as evil," the shadows whispered. *"You are the dark, as much as you are the light. You are of us, and we are of you—bound together before the beginning, and before the end."*

The darkness kept him impossibly close, as if it had always known him, never once letting go. It held him with a tenderness that made his skin crawl, and yet, Seren couldn't pull away.

"We can make you whole again," it murmured.

A shadowed hand traced the length of Seren's scars, and he shuddered. A finger brushed across his throat, then his collarbone.

"I have never been whole," Seren whispered.

"We can change that, Half-Light." A shadowy finger tipped his chin, and it leaned in, the cold brush of darkness against Seren's skin sending a shiver through him. For a moment, he couldn't move. The wings tightened

around him. The shadowed figure leaned in closer, its form hovering just inches from his face, where its mouth should have been. *"Let us in, Seren."*

And why shouldn't he? Nothing was as it seemed. Everything he'd ever known had been wrong. Who was to say this wasn't the right path? Who was to say this wasn't who Seren had always been? Not of the light, but of the darkness. Not holy, but corrupted—just like the world always had been. How was he any better than any of it?

Seren's head tilted back, eyes fluttering closed, his mouth parting in acceptance. It felt right. It felt familiar. His skin prickled as something brushed across his lips.

Her call nearly shattered him. *"Seren!"*

A burst of light exploded around Seren, so powerful that the shadows writhed and snapped apart, scattering like broken pieces of night. The darkness fled, retreating into the cracks and crevices it had come from. Seren collapsed to his knees, as if freed from a spell. The weight lifted from his chest, and warmth flooded him again, as though his body had thawed from the cold. His hands gripped the earth, his breath coming in jagged gasps.

Eventually, Seren stumbled to his feet. He looked up at the sky that awaited him. It was time to climb.

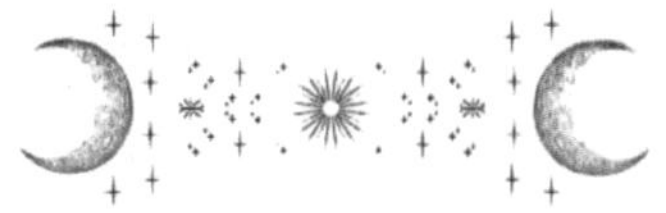

The ascent was steep. Seren strained, his hands clawing at the rock, fingertips digging into the wall as he pulled himself up. Strength rippled through him with every movement, pushing him further toward the top. He didn't dare look down, knowing the fall would shatter him all over again. Time was running out. He had to do this. And then, he would get to Jude.

He hoisted himself up onto another rock, sweat trickling down his back, and pulled himself onto the next ledge.

Seren thought of Jude's smile. Jude's laugh. Jude's kiss.

"Jude, have we met before?"

Seren's fingernails cracked beneath the pressure. How many lies had he been told?

"The Devil is no angel. He is a god."

How many secrets had his mother kept from him?

"When can I see my father again?"

How many memories were still buried beneath the surface?

"Why does he talk?" Seren asked, peering into Grimm's bionic eye. "Did you make him do that too?"

"I helped," Lumen mused, stroking Grimm's feathers. "When I found him, I wasn't sure he would survive. Half of his head was crushed in." His hand hovered over the raven's wing. "And he could no longer fly."

"Amazing," Seren whispered. "You saved him."

Lumen chuckled. "I defied fate. Not so terrible as it seems, is it?"

Seren released a yell as he pushed his chest over the top of the ledge, landing on the overgrown grass. He panted, turning onto his back.

None of it mattered.

Seren had to keep going. He forced himself to his feet, straightening up as a breeze rippled through his pale hair. He was still near the castle, the devastation of the fallen country all around.

Silence filled the air, only broken by the wind blowing through the crooked trees. Seren stepped over the debris, letting his feet carry him forward, trying to leave his thoughts behind. He would follow the path of memory. The temple lay in the opposite direction, at least a mile away, and the journey would take twice as long due to the rough terrain.

Seren stepped over crumbled marble, his gaze fixed ahead. He would get there. The power of a goddess lived inside him, the blood of a god coursing through his veins. He would not falter. A swell of power rose within him, and soft light emanated from his skin. A hiss sounded nearby, and any creatures that had lurked in the shadows retreated from the holy light he summoned.

He took a deep breath and began walking toward his forgotten past.

TWENTY-SEVEN

"The fox kills the hare out of necessity, not because it is thirsty for violence. A hare's luck can only stretch so far."

—the Scribes of Wisdom

The summers in Andanova had always been beautiful, a blur of gold and blue, with mountains that kissed the sky and celebrations that filled the world with color. Women dressed in silks as bright as peacock feathers in cerulean blues, royal purples, and emerald greens, while men wore white doublets trimmed with gold and silver.

The Midsummer Festival had been Jude's favorite. He would run between the billowing dresses of the women, snagging bread drenched in honey—more than his mother allowed—and stealing sips of the sweet wine. Jude always found the most fun in causing trouble at these types of celebrations and he was the *best* at not getting caught. Nothing was funnier than watching snot-nosed nobles point fingers at one another, wondering who had tampered with their drinks or stolen their jewelry.

But the best part of the Midsummer Festival? It was also the king's favorite celebration. He would indulge in wine until he was drunk and stumbling. Jude's favorite version of his father was the drunk one. He was kinder, happier, and took more notice of Jude's existence.

Once, when Jude was eight, the Midsummer Festival had just come to a close, and his father took him to the Temple of Gala. His bloated belly and ruddy face were a clear testament to the amount he'd drunk that night. Sober, the king never made time for his youngest son, but on nights like that, Jude had felt seen for the first time. He marveled at the golden tresses, the beautiful paintings, the kingly peacock crest, and the sun-shaped skylight. He remembered his father ruffling his hair, reminding him that he was named after an extraordinary man.

"You'll do great things, my boy. It doesn't matter how grand or small—they'll be great because you carry greatness in your name, in your blood, in your kingdom."

Even now, Jude could taste the wine and wisteria-scented air on his tongue. But the vibrant festival, the warmth of the past was long gone. There was no harp or piano echoing through the chamber, no goblet of wine filled to the brim, no nobles dancing in silks across the ballroom floor. No god to worship or call to.

Instead, there were only crumbling walls, left to an imposter. Bugs skittered up the walls of his confinement. It was almost laughable—imprisoned in a place of worship from his childhood, the home of his false god. And it was fitting. He was the false prince with no kingdom, no family, no purpose.

Jude pressed his palm against the gritty ground, trying to steady himself. His left hand had turned black, blisters spreading across his knuckles.

The necklace had burned him so badly that all the feeling in his fingers was gone.

He had already tried the door, but some kind of spell had locked him in. A rush of frustration flooded his chest. He had never felt like a bigger idiot. When he'd seen his mother's necklace in that chamber, he hadn't been able to leave it behind. Against every instinct, he'd taken it. Just one piece, he had thought. One piece of his past to carry, to remind him of the beautiful moments of his childhood. A stupid, moronic mistake. And now, it had doomed him.

Jude may never see Seren again. It was worse than the idea of death itself.

He could still feel Seren's hands, soft but steady, as if Seren alone could hold Jude together when he couldn't manage it himself. It wasn't fair. Nothing about Seren ever was.

And when Seren had kissed him, it had made everything seem worth it. It felt like he'd waited his whole life for that one perfect moment, the unspoken question always lingering between them.

Don't you see the way I look at you? As if you're everything. As if you're mine.

Seren's scent still clung to Jude, like the crisp air of a frosty winter evening, carrying the promise of freshly fallen snow. It was all Jude had left.

Jude curled inward. He'd always told himself he could live without redemption, without family, without a kingdom. But then came Seren, with his impossible determination, and suddenly Jude had wanted to believe in more. He wanted to believe he was worthy, that he could live for something more than just his own selfish fear. Jude had never believed in anything, in anyone, like he believed in Seren.

For so long, Jude had been full of emptiness. Loneliness had been his constant companion. He had found glee in pocketing extra coins from unsuspecting crooks, and sometimes, he had derived pleasure from hurting those who deserved it. It wasn't that he *enjoyed* it, but the act gave him something to do, a job to complete, a goal to achieve. It was a way to feel worthy of something when he didn't know how else.

For some time, those were the only things that brought him joy, the only distractions that kept him alive. Jude had no gods to pray to when the world felt too heavy to bear. Nobody to truly call his own to fall on when he was afraid.

When Jude and Mila had met, he'd felt a bit more alive, less alone, but still, that emptiness remained.

Until Seren.

How could Jude explain something he didn't understand? This belief. This feeling... He'd wanted to tell Seren that night in Aurelius, at the Grand Celebration. But how could he put it into words without sounding foolish?

Since the moment he met Seren, something had ignited in him, a spark that quickly turned into a burning fire. A purpose he couldn't let go of. If Seren needed to reach the stars, Jude would lift him to the sky. If Seren wanted to leave everything behind, to run to the edge of the world and asked Jude to follow, he would go.

Till the end.

And he would promise it again and again until his lungs were empty.

But this?

This could not be the end. Not yet. Not while Seren's name still burned on his tongue like an unfinished prayer.

With a rumble, the chamber doors swung open. Jude lifted his tear-streaked face, battling the fear gripping his heart. He loathed fear. Always had.

Long ago, he had shoved it into a box, wrapped it tight, and presented it with a smile. But now the ribbon had come undone, the lid had cracked open, and it was spilling out faster than he could shove it back inside.

The creature glided across the room, its bedraggled robes flowing behind it despite the absence of wind. Glowing blue orbs hovered in its sockets as it neared, and Jude's skin crawled when its bony hands brushed his cheek.

"You don't recognize your own father, Caius?"

Jude's blood chilled.

"Oh, my dearest son. We can all be together again now that you're here." His jaw clattered. *"The kingdom will rise again, because of you."*

Jude couldn't form words, a lump stuck in his throat.

"Let us prepare, my son."

From beneath his tattered robes, the monster extended a skeletal hand. Shadows writhed around its fingers as it muttered something low and guttural. A sharp flick of its wrist conjured a set of garments. They were pristine, the golden buttons glinting faintly. Jude's stomach churned as he recognized the insignia etched on each: a C.

"Put them on," the creature said, its hollow eyes boring into him.

Jude's hands trembled as he peeled off his dirty shirt and stripped his pants, bile rising in his throat with every motion.

"For you, my Caius." The monster's voice softened. *"We will finally be complete with you here, and all will be as it was meant to be."*

Jude knew he shouldn't have obeyed. He shouldn't have put the clothes on. He should have said *something*—a joke, an insult, *anything*. But who was left to fool? There was no one here to laugh with him, no one to hide from, except a demon that called him by his brother's name.

"Thank you, Father," he whispered, his voice barely audible over the sound of his own heartbeat.

The monster smiled—a grotesque, skeletal grin—and traced its bony fingers along Jude's cheek. Cold seeped into his skin, and he fought the urge to recoil. The demon's rotted hands settled on his shoulders, and a heavy haze enveloped Jude. His eyelids drooped, and the room blurred.

"Sleep, little prince," the monster murmured. *"Dream of gold and glory. Dream of what once was...and what will be."*

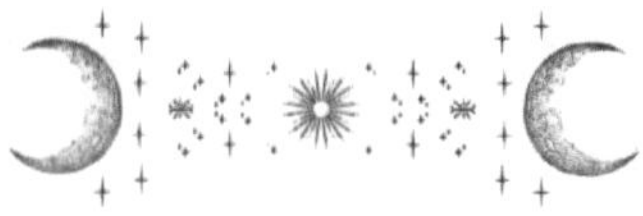

Multicolored wings unfurled from the peacock's body as it lifted from the ground, its glittering tail feathers cascading behind like a jeweled waterfall. Jude snickered mischievously as he crept forward, eyes locked on the bluish tail feathers. Then he lunged, legs pumping with determination, hands reaching out to grab his prize.

But before his fingers could close around it, something snagged his collar, yanking him back. With an undignified yelp, he tumbled backward, landing on the grass with a thud.

"Hey! I almost had it!" he protested, craning his neck to see who had stopped him.

Caius smiled from above, the autumn sunlight catching on his golden locks like a halo, his blue eyes glittering. "Shouldn't you be getting ready for the offerings, little brother?" He gestured to the peacocks pacing back and forth across the golden field. "One of these days, one of them might take out an eye. They're not exactly friendly birds, you know."

Jude crossed his arms over his chest. "Shouldn't you be courting princesses and plotting wars?" He stuck out his tongue. "Besides, Father said we needed to bring one to the temple."

Caius rolled his eyes, a half-smile tugging at his lips, and ruffled Jude's hair. "That's not what being a king is about, you little scoundrel. And I'm not king yet—but you'd best be careful."

Jude squealed as Caius tickled his side, sending him tumbling to his knees in the long grass. Caius chuckled. "Once I am king, I'll put you to good use. No more stealing from the guards."

"I don't steal," Jude insisted, rising to his feet.

"Oh, but you certainly lie." Caius raised an eyebrow, his expression pointed.

Jude sighed. "Okay, okay. I'll go get ready."

"And?" Caius drawled, drawing out the word with mock severity.

Jude pouted. "And I'll give Sir Uriel his signet ring back."

"Good," Caius said with a laugh, ruffling Jude's hair again with a smirk. "And don't worry about the bird. I already caught one for you."

Jude's face lit up. "You did?"

"Of course I did," Caius said. "It's caged up and ready for you in the castle."

"But father said we had to catch them ourselves."

"Then it'll be our little secret—just like you being my favorite brother is our secret," Caius replied, pressing a finger to his lips. "Now—go on. I'll see you at the temple."

"Fine," Jude sighed, his scowl deepening as he trudged toward the royal gardens. The long grass brushed against his trousers, its faded gold and orange reflecting the restless change of the season. Soon, winter's browns would smother it all. He paused, turning to the gaze of his brother, who stood with a flaxen eyebrow raised. "Caius?"

"Yes?"

"When you're king," Jude began. "Would you...?" He bit his lip. "Could you make me your knight?" He rubbed the back of his neck, warmth rising to his ears. "I can learn how to fight and use a sword. I've had enough of piano and painting lessons."

Caius chuckled and walked forward. "A knight, huh?" He cocked his head to the side, his nose pinched. "Knights are not thieves, Judas. Knights are honorable and disciplined."

"I can be those things," Jude piped, straightening his back. "I swear it."

A gentle breeze blew through the white oak trees and tousled Caius's honey hair. He smiled as he lowered himself onto one knee. The late afternoon sun sat on the horizon, basking his brother in a canopy of sunlight. "Then, by the will of our god Gala, I swear it." He lifted Jude's chin, his golden skin gleaming. "But you must make me a promise too, hmm?"

"Anything."

"Never lose that smile of yours," Caius said. "If you are to be my knight—you must be as bright as the sun above. Not just a knight but a prince that loves his kingdom. A beacon of light." He ruffled Jude's hair once more. "I couldn't have you by my side with an attitude like Sir Uriel, now, could I?"

Jude giggled.

"Now, run along and don't be late or father will surely hunt you down."

Jude's feet moved quickly beneath him as he rounded the corner behind the castle wall. Despite what he had told his brother, Jude wasn't heading to the temple for the royal family's blessings. Caius would be disappointed, but Jude knew his brother would forgive him. Afterward, Jude would discipline himself further, and one day, he would stand behind his brother in shining golden armor as bright as the sun.

Following a narrow path through the copse of trees, Jude made his way to the riverbank, the sound of rushing water growing louder with each step. An orange-bellied salamander crawled across a mossy log, leaving a trail of slime. Jude wrinkled his nose and picked it up between his fingers. Its buggy yellow eyes swiveled back and forth for a moment before Jude set it down with a bored sigh. He grabbed a smooth rock, tossing it in.

A small part of Jude hoped his father would be furious or, even better, worried. Perhaps the king really would come looking for Jude this time. He reveled in the idea, making up scenarios in his head, deciding what he would say to his father if he came searching for him. But an hour passed. And another. Until Jude finally tossed one last rock into the river.

The slimy salamander crawled across Jude's calf, its webbed toes tickling his skin. He picked it up and set it into the cool water. It swam against the rapids, going in the wrong direction.

"Stupid salamander," Jude laughed. He turned it around and watched as the creature disappeared down the river. He sighed and peeled off his boots, dipping his toes in the water.

Fallen red and orange leaves swirled on the water's surface, as if dancing. The river was lonely with nobody to share it with. Caius was always far too busy, as was Caspian. Armin had plenty of friends of his own that Jude wasn't fond of. Of course, Raima was a bore, always spending her time daydreaming about marrying the Prince of Kogarashi.

Jude didn't have trouble making friends; he simply had high standards for his companions. Last summer had been different. He had befriended a dark-haired boy whose father held the title of Royal Advisor. The boy, younger and slight, rarely spoke but quickly became Jude's shadow, trailing him through the castle like a lost puppy. Jude didn't mind. In fact, he was intrigued by the prospect of befriending someone with ties to political affairs.

Few children of royalty or council members were close to Jude's age, and most who sought his friendship seemed more interested in bragging about knowing a prince. But this boy was different. Before long, they were exploring the castle corridors together, their laughter echoing through the hallways. Though the boy remained distant and quiet, Jude had a knack for making him laugh—a small triumph that brought him endless delight.

Jude had even shown his friend his favorite spot in the fields, where he would stalk peacocks like a predator, crouching low and ready to pounce. Though he had regretted it. When Jude lunged at a young peacock, he misjudged his strength and clipped its wing. The boy had been furious, and Jude, overwhelmed with guilt, burst into tears.

The boy had scooped up the injured bird and carried it back to the castle. Together, they fashioned a splint for its wing and tended to it, both hoping it would one day fly again.

Then, one night, the boy and his mother disappeared without a trace, leaving Jude heartbroken. He sat beside the injured bird, sobbing, a hollow ache filling his chest as though he had lost something irreplaceable. His mother tried to console him, reassuring him with a smile that perhaps, someday, their paths would cross again.

Jude continued to care for the peacock, and when its wing finally healed, he released it into the open fields. As it soared into the sky, he desperately wished his friend had been there to see it fly.

The memory lingered for a moment before Jude shook it off with a sigh. He yawned and got to his feet, brushing fallen leaves from his trousers. It was time to head home. Of course, he'd be getting a scolding from his mother for not making an appearance. He kicked a rock on the trail ahead. If he was lucky, his father would want a word with him, too.

Jude dragged himself along the path toward the castle. A rustle in the brush ahead caught his attention, and a peacock stepped into view, trailed by five tiny chicks. He halted, crouching low in the tall grass like a cat. He grinned, preparing to startle the creatures. But just as he tensed to leap and unleash his most ferocious roar, a streak of orange darted between them, scattering the group.

A screech pierced the air as the mother peacock panicked, flapping her wings frantically. Feathers scattered like falling snowflakes. Jude met the glowing yellow eyes of the predator; its jaws clamped around a mouthful of lifeless peachicks. Only one remained, trembling in the dirt, its tiny leg twisted at an unnatural angle.

Jude clenched his fists, ready to scare the fox away—but then he froze. A sudden weight crushed his chest, stealing his breath and driving him to his knees. He doubled over, gasping as his lungs burned with each desperate gulp of air. Slowly, he forced himself upright, unsteady and trembling.

Overhead, the sky began to change. The serene blue dissolved into creeping crimson, bleeding across the horizon. It stained the sun and drenched the world in an eerie, blood-soaked hue.

The fox remained motionless, its unblinking gaze fixed on Jude as blood dripped down its pale, cream-colored chest. Then, with a flick of its tail, it vanished into the brush, leaving the carnage in its wake.

Jude forced himself upright, his heart pounding so violently it felt ready to burst. Without hesitation, he broke into a sprint, crashing through the trees and emerging into the open field near the castle. The air shattered with a terrified scream. Only when the burning in his throat became unbearable did he realize the sound had come from him.

Grotesque creatures loomed, their bodies twisted, spines jutting out at unnatural angles, limbs elongated, and mouths dripping with saliva. Jude stumbled backward, his heartbeat erratic, as he watched a horrifying monster with a twisted grin tear into a horse's throat, greedily gulping its blood.

Knights charged from the castle, blades glinting under the crimson sun. Jude felt a surge of hope as swords plunged into the monsters' chests. But then, a gust of wind swept across the land, slamming Jude against the tree behind him. Massive talons snatched a knight's torso, and he exploded like a grape inside his armor. The creature flapped its wings, made of jagged bone and rotted flesh, each ending in human-like claws. With a shriek, it reared back, grasping two more knights and crushing them without mercy.

Jude ran with all his might, charging across the courtyard, another scream rising in his throat. He needed his mother, his father, his brothers. He pumped his lanky legs, crashing into a pool of blood. His breath caught as he froze, staring into the lifeless eyes of a knight. It was Sir Uriel. Jude scrambled away, sobbing.

Getting to the temple was a blur. Jude didn't stop running even when his lungs felt like they were on fire. He burst through the carved doors, chest heaving, his eyes darting desperately for his family.

Jude froze.

He shouldn't have come.

He couldn't move.

He couldn't breathe.

Splayed out like dead angels, their hands like halos above their heads, blood spread behind them in perfect circles, like wings. At his mother's feet lay a white peacock, its bones jutting from its feathers. And then Caspian. Armin. Raima. All with dead peacocks resting at their feet.

"Caius?" Jude gasped. "Father?"

In the center, a writhing monster rose to its feet, holding the melting skin of its face, wearing his father's bloodstained robes. It turned toward

Jude, the air thick with the acrid stench of burning flesh. A grotesque hand, dripping with gore, reached out for him. Fear propelled him backward, his limbs moving on instinct as he fled through the doors.

Outside, a bloodbath raged. His screams mingled with the cries of others, the metallic tang of blood staining the air. Each footfall sent splashes of crimson across the ground as he sprinted.

A growl sounded behind Jude. A demon-dog's snarl snapped at his heels, its hot breath steaming against his skin. Panic surged through him as his footing faltered on the slick ground. His palms splashed into the warm, sticky liquid beneath him.

The demon lunged. Its teeth sank deep into his upper thigh, a searing agony that tore another scream from Jude's throat. He kicked wildly, his heel catching its snout. The demon snarled and released him. He pushed himself forward, but his leg gave way as the ground beneath him shifted.

The world tipped, and before he could catch himself, he plunged into a steep ditch. He landed hard, pain erupting as his leg twisted grotesquely beneath him. A sickening crunch filled his ears, followed by the white-hot stab of broken bone grinding against torn flesh.

Jude gasped, his vision blurring. Blood poured from the jagged wound where the bone had pierced his skin, soaking into the earth around him. His breaths came in ragged gasps.

There was so much blood.

Too much.

Jude sobbed, desperately clutching the golden grass, trying to lift himself up, but it was useless. He was going to die. With his fingers digging into the dirt, he wailed and tried again, his vision wavering from the pain. He turned on his back, straining to breathe.

Jude closed his eyes, feeling his heart slow, each beat a plea to hold on as his life slipped away, the ebbing pain slowly disappearing. With every faint breath, his mind echoed the same desperate thought.

I don't want to die.

I don't want to die.

I don't...want...to...die.

He longed for his mother, but above all, he wanted his brother. He couldn't die now. Caius was supposed to be king, and Jude was supposed to be beside him. Together. Side by side. A king and his knight.

Jude called for his god, his voice weak. "Please..."

And his god did not answer.

Just as the darkness began to take Jude, something wet and cold brushed against his nose, pulling him back. Jude forced his eyes open, and he met a pair of bright yellow eyes.

The fox from the woods.

Its front was still covered in blood. It stepped back, opening its mouth in a hideous, almost human-like smile. Its back arched as it began to writhe and transform, the orange fur flattening and vanishing entirely.

Before Jude stood a striking man, his hair almost white, pale yellow, and eyes like sunstones.

"Poor little prince," he simpered. "You're dying. And there are no gods here to save you."

Jude's voice was small. "Please, don't kill me," he begged. "I don't want to...die."

The man cocked his head to the side, his vulpine smile widening. "Another missing piece," He clicked his tongue, a laugh rumbling in his throat. "Isn't that unfortunate for your king?"

Jude's eyelids fluttered. The man leaned down and brushed his long fingernails across Jude's cheek. "Do you want to live, little one?"

Jude nodded weakly. He wanted to live more than anything else in the world. No matter what it took. He would give up his dreams. He would give up his freedoms. Anything. Everything.

Canines glistened in the red light. "I'll save you, child, but at a price," he purred. "You will never belong to anyone, not even yourself. Your soul will never be free, not in life, not in death. Is that a life worth living, little prince?"

Jude clasped the strange man's hand, lower lip trembling.

Anything.

Anything for life.

"Save me," Jude whimpered.

With a twisted laugh, the man's smile stretched unnaturally wide. He turned his head as his nose elongated into a snout, and a ripple of red fur spread across his skin.

"Don't let me die," Jude whispered.

After the plea escaped his lips, darkness followed. A long, hollow emptiness enveloped him. With no warning, agony coursed through his body, as if a razor-sharp claw was tearing at his very soul. A nauseating sensation overwhelmed Jude, leaving him feeling violated and exposed, as if someone had spread open his ribs and revealed everything he was inside. His fears and desires bled out into the void, no longer private.

When he finally opened his eyes, a figure loomed over him, pressing a cool rag to his forehead. His leg was gone, leaving nothing but a bloodied stump.

"Stay calm," an old man said. "You're lucky to be alive."

Twenty-Eight

"When the blood moon rises, and the moon children are born, the apple is eaten, and the serpents are forlorn. The past remains unchanged, the future ever present. For fate is a red thread, unravelling and incessant."

—Book Two of Metanoia

Kamil had been blue in a sea of red. Mila had always wanted to be blue. Blue was calm, the color of the sky on a pleasant day, calm waters, the flowers that Mila loved. She'd tried, thinking she had some sense of control over who she was, over the things she could do. When she'd dug her dagger into her brother's heart, she'd almost expected blue to flood out of his wounds. Instead, it had been as bright red as the veils the Sanguine Sisters wore.

She hated it, but it was the only color she could see now.

Red.

Red.

Red.

The sky was red. Mila's hands were stained red. Kamil had always said red suited her. She hated that he'd been right.

Mila trudged across the land, her pulse hot beneath her skin. She was out in the open, a wide target for any demons that might see her, but she didn't care. Let them come and fight her if they wanted to. She wasn't afraid. The sensation burning inside her was the only thing she feared right now. It was hot, hungry, a writhing pain deep within her. She walked past the castle, breathing in and out, forcing herself to ignore it. She had to keep moving north and hope that Felix and Cin were safe.

It didn't take long for Mila to see the temple in the distance. Pale and stark against the red sky, its domed top was covered in gnarled roots. As the sun neared the horizon, a dark purple crept up from the edge. With the darkened sun, the demons could withstand the light—but when night fell, it would be even harder to stay alive.

A streak of tawny collided with Mila's boot. Eyes like inkblots stared up at her. She reached a hand toward Theo, only to be met with a hiss. She withdrew her hand with a frown.

"He'll get used to you," Felix said, rounding the corner of the temple. He scooped up Theo and the weasel nuzzled against his cheek, then slinked around his neck. "Oh, and here." Felix procured the dagger from his belt, handing it to Mila. "I think you're better off with this than I am."

Cin stepped out next, her blade hanging loosely from her hand. "I hope none of that blood is yours."

"Not much of it," Mila replied.

Cin placed a hand on her hip, her pin-straight hair brushing against her chin. "We peeked through the windows. The temple is empty."

"Well, let's go inside then," Mila said.

"Take the lead, princess," Cin drawled, her eyes sliding over Mila's bloodied form. "Clearly, you can handle yourself."

The three of them crept toward the entrance, careful to step over the crumbled marble scattered across the ground. With one last glance at Cin, Mila pushed open the doors, the rough jewels scraping against her hands. A draft blew through her hair, tickling the back of her neck.

Crimson light flooded through the shattered, domed skylight. Knotted roots grew over the pews, splitting the wood where cracks had formed. Behind the altar stood a golden statue covered in cobwebs. It depicted a handsome man, his hands clasped in prayer, with peacock wings unfurling behind him, each feather glittering with sapphires and emeralds.

At the center of the chamber, intricate geometric patterns laced with gold overlapped on the yellowed marble floor. Strange markings were burned into the stone, reminiscent of the demonic script carved into Mila's back. As she stepped forward, her shoe nudged a velvet pouch, sending it spilling across the floor to reveal a scattering of shiny golden coins.

"Jude was here," Mila said as she retrieved them. "Which means the harp was probably here too. But...what would that monster want with Jude?"

Felix stepped across the threshold, Theo now at his heels. "The last Andanovan in existence?" he said, his voice low. "I imagine his soul would be worth more than all the gold in Aerithium."

Gooseflesh rose on Mila's arms at those words.

Cin knelt, brushing her hands against the burned runes. She lifted her chin, kohled stare steady on Mila. "You recognize these, don't you?"

Mila bit her tongue. "Yes," she managed. She walked around the circle of markings, pausing at two side by side, standing out from the rest. The centers weren't blackened or faded like the others. "These are sacrificial runes." Her eyes followed the fissures in the floor, tracing the burns that stretched like twisting veins across the marble.

"Guide my hands to them," Felix said from behind.

Mila nodded, carefully setting his hands on the floor. He ran his palms over the ground, his milky eyes widening. The air shifted, as if a freezing wind pierced through Mila's bones. She shivered, vigorously massaging her arms. Felix let out a choking noise, his fingers curling into the stone, his knuckles whitening. Theo trembled against his neck, digging his face into the hood of Felix's cloak. After several minutes, Felix pulled away with a gasp, his breath uneven.

"What is it?" Cin demanded. "Did you see something?"

Felix stood on unsteady knees while Theo nudged his cheek. "Yes, but it would be easier if I showed you," he said, extending his open palms. Mila and Cin exchanged glances before each took one of his hands. Felix took a deep breath. "Close your eyes."

Mila obeyed. A violent tremor ran through her as if the world around her were splintering. It was similar to Seren's teleportation but far more invasive, as though something were reaching deep into her mind. She gasped, her chest tightening, and her eyes flew open.

The temple had transformed. It gleamed, adorned with golden terraces and bathed in amber light flooding through the skylight above. Blue and gold carpets, edged with silver eyespots, covered the floors. Incense burned so heavily in the room that thick plumes of smoke winnowed through the chamber.

Beneath the skylight stood a woman, her skin glowing, her hands clasped in prayer. Honeyed hair cascaded down her back, and her dress began as soft blue before fading into ivory, pooling in delicate heaps at her feet. At the base of her gown rested a gilded cage containing a white peacock.

"What do you pray for, my queen?" came a voice.

The woman opened her eyes, revealing their sapphire hue. She bowed to the man approaching her, rosy lips pursed. "That is for our dear god to know," she said with a smile.

Fiery hair cascaded past the king's shoulders, braided down the middle. Upon his head rested a crown—the same one Mila had seen on the demon who had taken Jude. His mantle reflected the vibrant hues of a peacock—iridescent blues, purples, and greens shimmering beneath the light, trailing across the pearly marble.

The king placed a hand on the queen's shoulder, the gemstones on his fingers catching the light. "Are you nervous, my heart?"

"Of course I am," she breathed. "Solomon, perhaps we should reconsider? The Trinity Priests expressed concerns that worry me. After all these years—"

"Enough, Ymir," the king interrupted sharply. He sighed, pressing his lips to her forehead. "Do not let the slander of others cloud your thoughts. Trust in me."

Ymir's fingers closed around the blue stone of the necklace resting against her collarbone. "Ill fortune seems to haunt us at every turn,

Solomon," she whispered. "I dreamt of the livestock dying before it happened, saw the crops wither before they fell to disease..." She squeezed the gem until her knuckles blanched. "And a fortnight ago, I dreamt the sky bled and our kingdom crumbled to ruins."

"These are nothing but coincidental nightmares," Solomon said gruffly. "How many hundreds of years has Gala provided for us? He will continue to do so for hundreds more." He took her hands in his. "One day, he will be the one true god."

With a tender touch, he brushed a golden ringlet from her face. "You'll see, my queen. Gala is going to save our kingdom—and save us all." He kissed her knuckles. "Trust in him. If we follow his guidance, he's promised to restore our abundance. The crops will grow again, and the diseased animals will be healed. We must act now, before word of our misfortune spreads through the realm. Today, we'll meet him as a family, and you'll hear his promises for yourself."

"Solomon, these dreams—"

The king cut her off. "Are exactly that—dreams," he said. "Samael believes that after today, everyone across Aerithium will believe in Gala. No one will doubt our kingdom again. But enough of this, Ymir—I won't have you showing doubt in front of our children."

Darkness flickered over Ymir's features, but her lips remained in a tight line.

The temple doors opened, light flooding across the white floors. Mila stifled a gasp. *Jude?* He wore a tunic of white silk, its golden vest embroidered with oak leaves. Polished white leather boots gleamed in the sun as he stepped forward, bowing to the king. A golden circlet rested on his brow, blue diamonds glinting in its center. In his white-gloved hand, he held a large birdcage containing an ivory peacock, its train cascading through the ornate bars.

"Caius," Solomon greeted with a grin. "My dearest son." He turned to Ymir. "Are the others upstairs?"

"Yes," Ymir replied. "Except Judas." Her eyebrows furrowed. "Always getting into trouble, that one."

Caius's gaze flickered briefly to Ymir before he half-smiled. "Judas will be here soon," he said. "I spoke with him earlier."

"If he's not here in the next few minutes, we'll start without him," Solomon said, his tone firm.

Caius's smile faltered. "Father, I implore you to wait—"

"That boy has little respect," Solomon snapped, cutting him off. "If he's not here, we begin without him. He'll have to live with that shame for the rest of his life. Gala claimed the sun must be at its zenith and the moon visible in the sky. If he misses it, the fault is his own."

Ymir remained silent, her fingers clutching her necklace. Caius's fists curled at his sides, but he didn't challenge his father.

"They say only the kings of Andanova could speak with Gala," Felix said, snapping Mila's attention away. "Even the clergy were unwelcome. An entire royal family meeting with Gala was unheard of."

Felix's eyes were fixed on the king, and Mila realized that, in this vision, his domain, he could *see*. Cin stood silently beside her, watching as three figures descended the spiraling stairs. A young woman with hair as vibrant as the king's, and two younger boys who resembled Caius followed. Each of them carried a peacock in a cage, their feathers shimmering in hues of green and blue.

The king instructed the family to form a circle, placing their peacocks in front of their feet. They all obliged, exchanging nervous glances. Solomon stepped up to the dais, circled behind the lectern, and retrieved a thick, red-bound book.

"Where's Judas?" the young girl asked.

A muscle twitched in the king's jaw. "It matters not. Time is of the essence." He descended the stairs and directed his family to release the birds from their cages.

"Why don't you have one, father?" asked the youngest boy with a pout, rubbing a blooming bruise on his cheek.

Solomon's stormy eyes lifted from the book. "I only instructed what Gala bid. Now—let us begin." The king drew a dagger from his royal robes, its golden handle encrusted with sapphires. He stepped toward the youngest, grabbing his peacock by the neck. The bird writhed, its eyes bulging in the king's grasp as he lifted it from the marble.

"Solomon!"

The king turned toward his wife, his face red. "Do not interrupt the ceremony, Ymir. This is what must be done."

With his dagger, he plunged it deep into the bird's breast. The boy's face paled, but he remained silent as his father dropped the bird at his feet. Mila covered her mouth in horror as he seized the next bird and killed it. Blood stained the white marble.

Solomon stopped in front of Caius, and the young man stiffened, his knuckles white around the cage. He clutched the bird close to his chest, his jaw clenched, a flicker of fear in his eyes.

"Release it," the king commanded.

"Father, I don't know what this is," Caius protested. "But it feels wrong. You must stop."

"Release. It."

Caius hesitated, his breath shallow. "No."

The king's expression darkened and he grabbed the cage. But Caius held firm, refusing to let go, and the two of them struggled. The peacock's shrill cry echoed through the room, its wings flapping against the bars. The cage door swung open, and Solomon reached inside, pulling the bird free with a violent jerk. He lifted the dagger high, and in that instant, the room was bathed in an unearthly light. It flooded every corner, blinding and warm, as though the very sun had descended into the temple.

Mila shielded her eyes, barely able to make out Solomon's hand reaching for Caius before the light surged again, blinding them. Then, as quickly as it had come, it vanished.

Caius was gone—and so was the bird.

The birdcage lay on the floor, its bars twisted and empty. The air was thick with a hum, almost like the resonance of a distant song, fading fast.

"Caius!" Solomon's roar echoed. He staggered toward where his son had stood, his hands trembling. "Where is he?"

"What on earth is happening?" Ymir cried.

The king's eyes burned, his chest heaving. For a moment, it seemed he might crumble. But then his hand tightened around the dagger, and his gaze hardened.

"This ceremony cannot stop," Solomon hissed. "Gala's will must be done."

Ymir stepped forward. "But Solomon, our son—"

"Enough!" he bellowed, silencing her. "If Caius has been taken, it was by the will of Gala. We must continue."

With his dagger, he plunged it deep into the bird held by his daughter. The girl's face paled as splatters of blood hit her skin, and she looked away as her father dropped the lifeless bird at her feet. Then, he seized the next bird and killed it in the same swift motion.

Finally, he approached the queen. Tears streamed down Ymir's face as he grasped her bird. It was more beautiful than the rest, its train adorned with gold and flecks of blue.

"Solomon, please," she whispered.

Hers did not struggle. She flinched as blood poured from its chest, the bird's body going limp in the king's grip.

"I offer you blood," Solomon said, thrusting his hands upward. "I ask for your favor in return, mighty one!"

The peacocks' bodies stirred, the snap of bones echoing through the room as they contorted, gleaming white, bursting forth from their forms. All but the king writhed with the birds. Eyes rolled into the backs of their heads as their bodies convulsed, legs crumpling beneath them. Tears of blood traced jagged lines down their cheeks.

The king froze, mouth agape. "Ymir!"

He stepped forward, but his feet were rooted to the floor as if bound by some unseen force. Six scorch marks marred the marble, all darkening except the ones meant for Judas and Caius.

Solomon knelt, clutching his chest. "Ymir!" he screamed again, voice bubbling.

The royal family lay crumpled around him, arms thrown above their heads. At the base of each of them lay their twisted, dead peacocks.

As the sun waned, its brilliance fading, a dark red hue spilled through the skylight, as though the sky itself had opened a wound. A piercing scream tore from the king's lips, echoing with terror and agony before being silenced by a dreadful choke that swallowed it whole. His body convulsed in pain, hands clutching his face. The stench of burning flesh filled the air as skin melted away, revealing glistening white bone beneath, the horrifying transformation creeping from his face to his twitching fingers.

Mila couldn't look away. "What's happening to him?" she whispered.

Felix's hand gripped Mila's tight as he turned away. "Something terrible."

The king dropped to his knees, his lips frothing at the edges. "What is happening?" he gargled. "You vowed to grant me the power to protect my family! Reveal yourself, Gala!"

An icy voice slithered into the room. *"Foolish, greedy king—power always comes at a price."*

A figure stepped from behind the statue of Gala, wings of bone and heavy ore scraping against the ground. Cloaked in dark robes, its thin frame was barely visible beneath the shadow of a hood. As it emerged into the crimson light, a sinister, razor-sharp smile became visible, and the rusted ore adorning its body creaked with each movement. The wings, too heavy for its frail form, dragged behind it, while talon-like hands, marred with patches of discoloration, twitched at its sides.

Cin sucked in a breath. "The Fallen of Greed."

"You promised me six," it hissed. *"And yet, you only bring me four?"*

Solomon crumpled to his knees. "Ymir..."

A low growl, part strangled laugh, rumbled from the Fallen's throat. *"Foolish, foolish king. You will suffer the consequences of your error—and so will I. For this, I curse you."*

"I can't watch anymore," Felix whispered, his voice breaking. He let go of Mila's and Cin's hands as the illusion dissolved, revealing the temple's ruined, desolate state.

Felix dropped to his knees, trembling as he gasped for air. Mila knelt beside him, her hand firm on his shoulder. "That demon is Jude's father," he whispered.

"He killed his own family," Mila murmured. "That must be why he took Jude. He thinks he can finish...whatever this was."

"Yes, but what of Caius?" Cin said. "Wouldn't he need both of his sons?"

Felix pushed himself shakily to his feet, leaning on Mila for support. "Not exactly," he said, his voice grim. "Caius was a vital piece of the ritual, but everything changed when Andanova fell." He frowned, brow furrowing in thought. "Jude's soul holds more value now than it ever did before. There's many things he could plan to do with it."

Mila's shoulders sank. What Felix said was true. Souls held value for many reasons. She remembered how Seren's soul had been deemed priceless by the Shademother in the Veil: *"His soul is worth thousands."* If Jude truly was the last Andanovan—or even if his brother, somewhere, somehow, was still alive—then their rarity and royal bloodline would make their souls unimaginably valuable.

"What happened to Caius?" Mila whispered. "He just...disappeared." She could only recall seeing light like that once before, when Seren had used it to chase away the wisps. None of this made sense.

"There's no way of knowing," Cin said, crossing her arms. "This all happened ten years ago."

Felix nodded, his expression pained. "The mark never burned for Caius. Neither did the one meant for Jude."

Mila's hands tightened into fists. "How could he do that to his own family?"

"He was tricked." Cin looked upwards, red light washing across her deep skin. "Didn't you see the terror in his eyes?" She turned to Mila, her gaze distant. "It makes sense now why he doesn't allow demons in the castle. With the ritual being incomplete...a piece of his human soul most likely remains. Perhaps he is protecting it in his own twisted way."

A pang of sorrow filled Mila's chest. She thought of all the skulls facing the thrones, the way the thrones were perfectly untouched by the grime of the rest of the castle.

"Why would the harp matter to any of this?" Mila finally asked.

Cin stopped pacing, a sneer curling her lip. "The harp is the key to cleansing the Veil," she hissed. "Why wouldn't it matter? Do you really think the Fallen—or any demon bound to the Veil—wants it cleansed? If the Veil covered the world, they'd have free reign. Every human soul would be theirs to devour. That harp could stop them. *That's* why it's so important."

Mila drew a shaky breath.

"The Fallen are powerful, but they prefer manipulating others into doing their dirty work," Cin continued. "They're experts at pulling strings, calling on outsiders even beyond the Veil, guiding them. But it was only when the king performed the ritual and thinned the Veil that it could truly sink its teeth into this kingdom. Each step brings the Sundering closer."

"He'll kill Jude," Mila said. "We have to stop him."

"Yes, we do, because who knows what kind of power he'll hold if he kills Jude, if he hasn't already," Cin replied. "The king can't play the harp himself, so there's only one explanation."

"He's going to destroy it," Mila said, realization dawning on her.

"He'll try," Felix corrected. "Which could go very, very badly. That harp is tied directly to the Veil and..."

"To Seren," Mila finished.

Felix nodded. "That harp is as much a part of him as he is of it. If it's destroyed, I don't know what'll happen to him."

"How are we supposed to find them?" Mila asked desperately. "Jude and that monster could be anywhere, and we don't even know where Seren is. For all we know..." The words caught in her throat. It could already be too late.

Cin's lips tightened. "I have an idea where Jude might be," she said, her voice low. "On the edge of the Eclidian Ocean, there's a sacred burial ground for all Andanova's kings. It's a place held sacred—only the Andnaovans were permitted to step foot on the land. Jude is the last of them, the true king of Andanova. Where better to make the sacrifice?" She closed her eyes. "There's one problem. The ruins are across the country. There's no way we'd make it in time on our own—we might not even survive the night."

Mila's hand shot out, gripping Cin by the wrist. "We have to," she demanded. "Jude will die, and if the harp is destroyed, Seren can't cleanse the Veil."

"I know that," Cin hissed, peeling Mila's fingers away. "We have to use the stones."

Mila's eyes widened. "The stones." She delved into her pocket, her fingers curling around the cool, smooth rock.

"I was hoping we could save them to get as close to the border as possible," Cin said, grimacing. "But if we don't use them now, we risk leaving without Jude, Seren, and the harp."

Felix reached into his pouch and pulled out his stone. "Once the spell's activated, all the stones will glow. If Seren still has his, it'll pull him toward us. I doubt Jude still has his, but it'll work the same way for him."

"How do we use them?" Mila asked.

"It's simple," Felix said. "You call upon the location you want to reach and say a prayer to Zephyr. I don't know how far it'll take us, and it won't get us out of the Veil—there are limitations. Once we reach the location, the stones will break and can't be used again."

Cin shot Mila a look as she pulled out her stone. "We're probably going to die, you know that, right?"

"Of course I do," Mila said, her voice steady. "I'm not scared. Are you?"

A muscle twitched in Cin's jaw, but after a beat, a smile broke through. "Of course not."

"Alright," Felix said, holding his palm out, revealing the stone. "Zephyr, we call upon your magic and ask the wind to carry us to…" He glanced at Cin.

"The Sanctum of the Golden Kings," Cin replied.

The moment Cin spoke, the runes on the stones flared to life, casting a brilliant, pulsing blue glow.

"About time a god wants to help us," Cin chuckled.

A powerful whirlwind surged around them. Mila's feet lifted from the ground, her heart racing as her hair whipped wildly. The wind's cool fingers brushed her face, and for a moment, it felt as though she was truly flying.

The whirlwind carried them higher, the world below shrinking into a blur of dark greens and browns. Exhilaration surged through her veins, mingling with a flicker of unease as she soared further. Each powerful gust seemed to defy gravity, and Mila almost believed she could reach out and touch the clouds.

Beside her, Felix was laughing, though his voice was swallowed by the wind. His curls bounced with the wild movement, and Theo gripped his shoulders, screeching in fear. Mila couldn't help but smile. Cin's hands shot out to steady the three of them, gripping Mila's as the wind picked up speed, pulling them higher and faster.

Something dark appeared ahead, hazy at first, growing sharper with each second. Mila squinted, struggling to see through the thrashing wind as her hair whipped against her cheeks.

"What is that?" she shouted, her voice vanishing into the gale.

Cin's hand tightened around Mila's, her gaze fixed on the shape looming ahead. The air grew colder, and the brightness of the whirlwind dimmed as the dark mass drew closer. Then, a piercing, high-pitched screech sliced through the wind. The sound burrowed into Mila's skull, and she couldn't help but cover her ears with a cry.

The whirlwind lurched violently. Cin pressed a steadying hand to Mila's back, but when Mila glanced at her, she saw something she hadn't expected—fear.

Then, the swarm hit.

Hundreds of winged creatures poured in. Their gossamer wings were tattered, the edges torn and uneven, dark veins running through them. Their small, human-like faces twisted in rage, revealing sharp, pointed teeth.

Zephyr's wind veered under the assault, and the tiny demons broke through. Mila screamed as they swarmed. Small, clawed hands latched onto her arms, their thin wings buzzing around her. The tight space and the cyclone's erratic spinning left no room to fight them off. She flailed wildly, striking at the creatures, but more replaced the ones she tore away.

Her stomach dropped as the whirlwind spun out of control. In the chaos, a sharp elbow jabbed into her chest, forcing the air from her lungs. Her footing slipped.

For half a second, she scrambled, reaching out for anything solid—but there was nothing.

And then, Mila fell.

The trees below rushed up to meet her, their dark, gnarled branches reaching like skeletal hands. Mila braced for impact, but instead of the expected snap of wood and bone, something else caught her—an unnatural, sticky resistance. She dangled in midair, her limbs tangled in something silken yet unnervingly coarse. Strands stretched across the trees like an enormous web. Mila's heart pounded as her fingers brushed against the strange silk—no, not silk, *hair*. Her stomach lurched. The strands tightened around her legs, as if alive, sensing her movements. She thrashed, desperately reaching for anything solid.

"Cin!" Mila shouted. "Felix!"

Her voice sent vibrations through the river of hair, but she didn't care. Mila pulled with all her strength, the sharp sting of tearing flesh followed by the wet rush of blood pooling around her ankles. In the distance, Mila heard someone call her name. Whether it was human or demon, she did not know.

Twenty-Nine

"All gods have angels—just as a king has his knights. Before the fall, angels were great divine messengers, and protectors of the realm. Hundreds of years have passed since the last angel sang."

—Chronicles of the Gods

Strands of hair swayed beneath Mila as she crawled toward the nearest tree, her breaths strained. Her blood had freed her, but not before the strands had cut deeply into her leg. Though she managed to stop the bleeding, her leg throbbed with every movement. Glancing upward, she caught sight of the strange, small demons circling above, their glow casting a greenish light over the sprawling web of dark hair that stretched endlessly through the twisted branches of gnarled trees. The sun hadn't yet set, but the forest defied the light, its long shadows swallowing what little brightness remained.

As Mila scanned the dark forest floor, searching for the shimmer of her lost dagger, her thoughts flickered to Cin and Felix. She hoped they had landed somewhere nearby and were safe. If not for the heaps of hair strung between the trees, she would have broken bones.

After several minutes of slow, deliberate movement, Mila finally reached a branch and grasped it with a sigh of relief. Carefully, she eased herself down toward the next branch, the hair swaying and branches creaking under her weight. She froze, breath caught, every muscle tensed. The forest held its silence. When nothing stirred, Mila continued her descent, each movement cautious, each breath measured.

Just as Mila reached for the next branch, her hand slipped, and she lost her footing for a heart-stopping moment. She clung to the tree, huffing for air as her forehead pressed against the bark. Except—what met her skin wasn't rough or solid. It was soft, supple, and warm beneath her.

Mila jerked back, her breath hitching as she swallowed the scream threatening to bubble up her throat.

A face.

A human face, preserved in the tree's bark. It was a woman with deathly pale skin, her face framed by hair that stretched into the trees, merging seamlessly with the flowing strands. Her eyes were closed, as though in eternal sleep, but Mila could have sworn she saw movement beneath her eyelids.

Mila reached for another branch, lowering herself further. Her breath caught. Another face—a handsome male this time—fused into the bark, his hair tangled and twisted, disappearing up the tree.

Mila needed to get out of this forest. She moved recklessly now, her arms scraping against branches as she hurried down. Just as she was about to reach the bottom, something gripped her wrist. She yanked back, but it slithered further, coiling up her arm and then it pulled her upward.

Strands of hair snaked around her other arm, tightening their grip. They coiled around her legs and torso, dragging her higher. She thrashed, twisting against their relentless hold, but the more she fought, the tighter they constricted, lifting her further.

A limpid fluttering filled the air, a whispering sound drifting through the trees. Mila's heart pounded as her gaze locked onto a figure perched in the branches above. It stood like a human but was anything but. It resembled the small demons that had attacked during the whirlwind, only this one was larger.

Gossamer draped across its face, concealing it halfway. Beneath, its features were mismatched—a blue eye, a brown eye, and a grotesque patchwork of faces fused into a disfigured visage.

Long dark hair cascaded around its spindly frame. Its arms, knotted and rough like bark, seemed to be decaying, the forest slowly claiming them as its own. The creature tilted its head, its strange, wood-like fingers stretching toward Mila. Thin, mottled wings, resembling those of a moth, hung from its back.

"Let me go," Mila demanded, struggling against the hair.

"*Such a pretty face,*" the demon crooned. "*It has been a long time since I've seen such a pretty face.*"

Mila flexed her fingers between the layers of the hair, her magic landing on the erratic pounding of the demon's heart. The flow beneath its surface was strange, unnaturally slow. Reaching out with her power, she felt the familiar pull of its blood, ready to bend it to her will. But there was a resistance, like trying to command thick honey instead of fluid life. It refused to answer the call of her magic. Her brow furrowed as she concentrated harder, pouring more of her will into the pull. Again, she tried—and again, it resisted. Nothing.

The demon stepped closer, tilting its head as it reached out to stroke Mila's face. "*Such a lovely complexion,*" it whispered, its voice melodic. "*I must have it.*" It brushed over the scar on Mila's cheek. "*A bit damaged, but the beauty remains.*" With a sigh, it ran a finger through Mila's hair. "*Not enough hair. That can be fixed.*"

Mila's breath caught, unease spreading through her chest. The faces in the tree flashed in her mind: frozen in despair, their hair merging into the forest. It had to be the work of this demon.

Its hideous face clashed with the unnervingly delicate hum rising from its throat. Panic surged as Mila writhed inside the cocoon of hair.

"*Oh, don't fret, pretty one. I'll make it quick, but I cannot promise it'll be painless.*" The demon smiled, revealing small, pointed teeth. With a long, knobbed finger, it took the razor-sharp nail at its tip and sliced just beneath Mila's ear. A sharp sting bloomed, and as the demon withdrew its hand, Mila's gaze caught on a thin line of amber sap oozing from a small nick on its finger—thick and sluggish, glistening like syrup.

That's why her magic hadn't worked. It wasn't blood flowing through this thing's veins—it was something else entirely, something her power couldn't command.

Hot blood trickled from the cut behind Mila's ear, sliding over her scalp and pooling at her hairline. Upside down, the sticky warmth crept across her forehead, gravity pulling it in thin rivulets toward her face. The first drop finally slid past her temple, clinging to the tip of her nose before falling. She waited, holding her breath as the blood gathered—counting the seconds until it was enough to strike. When the demon brought its finger to her face again, the blood whipped out, severing its finger. The demon screamed, recoiling against the tree.

The blood sliced upward, tearing through the cocoon of hair. The strands snapped apart, and Mila plummeted, crashing into the heap of tangled hair below.

"*A blood witch,*" the demon hissed. Mila couldn't see it in the darkness of the trees, but she wasn't about to stick around and wait for it to find her. "*No wonder you have such a lovely face. I must have it. I want to wear it.*"

Mila crawled across the hair, reaching a tree. She slid down the rough bark, her fingers slipping, heart hammering. Sticky strands clung to her skin, and her breath hitched as she risked a glance at the shadowy branches. If only she had her dagger—she'd drive it straight into the demon's chest and end this nightmare for good.

She could use her magic, but relying too heavily on her own blood would come with consequences. She still had to save Jude; draining herself dry wasn't an option.

This was why the Sanguine Sisters created Hollows—broken, disfigured men, their souls torn asunder. A steady supply of blood without risking their own. Disgusting as it was, Mila couldn't deny that having one at her disposal right now would make all the difference.

"*Can you imagine how beautiful I'll be, pretty one, with your face stitched over mine?*" the demon called, its voice echoing through the trees.

If Mila defeated this monster, how much blood would she have to use? She clenched her fists, trying to focus. She could run. She hated the idea, but it was her best choice.

As quietly as possible, she reached for a branch, preparing to lower herself. She wasn't as high this time; if she descended just a couple more branches...she could jump. She eased herself down to the next branch, not daring to take a breath. Then the next. And finally, she jumped.

Mila's feet hit the ground, and she bolted into the dark. She had no idea where she was going—only that she had to get away. Then the earth slammed into her. Dirt filled her mouth, her breath torn from her lungs. Dazed, she blinked and turned.

Hair was wrapped around her ankle.

No.

Mila was dragged back, her nails scraping against the dirt. But it was no use. She was slammed against a tree, tendrils reaching out, pressing her against the trunk.

"Did you think you could get away so easily, little witch?"

From above, the demon dangled like a spider, suspended by strands of hair. Slowly, she lowered herself to the ground to face Mila. She stretched out her moth-like wings, her head turning to the side.

"You're not leaving with my face."

Fury surged inside Mila. She needed more blood. The thin, steady drip on her face wasn't enough, and she could barely move her fingers through the cords of hair. Closing her eyes, she steadied her breath. When she opened them again, the thin stream of blood hovered before her, as fine as a needle.

"And what will you do with that, witch?" The demon laughed; the sound almost delicate. *"It won't save you. You and I both know how this ends. Don't make this harder than it needs to be."*

"You want my face, do you?" Mila's voice was low, seething. "You think it's beautiful?"

The demon leaned closer. "*Oh, yes. The deep color of your skin, the darkness of your eyes, those soft, dangerous features. I'll take very good care of your face, little witch.*"

"No," Mila said coldly. "You won't."

With a controlled breath, Mila willed the blood and sliced across her cheek, the cut biting deep into her skin. Warm blood welled up and flowed down her face. She didn't hesitate and sliced again beneath the first wound.

The demon screeched. "*Stop! What are you doing?!*"

Mila pressed on, her lip trembling as she sliced across them. She smiled, blood staining her teeth. The pain was fierce, but she willed the wounds to stop bleeding, knowing they needed to scar.

"My face won't be pretty once I'm done with it," Mila spat. With a grimace, she sliced the other side of her cheek, the pain cutting deeper than before. She fought to breathe through it, but she wouldn't stop. Not until her face was a mess, if that's what it took.

"*You're ruining it!*" the demon cried. "*Stop!*

The demon's hands reached for Mila, and to her surprise, a sob tore through its throat. "*Please, stop! You're ruining it. You're ruining my beauty.*" It clutched at its face and wailed. "*Please, stop.*"

Please?

Had Mila heard that correctly? The thin blood blade hovered inches from her skin. "Let me go, and I'll stop," she demanded.

The hair loosened, and Mila ripped herself free. The demon stood before her, curling in on itself, sobbing. The sound coming from it was full of despair, so much sorrow. Mila couldn't help but stand there for a moment, confusion filling her. Was this demon truly…not going to even attempt to kill her?

Mila took a step back, keeping the blood hovering over her. "Don't you dare chase me," she said. "Or I'll make sure every inch of my skin is scarred, do you understand?"

A whimper formed in the demon's throat. "*Don't hurt my pretty face,*" it begged.

A flicker of pity flooded through Mila. She thought about the paintings she'd seen in the church, how every demon had once been something different. She never thought she'd feel sympathy for a demon. But now, she wondered what this one had once been, what kind of past had haunted it and twisted it into what it had become. The feeling was unwarranted—something she never expected.

The demon sounded broken. Destroyed. And with each cry, with each whimper, something twisted in Mila's gut. She took one more step back. And then, with a sharp breath, she ran, refusing to look back.

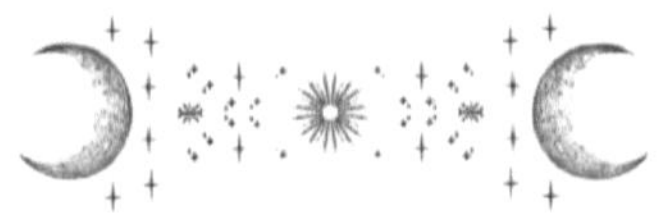

Thin branches snapped against Mila's body, scratching her arms and tearing at her clothes. How long had she been running? And where was she running to? Everything looked the same, and night was growing closer.

"Cin!" Mila shouted. "Felix! Seren!"

Her voice echoed, leaving nothing but an eerie quiet. She fell to her knees, her fingers curling in the earth. She had no idea if Seren's stone had worked or how far she was from the Sanctum of Golden Kings. She wanted to cry but didn't dare. She had to keep going or another demon would find her soon enough.

Mila staggered to her knees, toward the setting sun. A dark, purplish haze was coloring the sky. She was running out of time.

"Please, hang on, Jude," she whispered. "Seren."

Mila continued through the trees, her heart thudding tirelessly. She rounded a corner and came upon a pile of broken branches and a tangle of rotten leaves. As she reached down, her fingers brushed against the damp foliage—only to jerk back. Blood. She sucked in a sharp breath and looked up through the gnarled branches at the muddled sky. Maybe Cin or Felix had fallen here. If so, they couldn't have gotten far.

Something snapped behind Mila. She jumped to her feet and spun around. A shadow flickered through the cluster of twisted trees. She stepped back, fingers flexing as she searched for a beating heart—but found nothing.

A figure emerged from the descending darkness, cloaked in black, its hem brushing the ground like a whisper. Behind him, thin, skeletal wings—burdened by hideous ore—dragged along the earth, creaking with every step.

Fear coursed through Mila as the figure approached. She flexed her hand, blood rushing beneath her skin.

"*I am not here for a fight, blood princess,*" the Fallen spoke, lifting its head. Its eyes were...beautiful. Glacial blue irises, flecked with gold, set within a monstrous face partially veiled by dark, delicate feathers. They sprouted like fine quills along its cheekbones and brow, merging seamlessly with patches of mottled skin.

"I've been watching you. You are a valiant young woman. Dare I say, I am impressed?"

Mila said nothing. She backed away, her pulse racing.

"I have something of yours."

The demon reached into the folds of its robes and withdrew an object wrapped in ragged cloth. Slowly, it unwrapped the bundle, revealing none other than Mila's glistening dagger.

Mila searched for the demon's heart again, her fingers clenching as a strange coldness surged through her.

"Do you truly wish to fight me?" The creature glided toward her, its footsteps barely disturbing the forest floor. *"Or do you want your precious dagger back?"*

"Of course, I want it back," Mila hissed.

A wicked smile tugged at the creature's thin lips, barely visible beneath the shadow cast by its hood. *"Do you know this dagger once belonged to another?"* Its taloned finger hovered above the blade. *"It has been many years since I last saw it. The birds spoke of it—buried beneath the earth, never to rot, never to tarnish—yet forgotten. As are many things of this world."*

Mila remained silent, stepping back. For some reason, she didn't think the creature would chase her if she ran. And yet, something kept her from doing so.

The Fallen lifted its gaze to her.

"How did you come to possess this blade?"

Mila froze, her back meeting with a tree behind her. She blinked, caught off guard by the question. "I found it."

The air around Mila chilled.

"*I do not appreciate being lied to.*"

A bead of sweat slipped down her brow. "I..." She hesitated. "It was on one of the men brought to the Sanguine Kingdom to become a Hollow."

A man she had handpicked for a fate worse than death. Her mother had forced her to choose someone, and Mila had done so. She had found the dagger on him and immediately recognized it as a holy weapon—something her mother would have taken, perhaps even destroyed. So, she had kept it, hoping that one day, it would be the very dagger that freed her from Eden.

The Fallen tilted its head. "*I sense significant guilt in you,*" it mused. "*And yet, this dagger speaks highly of you.*"

Mila frowned. "The dagger...speaks?"

"*It is a Seraph blade,*" the Fallen said, voice softening. "*The whispers of the Seraph weapons can only be heard by the angels. It is strange that I can still hear it.*" The Fallen looked at the blade longingly. "*Though, it does not recognize me, as I do not recognize myself.*" This time, it did touch the blade, quickly retracting with a pained hiss.

Mila could have sworn she detected a flicker of something hidden beneath the Fallen's voice. Was this truly the same demon Felix had shown her in that memory? Was she losing her mind? Mila had no reason to feel a shred of sympathy for any of these monsters. They were pure evil, no matter what they had once been.

So why wasn't she running? Why couldn't she forget the dagger and leave?

"Many of the angels' names have been forgotten," the Fallen murmured. *"This dagger belonged to an angel known for his beauty, grace, and, most of all, his generosity."* His heavy wings dragged behind him as he stepped forward. *"It was said his wings were encrusted with jewels crafted from the stars themselves."* Mila's gaze traveled across the heavy ore that clung to him. *"The Mother favored him for his compassion, though others would argue that gods do not pick favorites. But they did. Just as the angels had their favorites—favorite gods, favorite humans they watched from afar."* The Fallen laughed, the sound like tearing flesh. *"Though his name... I have forgotten."*

"The dagger was yours," Mila breathed, realization dawning upon her. "If that's what you want, just take it and let me go."

The Fallen laughed again, raspy and dark. *"I have no desire for the blade, and it does not desire me."* Again, it touched a finger to the blade only to pull back in pain. *"As you can see."*

"Then, what do you want from me?" Mila spat. "If you're going to kill me, just get it over with."

"I am not going to kill you," the Fallen said, almost sounding amused. *"I am here to help you."*

"Help me?" Mila laughed. "I don't make deals with demons. Especially not with the monster responsible for the fall of Andanova."

The heaviness of the Veil thickened, pressing down on the air as if the very atmosphere were infused with rage. The Fallen stepped toward Mila, its razor-sharp mouth twisting into a grotesque frown, eyes burning with hollow fury.

"Andanova was built on greed, on sin," the Fallen hissed. *"Greedy kings who craved riches beyond belief ruled this land for centuries. When other countries suffered famine, do you think Andanova ever lent a hand? Judas was never lost in the Veil; I never tricked him. He knew exactly who I was. He built a kingdom on a lie, trading not just his soul but the souls of every king after him. And there's a pretty little secret about the Andanovan bloodline, princess. Something even the greatest kings of Andanova do not know."* The Fallen smiled, the anger seeming to dissipate. *"Though that isn't my secret to tell."*

"But there's blood on your hands, regardless," Mila argued. "They worshipped you."

The Fallen paced, its wings dragging through decayed leaves. *"Yes, I knew of Andanova's mountains—untouched for centuries, rich with gold and rare jewels hidden deep within caves. Though bound to the Veil, I led Judas to this wealth, to a place where he could crown himself king, at the cost of his eternal soul."*

"And then what?" Mila scoffed, taking a brazen step forward. "After collecting enough souls, did you turn on him, taking the souls of every Andanovan for yourself?"

The Fallen paused. *"We are cursed beings,"* it said softly. *"Angels were created to serve, and that need is carved into us. Even when we fell, that desire remained."* Beneath the shadows, Mila could've swore she saw sadness in the demon's eyes. *"And all I was given in return was a name. The Kings of Andanova gave it to me, and though it did not belong to me, it became mine—Galathrian."*

Mila's eyes narrowed, but the Fallen seemed lost in thought, the words slipping from its lips as though they had been waiting to be spoken. *"A king's soul is a treasure far beyond the reach of the common man, forged in the fires of worship and crowned with the weight of devotion. Gods are nourished by prayer, and a king's soul is nourished by the loyalty of his followers. The more his people kneel in reverence, the more precious his soul becomes—like a rare diamond lost in a sea of coal. And the Andanovans..."* The Fallen smiled. *"Are they not charismatic? Devastatingly charming? Easily loved? It is almost as if it's in their blood, as if they were born to be kings."*

Mila's heart skipped a beat. "Why are you telling me this?" she whispered, her voice barely above a breath.

The Fallen took a step toward Mila. It was so close now that she could truly see it for what it was. Something caught between terrifyingly cruel and horrifyingly beautiful. *"Truth is a rare gem, princess, one that's worth lessens with time. Perhaps it's time someone else knew."* Its voice dropped. *"And as for the fall...the Devil promised me freedom in exchange for the empire I built, yet I remain, empty-handed, waiting, restless. And the ruined kings that have kept me company for hundreds of years have been stolen from me."*

"Freedom?" Mila echoed. "What about the harp and the king?"

"I cannot play the harp. It holds no purpose for me. And the dead king now answers to the Devil, not to me. I was merely doing what I was told to do, and I failed." The Fallen's hands lowered, the dagger between them, so

close Mila could touch it. *"Not one, but two souls were missing when I came to retrieve them."*

Jude's brother. Mila swallowed hard, processing the words. "What happened to him? The eldest prince?"

"The gods have always had favorites."

A beat of silence took place before Mila spoke again. "And what does any of this have to do with me? I cannot give you freedom. I have nothing to give you."

"No," the Fallen murmured, the faintest trace of a smile curving his thin lips. *"You cannot. There is only one who can, and he is with you."*

Somewhere in the distance, a raven's caw echoed. The trees seemed to shift, a wind blowing through the branches.

Mila's eyes widened. "Seren?"

"There are many who wish to kill the Mother's reincarnation," the Fallen continued. *"Believe it or not, I am not one of them."*

"I doubt that," Mila said slowly. "Why would you want the Mother alive if there's a chance to cleanse the Veil?"

The Fallen sighed, a sound that carried an ancient heaviness. *"There is a misconception amongst demons: that if the Veil is cleansed, many of us will die or become powerless. The gods will rule again, and we will waste away. Yet, there is also the possibility that we will merely change back into what we once were. And I wonder...if that is truly such a terrible thing."*

"When I look into this blade, I glimpse a reflection of what I once was. I remember the Mother." It touched its bony wings. *"I remember what it felt like to touch the heavens. And buried deep within my broken, corrupted soul is a flicker of desire to become what I once was again."*

"You're lying."

"*I have no reason to lie.*"

"Just tell me what you want from me," Mila breathed. "I've no desire to hear your sob stories."

The Fallen's face lifted, another smile spread across deathly features, though it was as cold and mocking as ever. "*You and I both know the boy may fail. The Veil will continue to spread, and humankind will continue to fall. And I will remain the same, tethered to the Veil for eternity, my hatred and greed forever growing, leaving me empty. I merely want my place in this world. And I want you to take yours alongside me.*"

A laugh bubbled in Mila's throat. "You must be joking," she said, the words dripping with scorn. "Follow *you?*"

"*You misunderstand,*" the Fallen said, its tone changing, coaxing. "*The blood of Eden and Adamus runs in your veins. Did you know that they were the first two demons in existence? When they ate from the Mother Tree, it began to twist them—change them. You must wonder what that makes you.*" It laughed quietly, sensing her hesitation. "*Do not fret. As it stands, you are still human. You may think you have unlocked your true potential now that your bond is broken, but you have a long way to go, dear princess. You still need to defeat Eden. And you don't know how to do that, do you?*"

"I only want to free the Sisters," Mila answered. "I have no desire to be a queen."

"*You lie.*"

Mila's fists curled.

"*You want change. You do not wish for death.*"

"And I suppose you don't?" Mila scoffed, but even as the words left her mouth, something in her shifted. There was a flicker of hesitation, a memory of Kamil, of all the things she had already lost. "You're a demon. What do you get out of this? Because I'm not giving you my soul."

"I will tell you how to defeat Eden, in exchange you will give me my freedom from the master I serve. I would serve you. I would be the angel, to your god. You, the devil, I, the demon. A servant in a realm of darkness and death."

"No, I can do it on my own." Mila wasn't sure she believed it. She had no idea where to start, where to go for the answers she needed. She'd thought about Kitsune, but even that wasn't a guarantee.

"You will die—just as your brother."

Mila looked to the ground, to the rot of the forest floor. "Then, I'll die," she whispered. "I can accept that."

The Fallen's voice grew exasperated. *"If the Veil spreads and you die, it will be your mother who finds a place. Who will lead the mortals then? Who will keep them from getting lost forever? You could protect them. If you were queen, you could give them a chance. Even the strongest demons of the Veil would fear you. You can still be the queen you desire, even in a world of ruin."*

The blood beneath Mila's skin grew hot. What was this feeling that burned inside her? Her breath quickened, her muscles tensing. "I have nothing to offer you," she whispered, struggling to suppress the unfamiliar desire the Fallen's words stirred within her. "I can't."

The Fallen cocked its head, as if savoring the moment. *"You will have plenty to offer me when you are queen. I will never ask for your soul."* It extended its hands, the blade casting a glow between them. *"This dagger speaks of you. It has chosen you. And in turn, I will choose you."*

The Fallen placed the blade in her hand, curling her fingers around it. *"This weapon is the only thing that can truly kill me. If you choose to end my life, I won't stop you."* Its hands rose above its head. *"Trust me or not, the choice is yours."*

Mila stared at the dagger and then back at the demon. A strange calm washed over her. She kept the weapon in her grip but lowered it to her side, feeling the weight of the decision pressing down on her chest.

"And if the Mother succeeds?" Mila whispered. "What, then?"

"If the Mother succeeds, then I will touch the heavens once again and spit at the feet of the gods that abandoned me. Our deal will dissolve."

Mila's heart stuttered as thoughts of the little boys slaughtered and sacrificed across the continent flooded her mind. She had to defeat Eden—if not her, then who? Iris had warned her that Eden would not stop; eventually, she would find Mila and try to kill her.

A part of her screamed to walk away, but another part—the desperate part kept her grounded. "Okay," Mila said, her voice barely a whisper. "Help me."

The Fallen clicked its tongue. *"A proper deal is in place, don't you think, princess? I have returned the dagger and spared your life after all."*

Mila's jaw tightened. "I thought we weren't making deals."

"I will help you defeat Eden. I will guide you through the Veil. In exchange, I ask for your promise to seek me out when you have taken your place on the throne," the Fallen said. *"A promise in blood."*

Mila had no idea how to defeat Eden on her own. She had no clue where to even start. And the horrible truth was, even though every fiber of her being told her not to trust the demon in front of her, another feeling ebbed at her. She had no idea how to get out of this forest. She had no idea where her friends were. She had no idea if she would ever get the chance to face Eden again.

"No other promises," Mila said. "No souls. Nothing."

"*No souls.*"

Mila turned the blade in her hand, her fingers still trembling. "You'll truly guide me through the Veil?"

"*Yes, the answer to Eden's defeat lies in Andanova.*"

"Here?" she said. "You'll take me?"

"*Yes.*"

Mila sliced her palm. "I'm rescuing my friends before I do anything, do you understand?"

The Fallen was silent.

"You will not hurt them while we are here," Mila said, her voice steel-hard. "Not a single finger, not one move against them. And to prove your loyalty to me, you will tell me how to get out of this forest and you will tell me where my friends are."

The Fallen chuckled, a sound like the crack of bones. "*Valiant you are, princess.*" He pointed a weary finger in the distance.

Mila squeezed her hand, blood dripping into the dirt below. "Then, I will give you my promise."

The Fallen's smile stretched wider, its eyes gleaming. "*You have made a commendable choice, my queen.*"

The creature took a step back, dead leaves swirling around its frame. Birds erupted from the trees, flying around the Fallen before it disappeared.

THIRTY

"Otherlings came in many forms, and many of them had gifts to offer the world. However, one cannot share immortality."

−Histories of Aerithium

The trees warped and twisted, their grotesque faces oozing thick, blood-like sap. Mila spun, dagger clutched tight. How much time had passed since she'd spoken to the Fallen? An hour? Two? Longer? Maybe she was the world's biggest fool, led astray by a demon. She held out her dagger, its glow carving a path through the trees as she pressed forward.

A screech tore through the air. Mila froze. It came again. It was sharp and desperate. Not a demon.

Theo.

She ran. Branches snapped beneath her feet. Reckless. Loud. But she didn't stop. Dark shapes loomed ahead, their forms indistinct. A force slammed into Mila, driving her hard against a tree. Air fled her lungs. Cold steel pressed against her throat, stopping her dead.

Kohled hazel eyes locked onto hers. Then they widened.

"Mila."

Cin lowered the sword.

Mila broke into a smile. "You're alive."

But Cin didn't return the smile. Her gaze lingered on the wounds marring Mila's face before she stepped aside, her voice hoarse. "Can you help him?"

Only then did Mila notice the blood staining Cin's hands. And slumped in a heap on the forest floor, breathing heavily, was Felix. His left arm lay at an unnatural angle, bone jutting through torn flesh, glistening white against crimson. Theo was curled on his chest, his nose pressed to Felix's cheek.

Mila's stomach dropped. "Cin, I'm not a healer—"

"Try," Cin cut in. "Otherwise..." Her jaw tightened. "He won't get far."

Mila approached and kneeled on the ground, her hands hovering over the wound. It was miraculous that none of his major arteries had been severed.

Felix's eyelids fluttered, his mouth drawn into a tight line. "Is it really that bad?" he asked, his voice faint.

Mila swallowed the lump in her throat. "It's not that bad," she lied. She brushed back the curls from his sweaty forehead. She stood, voice lowering. "He's going to scream."

Cin stepped behind Felix and sheathed her sword. She removed the red sash from her waist and stuffed it into Felix's mouth. "Now."

Mila flexed her hand, and thin tendrils of Felix's blood coiled around the jagged bone jutting from his arm. The sight made her lightheaded. What if she only made it worse?

"I'm sorry, Felix."

With a steady exhale, she commanded the blood to pull, guiding the fractured bone back into place. Felix let out a horrible, muffled scream before his body sagged, unconscious. Cin didn't flinch, her expression set as she eased him onto the ground.

Mila willed the bleeding to stop, sealing the wound as best she could. Cin disappeared into the brush, snapping off a sturdy branch before returning and breaking it to size.

"Sit him up," she ordered.

Mila obeyed, holding Felix steady as Cin straightened his arm and wrapped it with her red sash.

"Are you hurt?" Cin asked, her eyes lifting to Mila.

"I'm fine."

In the trees beyond, an inhuman scream erupted.

"Good. The sun is down," Cin said, drawing her sword. "You'll have to carry him."

"Why me?" Mila scoffed.

"You're taking Felix, and you're running," Cin hissed. A strange tension crackled between them—something Mila couldn't place—until Cin's expression shifted into something almost soft. Then, she understood.

"Our odds are better this way. It's my turn to hold them off. Follow that star and don't stop, no matter what." Cin pointed to the sky where a large star hung in the distance. "And if there's a fighting chance you can get out of Andanova, don't come back for me."

Mila clenched her dagger. "I'll fight with you—"

Cin's grip tightened. "No. I've done this most of my life. I'll be fine." She closed her eyes for a moment. Then they both heard it—the creaking of branches drawing closer. The fur along the ridge of Theo's back bristled. The demons of the forest were aware of their presence.

Cin's voice dropped to a whisper. "Go."

Mila's jaw tightened. "I'll save Jude," she said, rising to her feet. "But I'm not going anywhere. Stay alive until then."

"Don't be a fool—"

But Mila had already scooped Felix into her arms. He wasn't too heavy, but his weight quickly became a strain. Her legs burned as she ran, adrenaline forcing her forward, but she knew she couldn't keep this up for long. Still, she pushed on.

The cries of demons filled the air, the clash of steel against flesh ringing out behind her.

The world was cold. Dark. Never-ending. But Mila didn't stop. She ran and ran, following the star.

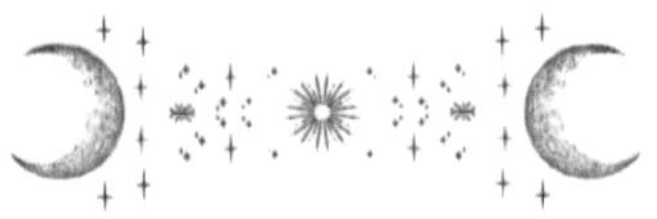

The trees parted into a clearing where fallen branches lay strewn like broken bones, and among decomposing leaves of tainted red and spoiled orange, a narrow trail wound forward. A bright star shone ahead of them like a beacon.

Felix was fading in and out of consciousness, growing heavier in Mila's arms with every step. She faltered, propping him against a tree. Thankfully, this one was faceless.

"Felix," she whispered, brushing his cheek. "I need you to walk. Please."

He barely stirred; his skin ashen beneath the moonlight. The weasel around his neck pressed its nose to his cheek.

"My...pouch..." Felix murmured. "Purple...flowers..."

Mila slipped her hands beneath his cloak, grasping the pouch. She opened it, rummaging through its contents—herbs sealed in tiny containers, smooth stones etched with unfamiliar runes—until her fingers closed around a small glass vial of delicate purple flowers. She hesitated, glancing at Felix, but he had already fallen unconscious again.

Without wasting another moment, she retrieved a few petals and pressed them between his lips. For a second, he didn't stir. Then, his jaw moved, his teeth grinding the petals to dust. A long, tense moment passed before his eyes fluttered open.

"What are they?" Mila asked. "Will they heal you?"

"No," Felix said. "But they'll dull the pain enough... Now, the red ones and the salve."

Mila found a vial of red flowers and opened it, ready to place them in his mouth, but Felix shook his head, his mouth tightening.

"No, for you," he said.

"For what?"

"You lost a lot of blood," he murmured. "They'll help. I slipped Seren some when he was sleeping."

"You lost a lot of blood, dummy." She shoved the petals between his teeth, then pinched a small amount for herself. They were profoundly bitter. While swallowing against the taste, she dug out the salve. Felix weakly gestured to the wounds on her face, and Mila applied it, wincing at the sting. Then, she shoved it back into his pouch.

"We have to hurry," she said. "I think we're almost there."

Felix nodded and wrapped his good arm around hers. She helped him to his feet, and they hurried down the path. Though his breathing was labored, he kept pace.

A glint caught Mila's eye among the dead leaves. She stooped, fingers closing around a small golden clasp. She held it up to the sky, starlight glinting off the delicate metalwork—a feather.

Mila reached for Felix's hand, setting it in his palm.

"Anything?" Mila asked.

Felix was quiet, his fingers wrapping around the metal. After a moment, he nodded. "We're going the right way. Jude was here."

Continuing up the winding path, they found the incline growing steeper as the forest thinned. The further they climbed, the air grew thicker with the scent of salt and the trees became fewer and farther apart. Night's first breath settled in, the sky deepening to a dark purple as a low, distant half-moon cast pale light.

Please be alive, Jude.

"I smell the ocean," Felix murmured.

They reached the end of the path, and Mila's heart quickened as the forest finally broke away. Before them, the jagged sea cliffs ascended, the land stretching out like a vast, open wound in the earth. Gravestones littered the surrounding ground, some toppled, others half-buried. The scent of the ocean was stronger now. But the view remained hidden and shrouded by the looming cliffs ahead. Mist glided across the land like ghosts, and for a moment, Mila could've sworn she felt the brush of stiff fingers against her legs.

At the base of the cliff, eroded stairs spiraled upward, carved into the stone. Mila's gaze followed the spiraling path to the very top, where a massive tree loomed. At first, it was nothing more than a dark blur against the sky, but as her eyes adjusted, she saw its vast branches stretching outward, reaching across the sky like skeletal fingers.

"This has to be it," Mila whispered. She glanced behind her, frowning at the stillness of the forest. Cin was still out there, and somewhere, Seren was too.

"Do you think they're okay?"

Felix squeezed her arm. "Fate will bring us back together. Yes, I think they're okay."

Mila studied his expression. It was impossible to tell if he was saying it merely to make her feel better. She hoped he was right.

The stairs were treacherous, each step requiring careful attention as they navigated over broken rock and gnarled, blackened roots that had pushed through the stone. Felix was exhausted, pain etched on his face as they climbed. As they neared the top, the sky was half-hidden with a blood-red hue, the massive tree above casting its crimson leaves overhead.

"We're almost at the top," Mila said. "Hang in there."

Finally, they reached the last step. Thick, black roots had overtaken almost everything—twisting and creeping through the ground, climbing over broken pillars and gravestones. Mila guided Felix, leading him through an arch. The arch itself was huge, made of white marble, though cracked and worn. Red plants spiraled around it, adorned with enormous thorns and spiky flower buds. As they passed through, the buds unfurled, revealing bloodshot eyes with deep-blue irises that followed their every movement.

Mila shivered.

"This place..." Felix breathed. He kept his hands close to his sides, avoiding touching anything. "There is deep corruption here."

Mila tilted her head back, eyes drawn upward. Now that she was closer, she could see the true scale of it. The tree towered, its bark as black as obsidian and its leaves the color of freshly spilled blood.

"Yeah," she murmured. "I feel it, too."

The two of them continued. A haunting silence reigned, interrupted only by wind rushing through the branches above. Mila guided Felix over broken stone and cracked gravestones. It was obvious that this place had once been magnificent, everything built around the enormous tree that loomed over the cliff.

Mila stilled, halting Felix as they rounded the corner. Light flooded ahead of them—golden and warm. She took a hesitant step forward.

Golden braziers lit a marble walkway veined with gold. It stretched toward the heart of the monstrous trunk, where a golden throne sat, half-swallowed by gnarled wood. The metal gleamed like trapped sunlight, its back shaped like peacock feathers. Chains snaked from the throne's arms, winding around the figure slumped within it.

His golden hair gleamed in the light, his wrists raw where the metal bit into his skin. A royal mantle of white and gold draped over his shoulders, partially concealing an embroidered doublet and matching trousers, their seams laced with intricate goldwork. A circlet of gold, set with sapphires that mirrored his blue eyes, crowned his brow while a matching necklace rested against his chest. He looked every inch a prince—a prince of gold. A prince of ruin.

"Jude's here," Mila whispered.

"Is the harp here too?"

Mila scanned the space within the tree. Her breath hitched. "Yes. I see it."

Opposite the throne, where the gnarled wood curled inward like ribs, an altar of twisted roots seemed to emerge from the tree itself. Resting upon it was a harp, paler than bone, glowing with a luminescence that reminded Mila of the birds Seren had created. Yet strange, dark veins stretched across its surface, and all Mila could think of were the twisting veins she had seen on Seren's back. The tree's roots coiled around the harp's base, not quite consuming it—but holding it hostage.

"It's quiet," Felix noted. "The demon isn't here."

"I'm going to free Jude," Mila said. "Stay hidden." She squeezed Felix's hand. "No matter what happens. No matter what you hear. Do not come out. Do you understand? If I... If the demon shows up, run and never look back. Promise me?"

Felix smiled. "You know my chances of survival are slim on my own, right?" He lifted his broken arm. "But yes, I promise, if it makes you feel any better. I'll run straight for the stairs and try not to plummet to my death."

"Thank you."

Mila slipped away, her steps muted as they struck the path. She darted past the fire, the flames cold, not hot. She reached the throne, her fingers hesitating.

Fear gripped Mila at the sight of him slumped, head bowed. She touched his wrist. Warm.

"Jude."

Jude's head lifted, blue eyes meeting hers. "Seren..." His voice was faint as if he'd just woken from a long slumber. He blinked, recognition setting in. "Mila."

"I'm here to get you out," she said, her hands reaching for the golden chains. She tugged at them, her brow furrowing.

Jude smiled weakly. "I suppose it's my turn to be the damsel in distress this time," he said, his eyes drifting toward the dark beyond. "Where is he?"

"Seren isn't with us," Mila whispered. "Neither is Cin."

Jude's face paled. "Is he...?"

"Felix says he's okay."

Jude was quiet, his honeyed hair falling over his eyes. "Mila, these chains are enchanted."

"You're an idiot if you think I'm leaving you here."

Jude let out a grim chuckle. "We seem to have made a habit of this, haven't we?" His head rested against the back of the throne. "Saving each other."

Mila reached for his wrists—then froze. His left hand was blackened, the skin cracked and burned. Her heart stuttered. Still, she forced herself to focus, searching for a keyhole—anything.

"I suppose we'll have to learn how to save ourselves eventually, won't we?"

Jude smiled. "I suppose so."

A gust of wind stirred, and the fires in the braziers flickered—then died. A shiver traveled down Mila's spine. She spun, scanning the darkness, dagger rising instinctively. In its faint light, a face emerged from the void—blue orbs glinting, unblinking. She hadn't heard it draw near.

She moved to strike, but she was too slow. A bone-crushing impact slammed into her chest, driving the air from her lungs and hurling her back against the stone of the walkway.

The demon stood several feet away, its eyes locked on her, its jaw rattling. All at once, the braziers flared to life again, the flames licking the air with an eerie bluish-green hue.

"Mila!" Jude shouted. The rattling of chains echoed as he struggled against them. "Don't touch her!"

Mila forced herself to her feet, but again, she wasn't fast enough. A thick, twisted root shot up from the earth, its gnarled form resembling a spine. It dug into her ankle, pinning her in place.

With a snarl, Mila brought down her dagger, and the root splintered, crumbling like dust. But before she could react, another root erupted, cracking through the walkway and wrapping around her wrist.

The dagger was knocked from her hand, clattering uselessly to the ground. Desperation surged through Mila as she flexed her free hand, searching for the rush of blood from the demon, the pulse of a beating heart to command—but all she felt was Felix's distant pulse and Jude's fearful heart.

"Silly witch," the king said, lifting a finger toward her. *"A dead man has no blood."*

The king's hand rose, and an unseen power snatched her off the ground, constricting around her neck. Mila's feet flailed, the sound of her gasps muffled by the suffocating grip.

"Mila!" Jude cried.

Mila flexed her fingers, and the wound on her leg burst open. Blood spurted toward the demon, wrapping around his wrists and yanking him back. He dropped Mila. She clawed at her throat, gasping for breath. Just as she filled her lungs again, the king's hand rose once more.

A rock struck the back of the king's head and ricocheted off. His jaw clacked together in rage as he whirled toward the source.

Felix stood, huffing, and reaching under his cloak. As the demon lifted his hand to strike, Felix dug into his pouch, yanked something out, and slammed it into the ground. A cloud of green smoke exploded, swirling around them in a thick, luminous plume.

That little liar.

Mila took a deep breath, her fingers twitching as she sensed the frantic beat of Jude's heart. She turned toward him. Through the powdery smoke, she could barely make out the faint outline of the throne. She willed the blood from her leg to move, guiding it toward the chains. Just as she prepared to strike, every bone in her body froze.

As the green smoke thinned, Felix was nowhere to be seen. The demon king had shifted, now standing beside Jude on the throne. He raised his hand, and roots shot from the tree, grabbing Mila and dragging her toward the trunk. She cried out as one root wrapped around her wrist, pulling her down. Another coiled around her waist, and a third snaked around her thigh, constricting her like serpents. Fear jolted through her. The sensation was all too familiar. Perhaps this was always meant to be—her true fate, the one Seren had tried so desperately to stop.

As the roots tightened, pulling her against the tree, Mila felt her body pressed into the gnarled bark, as though the tree itself were trying to swallow her whole. Though she had severed their bond, she still called for Seren—praying he would hear her.

Thirty-One

"My body will rot, and the golden rings on my fingers will not rot with me. Do we chase treasures for their promise of immortality? Is every man's secret desire to live forever? I have grown old, and sometimes forget—until I see the elder staring back at me in the gilded mirrors. I envy Gala for his immortality, and all at once—I pity him."

—The Third King of Andanova

The edge of the Elysian Ocean was a sight to behold. Seren had never seen a blue so clear, except perhaps the shade of Jude's eyes. The cerulean water beat against the jagged rocks of the Andanovan coastline, foam bubbling and catching on their jagged edges. Seren stood on the ledge, saltwater spray misting his hair, making the ends curl. He closed his eyes, letting the sting of salt and sand fill his senses.

"That one is Estellara," Seren's father said, pointing to an outline of dazzling stars. "You can see her wings if you look close enough."

"A horse!" Seren marveled. He reached upward as his father lifted him higher. He was so close. He could feel it. The brush of something impossibly distant, as if he could pluck a star straight from the sky.

His father laughed, warm and full. "A pegasus," he corrected. "A creature of magic."

"Magic," Seren repeated in awe.

Seren's feet met the grass as his father lowered him. The sea crashed against the ledge, spraying them both with a light, salty mist. Above, a half-moon hung in the midnight sky, surrounded by twinkling stars that resembled a string of thousands of diamonds.

Seren looked up at his father, admiring his amber eyes and the way they shimmered in the darkness. His father caught him staring and chuckled before lowering himself to the ground. Seren sat comfortably on his father's lap, resting his head against his chest. The scent of summer rains and roses enveloped him.

"There's magic in you too, Seren," his father said. "A magic unlike any other."

Seren lifted his head, searching his father's sharp features. "In me?"

Seren's father pointed to a bright star in the center of the sky. It flickered like a candle on the brink of burning out. He held out his hand, and in an instant, the star was gone. A brilliant burst of blue and purple light appeared, hovering above his father's open palm. Seren gasped. Rainbow hues flooded his father's skin.

Unsure if it was his imagination, Seren's heart thrummed with a rhythm that played in his ears, as if a song only he could understand was emanating from the star. Fragments of light danced in the air like sparks from a fire. Seren reached out to touch them, but then the star caved in on itself. Seren pressed against his father's chest as darkness swirled within, gradually swallowing the light. In its place was a swirling black hole, darkness that licked at his father's skin. Seren shuddered.

"Do not fear the darkness," his father said. "Light cannot burn forever."

The ocean crashed against the edge of Andanova, its roar snapping Seren out of his memory. Night had fallen, the stars blazing in the deep purple sky.

How many times had Seren wished upon the stars?

A god is not meant to love.

But his father loved his mother, hadn't he?

Seren didn't just harbor the soul of a reincarnated goddess; he was the flesh and blood of a god.

Half-light.

Seren was foolish for not realizing sooner.

Light cannot burn forever.

He turned his back to the ocean, an ache in his back spreading.

"You are the dark as much as you are the light."

And Seren could not deny this.

Stars die.

How many pieces of Seren had died? How many parts of him had festered into darkness?

It had been growing inside him for a long time, hadn't it? Since his mother had left him with Aiden. When he'd played the harp. All his lost time in the Godless City—stuck in Somnia dreams.

Seren had always known the truth.

He feared the dark in a different way. He wasn't afraid of the monsters that lurked inside it. No, he was afraid that he *was* the monster—that the dark called to him, and that maybe, a piece of him belonged to it. It was comfortable. It was safe. Deep down, he'd known. And when he'd played the harp, alone in the crypts, he had seen the duality in himself.

Even the Mother had known, and she'd wanted him to keep it hidden. She wanted to lock his darkness away.

Paradox.

How many times had Seren's mother made him promise never to lose the light? How many times had the reincarnated soul inside him whispered the same?

How many times had he already let the darkness in?

Seren should've been broken. Devastated. Not believing a word.

But now...

It was Adamus who ate the apple. Eden who had taken the blame.

It was a god they called a devil, and that god was Seren's father.

And there was something else, too—truths buried beneath his time in the Godless City. Things he couldn't remember. Things he wouldn't.

Not now.

Seren stepped over the rubble of long forgotten cottages that had lined the cliffs of the sea. Porcelain crunched under his foot, the near unrecognizable remnants of a child's doll. Amidst the broken buildings, all but one was still standing. It stood prominently on a gentle slope, miraculously untouched by anything more than the curse of time. The surface was covered in moss, and the roof had suffered a slight cave-in from weather damage. The fence that once surrounded the cottage had broken, and the grass all around the building was dead and withered.

With tentative steps forward, Seren headed for it. The door stood cracked open, split down the middle, and splintered. Trembling fingers peeled back the door as Seren opened it. Darkness shrouded the room, with the faint sound of rodents scurrying on the floor. With ease, Seren summoned light, tiny birds coming to life.

Everything inside was ravaged. Broken glass littered the floor, along with rotting wood. Books lay scattered on the ground, with bugs skittering across the moth-eaten pages. Seren stepped over debris, remarkably calm. He approached a blue door, the paint peeling and faded, and turned the handle.

Someone had flipped a child's bed upside down, leaving it covered in broken glass and dirt. Amongst the rubble lay a skeleton, wearing the same black-steel armor Cin wore. The armor was split open like a pomegranate, with the ribs of the skeleton crushed and broken. Seren leaned next to it, noticing something in its left hand. Carefully, he pried the fingers apart.

With a soft clink, a heart-shaped container rolled to the boot of Seren's shoe. He leaned down to pick it up. Ash and dirt had blackened the container. Using his shirt, Seren wiped the ocean mist and sweat from his skin and scrubbed. The grime slid off, revealing an ivory box underneath. Intricate designs of tiny doves outlined the sides of the object, their wings touching at the tips. On the surface lay a coiled black wyrm with a deep-red rose edged in gold resting in the middle of its coil. A strange golden circular piece poked out from the center. Seren examined it, his thumb rubbing over the ring on his finger. He lifted his hand and placed the jewel in the center, hearing a click.

The top popped open. Two painted glass figures danced across a night sky of dark blues and deep purples. A song played, slow and soothing as a lullaby. Seren closed his eyes and whispered the words that stirred in his chest.

"My little star
Even if you wander far
I am where you are
A dream within a dream
Is where you will find me
For I am one with the Mother Tree."

Sinking to his knees, Seren watched the figures spin across the starry glass.

What was so important about this? It was a piece of a buried past, a broken dream he'd once had.

Another lie.

Seren tucked the trinket into his pocket and rose from the floor. He stepped out of the cottage, the wind rippling his hair.

The turmoil that had once churned within him—the incessant waves of doubt, fears, and everything he'd lived with for so long—had grown still. Now, it was merely ripples atop calm waters, a hollow breeze through an empty forest.

A sky without stars.

Nothing.

Seren closed his eyes and took a deep breath.

And then, he let go.

The magic came easily this time. Before he knew it, he was soaring across the land, untethered and searching. He passed the royal gardens—only to find slaughter. Limbs of demon-dogs lay strewn across the grass, blood spattered on castle walls and broken stones.

He pushed forward, past vine-covered arches, through the canopies of trees, until he reached the temple. Ugly vines choked the curving motifs and sweeping arches, swallowing what was once a glistening white-and-gold structure. Now, it was cracked and weathered, a mere shadow of its former glory.

Seren burst through the doors.

Empty.

Seren willed himself to keep going, the journey feeling endless as he soared over rocky crags, dense forests, and barren fields—his energy thrumming with desperation. He pushed forward, searching for even the faintest glimmer of human life.

Then, he *felt* them—an invisible thread winding around his being, pulling him forward. Seren sensed their Aura. He moved through trees. Up stairs. Twisting through the gnarled roots of an ancient tree. And then, he saw them.

Mila, struggling against writhing roots, her body pinned to the trunk as if the tree itself were trying to consume her.

Jude, bound in golden chains, trapped in a throne nestled within the heart of the tree. And then blue orbs locked with Seren's. A weathered hand lifted.

"You. Are. Not. Welcome."

The world recoiled. Seren hit the ground hard, the breath ripped from his lungs.

No.

He reached for the spell, willing himself to teleport—but the moment he tried, something seized him and slammed him back down. His body refused to move, his magic wrenched from his grasp. The air thickened, warped, wrong—space itself twisting to reject him.

He fought against it, searching for his magic, but again, he struck something impossible. A wall that didn't exist yet sent him reeling as if he'd been hurled backward.

The demon had sealed this place.

No.

Seren tried again.

Blood sprayed from his nose.

Again.

Blood dripped down his lips.

He panted, sweat beading on his skin.

"Damn it," Seren whispered, his voice barely audible. "Damn it!" This time his words rang out.

He collapsed to his knees and squeezed his eyes shut.

"Damn it. Damn it. Damn it."

An icy touch ghosted across Seren's spine, like hesitant fingers brushing against bare skin.

"We can help you, little godling."

"Let us in."

Seren's eyes fluttered open, locking onto the wisp of shadow that curled around his wrist, skimming over his knuckles. It slipped between his fingers, tracing the lines on his palm.

"Do not be afraid of who you are."

Darkness swarmed, trailing down his throat. Seren leaned into it, the pull deep and aching, impossible to deny. It outlined the curve of his collarbone and swept over his bottom lip.

"Do you fear the dark, godling?"

"Take us."

"We can save them."

"We are yours."

"Mine." The words fell from Seren's lips, like a confession.

"We know who you truly are."

And Seren knew it too, didn't he? He'd never felt pure. Never felt perfect or divine. It was *impossible* to believe it. It was easy to believe that Aiden had made a mistake. That he would never be able to live up to the image of the Mother.

And where was she? She was nearly as absent as his own mother had always been. And when he needed her most, she always left him utterly alone.

When Seren had drunk the tears from the cauldron, he'd felt such anguish, such sorrow. But when he'd driven his sword through the lord, he had been ready to become the darkness that whispered in his ear.

Didn't Seren deserve the truth from himself? Or was he going to bury himself beneath more lies until he forgot how to breathe? And if he did, then it was no different than running away. He couldn't run. Not anymore.

Seren parted his lips. A chill enveloped him, familiar and cold, like a memory. He was four years in the past, his fingers violently strumming the harp. His mother's fever-bright eyes filled with fear as she reached for him. But all around him, the world dissolved into a single, enfolding darkness—an embrace that offered no escape.

Thirty-Two

"There lies a truth that none of us are taught. At birth, we are divided by many things—by blood, by belief. But nothing divides us more than the truths we cling to. The deepest truth is that all stories, all cultures, and all realms hold their own truths—and their lies. Bitter we grow, preaching of our gods and holding our blades at the throats of our brothers."

—the Personal Diaries of Felix Amos

Mila's dagger lay just out of reach, its blade glowing against the earth. The roots coiled around her wrists, biting into her skin with every twitch of her fingers. She tested them anyway, feeling the tension tighten, the bones in her hands threatening to snap. One more movement, and they would.

The king moved toward the harp, hands outstretched. Jude struggled against the chains as he neared.

"You're wasting your time with the harp," he said. "You can't play it."

"He doesn't want to play it," Mila said. "He wants to destroy it."

The king turned toward Mila, head cocked to the side. *"I am no fool."* He lifted his hand, jaw clattering. *"You are both mistaken. The magic of this harp is true. No living being, except the one it is destined for, can play it. But you see—I am no living being.*" He brushed his fleshless fingers over the strings. "*This harp was made to lower barriers—between realms, between flesh and spirit. When played by the one deemed worthy, it parts the heavens. But in my hands? It rips the soul from its shell, no bargain required.*"

Mila felt the blood drain from her face.

Jude struggled harder now, the chains thrashing against the throne. But it didn't matter. It was hopeless. And Mila was powerless to do anything.

"*Do not fear, my son,*" the king said. "*All will be well.*" He turned his face upward, lifting his hands. "*Gala, hear me! I stand before you in the presence of all kings who ruled before me beneath the Golden Tree. I offer you the soul of my blood—Caius, heir to Andanova. Grant me your favor! Bestow upon me the power to restore our greatness, to awaken the glory of a kingdom long fallen as you once promised.*"

A bony finger plucked one of the strings. The note shuddered—not music, something harsher, grating against Mila's ears and rattling her brain.

With another pluck, the king raised his hand.

Jude's face lost all color, turning ashen. His body tensed against the throne, muscles locking in place. He convulsed, his movements jerking in time with the harp's eerie sound. His blue eyes paled, then rolled back, and his lips parted in a silent scream.

"Stop!" Mila cried out.

From the corner of her eye, movement flickered. Theo scuttling into view, his wiry body creeping up the roots as he chittered. A voice rose from the shadows.

"Where's your dagger, Mila?" Felix appeared, breathless.

"Just a few more steps," Mila urged. "Hurry."

Felix's hand darted across the ground until his fingers closed around the hilt. Theo continued squeaking, guiding Felix to the roots. Without pause, Felix grabbed one and drove the dagger down. The root burst into ash, scattering into the air.

Jude's head slammed against the back of the throne with a dull thud. He kept twitching, the chains rattling with every violent jerk.

"Faster, Felix—keep going," Mila demanded, her voice raw with fear. "I still can't get my arms free."

Jude let out a shallow gasp. His body stilled, lifeless, his mouth hanging open as a radiant golden light poured from him. It dawned, soft as the first light.

The king reached toward the light. With a flick of his wrist, it twisted into a delicate string, coiling around his fingers like a living thing. His bony hands trembled as the glow danced between them.

"There it is," the king crooned, his voice dripping with satisfaction. *"A pure Andanovan soul."*

The blue necklace on Jude's neck slid off, floating into the air. It hovered between them, drawn to the king's call. He guided the golden light toward the necklace, pooling it into the center of the jewel.

Panic surged through Mila. "Damn it, faster, Felix!"

At that moment, Felix sliced through another root. This time, Mila was able to rip her arms free. She flexed her hands, free at last—but it was too late. Jude's body lay still, a cold, lifeless shell. The light that had once filled him was gone, and with it, their chance.

"No," she whispered. "We're too late."

And then, the jewel lit up—bright and blue, angry and alive. Golden light poured out, swirling into a vivid orange, twisting and taking shape into the grinning face of a fox.

"*Tsk, tsk, tsk,*" the fox taunted. *"This soul belongs to another."*

The luminous light plunged back down Jude's throat. He gasped, the sound strangled, as his eyes flickered bright once more.

"What is the meaning of this?" the king snarled.

Jude's lips curled into a shaky grin. "You can't take a soul that's already owned," he rasped, his voice weak. "It's not yours to claim—or mine to give."

"A trickster demon won't stop this," the king hissed, his glowing eyes flaring. *"Andanova will rise again."*

Jude's eyes rolled back as the king strummed the harp again. He writhed against the throne, his skin turning ghostly pale, lips parting as golden light spilled from his mouth once more. Blood traced down the corners of his lips, bright against his skin.

"Stop!" Mila sobbed. "You're killing him!"

She tore her legs free from the roots and snatched the dagger from Felix. Heart pounding, she rushed forward, but then—

Everything stopped.

The air thickened, growing heavy and cold, as if the very life had been drained from the world. Mila's breath hitched, her lungs aching with the effort to draw in the frigid air. A shiver ripped down her spine, rooting her in place.

The golden light drifted back into Jude, his breath slowing, evening out. But even still, the dread pressing against Mila's chest didn't ease.

Then, the shadows stirred.

They crept across the ground like writhing tendrils of smoke, curling in from the darkest corners of the space. Slowly, they rose, merging together and unfurling into vast wings, their edges twisting and curling as if alive. The wings spread wide, and the fire in every brazier sputtered and dimmed.

At their center, a figure emerged.

The shape became clear—slender, unsettlingly still. The shadows clung to him like a second skin. When his pale face lifted, the dim light caught his eyes. Amethyst, cold and distant like frozen stars.

Seren.

He flexed his hand, and the shadows responded, crawling up his arms, slipping between his fingers like liquid night. His expression was unreadable, carved from ice, as if the boy Mila knew had become something else entirely.

"You've stolen from me," Seren said, his gaze flicking from Jude to the harp. His voice had changed, as if a hundred whispers were hiding behind it.

Jude's head lolled to Seren, and a faint smile lifted the corner of his lips before his eyelids fluttered shut.

"Must I remind you—you are unwelcome," the king hissed. Lifting both hands to the skies, he swirled them above his head.

Far in the distance, where the stars burned bright and the ocean kissed the horizon, a dark mass formed. It thickened as it moved closer—closer—until Mila could just barely make out the shapes: winged creatures soaring fervently across the purple sky.

Mila stepped back, her breath catching in her throat. Hundreds upon hundreds of corrupted, bird-like demons were coming for them. Far too many to stop.

Mila gripped Felix by the shoulder. "Get down. Hide now!" she hissed. Felix hesitated for only a moment before slipping behind a broken pillar out of view.

But Seren's face showed no fear, no panic. He raised his hands, fingers gliding through the swirling shadows that curled around them. With a gentle flick of his wrist, a star blinked out from the sky. And then another. Soon, the sky itself seemed to fracture.

Shards of light rained down relentlessly, pelting the birds. Bursts of color exploded against feather and bone, falling into the unseen waves below. Some birds managed to escape, swooping low with ribs protruding from their chests and barnacles clinging to their massive beaks.

In the same breath, Seren's other hand moved with practiced ease, drawing his sword from its sheath. Shadows erupted from him like tendrils, stretching in all directions. They pierced through chests, yanking out hearts with ruthless precision, while his blade cut through anything that strayed too close.

Before the demon king could react, the shadows coiled around him, locking him in place.

Mila stared, stunned. Seren had destroyed hundreds of demons—as if it were nothing.

Was this the true power of a god?

The shadows held the king fast, his body writhing against them until Seren flicked his fingers. This time, there was no room for struggle.

"*Who are you?*"

"It doesn't matter."

Seren sheathed his weapon and stepped forward, raising his left hand in a delicate manner. His expression was strange—unfamiliar in its indifference. Somehow, Mila knew he was about to kill the demon.

"No!" Jude's voice cut through the air.

Seren stilled, his glassy eyes sliding toward Jude.

"Not yet," Jude breathed. "Please." He lifted his chained wrists, the metal clanking against the throne.

Seren hesitated, the shadows twitching at his fingertips, before finally lowering his hand and stepping toward Jude. A part of Mila wanted to throw herself between Jude and Seren, to scream at Seren not to touch him. But she stayed frozen, her feet rooted to the ground.

Why did she feel afraid? Seren had saved them. And yet, something in the way the shadows clung to him, the emptiness of his eyes... It made her chest tighten.

Seren reached for the chains, and with a touch, the shadows curled around them. But then he froze, his gaze dropping to Jude's hand—the blackened, burned one. For a heartbeat, his expression cracked, giving way to the fearful boy that lived beneath the surface.

"You're hurt," Seren whispered.

The chains broke apart. Jude was free now. He reached for Seren, but Seren flinched and took a step back.

Seren's gaze flashed to Mila, his eyes widening as he traced the wounds across her face. His breathing quickened. "You shouldn't have come here." The shadows around him writhed. "Neither of you should have come here."

Mila took a step forward. She knew that look. It was the same one she'd seen during the Trial of Nightmares in the Sanguine Kingdom. Back then, she'd had to stop his heart to prevent him from losing control in front of her mother.

He was losing himself.

"Seren?" Mila whispered.

Seren's fingers tangled in his white hair, tugging at the strands. "What have I done?" he whispered. "What have I done?"

The light in Seren's eyes began to fade. Black spread through his irises, swallowing the light.

"Seren!" Jude shouted. He rose from the throne, a hand reaching out, but Seren stepped back, chest heaving.

"Stay away from me," he demanded.

Then, everything plunged into darkness. Cruel voices hissed from every corner, their chill sinking into the marrow of Mila's bones. She forced herself forward, but it was as if she were wading through thick water. Wisps brushed against her hair and clothes. The insistent whispers, each one a breath of air against her skin, were so deafening that all other sounds faded into nothing.

Mila needed to get to Seren. That was all that mattered—because something terrible would happen if she didn't. She knew it. Felt it in every fiber of her being. She pushed forward, her legs heavy, as if the darkness itself clung to her. The cold gnawed at her bones, but she didn't stop, pressing deeper and deeper into the dark.

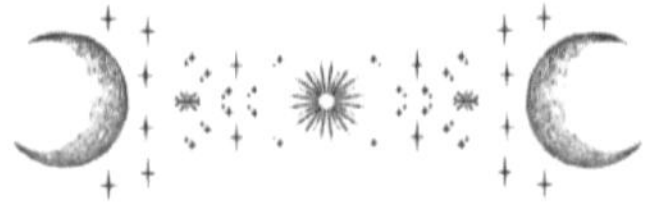

It was Seren's fault. All of it.

Jude's burned hand. Mila's cut-up face. His mother's lifeless eyes. The sword in Anna's body.

It all fell to Seren.

It didn't matter if he tried to deny the dark, if he tried to chase it away. The light in him was weak, a flame he couldn't keep ignited. He always had one foot in the shadows, the other in the sun. But the sun always sets. And in the end, darkness comes. It was why stars died. Light always had a source, and it only took one breath, one sinking sun, one collapse for everything to fall back into darkness.

It was unstoppable. It consumed everything. It was the beginning and the end of all things.

And it lived inside of him. It crept under his skin, tightened around his heart, choked him from the inside.

Seren's purpose wasn't to save the world from the darkness. How could it be? He only brought more of it. And it all made sense now. He'd been cursed with the mortal delusion of love, a thing he was never meant to know.

A god is not meant to love in the ways a human does.

That was it, wasn't it?

Love was too much for him. Too consuming. And Seren didn't deserve any of it. He didn't deserve Mila. He didn't deserve Jude. He couldn't keep them. He would lose them. One way or another. He always lost everyone—by death, by betrayal, by disappointment.

Always.

Always.

Always.

The darkness didn't just follow him; it had become him. It clawed through him, ripping him apart from the inside, stripping away every bit of light he'd once had. He was breaking open, remade into someone unrecognizable. Seren was certain now—if he ripped out his heart, if he wrenched free his soul, only then would he see himself for what he truly was.

He would know that he had been taught wrong. That he was his own worst enemy. That he was exactly what he was supposed to destroy.

Seren could feel the sting of Aiden's hand against his cheek and hear his words of scorn.

It's all your fault.

It's all your fault.

You stupid boy.

Aiden was right.

Maybe it would be easier to stop fighting. Maybe the darkness would be kinder than holding onto something that was never meant for him.

"Let us in."

"Let us in."

Fingers slipped beneath his ribs, prying and probing at his soul, desperate to unmake him. It whispered through his bones, his blood.

"We can help you let go."

"We can free you."

"We can make you whole again."

That's all Seren wanted. If he kept letting it in, then it could consume the light. Just maybe, he would be whole. He wouldn't be fragments. He wouldn't be pieces of a paradox constructed at the hands of gods that had abandoned him long ago.

"Seren!"

Someone was calling his name beyond the incessant whispers. It was distant, echoing like a forgotten memory.

It didn't matter.

Seren was drowning in the dark. And soon, he'd forget everything that had ever hurt, everything that had caused him pain.

There would be nothing left.

"Seren." Hot hands pressed against the sides of his face.

Arms darted beneath his, wrapping around his shoulders. Warm breath flooded the back of his neck.

Jude's face split through the darkness, his presence almost blinding—blue eyes brighter than any sky. From behind, Mila's grip was hard enough to bruise, her face pressed into Seren's back.

"Seren, come back to me," Jude pleaded. His hands burned against Seren's skin, but he didn't pull away.

He welcomed the pain. But all Seren could think was how foolish they were, how they should have run. How he was a monster and he was going to hurt them. No, he was going to kill them.

"Let us in."

"Let us in."

The shadows hissed, curling around Seren's throat and brushing against his lips. Yet Jude was untouched, shining like the sun in the heart of darkness, while Mila held Seren from behind—like the moon, having never known anything but the dark, radiant with a light of its own making.

They should have been afraid.

Why weren't they afraid?

Jude pressed his blackened hand against Seren's chest. "I see it, Seren. I still see it."

Even if you cannot see it, I can see the light in you. Even if you were to implode into yourself, collapsing into darkness like a star, I would still see it.

Tears flooded down Seren's face before he could stop them. "You're wrong," he whispered.

Jude brushed a tear from Seren's cheek. "Haven't I told you? I am never wrong."

Mila's lips pressed against the back of Seren's neck. He thought of sharing Sunbread and a fleeting kiss. He thought of dancing beneath an eclipse. He thought of Jude's laughter and drunken promises beneath a starry sky. He thought of desperation—of fear. He thought of how love was a thin, fragile line he had been willing to walk, even when it frayed beneath his feet.

Seren thought of his mother. She had loved him—he'd never doubted that. He'd felt safe in her arms, the world quieter when she held him close. Seren wasn't sure anyone would ever love him like that again, with a love so unconditional. But he knew, deep in his heart, that she would forgive him, no matter what he'd become. Because she had known. She had *always* known. And she still loved him with everything she was. Even when he did not deserve it.

It hurt.

Gods, it hurt so badly.

Though isn't that what love always did? It brought a fear deeper than any other? And where was love born? Wasn't it born in darkness and in light? It could come from any place, even in the depths of despair.

Seren's shoulders trembled as he clutched his chest, his breath shallow and uneven. More tears streamed down his face, unrelenting.

And they were here.

They were still here.

Even when Seren lost control, they hadn't run.

They stayed.

A sob tore through him. His fingers dug into his flesh, the pain almost welcome as blood pooled beneath his nails.

It wouldn't be fair to give up now. Not when they'd already risked so much. Not when they were holding him together.

But Seren wanted it gone. He wanted it all to stop. The hurt. The pain. The *hunger*.

Seren opened his mouth, and he wrenched something between a sob and a scream from himself, but no sound came—instead, writhing shadows, thick as smoke, poured from him. They scattered, a hundred forms stretching in every direction and vanishing into the night.

Mila's arms released from behind, and Jude's hands fell away. Seren gasped for breath, feeling a strange pressure lift from his chest, a sensation of relief that was almost foreign. But with it came an echoing emptiness, as if the shadows had taken not only his pain but part of himself. For a heartbeat, silence followed. The air felt thinner, as if the shadows had taken the very breath from the world.

"Are you both okay?" Seren whispered.

"We're fine," Jude answered, grabbing Seren's arm and hauling him to his feet.

As Seren rose, the ground trembled beneath him. The branches above swayed, creaking like bones in the wind, as if something terrible stirred. Seren's heart stuttered. The shadows were gone. The king was free.

"Enough of this, Caius," the king growled, stepping toward them, his strange eyes blazing. *"Do you not wish to restore your kingdom? To bring your people back?"*

"My name is not Caius," Jude hissed, turning to face him. His voice was low but seething. "You killed Caius. Just like you killed Armin, Raima, Caspian—and my mother. Have you forgotten your youngest son, Solomon?"

Seren froze. He had wondered why Jude had asked him to spare the demon, but had respected Jude's wishes without second thought.

The king halted. For a fleeting moment, Seren could've sworn he saw a flicker of humanity cross the decayed ruin of his face.

"We will bring them back," he whispered.

Jude stepped forward, his blue eyes burning. Seren reached out, gripping Jude's elbow. "Jude, don't."

But Jude didn't listen and ripped himself free. "You killed everyone!" he roared. "It's your fault they're dead. Your fault the Veil overtook Andanova! You destroyed our kingdom!"

"No!"

The ground trembled beneath them, but the king's voice rose above it, his fury reaching a fever pitch. *"I saved them. I saved us all!"*

In the distance, beneath the cliff, the crash of the waves below echoed, as though the very rage in the king's voice had caused the earth to move.

Jude's features twisted in fury. "No, you *damned* them."

The king's voice grew shrill, madness creeping in. *"You're not Caius. You're not my son. You're an imposter. A liar. A trickster demon with a rotten soul."* His hands lifted, trembling with distorted power. *"How dare you fool me? You will die for your deceit."*

Light flashed. A dagger pierced his chest from behind. The king froze, his gaze dropped to the blade that now jutted from his decayed body. But before a single word could escape, his form began to unravel. His body crumbled to ash, the golden crown and blue necklace clattering to the ground.

Felix stood, Mila's dagger clutched in his grasp, curls sticking to his forehead. "Is he dead?"

Jude inched forward, lowering himself to his knees. His thick, white mantle pooled around him on the ground, a soft, silent patch of snow against the rough earth. He grasped the necklace, turning it over in his palm before rising to his feet.

"Yes," he murmured. "He's dead."

From the hood of Felix's cloak, Theo poked his head out, nose twitching. The small creature crawled across Felix's neck, down his chest, then nudged Jude's boot with his snout.

Felix's voice came full of guilt. "I'm sorry. He was going to kill you. I know he was your father."

"That wasn't my father." Jude's words were empty as he slipped the necklace around his neck. "Let's get the harp and get the hell out of here."

Without a word, Mila and Seren moved toward the harp, still perched in the tangled roots of the tree. Mila's fingers brushed over the strange veins running across it, her touch hesitant.

"Do you think...it'll still work?"

Seren followed her movement, tracing the dark veins beneath the surface, like something alive, something waiting. He pushed his fear aside, forcing the weight of his thoughts to settle.

"I hope so," he sighed.

The two of them peeled away the roots. Seren used his strength to rip them away. The strange black and red tree stood still, unbothered by their presence now that the king was no longer there to manipulate it. Together, they hoisted the harp to the ground, its weight far lighter than expected.

Meanwhile, Felix was wrapping Jude's hand with a cloth he'd pulled from his pouch, speaking to him in a hushed tone. Seren and Mila stood together in the silence. The air on the cliff was still, no demons stirring. The half-moon and stars bathed the cliffside in a silvery sheen, casting long shadows over the landscape.

"Thank you," Seren whispered.

Though he didn't say for what, they both knew what those two words held.

Mila reached out, her fingers intertwining with his—her brown eyes meeting his. Seren frowned, tracing the horrible cuts on her face. With his other hand, he reached upward, his thumb brushing across the wounds.

"It's worse than it looks, I'm sure," Mila said with a wince.

Seren's hand fell away, his other loosening from her grip. "I'll heal you once we get out of here."

Mila's gaze dropped to the ground. "I'm glad you're okay."

"Yeah. Me too."

"Did you...feel it, Seren?" Her voice was barely a whisper. "I broke our bond."

Seren's heart stuttered. "You broke it?"

"Yeah, I think I did."

"No, I didn't feel it."

His mind flashed briefly. A dreamlike memory of Mila and her brother covered in blood.

Mila smiled. "Maybe because...in your heart, you didn't want me to belong to you."

"No," Seren said, voice heavy. "But I wanted to belong to you."

Their eyes met, and for a moment, everything else seemed to disappear.

Then Mila turned away. "Cin is still out there. We can't leave her."

Relief washed over Seren. He hadn't processed it before, but when he hadn't seen Cin earlier, he had feared the worst. "We'll find her, and then we'll leave with the harp."

Mila hesitated, turning her gaze back to him. Something in her expression shifted—softening, yet unreadable. Seren tensed.

"After everything?" she asked. "After all we've been through to get the harp, you really think this is a good idea?" Mila exhaled, her voice quieter now. "And Seren... you need to get out of the Veil before those things come back."

Her eyes flickered with concern. So, she didn't know. She didn't realize they were his doing. His darkness. Good. Maybe he never wanted her to.

Mila closed her eyes for a moment, then sighed. "I'm staying behind."

"What?" Seren's voice rose, his heart clenching. "No, Mila. You can't stay here."

Jude and Felix's attention immediately snapped to him. Both of them turned, concern flashing across their faces as they stepped closer.

"Stay behind?" Jude echoed.

Mila flexed her hand. "There's something I have to do here. I need you to trust me," she said, her eyes flicking to Seren.

Seren felt a tightness in his chest that he couldn't shake. He should have been relieved. The bond had given him control over Mila, something he hadn't asked for. Now, it was broken. They'd both wanted that. She no longer had any reason to be tied to him—she was free, just as she deserved. So why did he feel like this? Why was there this horrible ache of disappointment?

"Why do you have to stay behind?" Seren asked, his voice hoarse. "We can save Cin together."

"I hate to say it, Seren," Jude said, "but you said it yourself this couldn't be for nothing. And Felix says the harp can get us out of here. And..." He trailed off but didn't continue.

Seren understood. They all wanted him out of the Veil as soon as possible. He had frightened everyone. And who knew what was going through their minds?

Mila sighed. "I have a chance to take the Sanguine Kingdom. I can change everything." Her gaze swept over the group. "But first, there's something here I need to do. That includes saving Cin."

"Mila, we can help you," Seren said desperately. "You don't have to do this alone. It's too dangerous—"

"I *want* to do this alone." Her voice was steady, final. "This fate is mine and mine alone. We can't save the world all in one place at the same time. Do not fight me on this."

Before Seren could argue further, the necklace on Jude's chest blazed to life. It glowed a brilliant blue, rising from his neck and hovering in the air. A gust of wind swept through the space, making the branches above groan and creak.

"You cannot kill what is already dead." The voice echoed, deep and hollow. *"Bodies can be remade."*

Beneath broken headstones, the earth cracked open. A skeletal hand burst from the dirt, clawing its way free. More bones shot from the ground—spines, ribs—twisting and snapping together. But they didn't form a natural shape. Multiple spines coiled around one another, warped and tangled, bracing brittle bones that couldn't stand on their own.

Finally, a skull surfaced, its hollow sockets staring into nothingness as it fused with contorted vertebrae. A malformed figure emerged, its shape unnatural and strained. The necklace floated into the skeleton's open palm. Then, with a sudden spark, the eye sockets flared, blazing bright blue.

"Did you foolish creatures believe you could defeat me?" the king demanded, his jawbone hanging at an unnatural angle, garbling his words. *"How dare you fool me? You are no Andanovan. You are no prince."*

A bony hand, missing its index finger, pointed in Jude's direction. Jude dropped to his knees, clawing at his throat, gasping for air that wouldn't come.

"Stop!" Seren stepped forward, but the other hand lifted. Mila collapsed next, her hand clutching her chest, eyes bulging.

Seren froze.

"I don't know what you are," the king hissed. *"But you will watch them die before I take your soul as my own."*

Seren dug deep within himself, reaching for his holy magic—but something clutched at it. At first, he thought it was exhaustion, the strain of battle. But he felt unseen hands tightening like a noose around his power. His breath caught. Fear curled icy fingers around his throat.

"He's not an imposter," Felix said, stepping forward to stand beside Jude. "He is your son, Prince Judas."

The king stilled, his hands twitching. He loosened his grip, and Mila and Jude both took a ragged breath, though they remained rooted in place.

"You lie."

"No," Jude wheezed. "He does not...lie." He closed his eyes, a tremor in his voice. "If there is even...a piece of you left, Father, let us go."

The king's jaw twitched, his voice eerily calm. *"I cannot let you go even if what you say is true."* A pause, thin as a breath, and then his tone shifted—almost pleading. *"Without you, I cannot bring our kingdom back."* His jaw quivered, broken teeth clenched against the tremor. *"I'll fix you when I'm done. I swear it. I will bring you all back. Whole. Perfect. Just as before."*

Seren watched as Jude's face twisted in pain. He stumbled to his feet, his body fighting the weight of the dark magic that held him down. And somehow, Jude took a step forward.

"You can't bring them back, Father. They're dead." Anger seeped into Jude's voice as he took another step, his voice growing stronger. "And they should stay dead. If you bring them back, they'll be monsters—just like you." Jude stood taller now. "Some say it was your fault," he continued, his voice lower, "that your greed drove Andanova to fall."

The demon stilled, its hollow gaze locked on Jude. *"I only wished to restore our kingdom."*

Seren held his breath, every muscle tensed. Dread coiled in his gut as Jude continued forward.

"Jude—" Seren began, but Jude cut him off with a single warning look. Seren fell silent, his chest tight.

Jude took another step, now mere inches from the demon that had once been his father. He lifted his chin, the circlet on his head glittering under the moonlight, casting a faint shimmer over his golden curls.

"You didn't restore anything," Jude spat. "You took everything. How could you do it?"

"*I did not know,*" the demon replied, the words filling the space, raw and empty.

"You killed them all!"

"*No—*"

"Mother. Raima. Caspian. Armin."

"*I did not know, Caius!*"

Jude's voice broke. "And you killed Caius too!" His fists clenched at his sides as he strode forward. "*I* am the rightful King of Andanova now. Not you. King Solomon is dead," Jude said. "I am not an imposter. So, you will listen to me. You will let my friends go. And then I will give you whatever you want. I will tell you the secret to taking my soul."

No. Seren lurched forward instinctively, but Mila's hand tightened around his arm. "Don't," she whispered, her voice low. "Wait."

The demon king's gaze flickered, as if something deep and long-buried stirred within him. "*You speak like a true king, Caius.*"

Jude's jaw tightened. "I have one more request."

"*Oh?*"

Jude took a steady breath. "Look at me," he demanded. "And tell me who I am."

Again, that glimmer of something human passed through the creature's strange eyes. His head tilted ever so slightly, the barest recognition stirring. *"You are my firstborn son."*

"No." Jude raised his chin higher, his voice hard as steel. "Look at me. Tell me who I am, Father."

The world seemed to hold its breath as the two of them stared at each other. Jude stood tall, a prince in all white and gold, the light catching on his golden circlet, a stark contrast to the broken, borrowed body of his father. One alive, the other long dead. As Seren studied Jude's streaked face, he found no trace of fear buried beneath the confidence.

The king's malformed frame quivered, broken finger-bones twitching at his side. Finally, the demon spoke again, his voice hollow and broken. *"You are Judas,"* he rasped. *"My youngest son."* His bony finger reached toward Jude's face, brushing against the side of his cheek. *"How can it be? How have you aged so?"*

Now, Seren understood. The king's erratic shifts, the violent swings of emotion—his mind was shattered, twisted by the dark magic that had remade him into this *thing*. And Jude... Jude was desperate to reach him, to speak to the father he had lost.

"It's been ten years, Father."

"No." The king took a step back.

"Let my friends go," Jude said again. "I'll pledge my loyalty and my soul. We can bring Andanova back, just like you want."

The king's gaze shifted, and without warning, he commanded, *"Kneel. Prove your loyalty."*

Jude hesitated, but only for a heartbeat. Then, with an uneven breath, he began to lower himself, his knee hovering just above the ground. The king's hands rose, and the crown on the ground lifted into his grasp. Seren's chest ached as he watched Jude bow his head, the motion agonizingly slow. Jude's icy gaze never left his father's, the silence heavy between them.

"A great man once told me something," Jude said. "'A crown does not make a king; it is the sacrifices he makes for his people, the burdens he carries for those who cannot. A king never kneels, no matter how heavy his crown becomes.'" He jerked his head upward. "And I will not kneel."

Without warning, Jude pushed off the ground with his cybernetic leg, springing upward in a blur. A glow flashed from his hand—Mila's dagger. How had he taken it from Felix without Seren noticing? Before the king could react, the blade struck the glowing blue jewel embedded in the center of his chest. A crack split down the middle, and the demon screamed.

Seren blinked, unsure if his eyes were playing tricks on him. The stone beneath the king's chest pulsed, and the light at its center dimmed. It swirled outward, escaping into the space between the king and Jude. The light twisted in the air, rippling like a living thing.

And then, standing beside the king, there was a woman. Her hair gleamed like summer honey, and her eyes were deep and endless as the sea. She reached out and placed her hand on the king's shoulder.

Another figure materialized: a girl not much older than Seren. Her features were soft and familiar, her hair a blazing red braid thrown over her shoulder. Then, two boys appeared—one who couldn't have been older than twelve, the other fourteen—both with an uncanny resemblance to Jude.

Jude froze, his eyes fixed ahead. "Mother?"

The king jerked his chin upward. *"You see, my son? We can bring them back... Our family can return."*

Jude's hand trembled above the stone, his breath uneven, tears welling in his eyes. "No," he whispered.

Jude's mother's hand resting atop his. Her voice was gentle. "End this, Judas."

His fingers curled. His hand came down.

The jewel shattered.

Light burst forth, flooding the darkness, bright and unyielding. The force of it stole the breath from Seren's lungs, washing over everything in a brilliance too pure to belong in this ruined place. And then—silence.

When the light receded, a man stood before Jude. Not the withered corpse of a king but something whole, untouched by time or decay. His hair gleamed red, his eyes clear and calm, a blue like the sky before dusk.

"Judas," he murmured. "My precious boy." A hand reached for Jude's cheek, fingers ghosting over his skin with aching tenderness. "There are no apologies that can fix what I have done."

Then another touch—Jude's mother, her fingers threading through his curls as if memorizing the feel of him one last time. Her lips curved into something bittersweet. "We are proud of you, Judas. You have the heart of a king."

His sister smiled. "You've grown, little brother."

Seren watched as Jude's gaze darted between them—his mother, his father, his siblings.

"Where's Caius?" Jude whispered. His voice cracked. "Where is he?"

His mother's expression softened. "The gods saved him, Judas." Her fingers brushed back his curls, but the light that made up her form was already thinning. "And the gods have plans for you as well. It is time for you to go, my son."

Jude shook his head, his shoulders caving inward. "No," he choked. "Please."

His mother cradled his face, her touch feather-light, as if the world was already pulling her away. "Soon, our souls will join the Veil. We can protect you until then, but you must leave—now. Do you understand?" Her eyes darkened. "The true deceiver is coming, Judas. He's been playing this game for far longer than you know. You must leave before he arrives."

Her gaze shifted, locking onto Seren's with an intensity that made his breath catch. Something flickered in her eyes, a fleeting recognition that sent a chill through him. For a moment, she looked at him as if he were the deceiver himself.

Seren stepped forward, resting a hand on Jude's shoulder. "Jude," he whispered.

They were fading. Their edges blurred like mist unraveling in the wind.

"Live with the strength we always saw in you, Judas. Our love will follow you beyond the Veil," his mother whispered.

His father's voice sounded far away, but his words were like a final blessing. "You are more of a king than I ever was. I see you, and I am proud."

Tears fell freely down Jude's face, but he didn't move.

His sister's voice was the last to reach them, filled with certainty. "Do not grieve us any longer, little brother. Remember that our love is like gold—it does not tarnish."

Jude's hands clenched at his sides. "No," he sobbed. "Don't go. Please, don't go."

The light in the stone flickered. Once, then again.

And then they were gone.

Jude stood motionless, staring at the empty space where they had been, where their voices had just spoken, where their hands had just touched him. The moment stretched, unbearably long.

Seren tightened his grip on Jude's shoulder. "We have to go." His voice came out quieter than he intended, but it was all he could offer.

Jude didn't move. Seren wasn't sure if he would.

"Jude."

Blue eyes lifted, swimming with grief. "Oh, Seren," Jude whispered. "Caius wasn't there."

Seren eased Jude to his feet, throwing a glance at Mila and Felix. Mila's face was pale, tears streaming down her cheeks.

"Caius wasn't there," Jude whispered again, clinging to Seren. "He wasn't there."

"I know," Seren breathed, tightening his grip on Jude's shoulder. "But we can't stay here. Listen to your mother—we have to go."

Jude leaned on Seren as they moved to the harp. Mila was tense and alert, her eyes darting between Jude and Seren, but she didn't speak.

"Okay," Seren said. "I'm going to get us out of here."

Seren could now see where a string had snapped long ago, and his eyes traced the veins that pulsed through the harp's body.

What if it didn't work? Seren's magic had felt strange just moments ago, unreachable. He had no idea what song to play or where the harp would take them.

His hands hovered over the strings, and then his heart skipped a beat. He thought of the trinket in his pocket, its weight pressing against him, and the song it would play if he opened it.

His mother and father had wanted him to find it. It was something he was meant to remember. Something important.

Seren closed his eyes, running his fingertips over the intact strings. What choice did he have but to try? He knew this harp, and it knew him.

As he started to play his mother's lullaby, the flame within him stirred once more. His magic hummed, faint at first, like a heartbeat struggling to wake. Then it pulsed—alive. His fingers moved of their own accord, plucking the strings.

The soft notes swelled, overtaking the wind rustling through the tree above, drowning out the frantic beat of his heart and the uneven rhythm of Jude's breath. The sound vibrated through his bones, resonating deep, and as he played, the harp's glow intensified, casting a halo of white light around them.

But a sudden whisper of fear coiled in his gut. His fingers trembled, plucking faster. The halo warped. Shadows slithered into the spaces between, twisting and curling like unseen hands reaching for him.

Seren's breath hitched.

No.

He was in the crypts again. *Alone.*

His heartbeat pounded, a frantic drum in his ears.

"You're afraid. Do not be afraid," the Mother echoed.

"We are with you," the darkness crooned.

A sharp ache bloomed between his shoulder blades—then pain, sharp and shattering.

His wings burst free. Vast. But they were not pure, not the wings of a goddess. One was dark as night, feathers like the abyss. The other—stark white, as if cleaved from another being entirely.

Something was wrong.

Something was *horribly* wrong.

"Seren." Jude's hand closed around his shoulder, pulling him back. "You don't have to do this."

Seren's hands hovered over the strings, trembling. He hadn't realized he'd stopped playing.

"No." His voice was barely a breath. "I'm fine. I can do this. It's the only way."

Seren took a deep breath and began to play again. He willed his mind to empty, but instead, he saw the castle—Jude at the piano, his fingers gliding over the keys. He saw Mila, twirling across the floor in a dress woven from starlight, her hands reaching toward the heavens. And then, his own fingers moved, the harp singing beneath his touch, as if the music carried a will of its own.

Then, the air shimmered. A gate unfolded before him, a portal rippling like water, revealing a hazy blur of landscape on the other side—a glimpse of the world beyond the Veil.

"You did it," Mila whispered.

Seren could hardly believe it himself. "I'm not sure how long it'll hold without me playing. I'll go last."

Jude turned to Mila, his eyes solemn. He handed her the opalescent dagger, his hand lingering on hers. "This better not be goodbye," he whispered. "I've had enough of those to last a lifetime."

Mila smiled and planted a kiss on his cheek. "Not forever," she said.

"Not forever," Felix echoed.

It was a promise.

Jude's lips tightened, and he reached for Felix's hand. "Okay, then, I'll be seeing you."

"I'll be seeing you," Mila whispered.

And with that, Jude and Felix stepped through the portal, their forms disappearing on the other side.

Seren's hands lifted from the strings, and though the portal remained open, its edges began to shrink with a slow, steady pull. In a few minutes, it would be gone.

Seren stood and stepped toward Mila. "I'm going with you," he said. "We'll leave together after we rescue Cin."

To his surprise, Mila smiled. "You're predictable, you know that?"

Before he could respond, something cold pressed against his chest. Seren glanced down. The sharp tip of a dagger rose, trailing upward with aching slowness, tracing the line of his sternum, the hollow of his throat, before sliding back to rest over his heart.

"I could say the same about you," Seren murmured.

Mila reached out, cradling the side of Seren's face. "You're not coming with me, Seren. This is my fate, not yours. Besides, Jude needs you."

"Don't do this," Seren whispered, his voice barely holding together. "It's too dangerous."

"The portal's closing." Her hand trembled as she pressed the blade harder against his chest, though it drew no blood. "Kiss me goodbye."

Seren's heart stuttered. But he leaned in, his mouth meeting hers. The dagger stayed between them, its frosty edge biting against his skin. It was the kind of kiss that didn't ask for permission but demanded surrender. Deep. Possessive. As if they both knew nothing would ever be the same. As if they belonged to each other in a way no bond could ever tether them again.

Her lips parted further, breath mingling with his, and she stepped forward, forcing Seren back. The kiss remained unbroken. He grabbed her hips, pulling her close, desperate to hold onto her. But then Mila tore herself away, the dagger lifting.

Seren stumbled, realizing too late he was standing in the middle of the portal with green grass beneath his heels, the edge of Andanova just beyond his toes.

"I think a part of us will always belong to each other," Mila said, her brown eyes locked on his. "It was always real."

Seren swallowed hard. "Promise me this isn't truly goodbye." He pulled the ring from his finger, the purple stone glistening in the starlight. Taking Mila's free hand, he slid it onto her finger. He didn't need it anymore. "You can return it when I see you again."

But he never intended for her to return it at all.

Mila's fingers curled slightly around his. "Okay," she whispered. "I promise."

Seren's heart ached. But no words came, and none were needed. The space between them held everything they dared not say, promises they couldn't bear to make.

Mila reached out, giving the harp a push toward him. Seren grabbed it, his fingers tightening around the frame as he dragged it with him, stepping backward toward the portal, his eyes never leaving Mila's. Just before he crossed the threshold, something shifted in the shadows of the tree behind her. The obsidian bark rippled.

For a moment, he wasn't sure if he had truly seen it—scales, dark as the tree, catching the faintest glint of light. And then, just before the portal sealed shut, amber eyes met Seren's from between the branches.

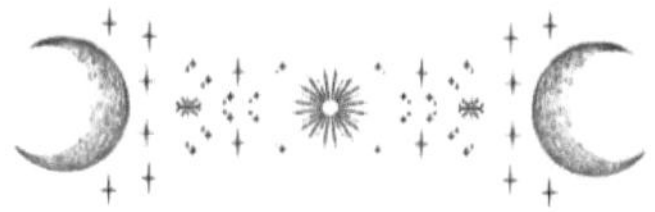

The moonlight spread across the horizon, casting a silvery glow on the undulating hills, their gentle curves illuminated like the contours of a sleeping giant. Shimmering starflowers adorned the landscape, their delicate petals catching the light and sparkling like tiny jewels scattered across the earth.

The chill of the Veil was far behind, replaced by the warmth of a summer night.

Beneath a weeping willow, propped against its trunk, Felix slept with his weasel curled on his chest, rising and falling with each breath. Seren had healed his arm, and now the boy was resting peacefully, Jude's royal mantle draped over him like a blanket. Beside him, the harp sat, casting a dim glow in the night.

Seren sat in a field of flowers, his face upturned to the sky. Soft footsteps sounded behind him, and before long, Jude settled beside him. He hadn't taken off the circlet on his head, though it was nearly lost beneath his sea of golden curls.

"Hey," Jude said.

"Hey."

Several minutes passed, the silence stretching between them. Jude reached for a starflower, his fingers tracing the petals.

"You're thinking about Mila, aren't you?" he asked quietly.

Seren sighed. "Yes."

"You care for her deeply." Jude smiled, and Seren could not read the emotion behind it. "And she cares for you."

Except now, she was gone. Though Seren didn't say the words. Seren glanced down at his naked finger, at their promise, and then back into the blue of Jude's eyes.

A pang of guilt twisted in Seren's chest. Was it wrong—thinking of Mila while sitting here with Jude? Had Jude seen Mila and Seren kiss from the other side of the Veil? Seren thought of Mila's mouth on his, and then he thought of Jude's. Even beneath such an unreadable gaze, he couldn't help himself.

"I think Mila will be okay," Jude continued. "Cin, too. Felix showed me something."

Seren raised his brows. "What?"

Jude sighed, the sound wistful. "I saw us. Mila, you and I. Together. Happy. We were different, yet the same."

Seren's gut twisted. "Do you believe it?"

"I have to."

Jude fell silent again, and Seren couldn't help but trace the lines of his face. He hadn't spoken of the darkness since they'd escaped the Veil, and though Seren supposed he should be grateful it had gone unmentioned, he knew it wouldn't last. He didn't want to pretend anymore.

"Something is wrong with me, Jude." The words came hoarse. "I'm not who you think I am."

Jude's eyes flicked to him, and where Seren expected uncertainty, there was none.

"Ah, well, isn't there something wrong with us all?"

Seren frowned. Jude was always too kind to him, too accepting. But he had a feeling nothing more would be said about it. At least, not now.

Still, there was something distant in Jude's gaze, as if he were searching for something beyond the moment.

"I wonder if he's out there somewhere," Jude finally whispered. "My brother."

When Seren didn't reply, Jude continued, "If anyone deserved to be saved, it was him." He brought his damaged hand to his chest. Seren's magic had failed to fully mend his hand, leaving it black and his fingers without feeling. "It's strange to think that maybe…he was just as alone as I was."

Seren reached for Jude's hand, their fingers intertwining. Jude sighed, resting his head on Seren's shoulder.

"You're not alone," Seren promised. "Not anymore."

"And neither are you," Jude said. "A few pesky shadows aren't going to scare me away. I find people to be far more frightening. Besides…" His finger traced Seren's arm. "Darkness tends to cling to those with the most light."

In the distance, a brilliant burst of light streaked across the sky, illuminating the landscape for a heartbeat before vanishing into darkness. A shooting star.

"So… What happens next, then?" Jude asked.

It was a fantastic question—one Seren had no answer for. He only knew the truths he dared not speak, not aloud. He couldn't. So, instead, he shoved them away.

"I suppose we keep going," Seren replied. "Find the crown and sword."

"Another deadly adventure? Count me in." Jude looked up at Seren, his smile radiant, warm as sunshine.

Seren gazed into the distance, past the rolling hills and into the deep dark beyond. He knew where he needed to go next—where to find the sword. He thought of the cruel blade he'd seen Lumen swing above his head, glowing with an otherworldly light. His fists clenched, the scars on his back throbbing.

Seren should have known he'd have to go back eventually. That fate had come full circle.

Even if the truth wasn't what he wanted to believe, he couldn't stop now. Not after everything. Not after all the bloodshed, after everything he'd endured.

Shouldn't he still try? If he could save the souls trapped in the Veil—Felix Amos, his mother, Jude's family, then he would. He would undo what his father had done. Even if fate itself tried to stop him. Even if his existence was a paradox. Even if he was the very darkness they feared and the dying light they sought.

"Hey, look," Jude said, peeling himself away from Seren. "What's that?"

Seren followed his gaze to a figure descending from the sky. It grew larger, then swooped down, ivory wings spread wide. Its talons struck the dirt with a thud. Seren blinked. Eldyir's falcon approached him slowly and lifted its leg, where a parchment was tied. Seren untied the parchment with careful fingers, unfolded it, and began to read.

Dearest Seren,

Though I have already asked much of you, I must ask once more. Eiran will need looking after, and if he has found you, along with this letter, it means I have already walked my last path. I trust that the bond you form with him will speak louder than any words I might write here.

Eiran is a beautiful judge of character and has served me faithfully for five wonderful years. I believe he will be of service to you.

As you journey forward, remember this: In all that you may face, you must put faith in yourself—and in those around you who have proven worthy of that trust. Do not lose yourself to uncertainty; it is far easier to lose your way than to find it again.

And, when doubt creeps in, do not hold yourself up to the flame of perfection. The gods are not without flaw. They created us, after all.

—Signed, Eldyir

THIRTY-THREE

"I always believed pure evil to be purposeless, but I now know this to be untrue. We are all driven by something—instinct, desire, or perhaps something greater. What purpose does the Devil serve? Priests and saints say his desire to become a god led to his corruption, transforming him into a being of pure malice. But what are we to the Devil? It is believed he is humanity's true enemy, and we cannot rest until he is destroyed, and evil is buried in ruins. Yet I cannot help but wonder: are we his true enemy?"

—Exorcist Damian Silver

There was once a time in Lumen's life when he wanted nothing more than to have a place beside his brother. It was a repulsive desire, born from a deep, pitiful longing for acceptance. A child's dream. As much as he hated to admit it, even to himself, walking the halls of the Church of Caelestis had brought reminiscent thoughts to the surface.

With every step he took, the doctor landed in the shadow of his former self—a pathetic boy with comical aspirations. Although, Lumen could never be like Aiden, even when he had tried. His brother had never questioned, always listened, and accepted all the lessons they'd been taught. Lumen had never been that way.

Lumen was a curious child, full of questions—a mind caged by doubts and wonder, shackled by his stepfather's rigid ways. His inquiries were born from simple childlike innocence. Yet, his father punished him for every question, as if curiosity itself were a crime. Even when Lumen's ribs were bruised, his throat raw from crying, and his thin torso marked with burning welts, he clung to hope.

One day, my brother will see me. My father will see me. And the gods will see me, too.

He believed it for so long.

Too long.

It was disgusting.

Lumen now believed only in himself. He was fully aware of what he had done—strapping Seren to that table and carving a piece of the boy away. It was an act that defied the gods, the priests, the saints, and everything Lumen had once held sacred. And when Seren had finally succumbed, his body a mangled, bloodied mess and his eyes hollow, Lumen had spread his remains on a table. His heart pounded in his throat. One wing was white—pure and divine, with red seeping into the feathers; the other, black—darker than night. He had looked back at Seren, reflecting on the boy he had brought to the Godless City, who had trusted him and listened to his teachings.

The boy had died, just as the child inside Lumen once had.

Lumen had dug his hands into the severed wings, clenching them, hoping they would disappear from the world. It should have felt good.

Amazing. No—it did feel good—that's what he told himself. That's why tears ran down his face *because* it felt so good. That's why his heart failed to pound properly, and his teeth remained clenched. It was what he wanted. Lumen was sure of it.

As he now held the sheathed sword, the very one he'd used on Seren, memories of that day flooded back to him. The weapon was abnormally light for a blade, one of the first things Lumen had noticed when he'd first wielded it. Grimm had no trouble flying it to him from Vavilon, and Lumen had sent a carrier dove weeks ago with a vial of the cure for the Auguries.

With a sigh, he set the blade against the desk. Grimm perched on his shoulder, head cocked as Lumen lifted another stack of papers. The mercenary was long gone. To Lumen's surprise, he had survived, and shortly after taking the cure, he had vanished into the night. The key had glowed in Lumen's pocket, signaling that the crypts would unlock for him.

Lumen knew that Aiden and his father had spent months in the crypts for good reason. Enchanted with magic, the crypts seemed to go on forever, a never-ending library with ancient archives gathered over hundreds of years by the Trinity. Half of the books and scrolls were written in languages that Lumen had no knowledge of. He had known he'd be spending a considerable amount of time searching for the information he wanted, but he hadn't expected the weeks to fly by so quickly.

Opening a deteriorating, brown-leather book, Lumen let out a frustrated growl. He slammed it shut and reached for a red book on his right. He winnowed through the aged pages, his hand resting under his chin, like a bored child. Then, he lifted his head, eyes widening with a smile. "Well, isn't this interesting?"

Lumen reached for his paper and quill, quickly tracing the picture and copying the text. It would be far simpler to take the entire book or rip the pages out, but the crypts were tricky. And Lumen was not in the mood to deal with the pesky repercussions of magic.

"What are you looking for, master?" Grimm said.

"I'm glad you asked," Lumen replied, reaching into his pocket. Grimm happily plucked a seed from Lumen's open palm.

"Gods are immortal, Grimm. They never age and can never be killed, or so it is believed." The raven tilted his head, absorbing Lumen's words.

"But consider this: the magic of priests and saints diminishes when faith wavers. I believe it's not just their connection that weakens; the gods themselves grow frail alongside it. People's unwavering belief keeps them powerful. What do you think would happen if people knew the biggest secret of the Godless City?"

And that secret was precisely why Lumen had released the virus in the east. The more death, pestilence, and unanswered prayers that were showered upon mortals, the less faith they would have in their deities. The less faith, the fewer prayers, and the fewer prayers, the less belief—and therefore, weakness. And in the weeks that had passed, the virus had spread rapidly through Kogarashi.

"You want to kill the one who powers the Heart of Vavilon?" Grimm squawked.

Lumen's grin widened. He always forgot how clever Grimm could be, always listening and paying attention like an eager child.

"Yes, my dear friend. Can you imagine if a god could be brought low by his own sword, wielded by the hand of a mortal man? All the faith would simply...fall away." He stroked the edges of the book's pages. "And isn't that what the gods deserve? To feel as insignificant as they make us feel?"

"And what of your subject?" Grimm asked.

"All in good time," Lumen assured.

News of Seren's appearance had spread throughout Lumina, and Lumen had overheard the townsfolk of Stellaris talking about him. It seemed that Aiden had finally revealed the truth to the Grand Priest, leaving Seren with no place to hide from his so-called fate. Truthfully, it had come as a surprise to Lumen, but it was only a minor setback. Seren would fail, and faith would continue to diminish.

Seren had dreaded the day that his identity would be revealed in Aerithium; in fact, he'd confided to Lumen that he hoped it would never come. On Seren's sixteenth birthday, Lumen had discovered Seren writing a letter to Aiden, stating that Aiden had made a mistake and that he would never be what Aiden wanted him to be. Later, Lumen had found the letter crumpled in the trash.

During the first year in Vavilon, Seren had been a hollow shell of a boy. Lumen kept his distance, though his curiosity about the boy's significance gnawed at him. He often wondered what had happened at the church and why Aiden could come to blame a child. Soon, Lumen heard rumors about the Unveiling, that a blasphemous priest could not protect his holy grounds. Still, Lumen had never seen Aiden with such rage in his heart before, and though he was tempted to poke and prod the boy, urging his side of the story to the light, Lumen did not demand anything from the child.

In the second year, Seren had begun shadowing Lumen, absorbing knowledge long considered forbidden. Initially, it had been a nuisance, and Lumen had even been tempted to send letters to Aiden demanding him to retrieve the boy, but he refrained. By the third year, with no communication with Aiden, Seren's layers of defenses began to fall away. And soon, Lumen learned many things about this mysterious child he had been observing. There were times when Lumen had thought he was losing his mind when he'd glimpsed a flicker of violet in the boy's eyes and shadows behind his form, as if he had seen a silhouette of wings, if only for a moment.

And then, there came a day when the truth bubbled to the surface—when Seren trusted him and Lumen saw the truth for himself. A gift had fallen into his lap. It was a chance to prove everything he had believed so deeply and, in turn, give Seren what he'd always wanted: an escape from the fate he had been given.

The sound of shattering glass tore Lumen from his thoughts. He jolted his head upwards and grasped the hilt of the sword. He rose from the chair and trudged up the stairs with Grimm gripping his shoulder.

"Aiden, are you up there throwing a tantrum?" he called. He hadn't seen Aiden in weeks. Perhaps his brother had finally returned.

Reaching the top of the stairs, Lumen swung the door open and peered down the hall. When he saw no one, he frowned, closed the door to the crypts behind him, and turned the corner. Pain exploded in his chest as a flash of blue struck him in his center. It sent him sprawling to the floor, with his limbs twitching from the burst of energy. His robes were singed, and by some miracle, his skin hardly burned. Grimm had leapt into the rafters above, squawking furiously.

Lumen struggled to catch his breath, his hand clutching at his chest. An Enforcer loomed over him, armor glinting.

"Well, that was certainly unnecessary," Lumen wheezed.

"I told him to do it."

A figure stepped from around the corner—a tall, bronze-skinned man with a monocle and slicked-back chestnut hair. He grimaced at Lumen, offering his hand, which Lumen refused. Instead, Lumen shakily pushed himself to his feet.

"Simon?" he coughed. "What are you doing here?"

"The question," Simon said, "is what you're doing here."

Lumen straightened his clothes. "It's none of your business."

Simon chuckled. "Ah, well, the Auguries have made it my business, Yukimura. It seems your secret Subject has drawn some attention. You're careful, but not careful enough." And from the pocket of his trousers, Simon withdrew a glass vial with two feathers, one black and one white, tucked inside.

Lumen flexed his jaw. "Do you make it a habit to collect bird feathers and electrocute people?"

"Don't play coy," Simon said. "It seems you've been keeping a lot of secrets." He smiled wickedly. "You've always been a snake, though, haven't you? It's why the Auguries favor you so much." He looked at the sword, laying on the marbled floor from Lumen's fall. "Did you really think it would be so easy, Doctor Yukimura? I truly thought you were smarter than that."

Lumen scowled.

Simon ruled over Sector Two as the head scientist in his region. He had always been several steps behind Lumen—never as good, yet always trying to step on his heels. Lumen wondered if the Auguries had given his job to Simon after his own absence.

"What do you want?" Lumen growled. "You certainly didn't come all this way to mock me."

Simon chuckled. "Well, certainly not. I wouldn't waste my time on something so trivial." He held up the vial. "It appears you could not destroy your evidence, Doctor. Though, I can't say I'm surprised."

Lumen gritted his teeth as two Enforcers hovered behind him. "The Auguries are angry, I take it?"

"Actually, they're impressed. Murdering Faith, one of your own? And then releasing the virus, knowing you're the only one with the cure, so they'll give you what you want," Simon chuckled, pacing the chamber. He twirled the glass vial between his fingers. "Finding a key to immortality and keeping it all to yourself? I can't help but wonder how someone so intelligent can also be such a fool. There is nobody quite like you, is there, Yukimura?"

Lumen was silent.

"Your creature is gone," Simon continued. "He's rumored to be in Andanova."

Lumen kept his expression blank. "Well, he'll be dead soon, then," he replied.

"But you don't believe that. Do you?" Simon asked, kneeling as he held the feathers to Lumen's nose. "You are soft for the child. For four years, you paraded that boy around as your nephew, then claimed he went back home. So, tell me, why did it take you so long to lock him up in your little lab? Were you too busy playing house and teaching him to hate the gods as much as you do?"

Lumen bit the inside of his cheek, blood welling up against his gums. "I didn't know what he was yet," he said. "I thought he was just a boy."

"I don't believe you," Simon said with a smile. "Do you want to know what I think happened?"

"Not particularly."

"I think you grew to care for the boy, and that feeling disturbed you. You've never been one to let the cracks in your armor show, Yukimura." Simon licked his thin lips. "I think you promised to help him, and then—you did what you know best. You manipulated him. Hurt him. Hoping he'd hate you just as you hate your gods." Simon sneered, "Am I close?"

"What do you want?" Lumen spat. "If you've come to take me to Lazarek, then get it over with. I don't have the energy for your petty speech."

A sly smile spread across Simon's face. "The Auguries agree that throwing you in Lazarek would be a waste. You see, the Auguries are going to have an audience with you." He grabbed the sword that now rested on the floor. "And I've been given permission to kill you if you refuse."

Simon dragged Lumen to his feet. "So, here's your first task. You're going to send your raven to find the boy," he said. "And with it, you're going to send a letter and tell the boy you'll give him the sword in Vavilon."

Lumen laughed. "And you expect the boy to come?"

Simon smirked and leaned in close. "You haven't heard the best part. You're going to tell him you can *fix* him," he whispered. "That you can give them *back*." He pressed the vial of feathers into Lumen's palm. "You've made him trust you once, Yukimura. And you'll do it again—but this time, not on your terms."

Simon pulled out a syringe from his back pocket, the bubbling blue liquid inside catching the light. Arms wrenched Lumen back, holding him in place.

"What're you doing?" he demanded.

"Fitting, isn't it?" Simon mused, as liquid squirted from the needle's tip. "Somnia dreams can be sweet, I've heard, but too much..." The syringe pricked Lumen's skin. "And nightmares and reality blur together. After a while, some go mad, and others...simply forget." Lumen winced as the icy liquid flooded his veins. "We can't have you forgetting, now, can we? So, why don't you sleep for now, and when you wake up..."

The rest of Simon's words faded as Lumen's vision blurred, his face swirling out of view. There was not enough energy left for a single last thought before the darkness swallowed Lumen whole.

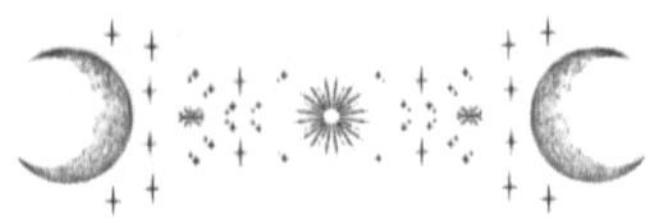

The stars were never visible in Vavilon, a fact Lumen had despised when he first arrived in the Godless City years ago. He had once found solace

in their distant glow, knowing they hung in the sky, untouchable though kindred. Both humans and stars shared the simplicity of hydrogen, the foundation of all things, and the inevitability of iron, forged in a star's final breath. Ash and dust they become, returning to the cosmos, just as humans returned to the earth.

That was something Lumen could understand—the cycle of life and death and the elements from which all things were made. Science followed its own set of rules, a language of numbers that defined the laws and boundaries of existence with precision and order. It was one of the reasons Lumen knew he could never deny the gods' presence.

The universe was too perfectly constructed, built upon fundamental formulas that remained beyond complete comprehension. And yet, despite this, the world was cracked and broken in a hundred pieces that would never fit together. These beings held so much power and still, the world continued to steadily rot, to fester with suffering.

That was something Lumen would never understand.

This strange boy knew what it meant to suffer. He had lost his mother, his home, and whatever life he might have left behind in Stellaris. And though Lumen could pity him, he chose not to. Suffering was part of the eternal cycle, the life the gods had condemned them all to.

Did all parents play a hand in the suffering of their children?

Lumen exhaled softly, his breath visible in the cool rooftop air, and turned his gaze to the boy standing at the edge. It was quiet, the stillness only broken only by the faint hum of Mechamobiles cruising through the streets below.

The boy hadn't spoken a word in days. He showed no awe, no emotion, even as they passed through the Vavilon gates—a sight Lumen was certain he'd never seen before. Lumen had told Seren that the city was alive in its own way, with a metaphorical beating heart that pumped energy through its concrete flesh and metal bones. It wasn't a place consumed by sin but a world beyond the gods' reach—a realm of innovation, change, and possibilities unlike anything anyone had ever known.

The boy had offered no response.

Now, Lumen had found Seren out on the rooftop again. He'd been avoiding Lumen, and he could not blame him. Truly, he had nothing to offer the boy.

The boy shifted, his foot dangling over the ledge and his arms spreading out behind him. Lumen hesitated before taking a step forward. His voice cut through the stillness. "Is that truly how you want to die, foolish child?"

Seren turned, his green eyes flickering faintly beneath the city lights as he pulled his foot back. "I wasn't going to jump."

Finally, the boy spoke.

Lumen sighed, shaking his head, and turned his back. "Then, I guess I'll go back inside. I better not wake up to Enforcers scraping your body from the sidewalk."

"Wait..."

Lumen turned, meeting the boy's gaze. "Yes?"

"Can I ask you something?"

When Lumen was silent, the boy took that as his cue. "Why did you...take me with you?"

Lumen paused, the weight of the question settling heavily between them. Truthfully, Aiden had never asked for his brother's help. Never. And deep down, Lumen carried the buried truth—he owed his brother for that day. The memories of the Veil's horrors stirred beneath the surface. So yes, he had come for the boy, just as Aiden had asked. But when he found them at the church, covered in blood, and his brother blaming a child for it all... Lumen didn't know what to think. He figured that when the time was right, he would ask the boy for the truth.

"You needed my help," Lumen said, almost mechanically. "And maybe one day, you'll be willing to tell me what happened."

Seren didn't respond. His eyes were distant, focused on something far beyond the city's skyline.

"You shouldn't have brought me here." Seren's voice trembled. "I hurt everyone. I should be dead, not them. Everyone would be better off if I was dead."

Lumen's face betrayed nothing, but inside, something twisted. His hand twitched at his side. "Don't be a fool," he warned.

Before he could say more, Seren's foot hovered over the ledge. Lumen lunged forward, his fingers stretching desperately toward the boy's shirt. But Seren slipped. The fall was too fast, too sudden.

Lumen hit the ground hard, throwing himself flat as his arms shot out. Just in time, his hands closed around Seren's arm. The boy dangled over the edge, his green eyes wide with terror as he stared at the city far below.

"Just let me go," Seren choked out, tears streaming down his face. His free hand reached for Lumen's, his fingers trembling as he prepared to pry them loose.

"Listen to me," Lumen said through clenched teeth. "I understand what you're feeling. Your gods have left you. You're alone." He gripped Seren firmer, pulling him upwards, his muscles screaming in protest. "Forget the gods. Forget what happened in Stellaris. You have to try to live for yourself. Not for them."

More tears spilled across Seren's cheeks, glistening in the city's glow. "But what if I can't?" he whispered, his fingers slipping. "What if I can't forget any of it?"

Lumen's jaw hardened, and his grip tightened. "Then I will help you forget," he said, his voice unwavering. "I will take away your bad memories. I will take away your pain."

He pulled the boy up, his breath coming in short, shallow gasps as they both collapsed onto the ground. Seren looked up at him, eyes wide with disbelief.

"You could do that?" he whispered.

Lumen huffed, rolling his eyes, though there was a soft edge to his voice. "Yes, foolish child. Many things are possible when the gods aren't watching." He pushed his glasses up the bridge of his nose. "But no more of that nonsense. Do you understand?"

The boy's chin rose toward the starless sky. "When will you do it?" He turned to Lumen. "How soon?"

Lumen scoffed, rising to his feet. "With time, you will change your mind."

Seren's eyes darkened. "I won't."

"We'll see," Lumen said. "Time changes many things."

As those words left his lips, the sky transformed. Thousands of stars ignited simultaneously, their brilliance blinding. Lumen flinched, shielding his eyes and stumbling backward. When the light finally dimmed, feathers began to fall around him, swirling like snow—black and white, dusted with blood.

Before him stood the boy, now a young man. His back faced Lumen, scarred and bloodied, with dark hair turned stark white.

Lumen blinked, his heart pounding. "Seren?" he whispered, extending a trembling hand. A white feather drifted down, landing on his palm, only to crumble into ash.

"The gods knew from the beginning that you were unworthy," Seren said, his voice echoing with another. He turned, purple eyes blazing. "You took more than you promised."

Lumen stumbled back, his pulse thrumming painfully in his throat. No words came. How could they? Nothing he could say would ever be enough. For the first time, he felt it fully—the raw, ripping sensation of his chest being torn open, the buried feeling exposed, the sin that was clawing its way through him. Apologies sat on Lumen's tongue, and he swallowed them down like bile.

Memories bloomed around him, fragments of the past taking shape like restless ghosts. Seren's awe as Lumen showed him a Holographus, demonstrating how information could be stored in an endless system. Seren peering into Grimm's cybernetic eye, asking the raven what it was like to fly. Lumen crumpling Aiden's hollow apologies—letters Seren would never see.

Yet, as the recollections faded into the background, nothing came of them. Lumen could not speak or make a sound.

Then, Seren's face began to shift, his features softening, his hair growing long enough to reach his waist. Before Lumen stood a woman, her hair flowing around her like a river of light.

"I forgive you," she whispered. "But he does not."

Something inside Lumen shattered. The ground beneath him crumbled, and he fell—down and down, into nothingness. No concrete to catch him, no city lights to break his fall. Only an endless, suffocating darkness, screaming with Seren's voice, echoing with his pain. Lumen's greatest sin, chasing him through the void.

Through the darkness came wintry whispers: "You took too much. You always take too much."

Lumen knew these words to be true. He knew what he had done. There was no hiding from it this time, no denial to blanket himself in. No. This was his doing. His damnation, his ruining. The gods had come to curse him, to condemn him for his sin.

So, this was how they chose to face him. After years of quiet, years of absence that had shaped Lumen into the man he was. After countless failings. He had already accepted it in his own way, molding his hatred and bitterness into a weapon of his own liking. He had challenged them to try and stop him when he'd carved the wings off a divine child's back—and they hadn't lifted a finger. All-knowing. All-powerful. And silence had always followed.

But now, for the first time in years, Lumen called out to the gods who had forgotten him. The words tasted poisonous and foreign in his mouth, but still, he called. Again and again, Lumen begged the gods to answer.

Acknowledgements

Thank you to Kaila Hiddleston, E.L. Maloni (Loricia), Olivia Renner, Dani Danker, Dylan, and Tabitha. Before I started seriously writing books, I thought it would be fairly easy—and I was wrong. I am incredibly thankful to everyone who has been willing to help me with this book and who has given me the confidence I needed to complete it. A special thanks to my family for supporting me throughout this process and always asking how it's going.

And thank you to the wonderful fans who took a chance on the first book, *The Wingless King*. I am so grateful for you all.

About the author

K.C. Wassem lives in Oregon with her four children, her dog, and her husband. She loves binging television, especially her favorite anime series, reading fantasy books, and spending time with her family. *The Ruined King* is the second in her debut series, *The Wingless King*.

You can follow her on Instagram or TikTok *@authorkcwassem*

www.ingramcontent.com/pod-product-compliance
Lightning Source LLC
Chambersburg PA
CBHW030543310726
48979CB00010B/2004/J